FIRST IN SERIES

S.E. ZBASNIK

DWARVES IN SPACE Copyright © 2015 by S.E. Zbasnik.
ISBN-13: 978-1508400356

All rights reserved. No part of this book my be used or reproduced in any manner without explicit permission of the author except in the case of quotations embedded in critical reviews. Any resemblance to people, creatures, or rather tasty pies is purely coincidental. I tried to form my own parallel universe where it did exist, but the chipmunks kept catching on fire and exploding. Chipmunks are not team players.

A Moment of Thanks

I'd like to take this blank space to thank my husband for putting up with me losing months creating this tale, and all my awesome beta readers: Adam, Grapeman, Dawn, and Mandaray.

Please forward all complaints to them.

Candy is hidden inside this book.

For More Information About Dwarves in Space Visit:

http://dwarvesinspace.blogspot.com/

See!
The Universe
with Constellation Cruise

PROLOGUE

Sulfur winds tossed vestiges of the colony across barren soil. After canceling the distress call, only two of the scouting party remained. With the rest of the team back on the ship, the rescue operation quickly turned to salvage. A man's armored boot kicked into a teetering gate, the plastic of the pre-fab homes grimy from the continual sandstorms of a planet that should never have been colonized.

Gods, what was anyone even doing here? Aside from dying.

The Knight-Captain smacked her fist against his hazmat suit. Even the bright orange rubber bore the crest of the enraged Bear lest anyone confuse them for common scavengers. He turned to face her and shrugged, not bothering to offer an apology over the partially functioning comm line. Terrwyn would have reprimanded him, but the little shit must have deep connections to rise this far up the ranks. If it weren't for the war, she'd probably be stuck saluting him.

"We make one final sweep, then arm the detonator," she ordered, staggering from another burst of wind. Her rubbery arm rose above her facemask as she stared into the horizon, the red giant of a sun slipping behind a set of MGC rich mountain ranges. The only reason anyone would bother putting down roots in soil that couldn't support a sapling was to mine all the MGC before the Corps got their connected tendrils in. And everyone, young men and women with gold in their eyes as well as the older ones selling the shovels, paid for it with their lives.

Purchase up the colonizing rights on some dust ball a salesman assures is full of energy-rich compounds and fail to pay the extra coin for a proper detox scan. A tale written across gravestones and in report footnotes that no one ever learned from. Normally, they'd find a few people clinging to life before someone wised up and sent out a distress signal, lack of nutrition or clean water being the major culprits. Once there was a pernicious strain of strangling vines that did not take kindly to being hacked away for the sake of a jousting court.

But this was quick. A virus or some alien virus simulacrum hidden deep in the soil, virulent enough to knock back every colonist within twelve hours. By the time the ship arrived, most of the skeletons were sand blasted clean of flesh from the tumultuous weather. The ship's resident field doctor poked his head out at the carnage, declared them "Dead, Jim," and hustled back inside the shuttle before anyone could argue.

It'd have been left as a warning for anyone trying to colonize planet P3-507, a few images encoded in a buoy, had it not been for the ministry official "accompanying" them on a final sweep through this backwater half of the galaxy before a necessary furlough. She ordered samples, evidence, data, all things that take time and risk other officers to whatever alien bug ate through these dead colonists. Knight-Captain Terrwyn Yates was thanked for her input, the best way of saying "fuck you" to someone who spent her life heavily armed, and sent back to the planet with one final order; destroy everything left.

She picked Lieutenant Dacre as her second, and blamed her choice on exhaustion the moment the atmoshuttle sunk deep into the shifting sands. He savored in the dead's final moments, poking and prodding about their hopeful homes like a child stumbling upon an ant to torment. A final sweep for any survivors, those were the regs, and a second to sign off on the lack of life.

"Dacre," her voice reverberated across the echo in her hood, "search through the few standing walls to the compound's west edge."

"Why bother?" His voice lilted with each vowel, a thick accent he'd have to smooth out before getting any higher up the chain unless his mommy or daddy paid for it.

"Because I gave you an order." Her voice didn't tremble, didn't hold any anger or rage. It was as immobile as stone.

Anyone without connections would have slunk back, maybe saluted, but Dacre merely shrugged again, "Very 'ell," and he slunk off towards the few standing walls. Terrwyn lifted a downed pipe from a stack, never inserted into the sewage system before disaster struck. Using the pipe as a walking stick, she measured her footsteps. The dying could not have made it far out of the compound; but there'd be a dump, close enough to make the trek easy, yet distant enough to hide the smell of human existence. Possibly, someone could have run before the bug got to her.

Her feet left half tracks in the shifting sands dancing in a mixture of gases their sensors assured them was breathable. She refused to believe a person could live in this; if the buffeting winds of sand didn't scourge your skin, the rising sulfur and ammonia levels would burn the lungs. Even implants wouldn't salve it all. Dacre's voice momentarily flared through her helmet, but the planet's high MGC levels wreaked havoc on their communications. She shut off the line rather than face endless static punctuated by "can you....me now?"

She paused before a crater, dug either by the colonists or a lost asteroid millennia ago. Their refuse only coated the bottom layer. They hadn't been living here long before the virus came a'calling. The walls lying upon the ground most likely were never even raised. A pathetic example of the entrepreneurially human spirit.

The Knight-Captain turned to leave, nothing could be hiding amongst the thin layer of garbage, when a light flared in the distance. She wiped off the film coating her helmet and stared across the crater at a dark figure. Its skin was thick as a cliffside with broken fissures that flared as if intermittent fires roared inside its guts. "Who are you?" she called out into the alien world, but the figure either didn't understand or couldn't hear. It raised its own arm slowly and placed a hand overtop its eyes as if to spy back upon the invader of its planet. Turning to look behind, two more lumbering rock monsters rose beside it, one far shorter than the others.

Terrwyn clicked open her comm, "Dacre, abort. Abort the mission. There's still life here. Dacre? Damn it!"

She turned from her new friend and raced back to the compound, unaware she was being followed. "Dacre! I swear if you don't pick up this comm line I'll strap you to the hood of the ship and parade your ass past the next station's embassy deck."

Her limbs grew weary with each step, the suit's scrubbers failing against the challenge of the environment. *Cheap pieces of shit.* That's military cutbacks for you. If they didn't get to the last shuttle soon, they may not get back at all. As her line of sight crested above the fallen scraps of what the colonists dubbed "New Avar," she spotted the Lieutenant hunched overtop the incendiary device. Burn everything to over a thousand degrees and scrap what remains for someone else's failed colony, those were the orders.

The Knight-Captain waved her arms, trying to catch Dacre's attention. He momentarily glanced up from his number punching and rose unsteadily. Patches of his voice clipped across the comm line, "Couldn't find...getting too hard...gonna blow it now before we lose sterility."

"Stand down, Lieutenant," she said, finally falling into comm range, "the orders have changed."

His weasel eyes slipped down to the bomb happily blinking away, and back to his commanding officer, "Sir?"

"There's people alive on this rock."

Dacre snorted, "I find that high'y doubtful. I get it, you'd prefer to find someone a'ive and play the big hero again, but your weary eyes are playing tricks upon you...Sir."

"You little, sniveling shit," Terrwyn cursed, her anger punctuating through the military fog.

A hissing sound, like water poured over burning coals, broke through their fight, and Dacre glanced past his fuming commanding officer to the rock monster breaking into the compound. His side arm slipped into his fumbling hands as he aimed upon its chest. Luckily, the bastard was a terrible shot. The quartermaster kept all of Dacre's weapons at a half charge just in case he accidentally shot at their side.

"There are more," the Knight-Captain said calmly, her mind flipping through the list of recognized aliens. This definitely fell into the miscellaneous category, but she was certain she'd seen something like this before. An alien with fire for veins and a suit of rocks...Gods she was terrible at this diplomacy shit.

"How many more?!" Dacre panicked, as if the little xenophobe never saw an alien before. Then again, the Crests did draw upon both the professional bigoted and terrified as much as those who wanted someone else to pay for their education or give them a bed at night.

"Enough."

Dacre's teeth chattered as he weighed his options, his gun waving about like a sapling twisting in the wind, "No one else knows they're here. We set the timer, head back to the shuttle, and let the planet blow."

"Let the planet blow? What are you talking about?" Regs were strict, they were to detonate the colony, not the entire rock.

Dacre rolled his eyes so hard the helmet slipped over his face. He took his balancing hand off his gun to try and get the rock monster back in his line of sight, "This planet is lined with MGC, the bomb's a fuel catalyst, not some old fashioned inferno. It starts a chain reaction and the entire planet blows. Sir."

"Then the plans have changed. There are clearly life forms, sentient and intelligent, living upon this rock. Setting off that bomb would be against the Accord of the Twelve Stars."

Dacre snorted again, "No offense, Sir, but if that Ministry official went to that much trouble to get a catalyst bomb drilled into the veins of this rock, she's not gonna give a shit about some musty old Accord and a walking island statue."

Terrwyn gritted her teeth and looked back at her new friend, the holes where eyes would be burned a staggering red. It seemed to know what was being discussed despite not responding. "Stand down, Lieutenant."

"Sir?" Dacre asked, uncertain. Surely she wasn't stupid enough to go against Ministry orders. They could make entire systems disappear.

5

"You heard me, stand down. I'll not destroy these people because some fat arsehole in Antilla says so."

"Those fat aresholes could toss both of us in the dungeon for the rest of our lives without anyone the wiser," Dacre's weapon shifted over to his commanding officer.

Terrwyn didn't flinch, her fingers slipping the catch upon her gun loose and arming in a single beat, "I said, stand down, Lieutenant. I will not say it again."

Dacre's gun bobbled, the barrel bouncing from her head then to her navel, but he wouldn't back down. He spent his life butting up close to the Ministry, rubbing elbows with people who'd keep things in their basements that would make most warlords vomit in disgust. He wasn't about to wind up like them. "No, Sir."

Terrwyn blinked once, "Fine," and she opened fire. The bullets smashed into the bomb's outer casing, kicking up sparks as the number pad crumpled into debris.

"You fucking moro..." was as far as Dacre got before the sparks caught and the bomb casing exploded, tossing the Lieutenant into the no longer standing walls and Terrwyn and the rock monster down the colony's hill.

High above orbit, the ship acknowledged the bomb's fire and slipped through the waiting wyrmpinch before it'd be caught in the planet's explosion. It did not care that one shuttle failed to return.

CHAPTER ONE

FIVE YEARS LATER....

"Station Eclipse 5... Eclipse 5, come in." The line popped and hissed as if someone pushed on the respond button before closing his side. *Amateurs.* "Coming in is code for answering the line, in case you forgot. If you can hear me, respond with absolute silence." Orn paused for a moment before smugly sliding open the comm line, "Good, glad that's all settled."

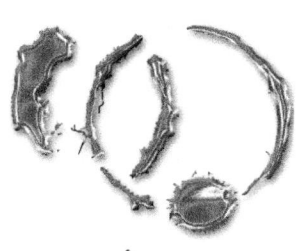

Orn leaned back into his chair, a highly sought after lower lumbar support system that could tip to nearly 105° before you'd find dwarf all across the bulkheads. Pilots were notorious sticklers when it came to *their* chairs and only *their* chairs, some even turning down vaunted positions on the most luxurious star cruisers because the chairs weren't customizable.

He thudded his right boot upon the excessive glass console, missing partially vital controls. Whatever idiot thought people would love seeing all the wires, diodes, and other electronic doodads to keep them from flying straight into a sun hopefully was tossed into one himself. Orn tried painting sections, but the shit always scraped off or melted when they dropped through a pinch. To remedy that situation, he took to "borrowing" the old-timey posters for acts on whatever floating hunk of rock the ol' girl set herself down on. A session of "Gabbing with Godot" hovered over the impulse drive he was supposed to be watching, but the traffic around the station was calm for once. It was the perfect time to sit back and...

"What's the situation?"

In the old days, Orn would have sat straight up and pushed a few of the less important buttons to look busy, but he'd been on this bird for nearing three (or was it four?) years now. The cap'n would see straight through it anyway. Instead, he swiveled slowly to her, unraveling the last of his stash of rope candy into a slightly stubbly mouth. "Not much," he slurped through the red goo.

The captain, as she hated being called, shifted back on her bare feet, more than likely roused from a nap by the proximity alarm. Orn preferred to do most of his dealings in the middle of the night. The graveyard shift asked few questions aside from "Where's the coffee and when will it be in me?" Her lip curled up, pulling with it the deep scar running down her right cheek; a landmark she refused to ruminate upon.

"Pull the other one, Orn. I can see the blighted station out the windows," Variel pointed out their too numerous windows at the orbiting waylay station, one of five above Samudra's ample coastlines.

Orn's excessive brows crocheted as he stared out the windows. They graced them with a near panoramic view of whatever existed outside the bridge; which for about 99.999% of the trip amounted to blackness, stars, then -- for a change of pace -- more stars and blackness. The things bothered him. Someone who spent more than a three hour cruise on a ship knew how easily a high powered nub of grit could shatter right through one...assuming the shields were down, backups were dead, and you smashed your noodle on the way to sealing the hole. Still, the mere possibility unnerved anyone with stardust in their veins.

"The station's out," the dwarf informed her, slurping down the last of his treat and reaching under his swivel chair for a drink of something other than thrice recycled "don't ask where it's been" water. His black gloves scattered around a few empty bottles of a drink decorated with fizzy bubbles.

Variel placed her hands upon a playbill about a dryad who thinks it's actually a man. She leaned out, staring into the carousel-like station rotating above the crystal blue planet. Most of the strip was dark, long since silenced for the families sleeping off their busy days ahead or behind them. Lights only burned on the lower maintenance deck and the top floors for those who think they're more important than maintenance.

"Flip the comm," the captain ordered, her voice all business despite the cottony pair of pajamas she'd waltzed onto the bridge in. Orn half expected to find an embroidered bunny.

"A'right, but it won't do you any good. They must have their gnomes in charge of docking." Despite his protesting, the dwarf pulled the switch, his right hand flickering momentarily over the blue tab covered in a fruit sticker.

"Eclipse 5, this is the *Elation-Cru* looking for a docking number. Please respond," Variel rolled her neck back, trying to blink away the last of her sleep. If this weren't the heart of "the safest ports in the galaxy" she'd probably be nervous about the quiet comms.

"Eclipse 5?" She continued before turning back to Orn, who lifted his massive shoulders and slipped another boot overtop his first. He'd pull out his PALM and start playing Spacecolony if the boss wasn't staring right at him. "I say, is anyone there?"

"We have coin?" Orn threw out.

The static popped and a voice, higher pitched than was typical for most organics, screeched across the flight deck, "This is Eclipse 5, oh bloody hell! Who let those little brats in here to dick with the controls?" some shuffling drifted across the space, a few pops answered back, and the voice returned much less like a rodent freebasing helium, "We have you on sensors, *Elation-Cru*."

"Sensors," Orn snorted, "look out a bleedin' window and we'll wave back at ya."

"Docking port 75-C is open. You'll be in the Happy Jellyfish lot," reported the man who was probably wiping sticky chocolate off his control panels.

"Joy of joys, we get to be a spineless blob of tentacles."

"Orn," Variel warned softly.

"Right, fine, uh," the dwarf flipped the switch back, "This is Elation-Cru, Ecstatic Jellyfish, got it."

"That's Happy Jellyfish," the weary voice stressed, "I see you're registered with the dwarven embassy. A proper customs officer shall be out in an hour."

"Right, Happy Jellyfish over and out," Orn mocked, flicking off the channel and punching in a few numbers. Docking was fully automated after one too many rich snots got wasted on Lavabombs while skittering about the galaxy in Leap-pods that somehow always wound up in the main director's lobby, the lady decals ripped to her nude waist. Pilots needn't bother with parking, but Orn liked to appear busy.

Variel sighed, this part of the galaxy made her itch. The surest way to snap was waking every day with forced joy and a shit eating grin. She laid a hand on the dwarf's shoulder as she leaned down to him, "Wake the others, I'm sure the twins have some unholy business they'll be getting to."

"What about *her*?" Orn asked, his eyes flickering to a smashed bulkhead that someone refused to repair on principle.

"Are you two...again? Fine, I'll talk to her. Gods know there's got to be something broken on this ship that'll cost all our money to repair."

Orn smiled, his overlarge eyes twinkling as he broke the comfortable silence of the ship by powering up the automated wake-up call. A charming cackle of a rooster bounded about the ship as bouts of twinkling music followed. The lilting, cheerful voice -- certain to have driven entire systems of people to utter madness -- chimed in, "Wake up sleepy heads! There's a big day ahead of you among the stars!"

The fact that everyone despised the thing with enough furor to power the ship across twelve light years encouraged Orn all the more to use it every chance he got. As Variel turned to leave, most likely to put on something that wasn't wearing to the point of being see through, the dwarf cheerfully called out, "Captain off the bridge."

She flipped him off before the doors could close.

Freshly clothed, Variel slid down the hatch to her quarters and straight into the chief and only engineer on the ship. Ferra thrusted a hunk of something black and slightly damaged into her face.

"Look at this!" the elf demanded, smudges from her latest discovery blacking the nearly triangular nose of her people.

Variel squinted at the oblong mass of what was not a piece off the back of a broken midden...probably. "It's bad?" she asked.

"The injector for the inertia deflector is half warped from SOMEONE throttling on the half burn while trying to impress star bunnies," her voice rose to a loud crescendo with each word.

"He can't hear you," Variel mumbled, wishing she wasn't caught in the middle of this.

"He damn well will when we're scraping bits of him off the forward windshields," Ferra screamed towards the bridge, locked off by two safety doors and a dwarf that was probably cranking up his music to drown her out.

"How much will this cost me?" Variel asked, turning the black pile of mutilated piping over in her hands. The elf was about to open her mouth when Variel cut her off, "Never mind, we're docking soon. Once we drop off the cargo, I'll forward the bits to the account."

The engineer finally noticed the leaking oil all over her icy pale hand and wiped it down her rubber apron. Just beneath it poked the pink frills of her blouse, unprotected from the hemorrhaging of a ship that should have been left to rust in its graveyard ages ago, as the engineer reminded Variel every time something snapped beyond repair. Not that the elf wouldn't curse out anyone who implied the same about her ship. Ferra was a continuous study in incongruity, usually in oil stained coveralls.

"It is my understanding we have reached our wayward point," this new voice was soft as silk, well honed to lull one into ease. It set Ferra's teeth on edge.

She turned from her boss to find the twins haunting around the edge of the galley, an area that was supposed to be off limits to

passengers. Not that the elves qualified as passengers anymore. They'd been onboard for nearly six months now, always returning like vermin after they'd "disembarked" on "business."

Ferra tucked the injector into the crook of her arm and muttered an, "Excuse me," as she pushed past the other elves on the ship, not bothering to look up as the oil soaked part gently collided with the girl's overtly expensive dress. "And tell Orn, he best be getting his hairy ass down here soon. We have words to share," Ferra shot out as she disappeared back down the narrow hall.

Variel tried to run her fingers through still knotted hair, but only got snagged and gave up. As the only technically paying customers, the elven twins dangled her over a disconcerting precipice. A small PR part of her brain said she should look somewhat presentable around them even though she was unaware what a presentable captain looked like. "Yes, we'll be docking soon. Will you both be long?"

Brena, the more talkative of the two, glanced back to her brother. He was in his usual blacks and greys, blending into the shadows; only the curls of orangey brown and white highlighting the dark skin on his face gave away his position. The sister favored the high fashion of the season, long droopy sleeves done up in velvets of purples and greens, her midsection cinched up so tight it was a wonder the girl could digest more than a grape. Then again, she wasn't paid to eat.

"No more than a day," Taliesin said, probably the greatest speech he'd given all day.

"Not a lot of people need murdering on the happy sands of Samudra?" Variel muttered more to herself than the twin, even though elf ears pick up on everything.

But the elf either missed the sarcasm or chose to ignore it, "Everyone has troubles."

"We shall not be longer than twelve hours at our assignments," Brena rescued her brother, "this I swear." Her own face was painted to accentuate the calico nature of the high elf twins, her eyes coated in enough eyeliner to incite the amorous affections of a raccoon.

"Good," Variel waved her hands and the elves turned silently, both vanishing back into the darkened mess hall.

"Them two give me the creeps," Orn's voice slipped out behind her, "It's what they're not saying that rattles my beard." He touched his poorly shorn chin and added, "metaphorically."

"Elves," Variel muttered, "Speaking of which..."

"I heard 'er. You'd think I never do anything proper around here." The pilot was in no mood for another redressing by the petite engineer unless some undressing was involved first.

Variel started the familiar tread through her ship, her freshly booted feet stomping across the fading red carpet laid by the previous owners. It takes a special committee of morons to coat a ship's decks in wall to wall carpeting. Orn trailed behind, twirling a spanner in his fingers and singing off-key whatever blasted through his ear piece.

The galley, mostly stripped bare save a lone table half-covered in bits from the ship that probably shouldn't be kept near food, gave way from what was once a "family fun center" turned storage to the disembarking room. This was the fancy term for a small enclave with a large, interactive plaque asking customers to wave any and all rights to sue in case of unexpected decompression, accidental alien pregnancy, or wandering bowel syndrome. And, of course, WEST was there, though technically WEST was everywhere.

Variel smoothed down what passed for her traveling business clothes, a not entirely billowy tunic and pair of cotton trousers in her standard brown, and looked towards the dwarf, "Where's your cape?"

"The cleaners," Orn muttered, his right hand trying to knot up the drawstring dangling down the front of his crimson vest. He avoided anything with buttons, snaps, or zippers.

"Do I pay you to spout crap back at me?"

"Consider it a perk," Orn grinned up at her, "We won't need it anyway. Why's a graveyard shift gonna expect a cape?"

"Orn..."

She was about to insist he waddle back and get the damn thing when the latch popped as the airlock finished pressurizing. Both the human and dwarf opened their jaws, trying to adjust to the inflow of station barometrics. The final safety seal unlatched

and the heaviest door on the ship swung open to allow a pair of humans into their little space.

They were each dressed in standard uniform whites and blues, brass buttons all along the chest at a Z angle, with matching pairs of flat caps to complete the look. If it weren't for the obvious age on the one, or the clipboard in the hands of the second, they'd have appeared identical clones to most other species and some humans.

"I am technician Partal of the spacial licensing and travel registration department. This is my intern, third technician Segundo. He shall not be allowed to touch anything upon, around, near, or in trans-dimensional proximity to this ship. Please nod your appendage of choice if you accept my terms."

The technician paused in his boilerplate and glanced towards the dwarf, who gulped a moment and then nodded. "Make a note the ambassador bobbed his head," he pointed to his intern's clipboard which flashed as his finger interrupted the data streaming from the kid's PALM. Something hidden in the unnecessary data struck a cord and he scrutinized the dwarven "ambassador."

"Sir, where is your cape?"

Orn grumbled, not looking towards his boss who could radiate smug annoyance at 10,000 lumens. "My pet rock ate it," he lied to the government official.

"Traditional garb consumed by sedimentary livestock," the technician pointed to an option in the scrolling list. It flared blue and disappeared into the mists of information. "This ship is listed as under the license of one Ms. Variel Tuffman. I assume that would be you?" He turned his tedious face upon the captain, who gritted at the last name but nodded.

"Sounds like a luggage brand. Make a note of that, Sec," he said to his intern, "No, not the luggage brand."

"Sir," Segundo spoke for the first time, his voice wobblier than Orn's attempts at hard boiled eggs, "it's flagged for immediate inspection."

"Don't be absurd," Variel pressed. "This is clearly an embassy sponsored ship. You dishonor our esteemed guest."

"Yes, I am very dishonored. If you do not rectify this dishonor we shall have to do battle in a pit of some type of sea creature. But not shrimp, I'm allergic," Orn rabble roused, shaking his falsely royal fist for emphasis.

"It's been over two years since a member of SPLITR has set foot upon this vessel," Segundo read off his report, afraid to make eye contact with the woman ready to tear his limbs off should he try.

Variel hoped to salvage what should have been a quick exchange. "The ambassador's been quite busy, meeting with various important galactic, uh..."

"Fusspots," Orn filled in, doing his best to not help. Was it too late for her to get an inflatable dwarf doll and fire the pilot?

"Eh?" a light flared in the first technician's ear. He tapped his own blinking PALM and spoke loudly to most likely not just himself, "Yes. Already? Very well."

He ended the call as quickly as it began and turned towards his intern, "Someone left the gnomes unmanned and the entire mermaid deck flooded with chocolate. This one's all yours. Try not to muck it up, cast off."

Before Segundo could argue, his mentor wandered back through the airlock, cursing about chocolate stains over his uniform. The technician gulped and stared down at the dwarven ambassador dressed in what appeared to be the ragged clothes pilgrims wore to show their devotion to a god by forsaking all manner of button. His PALM Board flashed over and over, the highlighted section in bright red font, "Inspection Required. Do not allow release without full Inspection."

"It says here," Segundo coughed into his fist, trying to lower his voice, "I cannot let you disembark until a full inspection is made of your vessel, ship, or domicile."

Variel cracked her knuckles, a move considered nonthreatening to most other species. The petrified human quivered, yet kept waving his official forms about as if they were a magical shield. As she was about to lay into him, their engineer bounded into the embarkation closet, her apron tossed in favor of a pair of canvas overalls.

"What's this little shit doing here?" she asked, eyeing up the scrawny human shrinking before her mighty five foot size.

"Pissing on the floor, mostly," Orn muttered, earning a small nod from Variel, a small quiver of defiance from the floor wetter, and recalled rage from Ferra.

"Shut your mouth, Orn, or I'll do it for you." Hell hath no fury like a woman facing a night of fully reassembling an inertia injector.

"Yes, Ma'am," he muttered, cowed by the only person in the universe who could get to him.

"Why aren't we going? The shop's gonna close soon, and I ain't trekking the twelve elevator stops for the next one." Ferra memorized nearly every mechanic shop's schedule in the three years she'd been keeping the *Elation-Cru* mobile. A photographic memory came in handy at times.

"Yes, why aren't we moving?" Variel's snake eyes turned on the exposed belly of the underling.

Third Technician Segundo coughed into his fist, "I don't have the power to override anything. I'msorry. I'd have to do an inspection before your ship can be released. Pleasedon'thitme!"

"Could you give us a moment, please?" the ambassador asked, yanking the elf and human slightly out of hearing range. "What's the problem?"

"I don't want any government grubworm poking about my ship," Ferra grumbled.

"What she said," Variel agreed. The thought of anyone digging through their lives unnerved her. It was why she burned so much coin getting the ship dwarf registered in the first place. They never asked any questions aside from, "How much money do you have, and where will you forward it from?"

"So one snot nosed brat wanders star struck about a spaceship, writes down a few notes about how clean the kitchen is, and then leaves a note for his superiors." Orn was trying to be the diplomatic one, which should have sent up red flags, but everyone was exhausted from a long flight.

"And," the dwarf's brown quartz eyes sparkled, "we have the only partially illegal thing on us the whole time. Most he can accuse us of is failing to replace the tail light."

"He damn well better not," Ferra growled. Inspection notes were a source of pride for any engineer wandering her way into a smokey bar on the edge of nowhere.

"The dwarf's making sense. I hate it when he makes sense," Variel rubbed her head, already planning a long stopover on one of those pleasure stations that has real running water. "You," she called to the kid, "Tech whatever. We let you onto the ship, you make your sweep while we take care of business on the station, yes?"

Regulations maintained that all occupants were to remain well cloistered within their cabins until a stamp of approval was received, but the small part marked as common sense warned Segundo that this was the compromise. If he didn't accept it, the next one was tossing his body into space. "I will require assistance as I cannot touch anything."

A cruel smile overtook Variel's ragged features, "I've already thought of that." She leaned over to the only control panel in the room, an ancient standing terminal, and asked calmly, "WEST, can you send Gene up here? We have a guest who requires his assistance."

The computer grumbled something, but before it could form an actual argument, the captain cut him off, "Thank you, WEST."

"Gene is a registered crew member of this vessel, then?" Segundo asked.

"You could say that," Orn muttered, feeling oddly sorry for the kid.

"Excellent," Segundo turned from the others and began to flip through his notes, waiting for his escort.

"If you're done shoving your thumbs up each other's asses," Ferra said, pushing past the pair of humans and one lonely dwarf, "I have a ship to fix." She waltzed through the open airlock without a second glance, her narrow stride moving at a near run to beat Crazy Al's Althernators & More closing time.

"After you, ambassador," Variel bowed slightly to the dwarf, letting him take the lead. He shook his stocky head, but set out before her, trying to play the poorly cast part of dignified dignitary.

For a moment the captain paused, taking in the knock kneed, barely out of -- or still trapped in -- his teens kid and felt pity, "Good luck with your inspection. You're gonna need it."

Before Segundo looked up, she was gone, leaving him alone with his guide.

It'd have been more appropriate if a ring of men, swathed in the filth they peddled to others, graced the back room of the office complex on some rusted dock while gambling away a poor urchin's legs. Instead, a scrubbed man unwound his tie and poured a dribble of antacid into a glass, slugging it down while his partner jabbed at his hand with fervor.

"Those boars never saw me coming!" he shouted as his hand erupted in celebration sparks.

Variel coughed into her fist, "Gentlemen." When the pairs of eyes turned to her, she lifted high a briefcase, "I believe we have some business to settle."

One-Eyed Joe, as the kids called him, rose from his pristine desk. Only the obligatory eyepatch and false leg dotted its metallic landscape incase a VIP family wandered in. Always stay in character, even when one's climbing your leg while you're trying to take a piss. That was life orbiting the corporate owned Samudra; clear skies, clear seas, and teams of underlings stampeding to keep it that way. It was inevitable that all beloved vid characters and childhood idols turned to the seedier strings of life if only to dull the endless cloying sugar on the palate.

His partner clicked off his PALM and turned, the more menacing of the pair when it came to the criminals Joe dragged home. While Joe reenacted scenes of his favorite movies to guys with more tattoos than a walking billboard, Eric would almost dial up the security force in the event something finally went horribly wrong.

"Did you bring it?" Joe asked, skipping past the woman nearly half his age for the case dangling off her arm.

Variel smiled and turned to her partner in minor crime and passed him the case, "Orn, if you'd be so kind."

The dwarf flipped the switch causing the false lid to swing open. One-Eye groaned at the sight of an empty case, but Orn reached inside to push the hidden switch and the illusion broke. A pile of cloth replaced the emptiness.

Joe smiled wide, "Jolly good show!" He was clearly enjoying this part. Eric dialed up another number.

Orn glanced up at his boss. Most clients insisted on flipping the hidden switch themselves despite not having the proper biometrics to see the damn thing. It was a challenge of bravado that could take hours and once led to a permanent case of cross eye. No one ever approached it like a magic show.

Variel motioned him forward; he was the star at this part. She preferred the dirty work, Orn was there for the show. Rolling his mountainous shoulders, the dwarf lifted the sack of cloth hidden inside the briefcase and shook it once. The hidden seams popped and shifted into place, creating an open basket ready to gobble up anything that could be shoved inside a 12x12 inch fabric box. "The deluxe backpack of storing contains not one, but two handles," Orn's voice oozed oily charm as he motioned to the two strips dangling off the edge. "It can store up to three hundred items that do not stack," he said as he grabbed up One Eye's leg and slipped it into the black void, then reached for a desk lamp.

Eric jumped to his feet, throwing off Orn's concentration. The dwarf's sticky fingers paused, but Joe waved his partner off, "Let him be."

Orn gripped the lamp anew, but Eric made the "I'm watching you" motion with his fingers. It was a very threatening gesture on the dwarven home planet, as it implied you owed someone money. The dwarf shook it off and shoved the lamp into the knapsack along with a pile of rocks he kept in his coat pocket.

"Once you've finished storing whatever you need to cart, simply push down on the sides," Orn struggled, forcing all his weight onto the EZ-Snaps, when one finally unlatched. Half of the bag slipped under, while the other half remained stubbornly upright. The dwarf cursed under his tongue and fought before snagging half the room in an unstable gravity field. Without breaking a sweat, and holding his sigh of relief in, the other latch gave and the backpack curled up in on itself, creating another pile of uninteresting cloth. Orn lifted the backpack high and waved it about as if it was a towel.

"Amazin'!" Joe crowed, carefully taking the thin sheet that now held his entire life, "How does it work?"

Variel stepped in, "MGC is laced into the fabric which top research mages use to create a small wyrmhole to the storage facility."

Orn's eyes slid back to his boss but he didn't move his head. Joe was shaking his new toy like a dog with a rabbit, blathering about all the things he wanted to squirrel away inside his new bag. "Amazing. See Eric, simply amazing!"

"Yes, love, amazing. How much does this amazing bag cost?"

"Two fresh cat videos and a picture of a domesticated animal in clothing," Variel said smoothly.

"One cat video, a hedgehog playing badminton, and three goats standing atop a crashed orc ship," Eric argued back, mentally ticking over how many meals out this was going to cost them.

"The price is non-negotiable," Variel replied, her fingers plucking the fabric away from Joe's and folding it up to place back in the case.

"Eric..." the old man whined, upset at having lost his highly illegal toy.

"Fine, two new cat videos and a bird singing along with a hamster," Eric relented.

"Sold," the captain smiled, thrusting the dangerous fabric back into the buyer's hands. "We have an off-planet dwarven account to transfer the funds into."

"Of course you do," Eric muttered, wishing his love would get back into building bottles on ships or something that didn't dirty their tapestries with the unsavory type. "Wiring them now."

One-Eye placed the bag on the ground, snapped it open, and reached inside. "Look, it's me leg!" He struggled keeping out of character whenever he touched the damn prop.

"Would you like to read the safety manual?" Variel asked as she snapped the briefcase shut, a thick flyer resting between her fingers. Paper was much harder to trace.

"No, thank you," Eric clipped as his grandfather's lamp appeared and then vanished back inside the bag.

"Suit yourself," Variel muttered, still laying the book down upon the edge of the desk. When they accidentally invert the gravity in the room, they can figure out how to solve the problem themselves. "Come on, Orn," she said quietly to the dwarf trying to pilfer the man's eyepatch.

His fingers dropped the famous bit of elastic and they wandered back into his pockets, "Yes, Sir."

As Variel eased out of the back office, dragging her companion along, she called out behind, "Pleasure doing business with you."

"'MGC woven into the fabric?'" Orn's voice bounced around the mostly empty promenade as Variel reached across the counter of the only open food stand, "I had no idea you humans could pull that kind of shit our your orifice of choice."

The professional weaver of near truth was impressed. His notion of most humans was that they clustered in groups, coated furniture in moisture at the first sign of distress, and broke down into a trembling pile of flesh upon a moment's scrutiny. Of course, prior to this job, his only major interaction had been shuffling groups of missionaries to their holy site. Possibly not the best cross section of the species, but Orn didn't match up well to the preferred example of dwarves either.

Variel thanked the gargoyle manning the food cart, one of the few species to prefer the endless night of space, and lifted the horrendous concoction towards her mouth. The fat still sizzled from the fryer as clumps of excess batter dropped off the weaving blob of meat on a stick to the pristine grates. She ignored the disgusted look on her pilot's face while wrapping a napkin around the edge of her dinner and commented upon the job. "Not a good idea to go blathering about gravity wells and microblack holes. That makes the customer jumpy."

"What was he expecting? That thing's illegal nearly everywhere."

She gazed up at the blinking lights of a security camera stashed into the high walls of the glorified floating shopping mall, "The ownership is. The sale is perfectly legal. Provided no one

catches you actually holding the damn thing." She spent a lot of her life skirting around the name of the law, sometimes by hiding for days in a frozen asteroid belt.

Orn curled up his lip and stared at the stomach churning image of the human chomping down on the wad of meat, "You're not gonna eat that are you? Orc food gives your intestines nightmares."

Variel shook her head. For being the people that took one look at the galaxy and said 'You're all welcome as long as you have the coin,' he was one xenophobic little turd, "There's nothing wrong with Orc food. It's quite nutritious and full of protein."

"And some guy named Ogg who didn't pass inspection," Orn grumbled.

"What would you want that isn't straight sugar?"

"Wolf, Bear, Jaguar, Snake? Anything that wasn't screaming about drinking my mother's blood before heading into the deep fryer," Orn shrugged, hunting around for a dwarf seat as his boss plopped the empty briefcase onto a rickety wrought iron table, scattering the triangles advertising the great fun they could have across the station.

Variel chomped down in the least ladylike way imaginable short of stuffing the entire thing down her throat and swallowing whole like a duck. Table manners were for something that didn't come on a stick. Orn drug over a hard won chair. He sat and pushed the "lift" lever to be about on eye level just as the last of Ogg vanished.

"I'm surprised you want all that human food," Variel said, clearing grease off her chin, "I figured you and Ferra'd go in for *haute elven cuisine*."

"Ha! She says it tastes like nothing but air and condescension with a wafer on top," Orn responded, dropping his hand to the table with a heavy thud. The thing was itching again.

Variel sighed, realizing the eternal story teller was gonna keep his mouth shut, "What was it this time?"

"Nothing. She just," Orn scratched at his bulbous nose and tried to find an untruth so he wasn't at fault for whatever repair bills Ferra was currently running up, "So, I maybe over-tweaked the last burn when we swung around the base."

"How 'over-tweaked?'"

"A few things caught on fire," Orn admitted sheepishly, "But nothing major, and it all went out like a light. We shouldn't need to test the fire alarm anytime soon."

Variel sighed, but any reprimand died on her tongue. It didn't matter much what she said to the dwarf, the elven engineer could dish it up tenfold and he actually had to listen to her. "I don't know how you two even got married, much less stay."

Orn stopped fiddling with his hand and brought it up to his lips, thinking. Slowly, he smiled and answered, "Angry sex. She gets that ship up and running after a long fight and...sweet ore. A pilot, an engineer, and a humming ship is the best kind of threeway."

"I do not need to hear this, or think about this," Variel muttered, wishing she could wipe her memory with something other than troll ale (along with her liver, spleen and lungs), "I'm never walking into engineering alone again."

"Probably for the best," the dwarf admitted. His last move wasn't the only time the fire systems had been prematurely checked.

The station fell silent as the two lapsed into a comfortable quiet. Only the soothing hum of "everything's still working" wormed up through the floor. It must be a deafening cacophony when the place was at capacity; boots trampling up and down the metal corridors, faces crying for food, water, those stupid sunglasses that give you "elven" eyes. Orn didn't do "family friendly." He could barely handle "friendly," and Variel seemed to keep the ship as far from the Pax sectors as she could. Peace and harmony didn't often call upon the likes of them.

A few spotlights bounded around the section below their outcropping, advertising for some show that wasn't to start for another three hours. If you have crowds of parents trying to find a place to sit down, you get a small stage filled with the kinds of people you'd normally never let your kid near. But, for five minutes the screaming stops as the kid watches wide eyed while a troll swallows bricks of flaming charcoal or a dwarf chops credit bits in half. It was one of those devil deals that leaves everyone soulless.

The station smelled of artificial baked goods, disinfectant, and the base note of urine. If it weren't for the occasional hurried run of someone in a drab uniform carrying a punctured hull repair kit, it was hard to believe you weren't actually trapped on a hell planet.

The gargoyle grunted, a low call of release, as it unsheathed its wings in the rare moment between shifts. Stretching long past its little stand, the thick stonehide that aided in gliding curled up and around the man's craggy head, bumping his carved curly locks. It was rare to find one this deep into shared territory. Permits weren't as easy to get for the lower species.

They weren't officially called that. Something like "Non-Organic Entities," which accounted for all the non-bipedal, greater than four limbed, occasionally non-corporeal beings that tried to carve a niche in the ever expanding universe. But everyone knew which way the solar winds blew. The only one lower on the pecking pole than the NOE's were the gnomes, but it's harder to get lower than dirt.

The gargoyle curled up his wings and tucked them back inside the apron decked with his stand's name, "Exotic Eats," and blinked his eyes rapidly. Orn slugged Variel on the shoulder and pointed excitedly, "He must have one of them new EyeScans."

"And..."

"No more lugging around a piece for the PALM to project onto when the imager loses cohesion, instant eye access, none of that scrolling through your hand," Orn sighed wistfully as if he was describing the perfect woman.

"And they drill straight into your brain to place it. No thanks."

"It's a one time installation. A one time, highly expensive installation." The dwarf dreamed of one ever since the big unveil Expo on Traltar, but coin was tighter with each passing month. If the cat market stayed the way it was, it could get much worse.

Variel shook her head, tapping her trusty hand and letting the screen wash over one of the PALM receptacles at every table, "It's one time, until there's a major hardware upgrade, then back into your skull they go taking gods know how many brains in the process." She tapped a few more numbers and, after exchanging their new riches into bank numbers, transferred it all over to Ferra.

Almost all. The bird and hamster duet would go into the ship's lease pot.

Centuries back, when meeting someone who didn't look like, sound like, or act like you was a novel thing, a few people had the brilliant idea to try a universal currency. Credits they called it, which confused most everyone who thought they were paying on credit and would wake up to a depleted account and massive overdraft fees. Then the gnomes came into play. After the vultures got them to a 10,000% interest rate, there was such an epic economical collapse the galactic community talked of trying to sell their universe off to an alternate one for scrap.

Oddly, it was the ancient elven tradition of trading stories for goods that took hold. Sure, the humans came back with coins, now in the form of holographic projections. Dwarves had an incredibly complex system involving the maiden name of your great-grandmother's clan, and most orc colonies had their own denominations of pressed heavy metals. But anyone could transfer a story to heavy currency.

Eventually, the stories simplified when one needed an epically epic poem to purchase bread. Filtered down due to anti-inflation laws, the most highly guarded mint in the entire universe contained a single man, a cat, and a video camera. There hadn't been a major crash since.

A sign across from their vantage point lit up: "Loqual's Trinkets and Tricks." The mood lights set to simulate day began to rise. Dawn was coming to the station. Variel motioned to Orn it was time to be moving on, avoid all the sticky fingered children and sticky chinned adults poking into business they'd never understand.

As she passed the gargoyle, she dropped a few limericks into his tip jar and nodded, "That was the best fried klak I've had in ages." The gargoyle's eyes faded to a pink as he accepted the comment.

"You know what your problem is," Orn started, walking beside the human who learned to shorten her stride years ago.

"That I have a government official poking about my ship, a ship I'm still over 10% on the line for -- assuming it doesn't crumble to ash before then -- and a dwarf trying to psychoanalyze me?"

"I was gonna say you're too cynical, but that's good too."

CHAPTER TWO

Ferra tapped her finger against the pale blue button, a small charge bouncing through the air. Most people would wait patiently after shocking up a summons, but the elf had already laid into it five times and was about to go for a sixth when an exhausted human stumbled forth. The facial fur of their kind had something pink stuck on the cheek, but for all she knew it was a common fashion trend.

"I need to replace the seal on this inertia injector," she said in her most colloquial tone.

Probably-not-titular Crazy Al slipped on the store's pair of discharge gloves and picked up the part, micronodes of excess MGC dissolving into the atmosphere. She barely felt anything above a deca-mage anymore. He turned the piece over in his hands and placed it back on the overloaded counter, "The seal's broken."

"No? Here I thought it was a perfectly functioning injector that wanted to go for a stroll, see the universe and all before it bloody cracked in half," colloquial was quickly slipping into snippy. After that came sardonic, then vitriol. Most people never lived to see stage five.

But Crazy Al's minion didn't get the nightshift because he feared the light, "A-yup, have to order a whole new part." His fat fingers slipped free of the gloves and called up the inventory screen embedded in the counter. "What class is your vehicle or traveling structure what needs a new one?"

Ferra's fingers slicked her nearly transparent eyebrows in place as she tried to calm the rising fire, "I don't need a new injector, all I need is a seal." She flipped apart the coil and bounced up the rubber piece fraying to near breakage. "See, seal, little rubber thing what goes on the injector and keeps excess inertia from shattering across the deck."

"I'm afraid we don't have excess seals...Ma'am. Only entire parts."

That little pause before he settled on ma'am told her she wasn't dealing with a human used to elves. They worried to an excessive degree about getting gender correct, as if elves gave a shit. Humans could keep their concerns about everyone's genitalia to themselves. If he'd called her a dulcen though they wouldn't be finding the body until all of the galaxy compressed into a black hole. "Then go get another injector, take off the seal, and sell me that!"

"Then that injector would be missing a seal."

Ferra bounced her head against the counter, causing the inventory screen to jump, "This is when I'd ask to see the manager but..."

"I'm the manager."

"I feared as such." She rose, her large eyes quickly narrowing as she asked, "How much for a new one, then?"

"For the entire part, we don't sell seals."

"By all that...yes, the fucking part. How much for the entire injector and not the three inches of colon I wish to shred out of you."

"No reason to be using that kind of blue language...ma'am," the barely sentient clerk shifted over to the locked down transaction screen, poking at a few more buttons until a range of injectors appeared beneath Ferra's fingers. "Please select which size to continue," he said just before the helpful computer chirped up *"Select which size to continue."*

Ferra flipped quickly through ten pages, her eyes not scanning as years swam by until a good five decades were gone. Barely a blink for her kind, but the human in front of her had probably only gotten out of diapers, or something like that. "Species relating" was for ambassadors and salesmen. Larger, sleeker ships passed under her fingers; the fancy ones aging people buy to impress their younger not-technically-peers. The clunkier ones, still sturdy as rocks, and enjoyed by those with a nostalgic touch also vanished with each scroll of the menu. Finally, she came to the "Commercial Class" of ship.

Pushing the button, she looked up at her current tormentor and said, "That one. How much?"

He paused, waiting for the computer to tell him his job, "Five hundred chickpeas," he said, his dull eyes casting down upon her.

She thought of asking for that in "universal please," but knew how well it'd go over and did the calculation in her head. The captain was going to blow about ten inertia seals herself, but it was better her than the ship. "Fine," she relented to the man.

"Excellent," he punched some numbers into the computer, "would you like delivery?"

"Delivery? I'm standing right here."

"Oh no, no, no. We don't keep parts like that in store. It would be too dangerous."

"Too dangerous for whom? It's a hunk of plastic and rubber until the charge is run through."

The finer points of space travel passed over the clerk's head and he repeated, "One of our gnomes will have to retrieve your package and deliver it to your ship within a business day. Or you could return here."

She thought of just how much damage a second return to this shop would cost her and shook her head, "Delivery, fine, tack it on."

The clerk tapped happily into his screen, "And the name of your ship for delivery?"

"The *Elation-Cru*, it's on the," she tried to tamp down her own shudder, "Happy Jellyfish deck."

"Thank you, Sir. I mean, Ma'am," he banged furiously against a holographic keyboard, trying to hide his own blunder before unlocking the scanner and passing it over, "If you could be so kind as to give me your PALM."

She held out her pale hand and felt a small tingle as it accessed her internal data, decimating the already paltry bank account. He took the scanner back and she flexed her fingers, always afraid of the day there'd be a major blowback from one of those damn things. "Someone will be around with your inertia injector in 12-25 hours. Be certain you have a sentient adult or gnome with legal guardianship waiting to sign for it."

"So, no ship of hyper-intelligent chicken children, then?"

"Is that what this part is for?" he asked seriously, as if he were about to report her for poultry-napping.

Ferra's mouth hung agape, "We're you born this stupid or did a troll sit on your head as a child?"

"Ma'am?"

"Put it away," she mumbled to her fists as she shook her head. Lifting up the old injector that could be cannibalized later, Ferra marched towards the door crowded with fading stickers from part manufacturers; a few far too familiar to the old engineer. "I'm leaving before I put your head through something it's not actually thicker than."

As she passed over the threshold, pausing for the few seconds it took the door to whoosh open, his cheerful voice carried across her last nerve, "Pleasure doing business with you. Please come again."

Third Technician Segundo tapped another set of checks off of his endless list as he placed the bags of flour and sugar back inside the galley's peeling cabinets. "Labeled properly," he muttered aloud to himself to overcompensate for his silent guide.

He switched on the drinking sink, a pitiful stream of water burbling out, its shade an appeasable yellow. Another checkmark down, 786 more to go by his count. "I believe I need to visit the 'Crew Storage' next," he said and looked up and then up some more at his silent guide.

The monster...No, the training was very explicit. When meeting a fellow sentient it was best to address them as alien and later determine if they are in fact someone's pet or grandmother. He failed that test every time he opened his mouth, his previous life failing to prepare him for much of anything aside from sitting quietly and being holy. His guide, Gene they called it, towered a couple of feet above Segundo, putting him somewhere near the eight foot tall ceilings the ship boasted. But it wasn't the height that bothered the technician, nor the fact its skin was composed of an igneous rock substance cleaved to reveal ever shifting fires below. It was the eyes, the only gaps in the head portion of the monster, that flared an eternal red, occasionally clouding over in puffs of grey smoke. Like when the mon...Gene laid red gaps upon the kid it'd be touring about the ship. He could almost swear the smoke rolled like a tornado when he asked the Gene for its PALM scan.

Segundo wasn't prepared for this. Technically, he wasn't even prepared to be a technician. He'd been bumped to intern in the training program after his predecessor jammed his head inside an aft engine burner when the ship was in the middle of pre-space flight checks. It took days to properly scrub the ship and hours for the government's lawyers to lay blame at the feet of the ship's owners; a nice couple from the rolling farm systems who were doing time in a troll prison up-galaxy.

The death or dismemberment of a technician was always ruled the fault of anyone other than themselves. Even a few suicides were found to be the cause of too well constructed rope, far too copious pharmaceuticals, and -- in one landmark case -- the deadly overabundance of gravity. After dwarves, elves, and humans all laid a stake to Samudra, terra and ocean forming it up to match their preferred water getaway, they realized it was far easier to found its own interspecies government rather than getting the other species' ruling classes to communicate. Being traditionalists, the elves demanded a proper coup before the official documents could be signed. A single bread stand was tipped over. Every year the stations celebrate the triumph of freedom over imagined tyranny by lighting explosives and tossing bread.

So here was poor Segundo, barely out of his pupal stage and already poking about dwarven ships. "Are there any rickety staircases that are not up to the Aliens with Disabilities code?" he asked the Gene leading him through the narrow galley with its slightly wobbly but acceptable table, out past the heat exchange and MCG expansion pipes, towards what would hopefully be storage.

The monster swung his head in a wide "No," emphasizing the movement so the technician wouldn't have to ask twice. Not that it helped.

"So there are no cases of anything stair that could impede a gnome with a broken back?"

Steam hissed through some of the glowing cracks in Gene's back as he swung his head a harder no and kept pulling the babbling child forward. Segundo's paper thin boots skidded across the carpet. He'd never seen cloth laid across the floor before and was uncertain how to react to it. Currently, he was building up such a static electric charge his visit to engineering should be very hair raising indeed.

A few curious trappings remained from the old ship's early days. A pair of curtains hung over what had once been a viewing port long since covered in scrap. A phrase etchinged in five languages hung over the door to direct people who didn't spend their lives on the ship to the lavatories. And in every room, a happy blue and gold panel with a bright washscreen of a rising planet's shadow greeted the entrance.

As Gene stomped onwards, his bulk skimming across the cramped walls of the shunted sails, Segundo paused at the eternally open doorway to the "Entertainment Deck." His fingers scrolled through the inventory list, never letting it fade away from his PALM incase it couldn't come back. There was nothing about testing a door system, aside from making sure no limbs were recently mangled, but a small pique of curiosity got the better of him.

He approached the blue screen, larger than his face, with a hefty speaker system grate embedded below. Segundo tapped the small image of the cruise ship zipping around an asteroid belt. A calm voice chirped up, "Good day fellow star traveler. I am your Welcoming Engine of Spacealogical Tours. Whatever your heart desires, I shall endeavor to make available. What do you wish?"

The soft screen faded and a narrow tan box appeared. A pair of wheels of varying size took the place where eyes would be, while a foul zigzag of wiring created a mouth. For some reason, it also wore an eyepatch and a tri-corner hat. The zigzag opened and a foul, echoing voice asked, "Whatcha want?"

Segundo stepped back. He'd been expecting a human face, formed from the users own sexual preferences. It was a coming of age experience for children near puberty to rag on whatever the computers picked for their friends, and secretly hope what it chose for them was acceptable and not, say, a gargoyle in fishnets. He'd never interacted with a talking box before. "Who are you?"

The talking box cranked its wheel eyes and said, "Read the watermark below your fat lips, detective."

"W.E.S.T? Oh I get it, Welcoming Engine of Spacealogical Tours. You're west."

"It's pronounced Wee-st," the computer snipped, stretching out the vowel as if it were a game to pass the time.

"Why?" Segundo's hospitality instructor would have just thrown him into an aft engine.

The wheel eyes spun quickly, creating the animation of smoke pouring off them, "Because Mighty Overlord of Organics was already registered."

"Oh," he tried to make a note of that in his likely never to be read report, but the tablet kept flashing at him every time he etched in "overlord." Even the slightly-less-sentient-than-a-toaster word document picked up on the sarcasm flying right over the human's head.

WEST sighed by activating the air compressors to clear out its interface in the inevitable event of an undeveloped organic jamming crispified potato into its airports. The air whooshed right over the technician's head as he leaned down to pick up an errant bit. "Was there an inquiry you wished to make, or must you drain the life out of every thing you interact upon?"

"Tell me about this ship," Segundo stuttered. Not that the technician had any plans to cut short his first inspection by asking the onboard computer to do his job. He just couldn't think of anything other than, "Why is the sky black?"

"It is a ship," WEST began, "it is made of various metallic ores and alloys, shaped and formed to create something that others would generously call a 'bedpan with wings.' Most scientists believe it exists primarily within the four dimensions of space except when opening a wyrmhole where it slips either down to two or up to five. These scientists are, of course, wrong. A few calculated that in order for the sheer energetic magnitude of folding space to fit within a two dimensional view of..."

"Where are the bathrooms?"

Another blast of air hit Segundo in the chin. WEST's voice, always a bit shrill from age, raised a few octaves higher in its perturbance. "The commons bathroom is located behind the shuffle board, which was torn out. A second family and non-organic friendly one is towards the back of the deck near a gaping hole no one bothered to cover over," as the computer lapsed out of its script, the eyes spun slower and it asked darkly, "Would you also wish to know where the exits are located and how to squeeze your soft, squishy form into a life suit?"

The technician shook his head and poked at his concave stomach with his licensed SPLITR stylus. It was the first time his form had ever been referred to as soft. The head was a different matter. He could almost swear the jagged wires smirked as the welcoming engine lapsed into bemused silence. Computers were supposed to be helpful, not revel in getting a rise out of every organic that woke it from its slumber.

Segundo flipped to the ether and did a quick pile on for anything calling itself 'west robot.' After about fifty hits for a very prolific porn actor who had a particularly entertaining handicap, he found what he was looking for, and hoisted his PALM illuminated clipboard at the computer screen. "Says here your entire lot was discontinued, ripped apart chip by chip and sold for scrap ages ago. You're the only one of you in the entire universe."

WEST's eyes rotated slower, the left one coming to a halt before it responded in a chipped voice, "That makes me special, mammal."

A crack resounded from behind the technician and he flipped away from the computer that he could have sworn flared an animated tongue at him. His guide stood in the doorway, its knuckles firmly gripped upon the half closed door, digging into the metal alloy. Segundo nodded solemnly to his silent guide, turning his soft chest away from the computer.

But WEST wasn't finished with him, "Hey, djinn!" Gene's eyes smoked up rapidly as it focused on the blathering box, "Would you kindly stomp this puny human to paste?" Segundo gasped, his head flapping about like a terrified chicken, but Gene only folded his arms up and tapped his crackling foot against the carpet.

"Damn," WEST complained, "It used to work on the last guy."

"What did you call him?" Segundo asked the computer trying to turn him into paste. There were subsections inside of subsections on the legal transportation of specific species not recognized in the Intergalactic Book of Not-Making-An-Ass-Out-of-Yourself. Most came down to "You can't do it."

"Djinn, or if you'd prefer the colloquial jinn spelling," WEST teased, even though both sounded the same to the organics unequipped with verbal grammar check.

Segundo's fingers sped through lists: pixies, pictsies, sprites, can of sprite, brownie, brownie scout, pan of brownies...There was nothing under a D or a J for the jin. He tried not to hyperventilate at the idea that he just discovered an unknown species, conveniently forgetting it was on a ship docked at an orbiting vacation spot and more than likely it was aware of, and had discovered its own species some time ago.

He flipped his PALM over to document mode, preserving five images of his thumb and a video of his nose for posterity before lining it up properly over the now steaming hulk of rock, seething at the attention and interruption. A few flashes bounced from his hand, held up as if he were waiting for a very low high five. He pushed send, launching the images off into the ether with the epitaph "Gin." "I cannot find anything in the lists for the feeding or housing of a Dah-jinn," he mused to himself as if he weren't surrounded by two people who cared little for what passed between his ears.

WEST's eyes rolled quickly, giggling to itself, "Perhaps you can find them listed under 'genies.'"

Gene shifted back as the technician's head swung up, his dust cloth eyes as agape as his mouth. A few gurgles dribbled from the drooling maw, but nothing coherent escaped. The information seemed to have pushed the human over the narrow edge it teetered upon. Even WEST hadn't anticipated this utter mental breakdown. It was looking to be a much more entertaining day after all.

"You," Segundo pointed to the hulking rock, "you're a genie? But you don't live in a lamp, or have a beard, or wear pointed shoes."

A large gasp of steam blew, the heat bursting dangerously close to Segundo's face as the djinn leaned in close. His red eyes burned hotter than seemed physically possible as small sparks of blue overtook the middle flame. Slowly, with emphasis, Gene shook his head. A very definite and clear there-will-be-no-follow-up-questions "No."

Segundo gulped, settling back onto his heels, trying to put all those old books he read as a child out of his mind. But something stuck deep, a fervent dream more than anything else, and --ideology overriding the self preservation instinct -- he looked up at the quickly defusing djinn to ask, "Will you grant my wishes?"

"Satellite."

"No way, look at that gait. He's never stepped foot off planet in his life," Orn tossed another piece of fried close-enough-to-chicken into his mouth. Ferra would have him sleeping with the genie if she knew what was failing to travel his digestive tract. Dwarves were supposed to be loyal, hardworking, and concerto ass flautists. Orn failed at the first two, so he doubled down on the last.

"His knickers could be trapped in a gravity well inside his ass," his captain said, snagging one of the dwarf's bits of fried sea bug. "There's no way you can tell who's a virgin from their walk."

"Oh my cynical, Sir," he said, mocking a small bow as he balled up the last of the sack and tossed it towards a recycle bin. It called out a cheery "Only You Can Prevent Decompression," as it flared up his trash. They moved their 'basking in the glow of a job well finished' party onto the main thoroughfare, watching the early risers pass through shops over-crammed with every tacky piece of paraphernalia the designer could stamp "Samudra: Gateway to Relaxation" onto. Most denizens were decked in gargantuan sun bonnets, some with high frills thanks to a passing fashion interest in the headgear of pilgrims making their way through the nebula havens to find god or something. If it can't be exploited, it isn't fashion.

Orn hitched up his waning belt -- the canvas knot of his traveling pants slipping loose from their employment famine -- and gestured toward a young man, human from the size of his legs and lack of brains. The example tottered about, failing to adjust for the microshift of gravity with each pass of the balancers. "Like watching a baby varg take its first steps before it bites your face off," he said to Variel.

She smiled politely, her own calculating eyes picking through the piles of tourists, some dragging still groggy spawn towards the shuttle deck. Another dawn, another day of fun; even if the kids screamed the entire time about not wanting to go, the parents screamed about not wanting to take them, and the vendors screamed about spending another 10% of their monthly income to rent a scubaship. Fun. The middle class: backbone of the galaxy. It was a world she only ever saw from the outside, more alien to her than a ship full of elves, a dwarf, and a mute djinn.

"He may not be a space virgin," she said diplomatically to her pilot, "perhaps he suffers from a debilitating inner ear infection and he cannot remain standing still for more than a few moments before he takes a pathetic tumble to the floor." The dwarf looked up at her deadly serious face, his mouth drooping, "You could have just committed seventeen violations of the ethics code for this quadrant."

"Are you shitting me?" Orn asked, his hand slightly trembling at her stone face. Whenever he saw her this focused something was about to explode, occasionally something important.

She glanced down, one eyebrow raising in an elven maneuver, "What do you think?" And failed to maintain her straight face as a laugh broke.

Orn laughed himself, shaking off the momentary fear that she'd toss his dwarven ass into some ethic's reform jail for breaking part of her ship, "Never shit a shitter."

"I'll remember that the next time I meet a toilet." She shrugged her shoulders, trying to crack a bit of life into stiffening joints, and checked her hand, "It's been nearly three hours. Do you think they've finished the damn inspection?"

Variel and Orn were allergic to government oversight; one by habit, the other by genetics. Even seeing a badge sent them both into hives. It was one of the few things they could actually share aside from food so greasy it could bottom out a golem's gastrointestinal tract.

Orn's trademark impish grin returned, "I figure your husband's got him pinned in a corner and refuses to let him come out. We'll find his body, three months down the line, stinking up the place after he died in the walls."

"Very funny. You're a regular Braxl the Red, you know that," Variel responded, hoping the dwarf wasn't even a quarter accurate. "The last thing I need to deal with is wiping a 'Death of Technician' off my record. I'm only a few more months, half a solar year at the most from finally getting out of this lease."

"You know," Orn tapped his greasy chin, "if we took a few jobs from the Quest Log...."

"No," she interrupted him in what had been an ongoing and never ending argument. Orn was about to make his standard rebuttal when her PALM chirped. WEST's signature chaotic beeping promptly came over the line as he hacked the accept button. "Good, they're done," she lit her palm up against the wall as the computer interface on the other end appeared.

"Owner number 23, I have news," WEST's voice was more obstinate than usual. The technician must have been talking to it.

She bypassed the Owner 23 remark and asked, "Good or bad?"

"Let us settle on chaotic neutral. Your dimwitted friend asked our resident djinn a question."

WEST was clearly enjoying the show, hoping to drag this out for his amusement. "And," Variel prompted, "what was it?"

"If he could have any wishes."

The captain didn't bother to disconnect her PALM while her legs pounding through the busying corridors, a flustered dwarf hot on her trail. By the time she got to her ship, she'd shoved aside families dragging novelty air dragons, past a pair of gnomes collapsing down for a air break, and batted away a pair of lost virgins hunting for their bus mistaking the happy jellyfish for the disgruntled cuttlefish.

The airlock door hung wide open, WEST's doing, as she bolted through, and zipped past the embarkation room towards the sounds of her computer crying out, "Warmer. Warmer. Hot!"

She skidded to a very out of breath halt at the not-so-law abiding sight of her djinn dangling the whimpering technician by his suspenders. They were wadded up inside his raging fists while smoke poured from the cracks in the djinn suit, clogging up the technician's eyes. Murmuring sounds whimpered from the kid as his pathetic discount shoes bounced into the djinn's immoveable shins. On the plus side, no one was dead yet.

"Gene," she started calmly, holding her hand up to show she was unarmed and accidentally projected a smarmy WEST onto the standoff. The flicker of the computer pulled at the djinn's vision and the craggy head turned towards her, the fire raging so bright his eyes were nearly blue. Oh boy.

"Now, Gene, we don't want any unnecessary bloodshed," she said cautiously to her oldest friend. But the djinn was barely listening, all his rage burning for what amounted to the greatest racial insult anyone could make to his people short of "You look like you could use a glass of water."

The technician kicked valiantly against thin air, his soles providing little traction to the rising tide of an angry giant. "Help," he gurgled to anyone within hearing distance, unable to see thanks to the acrid smoke tearing up his sclera.

"Come on, we've been through a lot. Seen things someone like this flameless candle can only dream of," Variel soothed. "Pebble like this can't understand what lava he's jumped into."

The giant jerked a moment at her but still he stared the vertebrate child down, willing all his malice into a few flicks of the inner flame. Orn skidded to a halt behind his boss, trying to get in enough oxygen to fuel his very un-dwarflike sprint. He took in the vision before him and stuttered, "Right, well, I have some very un-murdering things to be doing on the bridge," and backed away as quickly as he came.

"Gene," Variel laid her hand across the rock suit, despite the scorching heat, "put him down."

Steam hissed through his shoulder cracks, but he lowered his arms until the technician's boots met deck. He unclenched the fists, snapping the suspenders into technician shoulder. Segundo plummeted, his legs losing most of his pounding blood after hanging suspended in the air for twenty minutes. The computer took its sweet time in calling for help.

"Thh...thank you," he muttered to the captain, rising unsteadily like that baby varg.

"It's not me you should be thanking," she looked at Gene still smoldering, but the blue was fading to a safe red-orange. "By his people's laws he could have ripped out your intestines and smashed your face through a wall for those remarks. It would be in everyone's best interest if you apologized, now."

Segundo shook his entire body, but looked from the woman who he thought saved him, back to the one that was trying to kill him, "Ss..sorry, Sir."

"Are you injured?" she asked, eyeing up some scuffed marks on his striped uniform.

"Nnnoo." Any thoughts of faking a minor injury for something major vanished in the face of aged experience in dealing intimately with the criminal scum he was supposed to stop but wouldn't recognize if they wore stripped uniforms and eye patches.

The proprietor and only person between Segundo and a crushed everything crossed her arms. She very slowly asked the still trembling technician, "And you're not going to make a universal case out of this, are you?"

Before the technician could respond, Variel uncrossed her arms and called out, "ORN!"

By all rights, the dwarf should have been long out of range, but his shaggy head poked around the corner, "Yes, Captain?"

She let the barb pass, not in the mood to rise to the dwarf, "You shall escort our guest through the last of his tour, making certain to answer any and all questions he has, then you shall escort him off my damn ship." Variel rose up on her toes, making her average height all the more imposing as she stared down the technician. "Do we have a problem with that?"

"No, Sir," Segundo saluted despite himself, his palm displaying the inventory checklist against Variel's face. She didn't blink in the blinding light, only leaned back from him as Orn scooped in, grabbing the shaking kid's hand.

"Come on, Squirt," he said to the human towering a good three feet above him, "Best be getting out of here fast like." He peered over the checklist on Segundo's hand, skipping past long swathes of ship he had no interest in.

"Boring, boring, who cares, lost that, sold that, ah! The Bridge, now she's a thing of beauty. Come with me," and hauled Segundo away from the gathered masses.

As the technician's head knocked into the low hanging ceiling of the hallway, a chirp called out from WEST, "A virus upon you. I had ten gigs on the djinn."

Variel glanced over at her mute friend, and said, "Try not to kill anyone else for the day."

Gene shuffled upon his feet, perhaps the only other one aware of the line the pair walked each day, but said nothing. His fingers fell towards his hips, silenced in shame. The captain touched him once on the cracking shoulder, despite the still raging heat, and smiled wanly. There wouldn't be any shoving someone out the airlock, unless the technician tried to get cute.

Before she could turn to walk away, the airlock door slammed open hard, the operator too impatient and overpowered to wait for the computer to finish its job. A flurry of color burst into the bereft storage room, empty of anything but a few of the cruise ship's accoutrements Orn convinced her to hang on to just in case.

The elf paused, trying to catch her breath as she eyed up the room. Her multi-hued skirts came to a dramatic flair, hovering like the wearer was caught in a perpetual wind. The pink stars sparkled with each triple beat of the elf's heart. This was the most panicked Variel'd ever seen Brena, her stage makeup smeared until the fuchsia patterns mushed to form the half eye mask of a super villain and the pre-programmed hair color slipping back to black.

"My commander," the elf called out, the closest the race could come to showing respect to something that didn't share their particular brand of ears. It wasn't a good sign.

"Yes?" Variel asked, strain in her voice.

"I request the aid of your hands."

"I'm not an enchanted fop with more money than brains. You can speak like it's 500 DC," Variel shook out her words, more cutting with her local bard than usual. Usually, she'd let the wordsmith get a few purple sentences out before dragging the girl back to her preferred century.

Brena's tiny mouth turned further down, but she buried whatever curses floated through the devious brain, "My brother, he is in danger."

"Maybe he shouldn't have become an assassin, then," Variel waved her hands as if the elf told her Orn got into the stash of licorice again. The captain moved to WEST, who watched the exchange curiously, and punched in a few commands but mostly waited for the elf to bounce off.

"You do not understand. He could die."

"Oh no, I got that. Death and dying, they tend to follow assassin's around. Maybe you should take it up with his guild instead." To emphasize her "this discussion is over" she began to hum softly under her breath, horrified to realize it was the same damn tune playing across every single elevator on the station.

But Brena reacted with the most force Variel ever saw from a dulcen. The elf spat upon the floor, her drawn on eyebrows pulling into a sneer. "That cursed guild, may it burn within the darkness of the forgotten sun for a billion turns. It was their foolish and failed espionage that led him astray."

Despite every neuron in her brain telling her to keep ignoring the elf and wait for the latest crisis to pass, Variel turned back to the girl. This was enough of an invitation for the dulcen to launch into the mantra she'd probably been preparing on the entire shuttle ride back.

"The guild marked the intended as a grade two at most, but the moment the entertainment began it became evidently clear he was a grade seven!"

"Yeah, my translator doesn't speak murder," Variel said, "Could you try explaining that one again?"

If her fury wasn't burning for a distant bureaucracy of some of the highest security elves in the universe, she'd have turned on the captain. Instead, Brena flapped her arms in consternation, blowing off the air of calm centuries of training forced upon her, "A grade two is 'no combat skills, nearly null security.' Supposedly wanted for gambling debts. But Magalar Dacre is clearly a retired member of the Crest Knighthood. Any moment of espionage would have informed one of such."

"Dacre?" Variel asked as deadpan as possible, her past flaring up from behind a wall she erected, then armed. The djinn behind her hissed as well, sensing the shift in his old friend.

The captain rounded upon the bard, grabbing onto the bare skin of her shoulders and pulling the oversized eyes to her own, "How do you know he was a Crest Knight?"

"The arrogant cricket had the sword placed above his mantle," Brena answered, confused by the turn of events. It'd been a long shot trying to get the captain's help. She rarely spoke to either of the elves unless rent was due, but Brena was still grateful for the change in demeanor, even if it tugged on her fractured brain.

Variel searched through the elf's eyes, looking for something, an explanation, a revelation that this was all some elven joke and her brother was caught between a set of dumpsters, unable to finish his job, or sitting inside a Samudra prison, etching elaborate wood carvings into the walls with his homemade shiv. But even as she dreamed up the magical scenarios, she knew the truth. The assassin in her midst was good. Too good for the jobs he did take. That fact always bothered her.

"WEST," Variel called to her ornery computer, "search through the shuttle schedules. I'll need to break atmo over..."

"The northern hemisphere, in the Tau cluster of islands," Brena filled in for the captain.

"Find the earliest flight possible," Variel said, clicking off the interface before it could argue. Instead, she pushed open her PALM and called for a connection to Ferra.

"Aye, I can explain," her engineer's voice was frazzled, obviously not expecting to hear from Variel so quickly.

"Did you get the injector doohickey replaced?"

"Yes and no."

"Explain." Any joviality drained from the captain's demeanor. This was all business.

"Yes, I ordered it. No, they haven't delivered it. It'll be another 12 hours to whenever some lazy shit gets off its tiny furry legs and sends it," Ferra's measured tone echoed through the storage room, occasionally overridden by the heavy whirr of machinery on the elf's end.

"Are you onboard?"

"Course. I'm back in the engines, seeing to my gardening," she said as if Variel inquired if the elf ever visited the bathroom.

"Good. Tape up whatever you can on the injector and stick it back in until we get the replacement."

"Now it's gonna cost...what? You can't be serious, this thing's gonna crack in..."

"Do it." Variel cut the line before Ferra could complain, but she still got some prime cut cursing before the PALM flashed dark.

She shoved past the deadweight bard, her mind flicking through all the possible security systems a man with a Knight's pension, or more likely illegal pension, could pull off. Her feet thudded through the storage room forwards to the galley, Brena trailing behind. The elf said nothing but watched her captain try to scrape together a plan from half forgotten tactics and something she'd found on her shoe.

"WEST," Variel's voice cut across the narrow hallway as she stepped through the porthole into the kitchen, "any luck on the schedule."

"Yes, Owner 23. If you move your oversized flesh tube quickly enough you can take the shuttle at hanger G-75 in fifteen minutes."

"Thanks," she admitted, glad to be able to leave one bit of this madness to something else. Fifteen minutes to get there, another hour on the ride down. Brena better pray her brother's a better hider than assassin.

"Did you call Taliesin, warn him?" Variel asked, surprising Brena. She suspected the captain knew neither of their names.

"He slipped into silent mode the moment he breeched the perimeter. There is no way to contact him."

"This just keeps getting better and better."

"Youngling," the elf's voice started as her captain stuck a hand inside the dishwasher lock, a loud whirr reading all the data it could off her lifelines. "Captain, it is perhaps the wrong time to inquire this, but why are you extending yourself to assist?"

The dishwasher cracked open, ancient steam escaping as what were clearly not dishes shot out upon the white racks. Variel's fingers weighed the options before her, pocketing a shield generator and scanning the ammo charges. "Dacre," she said the name as one would an intestinal parasite, "whoever he is, is clearly hiding more than a Knighthood."

She extracted a pistol, slipping a few excess batteries into her pockets, and a small submachine gun from the dishwasher armory. It was the only thing on the entire ship that required DNA and a palm print to unlock. She altered it ages ago to hold her few weapons. People could wash their damn dishes by hand, anyway. Variel eyed down the sight, always leaned a bit to the left, but if shouldn't be a big problem with the mess she was about to jump into.

"What do you mean?" Brena asked, shirking momentarily from the arsenal before her. She'd never seen the options hidden in the dishwasher.

Variel cocked the pistol before slipping it into the hiding briefcase so no detector could find it. She paused and looked one last time into the elf's eyes, "Knights don't retire."

She dashed out of the galley, calling out to her computer "WEST, get me those damn tickets now," probably heading to her death for someone she'd traded only a few words with.

CHAPTER THREE

A shudder rocked the atmoshuttle, eliciting a squeal from the young child bundled up in a sea horse themed bathing suit to Variel's left. She spent the entire trip bragging about the rag she propped upon the window, a Mister Turtle who neither looked nor acted like a turtle. The greater problem was the hulking man to Variel's right squeezed into a too tight seat. As the ship began its takeoff, his countenance shifted to a disturbing shade of mossy green and hadn't slipped back to normal. Possible vomit was almost a nice distraction from the certain death awaiting her on the ocean below.

Samudra sparkled as the shade of night pulled across the ocean planet, the waning light bouncing upon the handmade islands scraped together from piles of space junk. Most of the universe's derelict satellites, space stations, ships, fuel depots, and chip shops all wound up on the bottom of Samudra's seas. The beauty of the planet lay in the brains of its exterior designers, a set of very serious dwarves and elves who only smiled if it added to the ambience of a space. By piling together the garbage of the universe they were able to craft the islands that made living on the water planet possible.

The shuttle shook again and the automated pilot's voice cracked over the intercom, "We will be reaching your destination of TAU CLUSTER in five minutes. Please have all hands, legs, and tentacles properly secured."

Variel slipped her arms to the side as a set of cuffs slid over, locking her limbs in place. The girl bounced in her seat a few times, but dutifully plopped down when her mother glanced from across the way, strangling Mister Turtle in the restraints. Mr. Green glanced down for a moment and then his eyes rolled back up, as if he were about to pass out.

"Hey!" Variel called out to him, "Think of grass, trees, mud, the feel of wind on your face after a rainstorm."

Mr. Green gulped down what they were all grateful didn't join the cabin and nodded slowly, his rolled eyes shut tight. The other passengers, a few families and an elderly couple, gazed down at the sight below their sandaled feet.

Every atmoshuttle on the vacationing worlds was equipped with a solid "glass" bottom. The blue bauble grew beneath their feet as she expanded to solid land. Mostly solid land. Waves that could destroy entire cities looked little more than ripples from their height, but soon enough they'd be sloshing about in them as the shuttle made a crash landing. It would be breathtaking to anyone who hadn't survived an emergency sea dive a dozen or so times before.

Variel closed her own eyes, yanking her mind far from the ordinary of a piece of metal hurtling towards a planet's junked islands and back to her own troubles at hand. WEST was scrounging for the house plans, but basically told her unless the architect really loved to brag about his work on missive, he wasn't gonna find jack shit. It was unlikely the planet's security would get involved for a little breaking and entering, Dacre wouldn't want that kind of attention brought down on his squatting ass.

Still, she was heading into an unknown situation, with no intel, no maps, no knowledge of enemy combatants, and just enough ammo to get herself in deep. If she was a decade younger and tripping through a rainforest while loopy from an excess of implan this might make her misty eyed.

A loud whirr replaced the gentle shushing sounds of the engines as the inertia dampeners flowed all their precious cargo into the atmosphere where it could be collected later and scrubbed. The shuttle plopped to a gentle splash as it broke the surface of the landing sea, cordoned off by a row of flashing lights. Mr. Green's eyes flashed open as the water rushed past the ring of windows, and he promptly shut them tight.

Afraid of heights and water? This guy's superiors must really hate him Variel thought as the restraints snaked away, releasing each prisoner from their purchased seat. She shook her hands and grabbed for the briefcase, still empty for "shell collecting" as she told the gate guardians. They mostly shrugged, not in the mood to point out there were no shells on Samudra.

"We have arrived at the dock," the automated pilot croaked out. "Please collect any and all valuables or offspring lest they be sold off to the NERATO company. Thank you and have a pleasing day."

The little girl bounded off her seat over Variel and straight into the lap of Mr. Green. As he opened his eyes, saying a prayer to the gods of water, he glanced down at the girl as she thrust Mister Turtle in his face and shouted, "Can we go again?"

The taxi to the Dacre residence was blissfully uneventful and uninhabited. The driver, one of those people the landlubbers call old salts, asked his passenger only one question after, "Where do you want to go?"

After Variel gave him the location he looked at her aging face, the utilitarian hair cut and clothes just baggy enough to hide a figure but not get caught in anything mechanical and followed up with, "Are ya sure?"

The boat docked quickly with the solitary island, the setting sun bursting upon the bright white eyesore. It was as if someone lifted one of those pristine ideals of future living out of a science fiction movie and dropped it on top of a garbage heap. Windows, each with a well guarded and barred off balcony, encircled the top two floors. A giant picture window covered almost half of the first floor, only reflecting back the sea behind her.

Variel dodged its line of sight, fully aware that it could be switched to open reflection. Knowing Dacre, she suspected it was projecting something of a more carnal nature. The way the kindly driver all but begged her if she really wanted this place to see this man told her how little time changed her target. A pair of stone bear faces hung above the doorway, their eyes lit up from the sensors of the turrets hidden inside the mouth.

People, most dressed as if they wandered in drunk from the beach after getting kicked out for forgetting how to properly attire themselves, milled about in front of the bears. They were all human. A lone troll, painted up with a black suit coat, guarded the entrance to the house.

Great, a bouncer. Variel squared up her shoulders and put on her best "course I'm supposed to be here" face. She stepped around the pair of humans leaning into each other asking if they'd ever touched the stars and looked up into the troll's beady eyes. Granite shifted as its forehead cragged, a large fist nearly the size of her torso rose in front of her.

"You're not on the list."

Variel turned her own beady eyes upon him, the fading sun giving them a troll-attractive black matte quality. "Of course I'm not on the list."

"Then you can't go in."

She tapped the side of her briefcase and lifted it to his nearsighted face, "You see this?" The troll nodded slowly, uncertain if this was a trick question. "You know what this is?" she asked, still dangling the case.

"A briefcase," the troll answered slowly, his eyes slipping over her form trying to spot any hidden weapons.

"A briefcase," she said softly, luring him closer as she flipped the latch, opening up the false top, "with nothing in it."

The troll scratched his chin in thought, then smiled wide. "Oh..."

"Now you're getting it. I'm here to see the man of the house about what's not inside this case."

The bouncer smiled, obviously used to ushering in all manner of people dressed as if they'd flown in from slumming across the galaxy while escorting empty cases, "Of course, Miss..."

"Miss Swiss," she lied poorly, forgetting to make up a false ID incase she could waltz in through the front door. She may not need those siege grenades after all.

But the troll smiled warmly, unused to the overt squishiness of human names and customs. "Let me wave you through," he said to Miss Swiss as he entered a code into his security tablet, momentarily disabling the bear turrets.

"Thank you, kindly," she said, nodding towards the troll and entering into the house of sin.

The pristine door slid open to a darkened den. A track from one of the more bass heavy rock species thudded across the plastic floorboards while streams of light bounced across the walls and ceiling portraying various scenes and small animations from popular...you know, that wasn't really the point. A handful of women, having clearly escaped from a death defying fight with a shredder based upon their attire, stumbled past Variel, giggled at the bore clogging up the doorway, and moved on to a pair of men who didn't acknowledge them.

This is where Brena performs? She didn't seem the drug den type. But if you wanted to appear sophisticated in front of a bunch of other sets of new money, an elven bard that sung you the plots to classic movies was the way to do it. Assuming you couldn't get a fancy cheese plate with those triangle squares.

"WEST," Variel whispered to the air, tapping her PALM against the briefcase's handle. She knew it was listening, it was always listening, "can you find our wayward elf?"

"His communication link is severed," WEST responded loudly into her ear, either trying to overcompensate for the noise levels barraging her hearing or to be an ass. It was hard to tell.

Variel smiled at a pair of gnomes of all things, dressed in royal robe costumes, passing flutes of what was probably moonshine to the milling guests. Dacre took skin crawling to depths only a racist flesh-burrowing worm could reach. She accepted a glass and, through gritted teeth, asked her damn computer, "You're telling me you can't track the heat signature of everyone who ever set foot on your ship?"

"It is written in my technical specs that I should not," WEST said diplomatically.

"Should and could are two different things. I've seen your damn algorithms," her whisper shout caught the attention of a half drugged dwarf probably trying to figure out what the blob still crowding the door was up to. "I have to mingle, find him. Now."

She cut off the contact just before the dwarf began to rise from his seat. Variel hoped to lose him in the shuffle of guests as the song momentarily switched to a slow dance. The women in triage dresses tried to drag their various escorts and most likely high rollers out to the floor in the hopes they'd get a better tip, giving Variel the perfect chance to flutter around the walls and make for the looping marble staircase.

Her rubber soles were far softer than the seven inch eye gougers the other invited women preferred, allowing her to slip quietly up the winding case, her free fingers lightly gracing the gilded banister. She couldn't see a fireplace, but if Dacre really had a sword and not some cheap space-port knock off, he'd have it locked up in an office. Which is most likely where dirty deals were going down under cover of morons partying their narrow lives away.

She paused at the top of the staircase as her PALM buzzed. WEST found something. Shifting the case to her other hand, she bumped the trigger across the observation deck's banister, pretending she gave a shit about what happened below. "What is it?" she asked the computer.

But the dwarf, who followed stealthily behind the newcomer answered back, "A relic of the lost kelpie nation, pre-contact I believe."

"What?" Variel flipped in shock to find the man just a little to her midsection coyly pointing to some weird horse statue gracing the entrance to the house. Hands stuck to the metallic green horse -- at least a dozen -- the owners long torn free, leaving a few of their arm bones behind.

"I assumed you were admiring the art," the Dwarf continued, twirling about a glass of something that apparently wasn't strong enough. He kept his attire a bit less mob, favoring the half out of a suit look. Never a good sign. "Our host has some interesting tastes."

"You could say that," Variel mumbled to herself, trying to pull the screaming computer out of her ear. The damn dwarf kept talking overtop every time it started to give a report.

"Ah," the dwarf turned from the Kelp-thing to look into her eyes. Probably her eyes. It was hard to tell with dwarves, "Then you are familiar with Mr. Dacre. Intimately so?"

"I'd rather shove my head down a kraken's beak and shave my skin off with a vegetable peeler." Variel could probably use a few lessons in tact from the high elf who managed to infiltrate the party and escape without anyone the wiser. She'd only been in for five minutes and already had the ear and eye of someone trying to not look like he was in charge of something nefarious, which meant he most certainly was.

The dwarf laughed, the hearty "we could all be hurled violently into the sun tomorrow, may as well live it up" laugh his people were famous for. He folded his fingers below his box jawline and said softly, "I find it most interesting that a woman with, if I may be so blunt, more than a generous share of wear and tear to her face..."

"Flatterer," Variel interjected, too busy to be bothered by the accurate statement. She had decades to adjust.

"Ah," it momentarily threw the dwarf, but he rebounded beautifully, "A woman who enters unannounced and far into the festivities carrying an all too familiar briefcase favored by the type who do not like to answer too many questions."

The dwarf paused, savoring in his deductive skills just long enough for WEST to blurt out, "The fifth east room on the second floor. He's moving through the maintenance system. About to find a messy end thanks to a...oh, disabled that one. Hm. Well, there are still a whole lot of..."

"I believe we skipped past the introductions," Variel said to the dwarf.

"I am not the type to give my name freely," he responded, not enjoying the way the game turned.

"Nor am I the type to care. What is your relation to the master of ceremonies?"

The dwarf's lips twisted up into a half smirk, "It is, as you humans say, 'on the ice' at the moment. And I fear it shall be irreparably damaged."

Variel nodded and flipped open the true bottom of the case, revealing her treasure inside, "Then, Mr. Nameless, I believe you and I can be of great benefit to each other."

He stepped back from her packed arms, a rather outdated model by the size but much beloved for its steadfastness in the event of jamming. A heavier handle made for a heavier blow to the head after the battery ran down. The dwarf looked up into her eyes and smiled wide. "Madam," he hoisted up his manicured hand and she grabbed it, shaking, "it was a pleasure making your acquaintance."

Then he hooked a well trained arm through one of the blindly wandering women and said loudly, "I was hoping to have a word with our host. Is he still sequestered in the back office with his guards?"

The woman looked down at the man with his arm around her waist and blinked slowly, "Wha' are you talking about?"

But Variel got the message. She slipped down the hall, counting the doors, and hoping WEST meant from her position and not the other. One. She opened the case. Two. Three. She slipped the pistol into her holster. Four. Yanking out the submachine gun and regrettably tossed the case aside, she stopped before the fifth door. She steadied her nerves, hugging the edge of the wall as her fingers tapped against the locking mechanism. The panel beeped a calming blue as it gave in to a universal command. Just as she was about to rush in, a shot cut through the air.

Another set, blam blam, burst through the end room, tearing apart the walls and splintering wood, as a pair of black jacketed guards rose from the rooms adjacent to the end. The office. Where Dacre was.

"Fucking, son of a lich," Variel cursed. Without pausing, she lifted her pistol from the holster and flipped off the safety.

A red light flared beneath her finger just as the first guard reached the door. She pulled the trigger and a bullet laced out, striking him in the head. His second turned, getting one in the neck. Variel broke into a run, her steps heavy against the marble facade floors as the party goers finally woke from their stupor to find bullets whizzing past their heads and into the stereo system.

The entire bass sputtered and collapsed, waking them from the Neverland.

In the rising cacophony, Variel failed to hear the third guard as she approached the office door. She turned just as he lifted his own gun to her head. Her arm rose but she wouldn't be fast enough. As his own red light flashed, ready to fire, a shadow broke from behind the dimly lit guardroom and a pair of black hands slipped around his head, snapping the neck like a piece of celery.

The crunch was a little hard to stomach as the broken body collapsed in on itself. Variel held her gun on the killer but watched the guard to make certain this wasn't some trick of a party necromancer.

"Captain, what are you doing here?" Taliesin asked as if he just ran into her outside the bathroom. The elves must have ice for blood.

"Saving your hide," she said like he hadn't saved hers.

The elf's crystal fine features crumpled. He glanced to the two guards she got, like she broke some strict assassin code, "I do not understand."

"Your target, Dacre, turns out he's an ex-knight." The assassin's pout puckered at the fresh information but he did not interrupt. "Your sister seemed to think it was important you not die, so here I am. Let's go."

The elf could have argued, she'd even anticipated a bit of "I must finish my mission" bravado, but he nodded deeply, a few strands of his pulled back hair slipping in front of the yellow eyes. "Yes, that is wise."

Well, that was easy, she thought, about to holster her pistol and try to slip out with the panicking guests when the office door to one Mr. Magalar Dacre slid open. The man wiped his hands slowly on a white towel, dabbling off the blood of mobsters come to collect their cut as he boasted in front of the men who did all the work. Slowly, he looked up at the woman and elf hovering around his doorstep. Variel squared her shoulders, but she was at the wrong angle, and his eyes stopped upon her scar.

The mouth of the endless night could not match the cruel joy that took Dacre's lips as he remarked first to himself, "You," then to his guards carrying enough ammunition to take down a squad of orcs, "Kill them."

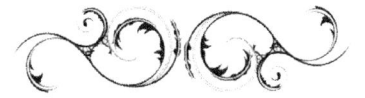

Variel shoved Taliesin into the guard room just as Dacre's goons thought to open fire. Bullets bounded across the hall, slipping above the tumbling pair as the elf's leather-bound hide crashed through the card table, scattering dice to the four corners. The door slammed shut. Variel jammed her hand into the locking mechanism, her fingers flipping through for the manual override.

The assassin hopped to his feet, seeming embarrassed by the destruction his ass caused, just as Variel found what she wanted and yanked on a blue wire. Flashing momentarily, the locking mechanism stuck, unable to be compromised by anything short of a battering ram...or a pair of men armed with state of the art Crest weaponry.

Sounds of batteries being replaced and slotted in eclipsed the fallen silence. Taliesin grabbed Variel's wrist, dragging her to the ground.

"What are you doing?" she hissed, counting the time it took for the oafs to cock their guns. A familiar warning beep turned up the corners of her mouth. That damn safety was so touchy.

"Their weapons can shoot through the plastic of the doors and straight into us," he annunciated as if speaking to a green recruit or a child that peddled its school candy to the very wrong house.

But Variel shook her head, "Nah, it's triple frictionless. The energy from their weapons will absorb." To punctuate her point, they fired on the door, the rat-a-tat turning into a reflected rainstorm of pings as the magic plastic did its bulletproofing job. She smiled smugly when one bullet slipped through the micro-gaps in technology and shot directly above the pair's heads. No safety feature is absolute

"Mostly absorb," Variel admitted. She crawled back from the heating door, the plastic white burning to the dangerous red of Gene's eyes. "How'd you get in here?" she asked the assassin as she pushed the table against the melting door. Another hour of charge and they might actually get through.

Taliesin pointed above her to the narrow air duct, just wide enough for one ass at time. "Perfect," Variel muttered, and tossed him the pistol, "Here. I hope you know how to use one."

He nodded and slipped it somewhere hidden beneath the black folds of his clothing. They were stained with grey dust along his knees and sides. The work on Samudra required finesse and skill, and the lack of any firearms due to strict travel restrictions. Apparently, the captain could work marvels on even that.

"I'll go first," she said, tossing the submachine gun into the duct where it made a satisfying thud. "Give me a boost." She stepped a foot up, expecting him to create a ladder with his hands.

Instead, the elf lowered down and wrapped his taut arms around her hips. As if she weighed less than a small child exhausted from a day at the beach and wanting a piggy-back ride, he lifted her body high above his head. Her fingers gripped the stainless sides of the duct and she wiggled in, pushing the gun before her in the rising darkness of air supply.

"Do you need help?" she asked the echo in the ducts, uncertain how she could supply any with her ass wedged dangerously tight in the duct.

"No," the elf was calm, calmer than he probably should be given the situation, "but please move forward a few meters."

Variel crawled on her forearms, nudging the gun along. Behind her she heard the endless rapport of bullets meeting with immoveable plastic and a few slicing through the armoire probably containing enough contraband to get her a new ship if she had time to loot. "Taliesin..." she whispered to the elf.

A loud "**whuf**" bounded through the air as the assassin's hands grabbed onto the slick air duct, his gloves implanting microspikes to support his form. From a straight almost four foot jump, he clawed his way into the duct, barely out of breath and fitting inside the damn tomb much easier than her.

"I am inside the air vent," he called as if he just informed her dinner was ready.

"Elves," she muttered and slipped her middle finger down to her PALM to start it up. Her projecting fist smashed down on the duct, moving her ass along. A small movie about a girl who meets a boy that turns out to be a clone of an infamous tyrant cued up on its own. It skipped forward a scene every time her hand met with ground.

"How do we get out of here?" she asked, despite being in the lead.

"I generally prefer the doors," Taliesin admitted sheepishly. This was not supposed to be so difficult. Get the intended alone, perhaps waiting until there is a lull or he excuses himself to the bathroom, finish the job quietly, then walk out the front door with none in the house the wiser. He preferred the bathroom kill, cleanup was easier for himself and the inevitable ghoul squad. Any use of gun play would typically forfeit a bonus, but this was such a low level kill the extra cherry was a coupon for a free sandwich from any of the universe's "Shuttlecocks."

Variel sighed loudly and, trying to shout overtop the clone discovering his past, called to the only one who could help, "WEST!"

"It looks like you are trying to escape utter annihilation. Would you like some assistance?" it responded.

"A path to the door, give me one," Variel ordered, thinking she'd either throttle the computer or give it a fat kiss when this was all over. He'd probably hate it either way.

Variel paused in the flickering light, trying to raise her only source as the movie projected onto one of the suffocating walls. It was at the obligatory "even though we just met I am madly in love and pledge my life to you" songs. The reason she was in this mess in the first place failed to notice her cessation of movement and his bowed head plowed into backside.

"Please, forgive my intrusion. I did not intend harm or contact." This was the first time since the whole flying bullets started the elf actually sounded flustered, even embarrassed.

She may have been a bit flattered to be the first to break through the ice veins, but WEST beeped up, "There isn't one."

"What do you mean 'there isn't one?'"

"One, a noun of the singular variety, in this example referencing a previous request i.e. escaping through a door. Isn't, a contraction of is and not, implying the one cannot be achieved. That which you requested is not an available option."

"How can there be none? This house cannot be placed under lockdown," the elf's voice cut into the fight.

WEST bristled at the interruption, but his smarmy algorithms rebounded, "No, but a very sophisticated anti-theft device can be pumped through any and all door mechanisms and other switches at a moment's notice that, when touched by human or *other* hands, would render the escapee very very inert."

"Shit," Variel cursed to herself. How a little asswipe got his hands on that technology...it was in prototype last she'd heard.

"Which the proprietor of your little extravaganza has just activated," WEST added.

"Doors are no longer an option," Taliesin pointed out for himself. "What of the grates or ductwork?"

"If it affected grates wouldn't 20,000 volts be racking through your puny electrical system right now?" WEST was having the time of its life, being able to calculate something other than time tables and the selling weight of aged centarian cheese.

"Up," Variel's voice cut through the pair arguing and the movie getting to the first big action fail before rebound and triumph! "Find me a path to the roof," she ordered her computer then clicked over to her miniature address book, scrolling through to find Orn.

Her end rang once, twice, then a third without a pickup.

"Perhaps he's away from his hand for the moment," Taliesin said, catching onto her plan.

"If he is we're in bigger trouble than I thought. It's implanted in his good one."

A buzz clicked as the dwarf finally answered. Orn got as far as "Who is..." before WEST butted in.

"Take two rights, one left and you'll find a ladder at a small maintenance hatch. Take it up. There you should find the roof. Or the basement, if I'm holding this wrong."

"Thanks, WEST," Variel said, holding her palm out before her, and shoving the beleaguered gun to the right passage. The elf trailed behind far more softly.

"Do you require any more assistance, Owner 23?"

"Yes, get off the damn line!" The computer huffed but clicked out, letting the original line pick up. "Orn, you there?"

A gust of music, like someone threw a cat against a guitar and played the mess backwards, blasted out of her hand directly below whatever room they hovered above. "Crap, crap, crap," she tried to fumble for the volume in the dark, but could only scroll the damn movie back to the obligatory musical number.

Her assassin laid his lavish ears against the floor and said, "Many voices, muffled but stern. I would recommend moving quickly."

His calm assessment was reinforced as a bullet pierced through the plaster of the ceiling and into the ductwork, traveling to the roof they were hoping for. Another inch to the left and she'd have been short a lung. Variel scrabbled through the duct work chanting, "right, right, left," still shoving the gun as if it were an errant child. "Orn! Turn that shit down!"

The music continued to blast, as she rounded on another corridor of duct, cursing her bad everything. *How fucking long was this damn house?* Below her hand Orn's noise dimmed and his out of breath voice came over the line. After their earlier discussion, Variel decided to not ask what he was doing.

"What's up, Cap?"

"Get your ass in the pilot's seat," she ordered, halfway down the long corridor, leaning to the left. More boots and fancier shoes trampled below them. Hopefully the lost and drugged out party guests made havoc for the guards.

"Already am," Orn said and probably tipped back, his shoes scuffing up very expensive controls.

"I do not need to know that," she shuddered, wishing she'd avoided the trip into his marital relations.

"Pardon?"

"Break orbit. You're gonna do an atmo break over the islands Brena sent me to. Tee or something. Ask her."

"Tau cluster," Taliesin's calm shook a moment as the superior elven hearing picked up what sounded like the wheeling of a very heavy machine.

"Yer shitting me, right? This is one of them big tests to see how loyal I am."

Through the conversation, Variel pushed on, shining her PALM light around the edges, then pulling it to her face to curse at her pilot. "I'm serious, Orn. This is my serious voice. Get your fat, dwarven ass in the sky and down to the planet."

"An atmo break, on Samudra," but even as he shook his round head she heard the heartening hum of controls booting up.

"There's the left," Variel said to her caboose and turned.

"Cap'n," Orn's voice carried across the warming of engines, "we, uh, the thing is, we still have..."

Variel spied the maintenance shaft, large enough to stand hopefully two to a person, just as Taliesin heard the tell-tale click of an ammo round fitting into the turret. They were going to rip through the ceiling, like killing a fly with a warhead.

Without saying a word, the assassin's gloves gripped deep into the shaft before him. With all his might, he propelled himself forward, shoving Variel further into the shaft. His own body crumpled atop her when the gun turret fired up, showering the previously occupied area in bullets, plaster, and metal shrapnel. That was gonna be a bitch to explain to the home owner's association.

The assassin popped up onto his legs and offered a hand to the captain nursing a bruised sternum thanks to the submachine gun breaking her fall. "Are you all right?" he asked while guiding her up.

"Peachy." She'd hurt later, "Orn..."

"Still here. Wasn't certain if you were, though."

"Get the skyskiing jackets out, have Gene man the crank. And you, reserve a good wyrmroute. Hopefully we'll leave the system before security even notices anyone broke atmo," she tested the ladder as she spoke to Orn, her light shining to an obvious lock at the top.

She turned to Taliesin and lifted the pistol from his hands. Aiming haphazardly, she shot at the lock, blasting a hole large enough for her hand to fit through. Variel passed it back to him, her PALM lighting up his dark face. She thought perhaps she should reassure him that everything would be all right, then she remembered he kills people for a living. Maybe he should be reassuring her.

"We head up. I'll go first."

"Why?"

Variel tapped the submachine gun, a spray of bullets against a room of unknown enemies worked much better. "Stay low. It'll take the Elation five minutes to get through the atmo at least. If Orn's still bitching about his driving record, more than likely ten. We find cover and hold our ground," she dug through her pockets, fishing out the handful of batteries she saved. "I have enough for three charges, maybe four if we're lucky."

"I see no reason for luck to start now," he said as he accepted the batteries, slipping them into a series of vest pockets expertly hidden in the field of black.

"Right," she balled her fist to shut off her PALM. The shaft fell dark. The assassin's heavy breath brushed across unhindered skin as her heartbeat increased in tempo. Her fingers slipped around the ladder's rungs and she climbed slowly, boots clanging against the gnome sized lift.

Taliesin followed close behind, his own weapon at the ready as Variel's fist punctured through her damage, searching for the handle. Gah! The puckered metal sliced through her shirt and into flesh as she reached deeper in, her fingers falling across the handle. Sucking back a grunt of pain, she jammed her arm the last few inches and turned the latch. The door lifted up and she snaked her arm in.

"On the count of three. One. Two. Three!" She threw the door open, the end of her gun meeting a clear night sky.

Variel climbed quickly, spinning about to sniff out any enemies hiding in the piles of air and heat vents littering the roof, but none appeared. Only a few clouds lilted across the starry sky. Two of the three moons were nearly full, giving a full cast of light to the dirty work before them.

Taliesin appeared behind her -- his pistol raised -- as she took in the surroundings. Given time, even Dacre had to realize they were on top of the roof and come for them. "We need to fortify," Variel pointed at a massive pile of old pipes, probably thick enough to absorb most handheld weapons. "That should be the base. Drag some of the excess metal whatever to the sides," she pointed to the scrap and the elf obliged, his fingers slipping around an edge.

The only main entrance was a door, probably sealed by the anti-theft system. Well, she could help that out a bit. Pulling a pick the size of a pen from her pocket, she inserted it below the doorknob and pushed a button. Rods ten times the strength of iron dug deep into the floor, walls and frame of the door. It wasn't gonna be easy getting through there. She walked about the roof, glancing over the edge. The walls were too sheer, almost no chance of anyone attempting to climb from the bottom, but there were a multitude of windows. It was all the rage to boil in natural light over a never ending sea view. The waves crashed harder against the floating foundation of the house testing the balancers; a storm was rising.

As Taliesin pushed the last of the fortification walls into place, her PALM lit up. She tapped it quickly, not bothering to check who it was, "What?"

"If you run this hunk of shit on a cracked inertia injector..." she closed the line before Ferra could finish her rant. Variel knew the engineer could argue a saint to death for his perceived sins, but she'd also listen to her boss. As her still flashing PALM light swooped across the sleeping roof, it lit upon a familiar sign. The orange and black triangle warned any and all organics to refrain from combusting near this pile of...*Oh Dacre, you've been a very bad boy.*

She marked the location of the dump and returned to her assassin. He settled down into a crouch, probably praying to his plants for guidance. She whistled softly, "There's an entire pallet of weapon's grade explosives sitting behind the attic door. Enough to send this entire house up in flames."

The elf rose up from his small prayer bow and said quietly, "Then I best be extra careful what I shoot."

It was either the endorphins or the brain in full on fight mode, but Variel laughed at her nearly silent elf and he in turn smiled back. "I had no idea your kind could do that?"

"Do what?"

"Show emotion." A bang broke from below the attic door.

Taliesin blinked slowly and aimed his pistol towards the door, "We reserve it only for special occasions, or if someone is losing poorly at cards."

She laughed again and raised her own gun. The door buckled against whatever man bear they persuaded to play battering ram. "You think they forgot to turn off that zapping door thing?"

"I fear I was not born under a lucky star."

"Yeah, me neither." With her words, the door finally splintered in half and a head poked through. Without pausing, she unleashed a round straight into the questing face. It roared and tumbled back into the crowd behind it. While Variel cocked her gun, trying to burn off some heat, Taliesin took aim, popping off the next two guards climbing over top the first, each falling like a sack of lembas.

Maybe this wouldn't be so hard after all, if those witless wonders keep funneling through like that. Another round of the machine gun ripped through the half door one used as a poor shield and down he went.

A shot clanged against the metal pipes, sending both of them down to the ground. Someone broke through in the blue of night. It was enough to trigger the assassin instincts, and he popped off the guard before another shot was fired.

For a moment the guards paused, trying to regroup and replan. As far as they knew, their prey were trapped. No reason to risk a bullet to the brain to get to them fast. Variel checked her battery level: low. Damn things were getting too old to handle a charge. She slotted it back in and cocked the gun. *Come on Orn, get the fat foot of yours in gear.*

The assassin shot wildly at a guard exploring, getting nothing but ceiling and a puff of white plaster into the rising winds. He turned to the woman fighting beside him and replaced the battery in the pistol. She got the count. But how many guards could Dacre possibly have?

In response, the entire roof below the door collapsed revealing a jagged staircase like a broken set of teeth. Out jumped ten men surrounding the man of the hour himself. A sword with a brilliant blue edge shone out of one hand while the other sported a micro-gattling gun. Taliesin popped off the guard on the edge while Variel whittled down a few just as Dacre started to return fire. The pair bounded down to their cover, turning back to face the still shipless night.

"Shit, shit, shit, shit, shitshitshit!" Variel cursed over the sound of bullets pounding into the metal pipes. Her ear drums were going to take days of reconstruction therapy.

"He is carrying the sword," Taliesin stated the obvious.

"I know," she shouted, angry at the reason she was in this mess in the first place. "Get anywhere near that thing and we're all dead."

The elf pulled a blade out of his pocket; a small thing, nowhere near as powerful as the one Dacre wielded like a sickle. He weighed it softly and whispered, "If you distract them, I slip in behind and pick off some of the guards."

"With the gattling-gun? That's near suicide," she said to him, already aware of the "but we're nearly out of bullets argument." Variel dug into her pocket and pulled out a round device, slightly larger than a quarter, and pushed her finger into the middle. A sheen overtook her form momentarily, then vanished.

Without waiting for the elf to say anything, she stuffed the shield generator into the front of his pants pocket, the shield enveloping him. It wouldn't stop the sword, but it'd at least keep most of the bullets away from his vital parts. He looked down at his hands, slightly shimmering in the sparks of the bullets beating against the pipes, then to Variel. Nodding, he passed her the pistol. Extracting his blade, he inched along their sidewall and vanished into the night.

All right, Dacre, let's dance. She shouted into the stars as he momentarily paused to rest his trigger finger, "You were always a weasel! A shitless nothing!"

A few more bullets bounded into the pipes from the guards at her comments, but Dacre stopped his storm. "And what of you, *Sir*. Hiding, running, scared of the big bad Crests coming for ya? You can change the whole face for the right coin, but that scar's forever. Tha's what you get for lying down with orcs."

Through Dacre's peacocking a shadow moved around the shifting shade, his blade biting into the exposed neck of a guard swooping towards the uninhabited section of roof. One down, four more to go. A crunch shattered the eerie calm and Variel popped up, the last of her machine gun emptying into someone trying to invade her cover. His body tipped back, more meat than man now.

Dacre restarted his fire, trying to melt the pipes with enough friction. Grabbing one of the side walls, Variel slotted it into place behind the pipes who gave it their all against superior fire power. Another guard bit the dust as the elf stabbed him through the back, straight into the heart.

Three more left and still no sign of her ship or that blasted dwarf. He'd better not be under fire from his wife or, so help her, she'd haunt the shit out of both of them for an eternity. "I should have killed you," Variel's shout managed to make it over the rapport of bullets.

Dacre paused again, wanting to savor what was a long time coming. "Is that why you're here now? To kill me?" A small light flashed on her PALM, and she pushed it, holding her hand up to her ear to muffle the voice.

"I knew it," Dacre continued to gloat even as another of his guards fell to the assassin's blade. "All those companies sudden interest in 'em. It had to be important. And what do you have to do with it? Are you working for the corps now? Tell me!" The man jumped from the kiddie pool into the deep end of insanity.

Variel touched the "answer" button on her PALM and a familiar voice chirped, "Honey, I'm home."

The rising winds buffeted everyone to the floor as the stars descended, lining the rim of her beautiful ship. She rose against the winds to her knees, Orn's few skills paying off as he hovered over the correct house. Dacre screamed and tried to fire up but the gattling-gun couldn't maneuver directly above him. He tossed it aside and began to stalk around the roof, his sword drawn.

The docking bay opened on the *Elation-Cru* and a crackling red fire form dropped an anchor strung on thick cable towards the roof. It scrapped above their heads. Variel broke cover and jumped in the confusion, but couldn't reach it. "Damn it, dwarf. Lower the ship."

"Fine, fine. If I'm gonna break one law tonight might as well go for all of them."

Taliesin inched around the roof, slipping the knife into his pocket as he joined his captain. The swinging anchor pounded through their cover, finally smashing the poor pipes to bits, but Variel grabbed it before it made another pendulum swing. She undid the locks and broke into the padded jacket for the skyskiiers. "Put it on!" she shouted above the buffeting winds to the assassin.

He shook his head no. *What a time for chivalry.* "I'll need you to hold me! Put the damn thing on." The elf nodded and slipped his arms into the jacket just as she locked the vest in place. A shot zipped past her exposed head as the last guard rounded on her. She pulled the anchor chord loose and Taliesin rocketed into space.

Variel dodged, ducking and running around the roof as the guard fired madly towards her. Two targets and one bullet left. This was a good time for a miracle of some sorts.

High above their heads, the elven assassin flipped upside down, wrapping his legs around the tether. He dangled his arms down. "Lower!" Taliesin screamed into his PALM. The *Elation* dropped, and he swung over his captain, the shield momentarily deflecting the guard's bullets, but leaving her exposed as he continued the arc.

The guard stepped closer, grinning wildly at the trapped prey, and failing to notice the return of the very athletic elf. Taliesin grabbed onto the guard's arms and pulled the now screaming man with him off the other edge of the roof. Once free, he dropped him into the seas below.

The weight was enough to throw off his swing and he went wildly left, slightly corkscrewing. Dacre laughed at the show, slicing his sword through every duct and piece of long tossed equipment on the roof.

"Are you scared, *Sir*? Is that fear running in your veins? Or piss down your leg?"

Variel shifted, running low towards a specific spot. She'd get one shot at this and she needed things to be perfect. Taliesin swung his hips like a pro, trying to direct his body towards her. He passed close, only fingertips away, but moved past. It gave Dacre enough time to walk near her and the pile of orange warning stickers below her feet.

He raised his sword, the sword of a Knight, high above his head like a meat cleaver. "You were such a disappointment," he crowed just as Variel jumped back.

"I'm making up for my mistake now," she said as she shot at the explosives. Twisting, she leapt towards the sea and the swinging elf.

Her questing fingers grabbed Taliesin's forearm, just as the excess pile ignited. The fireball claimed the roof and the screaming corpse of one Lieutenant Dacre. The elf gripped deep, his gloves biting into her flesh, but she didn't register the pain. Her eyes followed only the arc of the swing that would pull her back overtop the flames bursting off the roof.

"Up!" Variel screamed into the night sky, and hopefully her PALM, "UP! UP! UP!"

In the darkness it was impossible to tell if the order reached any ears. The flames bit down into the roof tiles and the metal stashed on top it, crackling and spitting like a fireplace, shooting shrapnel back at the night. The tether reached the end of its pull and began the swing back. A series of very family-inappropriate curses racked through her brain and probably out of her mouth as Variel watched her dangling feet swing nearer to the inferno. Even as the assassin gripped her with the strength of a hungry constrictor, she still clung back with her legs pulled up to her stomach, just passing over the fire on the swing out.

By the second pass over the fire, only the heat nipped at her heels. Variel slowly relaxed her legs, letting them dangle to not throw off the elf's grip. His eyes seemed to be bulging a bit as he dangled inverted out of a spaceship pulling higher into the atmosphere.

But up they went, the tether retracting back into the *Elation*. For a moment, Variel broke the first rule of skyskiing and looked down. As the light of the ship pulled from the black water below, the famed moon plants erupted. Cascading pinpoints of dancing green light floated below the ocean's depths. The wisps of the water signaled their goodbyes.

The endless rushing of air was replaced by faint voices as the tether inched closer to the ship, their bodies dragging along the hatch. A loud beeping started, and the hatch closed as the cabin tried to re-pressurize and seal before Orn got any bright ideas. With the final beep, a green light flooded the mostly empty cabin. Finally, Taliesin let go of Variel. They lay on the rocking hatch, trying to breathe life into shaken lungs and acid out of stretched muscles.

A heavy hand dropped to the captain and curled around her fingers. Gene lifted her surprisingly tenderly, and she leaned into the djinn, inspecting her arms for damage.

"Not to be a pain or anything, but we've got a good ten Sec. ships blaring out of their hidey holes," Orn's voice echoed through the shuttle-less docking bay.

Variel coughed, and whispered to Gene, "Tell him to get us out of here."

This would not have been very helpful from the mute djinn, but her comm line still sat open, and Orn didn't need to be told twice.

"Hands on yer bums people, this is gonna be a rocky one," Orn's voice clipped before he severed the line and punched in the vey illegal atmo-burners.

Variel stumbled at the increase in inertia -- Ferra must be keeping the thing off-line as long as possible -- but Gene caught her. The assassin unhooked himself from the jacket and rose despite the gravity boost, inspecting himself for damage. As his eyes moved off the tattered remains of his vest up to the teetering captain he caught the eternal damnation glare of the fire golem. It was supposed to be near impossible to read the emotions of a djinn, most never tried, but Gene made it painfully obvious how little he thought of Taliesin.

"Damn it!" the captain's cursing broke the elf-djinn stalemate, "Orn! Pinch the wyrm," her fingers poked around her side, trying to knot up a stitch from that burst of exercise.

"Breaking atmo...now!" Orn's triumphant voice called to the ship as if anyone was impressed he managed to find "up." "Fine, fine, pinching the wyrm. Prepare to have your molecules rearranged."

The air grew metallic as if it filled with ozone, and very humid. Variel's saliva glands tried to make up for the excess of magic rushing through the ship's divergence systems, altering the fabric of space. Her stitch searching hand flew up to her forehead as the tear opened. Damn things always gave her a headache.

Without waiting for an on the ball security guard to wonder why a ship that rose from the planet suddenly opened a hole right outside the ancillary zone, Orn drove the ship in. The wyrm collapsed behind them, zapping some excess MGC back through the circuits as she raced through to a point on another side of the galaxy.

As normalcy replaced the magic burn, Taliesin glanced towards his captain and paled. A swathe of blood trailed along her forehead where her hand left a path. He walked quickly to her side but the djinn grumbled.

"She is injured," the assassin said, having trouble hiding the blame in his voice.

"Oh shit, am I?" Variel complained as if she got a summons for justice time, and she poked at the wound. "Must have been a stray bullet." As the endorphins drained from the chase, a wave of nausea and pain hit hard, "or a few. Medical, better get there. And Monde, he's probably hiding somewhere safe. Find him."

The djinn nodded to her. Like a gorilla picking up a kitten, he hefted her into his oversized arms. She rolled her eyes and muttered, "I didn't mean that," but was losing enough blood she didn't have the energy to argue.

Taliesin paused, uncertain if he should follow, when his own PALM lit up. Curious, he touched it and an automated message scrolled quickly, the white text legible against his black skin.

"Congratulations on finding and destroying your intended, MR. DACRE, the fee has already been wired into your account."

He flipped the message off in disgust and followed after the captain.

CHAPTER FOUR

The dwarf flipped the "reality" switch -- a word he sketched over the fancy mage term for zipping up the universe's fly -- closing the wyrm behind them and gargled the awful taste of the galaxy out of his mouth. He waved his hand and raised up the three dimensional map, zooming into a particular spec of nothing in the grand scheme of things. A few holographic planets whizzed around his ear as he charted the time it'd take to swing into the next station. Vargal (so named after the sound someone choked out upon seeing it) was about all that interested this backwater shiphole. She wasn't going to be happy about it, but Ferra'd learn to adjust. The Captain; however, was going to go spare this close to the old demilitarized zone.

Orn yanked down the map -- after digging some planets out of his hair -- and set the course in, flipping on the autopilot. WEST grumbled in a jealous rage. This gave Orn no amount of glee every time he informed the glorified concierge that the autopilot had the bridge. *Well,* the dwarf thought, turning to the person shaking like an avalanche beside him. *Time to go break the bad and worse news.*

The med-bay -- also known as the closet stocked with bandages, black market morphine, and that damn pool table they couldn't find a use for -- was nestled off the mostly empty crew quarters. Only the twins haunted the area, laying claim to some of the "rentable rooms" not torn out. Rounding past the galley, Orn snagged a piece of ice rock candy from his drawer and jammed the entire fist sized lump of sugar into his maw. His companion was silent but still mobile; a plus in this line of work.

They turned the corner, ducking down the incline to the "customer deck" and paused as their assassin paced back and forth outside the shuttered door like a father or widow to be. Orn caught the elf's eye and shrugged, "She's been through worse."

The elf grimaced, his tiny mouth sucked so deep in consternation it vanished, but he said nothing. *Quieter than the grave, that one. No wonder he got into the stabbing people in the night business.*

"A few rub downs, a new coat of paint, an oil change, and she'll be right as rain," Orn said, patting the elf on the back.

Taliesin's clouded face turned down on the dwarf and his buttoned mouth actually broke, "You are referring to the ship."

An alien pull of concern overtook the elf's eyes. It was rare for them to feel anything beyond ennui or a flower-scented passing of gas for someone that didn't sport the right brand of pointy ears. It caught Orn by surprise and he slightly assured the kid, "She'll be fine too. Saw her take on a midgard serpent once. Bare handed."

"Those do not exist."

"Exactly," Orn winked as if it was comforting and pushed on the admittance panel to the med-bay.

Variel lay haphazardly across the pool table crackling the protective tarp now dotted vivid crimson from her injuries. Her pet hovered over her, taking up space as the Doc buzzed about, his nimble fingers slipping in and out of jars labeled in one of the non-universal texts. He liked it that way, made looting much harder if you didn't know what pill you swiped.

"Cap!" Orn said cheerfully as if she weren't half naked and bandaged like a pharaoh mid-mummification. "We're out of the

Samudra system and nearing a fresh new station so my lovely wife can acquire the part we need before she gets excessively stabby."

Variel slowly rose to her IVed elbows looking over her pilot. A few dark circles sunk in her eyes and that olive skin was paler and waxier than normal, but otherwise she looked fine. Mostly fine. Mostly not dead, at least. "That'd be the good news. So what's the bad?"

Orn tilted his head, a pile of knotted hair falling into his eyes as he chided, "So cynical, my captain. It just so happens there is no bad news. The station we're two days from would be the 'famous for its active nightlife' Vargal."

"You WHAT?!" she threw her arm up, scattering an injection from Doc's fingers clear across the room.

"We needed a quickly registrable, no questions asked flight path near a station. It was the best I could do in, oh ten minutes notice," Orn folded his arms and pouted, "And you're welcome for me saving your ham hocks by the way."

It was either the heavy dose of painkillers or the lack of blood, but she actually slumped back, willing to let him win one for once. "Yeah, yeah, you're right. It could be worse. We could have wyrmed into a dead system or dark space."

Orn turned to leave but then paused. Turning back over his shoulder he added, "One more tiny, small, so insignificant you'll never notice little thing."

"Orn..."

The dwarf reached into the waiting area and grabbed the arm cuffs of his fellow bridge partner, "The technician's still on board."

Segundo blinked into the heavy operating lights, which used to be for the vacant shuttle bay and slowly turned his "so out of its depth angler fish swam around it" head from the injured registered owner, to the genie that tried to kill him, and finally over to the doctor. That was when he started shaking again.

"That's an...an...an..."

Doc put down his tools and turned, the polyester lab coat snagging on the ball return jammed with tongs. "An orc?" he asked softly, raising where an eyebrow would be if his species sprouted them. His pale orange eyes, double lidded, blinked twice in rapid succession as the newest crew member, or stowaway, gave him the once over. Human gawking was standard fare, and why he preferred to remain hidden in the bowels of the ship when they docked.

Segundo trailed across the row of spikes descending in size down his skull, a deep green skin with shades of grey. The underbite was not as noticeable as one expected, and the razor ripping teeth were barely longer than human canines. Even the orc's size was something of a disappointment; slightly shorter than Segundo himself and only a bit thicker, most of that in his upper shoulders.

"But we were at war...?" the technician asked, turning to the only other human on this cursed ship.

"And it ended," the orc said, "as they are wont to do."

Variel butted in, knowing how this could trail on for hours, "This is Demi Monde, resident practitioner of ointments and boo-boo patches. He won't rip your legs off to beat you over the head with them, or chew your ear off and drink your blood."

"Unless I missed meal time," the orc smiled, highlighting the teeth that didn't look so harmless now.

"A..." Segundo fought back the shakes and held out his hand, "a pleasure to meet you Demi."

The orc watched the hand, uncertain what to do with it. He settled on giving him one of the ancient lollypops left in the healing lounge after the ship's decommission. As the human putzed about with the treat, he returned to the bleeding captain, "It is Monde, actually. Demi is my kin name. And what shall you be known as?"

"Getting off this damn ship," Variel interrupted. The orc problem having solved itself with sweets, she got to the marrow.

"I," Segundo faltered in the face of raging pain looking for anything to take it out on.

Surprisingly, the dwarf stuck up for him, "It was my doing. You called in the middle of his inspection."

"The middle...you were in my home for over five hours!" she continued to press the kid.

"We were, that is to say, I..." Segundo put his hands behind his back and stood rod straight, mentally trapped in his previous life. All business, with his eyes screwed tight, he said, "I inquired of the dwarf's preferred activities outside of piloting and he indulged my curiosity."

Variel sagged at that, knowing when she lost a battle, "You asked Orn a question?" She shook her head slowly, trying to clear through the medicinal fog.

The orc chuckled at that, knowing all too well the dangers of engaging the dwarf on anything he had ample opportunity to showboat over. Even the djinn shifted on his steadfast feet, as if he too was once caught under Orn's spell. "All right," Variel said, coming to a decision, "We get to Vargal, get a fresh part, then wyrm to whatever station has a direct line back to Samudra. So, in the meantime I suppose you shall be able to enjoy the fine elegance of the *Elation-Cru* for free."

Segundo looked down at the dwarf, who nodded as if he somehow just defended the kid against the death penalty. Surely she wouldn't have tossed him out the airlock for failing to disclose his existence upon her ship...which made him sound exactly like a stowaway, who were traditionally tossed out airlocks. The technician realized it was in his best interest to thank the captain profusely for her stay of execution, but she cut him off.

"Orn, find the kid some quarters. Some place not overrun with protein. And then get your hairy ass back up to the controls. I need your eyes watching for marauders. We're flying in purple space, and their ain't no corps we can run crying to."

The dwarf bowed deeply, as if he received orders from a god or loan shark. "Come on," he said, tugging on Segundo's shirt cuff, "I know a cozy little place that'll be perfect for you. Rat dropping baseboards, mold encrusted fixtures, and wainscoting -- whatever the hell that is."

Segundo began to trail after the dwarf, but he paused and turned towards the orc. "My name is Quito Segundo, but I do not have a kin name." He toddled after Orn onto his forced detainment on a ship full of aliens.

As the door closed, Monde swirled a finger in his ear and asked, "Either my translator's on the fritz, or that human is named Fifth Second?"

Variel laid back, trying to find some sleep to pull her away from the mounting headache that was her life.

Segundo collapsed onto a creaky, "ultra-deluxe" foldout bed, careful to keep his elbows away from the razor sharp edges. After perusing through his quarters' collection of reading material he waded the ether, trying to find any mention of a possible kidnapping of a government official on Samudra. Not a peep, though there was edge to edge coverage of a giant fire at a local dignitary's home and something about an adorable kitsune kit curled up inside a spacesuit glove being the next big monetary denomination.

So this was life on the outside. He gazed at the "vanity" mirror, clouded and warped from the fumes of sterilization sprays. Only the blues of his uniform were visible through the grunge. Space travel was supposed to be excitement and mystery; traveling to uncharted worlds, discovering the soup you stood upon could talk, falling madly in love with a princess with vibrant skin pigment, and catching a foreign disease that caused you to devolve into a hairy amoeba. Seven months out of the commune and all he saw was the inside of the toilets, the windowless claustrophobic deck of the bus, Samudra's open office inside a storage bin, and here. This ship would have been declared obsolete and a health hazard over a decade ago. It was a miracle the thing could run in its time much less now.

The paper thin mattress shook below him as the ship probably inched another step closer to its death. Or maybe that was Segundo's stomach. *Were they supposed to feed stowaways or let them starve to death locked inside an economy cabin on an ancient star-sight cruise ship?* The old Segundo -- the one that dutifully shaved his head each rise of the week, that placed his faith in whichever vague god he was supposed to, the one that wasn't chosen to succeed -- would have patiently waited it out and probably starved to death before anyone on the ship came to check on him.

But he learned a few things in the sparse months he'd been set loose on the universe. It was an orc eat orc world; or galaxy, universe, something like that. Screwing up what passed for courage for a third grade technician, Segundo rose off his bed -- which snapped with a dangerous bolt behind him -- and tested the door to his room. He anticipated a lock needing to be smashed open, perhaps that djinn standing guard, but it wooshed open without trouble as if recently oiled. Poking his cropped head out the door, he checked both ways expecting guards rushing to pound his peg back into place.

Only a rickety but empty hall answered back, the few lights that did work flickering above his head. Stretches of inky emptiness filled both sides of the corridor. Stepping out of his momentary quarters, Segundo retraced his steps back to the galley. The pilot had been blathering about the last time his boss discovered a stowaway onboard. There was something about dragging him out of the shuttle bay and lightly breaking atmo. It was so outlandish even the sheltered technician suspected it to be a fabrication, but he couldn't take his chances.

The plastic shoes he still owed coin for trampled over the few metal grates until they found fading carpet when Segundo turned a corner; he must be getting nearer the commons area. A few more of the lights reflected the filthy walls, and a half faded sign called this the "arlor Roo." Must be foreign.

"What are you doing here?" the voice stopped him in his creeping tracks, "You're not supposed to be here, you know."

It was the brash voice of that elf. The loud one that burst onto the bridge while the pilot flipped through his music collection, cursed out the dwarf, and stomped away. She turned Segundo's spine to jelly with only a narrowing of her eyes.

Despite himself, Segundo inched into the new room and peered around the corner. Judging by the single track machine and handful of free weights, it must be the onboard gym. The elf stood next to a panel, her arm halfway inside, while the other batted at a walking light fixture. Its scrap metal arms, little wider than a thumb, repeatedly bumped into the increasingly angry engineer.

"WEST!" she shouted, causing Segundo to jump. "Get this damn thing out of here."

Without waiting for the computer to respond, she picked up a spanner in her leather apron. Ferra swung at the steel grey walking mass of lamp parts, putting a dent into the structure and knocking one of the arms free. It clattered to the floor while the robot stared forlornly at its loss.

"You will be fixing that, you know," the computer's voice piped through the panel she was arm deep in.

The engineer pushed up some of her errant ice blonde hair slipping free from a back knot. Digging in, Ferra yanked on something inside her panel, her elbow whipping out. Like a fasting holiday, rows of lighting burst into operation, scaring away the crypt gloom over the corridors. The elf smiled smugly and began to replace the panel.

"No, I won't," she said to the computer, who seemed to be mulling over its options.

After knocking the panel back on, she collected her tools into a box and turned to find Segundo watching her. The technician faltered at her piercing stare, but she only rubbed the back of her hand across her forehead and picked up her box. "Are you lost or something?"

He sat through the lesson on elves everyone in technician training did that amounted to "just never ever run into an elf, ever." His station rarely if ever saw the *fair-folk,* being more of the human and preferring-to-sell-to-human variety. The training session had been very exact; only use the minimal amount of words necessary to convey your deepest needs. The elves looked down upon waste be it in energy, space, or words.

Pointing to his mouth, Segundo shouted, "Food!"

Ferra stepped back at his outburst and eyed the human over, "You want it or you're storing some in your cheeks?"

The technician blinked slowly, afraid this was another test. "Hungry?" he tried.

"Uh-huh, the kitchen's right through here," she gestured with her stabby tool out the door. "Most everyone's gathered for dinner, supper, whatever."

Segundo bowed deeply -- always overplay your actions around the elves, they do not understand subtlety -- and motioned for Ferra to go first. Her eyes bounced to the doorway and back to the human half bent over to stare at his shoes, eyeing up her chances before sighing. "All right." Crossing in front of the bent human, she walked towards the galley where the din of her husband easily overtook the bangs of pans sloshing into the sink.

As the technician fell behind her, she called over her shoulder, "Are all technicians this way or did you lick an engine on accident?"

Segundo tried to parse through the cryptic question, an obvious test, but his brain stopped short as the over abundant and eager voice of Orn carried across the still clanging galley. He'd propped his boots on a catty corner chair, having cranked his ornate dwarf seat as high as it could go. The captain was seated across from him, a plate of varying earthy colors before her. She looked a lot less dead than the last time he saw her.

"I shit you not," Orn said, waving his arms about for emphasis, "we'd been staring at each other for an hour, hour and a half. Just as I was about to crack, that dulcen let out the wettest belch I'd ever heard. I thought I'd be picking pits of sunshine out of my hair for a week." His side of the table was empty aside from a few discarded candy wrappers. He only came to the galley for the readily available audience.

Variel smiled into her food, nodding to the story as if some kernel of truth rested inside, but Ferra butted in, "Don't believe a fool word this lump of flesh says. The only elf he sees is me, and he'll be lucky to have that chance again."

The pilot shifted over to his blushing bride, throwing his arms open as if she wounded him, "My love, apple of my adam..." The elf eye roll is a sight to beheld given how large their orbs grow to. Ferra honed it into an art.

"I'd believe it," Variel butted in, stabbing her fork into something crunchy and bringing it to her mouth, "I once attended a dulcen state dinner, or high fancy blah blah blah with gold lettering. Five hours with eleven courses, not a word, not one bleedin' word escaped a single lip. I'd have feared I went deaf if it weren't for the clattering of spoons. Elves sure love their soups."

A stirring spoon banged against the pot at that comment as Brena tried to as un-elvenly as possible finish her dinner soup. She'd probably cough or something to remind the rest of the crew of a fellow dulcen's existence, but that was the height of uncouth. Instead, she quietly pulled the ladle out of the cutlery cup causing a screwdriver stowaway to flop to the counter. Brena picked it up cautiously, getting a shrug from the engineer. Without asking, she put it back with the other spatulas and cooking paraphernalia.

"Just 'cause you met one set of ears doesn't mean you know them all," Ferra said, surprisingly diplomatic for her, before adding, "Rock licker."

Orn placed his gloved hand to his scarlet vest and mocked a myocardial infraction, "My love, she does wound me so."

"Don't tempt me," Ferra muttered, folding her arms and shaking the heavy tool box.

"I've never met a light elf before," the stalemate broke by the overeager technician who wanted the awkwardness of a couple's fight to go away lest someone get in an airlock kind of mood. And then he turned to Ferra -- who squished up her face as if she smelled something rotten -- and stuck his foot right into an ancient trap. "I had no idea dulcens would service as engineers on human ships."

The elf reacted as if he reached out to shake her hand with a rattlesnake, brandishing her spanner at him incase he was about to attack, "What did you call me?!"

Fully forgetting her manners, Brena chuckled a most unbecoming snort from the stove as the engineer all but shot djinn steam out of her nose. The technician cowered before the five foot nothing of the elf's fury. Segundo fumbled for words, "But, your skin and your hair. I thought light elves looked..."

Ferra grabbed his uniform, popping off a few of the mostly decorative buttons. "I ain't no la-de-dah high elf, and you'd do well to remember that unless you want to become good friends with your intestines," she hissed into his face. Waving her spanner towards his head once, she released him. Grabbing a handful of nuts off the table, she loudly tramped out the door to one of her hidey holes in the guts of the ship muttering about things that drained the blood from Segundo's face.

He trembled, slowly dropping to his knees at the fury of an elf's reputation scorned. Variel shook her head, "What do they teach kids these days?"

It was Brena that interceded, happy to correct the miscommunication as if she were on the clock, "High or light elves do not reference our coloring: skin, hair, or otherwise. It is to represent our familial lines. One that is a light elf exists high within the branches of life, while the dark, or Tennens, reside amongst the roots. Structurally, we are more similar than distinct."

"And space save you if you ever mix them up," Orn said, speaking from a lifetime of experience.

"Yes," Brena whispered into her cup of soup, "some of us take it more to heart than others." She swept past the slowly rising Segundo back to her quarters.

Variel crunched down some more on her dinner, trying to get back the blood Monde was still scrubbing off the felt, while Orn watched their high elf go from the side of his eye. "Don't care what she says, them dulcens still give me the willies."

"I'd rather not hear about the state of your willy," Variel quipped.

"Come on," Orn slipped his boots off the chair and inched closer as if in conspiratorial mode, "You can't tell me there ain't nothing a bit *off* about those two? Always scurrying about together, never saying more than a few words a day, taking meals in the middle of the night to avoid everyone else."

"They eat the same time we do. You're the one who scrounges for something besides processed sugar at 4 in the morning," Variel tried to wave the dwarf off his wild theories. They all heard enough over the years about Monde, and Gene, and even a few about his wife being a secret double agent for the Elven Intelligence Force. Only the elves would create a bureau named EIF; sounds like something a person says when getting smacked in the gut.

"Still...I hear they were forced off of Cangen for being, you know, a little too close, if'n ya catch my meaning," the dwarf's eyebrows bounced up and down. Variel leaned back in her chair and crossed her arms. If he'd been closer, Orn would have started nudging her in the ribs screaming "Get it?"

"And I assume you heard this from your own two lips," she said, her voice rising to compensate for the dwarf's whisper. Gossiping about your crew was a good way to ensure a mutiny or by instituting every Tuesday as steamed cabbage night.

"It all makes sense," he said, sitting back in his chair. "Why else would a bard and a registered assassin sign up on this flying rock?"

Variel pushed her chair back and grabbed her plate. Rising stiffly and walking towards the sink, she dropped her mess in and said to Orn, "You better never let your wife hear you say that."

"Psh, she says it all the time, typically when she's half inside the rock."

"But it's different when it's her rock. And forget the dulcens, they'll be gone before too long. The bard keeps saying as such." She scraped her excess rinds into a bag and whacked on the sanitizer. A heavy whir overtook the conversation as focused light blasted away at the filth coated plates.

"To elves, 'too long' could be five of our lifetimes," Orn muttered. The twins made his life even more of a living hell than usual. His wife turned into a feral cat around them, especially the female one. She seemed to hit every ancestral hate button by merely breathing. The fact Brena talked like she fell out of an En Faire and dressed to the nines to take a shit only made it worse.

Still mulling over his bit of homemade gossip, Orn turned to his new victim, "Seggie, come and have a seat." He patted the chair his boot previously occupied and Segundo slipped down, "What can we do for you? Fluff your foam indent? Change the tinfoil blanket? Replace all your little soaps with roaches?"

"I," the technician wadded up his hands, somehow knotting his fingers, and said, "I was hoping for some food."

"Well you, *Sir*, are in luck. The captain here happens to be a world class chef. Mind you, that world evolved without tastebuds."

"Shut it, dwarf," Variel muttered, but dug into the other pot still warming on the tiny stove and plopped a serving onto a plate. It saved on her having to store it later. She limped a bit, but otherwise shook off most of the damage from the firefight. A few more pieces of shrapnel under the skin weren't gonna make a big difference in the long run.

"Here," she said, sliding the plate before the technician. Mostly brown lumps with a few white lumps to spice it up gurgled below him.

As he explored the pile with the metal spork, a curious crunch answered back. "Can I ask what it is?"

"You can, doesn't mean I'll answer," Variel said straight laced, but relented at the kicked puppy eyes, "I believe tonight we dine on grasshopper."

"Good," Orn said, "those bastards were keeping me up."

"G..grasshoppers?" Segundo's utensil wavered above the mass. His mind whipped back to thousands of tiny legs twitching in harmony around the tall grass blades of the commune. Of course, there the 'hoppers were about five inches long and occasionally breathed fire, but they still made lovely songs in summer.

"Yeah, grasshoppers. The ants aren't ready yet, probably another week." At his wan face she asked confused, "What's your problem?"

"I've...why do you eat bugs?"

Variel folded her hands up as she stumbled back into her chair, a small groove already molding to her form, "Let me guess, you're from the Ring."

"The ring?" Segundo had no idea what jewelry had to do with not consuming insects.

"Well, whatever high falutin' fancy breeches planet you hail from, out here in space we eat bugs. They're an easily farmed and quickly harvested source of protein."

"You mean there are bugs on this ship?" A squeal probably would have slipped from the technician if he weren't under the scrutiny of a woman who just jumped over an explosion and survived.

Variel responded like he questioned the existence of gravity, "Yeah, millions of them. But they're all safely locked in their enclosures." Then she turned on the smirking dwarf, "Right Orn?"

"Yeah, right."

"We won't have any repeats of 'the accident,' now will we?"

"No, no," he looked away from her, trying to hide a grin at the memory of a thousand ants crawling across her arm sending her into a near panic, "of course not." He'd kill to have video footage of the great Cap screeching as she tried to jump out of her own skin. That would have set him up for life.

"So eat your bugs," Variel said encouragingly, "Or, if you'd prefer something green, we have an overabundance of kale."

"I'll stick with the grasshoppers, thanks," Segundo said, digging his spork in deep and shivering at the crunch. As he brought the protein to his lips he tried to not think about a bug splattered across a windshield or smashed beneath a shoe. Closing his eyes and chewing slowly, a meaty and soft texture garbled his tongue. The mass almost reminded him of the crispy meat pies the commune had every fifth day, fried onions mixed into the gravy. Come to think of it, exactly like it.

With the bug crisis over, Orn began to probe the newbie as he always did when a fresh pair of legs joined the table. "So, Segundo. I gotta ask, what's with the name? Half the time my little brain bug turns it into Second."

Some of the slop vanished into his lips as he swallowed, but most dribbled off the chin as he quickly answered, "Segundo is a registered name with the list of untranslated proper nouns."

Orn glanced up at the captain. She shrugged her shoulders. She didn't much care what the kid called himself as long as he was off the ship in a week. "Thanks for the software update. So, why are you called Second?"

"Fifth Second," Variel butted in, despite herself. The doc pottered about the name as he injected the burning stuff into her veins. She played the same mental game to keep the pain at bay while the morphine wore off. What sort of society goes with a numbering system for their people? She'd never heard of any of the various Crests going that route. Well, maybe the Narwhals, but they were always a bit special.

"Yeah, Fifth Second. Sounds like a cyborg baker," Orn added.

Segundo swallowed his grasshopper pie slowly and bounced the end of his spork on the table. It wasn't anything to be ashamed of, they stressed that repeatedly while throwing all their washouts out the door. "I was raised by the Society of Prophet Placement," he said as if confessing to enjoying the burn of sandpaper across his bottom.

Dwarf and captain shared a look before Orn turned to the kid and asked, "What's that mean? You were an accounting intern?"

Segundo shook his head. How could these otherworldly types not know about the prophet school? It'd literally been his entire life up until a half a year ago. To think anyone outside its beige and padded walls had no idea of its existence paralyzed his entire existence. "It's a school, a siphon, set up to educate and nurture the chosen one."

"Which chosen one?" Orn's grasp of religion ranked somewhere above his knowledge on interstellar banking and unreal estate law.

"Any chosen one. Many religions contract with them to save on time and resources in their hunt for the new prophet," Segundo sounded like he was reading off the brochure.

"So, you were raised by these prophet middle men instead of on top of some unrepentant monastery high in the mountains on a planet that rains glass?" Variel asked, curious enough to draw some weep from the technician's wound.

"There were fifty of us, taken from our parents because we were all born under a certain star across the universe. The eldest was almost ten and hated every moment of it. I wasn't much past six or seven months and can't remember my biological donors."

"Parents would give up their children like that? No questions asked?" Variel was surprised, especially if there was no compensation.

"The 'leaders' spoke of a great light touching the one who would lead the People of Salvation, granting him the ability to heal with a word and balm the soul of suffering. What parent wouldn't wish that for their child?" Segundo had a lot of time to try and forgive his parents, which was much easier than the others when he couldn't remember them. It was a bit like praying to a black stain on the wall.

"We were trained, not in the religious doctrine of the Salvagers, that would have made choosing the chosen one too easy," Segundo's bitter words caught in his throat. Perhaps he wasn't as over it as his superiors hoped. "But in sitting still, being quiet, listening to the words not spoken, contemplating the pain of trees being felled with no one around, and sweeping. Lots and lots of sweeping."

"Sounds like prepping a kid for a life of accounting without ever letting him crack a math book," Orn butted in.

"And if you didn't eat all your meager rations and happily go to sleep on the floor were you beaten and kicked out?" Variel asked, knowing where this was going.

"Oh no, of course not. We were all treated with the same level of dignity and grace afforded a person of import because they had no idea who was the actual chosen one. To be on the safe side they assumed it could be anyone, even the boy that tried to flood the boarding house by clogging the drains with copies of the rule tapestries.

"After eighteen years in the commune, they gathered us all together and announced it was time. Some old man, foreign to all of us, waved a stick dotted in crystals over each of our heads. With it, he determined the worm eater was the One. There was lots of celebrating from our Fathers, crowing about how from now on he'd be the Chosen One destined to save the universe. Most of us kept blinking up at the kid on the podium asking 'him?'"

"No miracles or feats of anything associated with this kid, I take it," Variel said.

Segundo tried to think. There'd been an obvious hierarchy as was bound to happen when trapping fifty boys together, but The One ran to the middle of the pack. Not strong enough to be a leader, not weak enough to be a follower. Certainly not weird enough to be an outsider. Just was. "He did eat almost twenty worms in a sitting once, hence the name."

They'd been stripped of their previous identities the moment they crossed the boarding house's threshold. Names could place undo significance on a child and throw off the results, so everyone was simply called Brother Salvage. Of course this lasted all of two, three weeks at the most as each brother tried to carve his own sense of autonomy -- hence the names of skill. For most of his life, Segundo was known as "Triple Jump" after he took three giant leaps back to avoid a spider. It could have been much worse; poor "wet pants."

"And they all named you Second because you weren't the first?" Variel continued after the kid lapsed into silence.

Segundo nodded, "They lined us up, gave us a number, the surname of Second, and told us where we'd be reporting for an apprentice or internship."

"Okay, wait," Orn interrupted, "So, you're the Fifth of the seconds. Does that mean in the event the first four fail to perform their duties, get caught taking naked pictures of saints or what have you, you get the title and crown?" His dwarf eyes lit up, "Oh please tell me there was a Chosen One runner-up crown! With lots of those stick on jewels on colored cardboard paper. And a scepter!"

"I'm glad you find my life so amusing," Segundo showed his first sign of teeth as the dwarf gleefully crafted a crown in his mind. But Orn was too far gone and failed to miss the glares of the barely into adulthood technician who never really came up against adversity in his life, much less from a dwarf who didn't care if he hurt anyone's feelings.

"Well," Variel said diplomatically, "Life sucks for everyone, unless you used to eat worms." She rose from her seat and added, "Don't forget to sterilize your plate when you're finished. No free rides on this ship." Panic claimed the face of the more than likely penniless kid and she amended, "Figure of speech."

The intercom buzzed to life and the surprisingly dulcet tones of WEST carried across, "Message for you, Owner 23."

"Send it to my PALM," she said, wondering why the computer was bothering her with it.

Orn broke from his little chosen one pageant reprieve and noticed WEST's less confrontational nature, "Fer must have drugged it again."

"You misunderstand, Owner 23," WEST continued. "The message is coming from a ship floating to the starboard bow."

"What? Orn, you swore space was empty!" She cursed at the dwarf as he tumbled out of his chair.

"It was, last I checked," he tried to defend himself as he chased after the captain, "A few hours ago, anyway."

"If we get blasted out of space, I'm holding you personally responsible," she admonished Orn as she dashed through the bridge doors, partially open from a lazy pilot.

"Yeah, yeah," he grumbled, "What else is new?"

Orn's backside slipped into his chair as he hit the rise button and swung about trying to find the comm line. The captain tinkered with something on the side, near one of the non-functioning panels the old cruise-line put in to let passengers live out their "space pirate" dreams. Sure, you totally decimated that Dragon ship by pressing a few buttons that are connected to a child's busy box. Congrats. Now, why not head back to the buffet line while we handle the important stuff?

"It's not a Crest ship," Variel said, relieved.

"Why in the rockslide would it be? Patching through to the hailing ship's comm," Orn said, as he pushed down on the wrong switch.

A screen rose from the depths of the control panel and fitted itself into the viewing windows. Orn gulped and glanced to the captain. He waved his right hand in consolation and said, "Sorry, clumsy fingers."

Variel ran her fingers through her "pool table" hair and tugged down on her fresh change of shirt, the tunic even more billowy than the last to allow for air movement across the still healing wounds. Orn was never ever supposed to call up the viewscreen. It was like telling your enemy where you stuck your battleships and then letting him go first.

At first the screen remained white, a small bit of fuzz warping the edges, then the white pulled back and a gigantic pink monster with two deep black crevices for eyes came into view. Captain and dwarf recoiled, both searching for a weapon, but the view continued to pull back until the monster focused into a nose linked to a face and then a man. He was thin, his cheeks passing from gaunt into skeletal, as limp salt and pepper hair dangled from below a white hood. But his eyes sparkled, like the joy of someone who'd found either inner peace or total madness. Possibly both.

"Can we help you?" Variel asked slowly, hoping the answer was no.

The man smiled wide. Madness, definitely madness, no one can smile that big without pulling something in his brain. As he beatificated first over the woman in brown, then down to the dwarf in red, the smile actually rose higher, "It is I who have come to help you."

"Beg pardon?" She would have made the "kill the line" gesture but the skinny grinning man was staring through her, as if she left her face on the back of her skull.

"Is your life languid and limp? Do your limbs dangle from your nearly lifeless body?"

"Nope," Variel leaned over Orn's shoulder, moving to shut off the line, "We're all limpless here."

"Well, that's not strictly true now is it Cap," Orn grinned wickedly.

She bit back a few choice curses and, shifting to her right foot, kicked Orn's chair hard. "What do you want, Mister...?"

"Me?" their caller touched his robes in feigned simplicity, "Oh, I am a humble servant of The Way."

"Thank you, but we really don't need any-" Variel moved to click off the line, but Orn wouldn't shut up.

"The Way?"

"You have not experienced The Way?!" He sounded like Segundo now, so certain a pair of space debris would know all about an obscure sect on a planet far flung in the nebulous fields. "But of course, it is obvious from your lackluster hair and the dark circles rimming your eyes."

Variel leaned back, trying to not feel insulted. She just donated a pint or two of blood to the med-bay floor, which wasn't about to become a favorite beauty treatment. But it was hard to shake off the barb to her pride. Healthy was about the best she could hope for anymore.

"Do not fret, young...ish one," the stranger continued, "for I bring salvation from your curse. All you need do is renounce the devil in all its beguiling liquid forms, then the light shall shine within. Water!" He tried to spit, but was so desiccated from his devotion only a mote of dust escaped, "It is home to disease, destruction, and will make you bloat with fluid."

Oh gods, Variel massaged her aching temples, just what she needed, a dietst. She thought about asking him just how long he intended to survive without any water in his body, how water could possibly be a devil, or if he'd actually passed any of the sanity tests required to purchase a space vessel. Instead, she focused on getting this problem out of her hair as quickly as possible.

"Yes, thanks, I'm afraid we're all full up on religion, gods, deities, and any other floating disembodied sky being that will destroy us all for failing to accomplish his nebulous goals, but we'll take your instructions under advisement."

She leaned over to sever the line but not before their new friend could pout and ask, "Okay. Can I leave some literature on your--"

And the screen blissfully fell dead as she turned the thing off, letting it retreat back into the console from which it should never escape again. Maybe if she put tape over the damn thing, or got a pilot with a working hand.

Orn shrugged and smiled up at his beleaguered captain. *Could anything take down that dwarf's spirits?* "He seemed a bit thirsty."

"Ha," she barked a solitary laugh and returned to the starboard sensors, watching the water dietest pull out of their orbit and off to harass someone else.

"I've always wondered though," Orn mused aloud, "what does God need with a starship?"

"Are you going to make that stupid quip every time we pass a missionary ship?"

"Until they learn a new position," Orn grinned wide, but the captain only waved her hands in defeat.

"I'm too exhausted to continue this..." her hands circled for eloquence as her exhausted brain hunted through her internal thesaurus, "thing. I'm heading to bed. If anything catches on fire have Gene take care of it." She slid towards the exit of the bridge to the small recessed ladder on the left. Orn's humming accompanied her slow climb.

The door to the Captain's Quarters whooshed open at her life signature, and she stumbled into her room. Most proper captains kept their quarters as far from the bridge as possible. They already spent most of their life hovering around it, no reason to sleep there as well. But this ship hailed from an archaic romantic period; the stoic bachelor going down with the ship, chasing white dwarf stars, avoiding love except for the ship and all that. It was also one of the few rooms she could lock the dwarf out of. As the lights rose to greet her, a shadow jumped from the darkness.

Variel recoiled, still on high alert from the near miss with authorities. Her hand clawed for something heavy on the desk. Being a spaceship, the heaviest thing allowed to roam free was a small book of ancient postcards. She still wielded it like a pro, but it was all for naught.

As the lights above her narrow bed rose, the familiar face of her resident killer lifted to meet hers. The postcards slipped back to her desk, a joke gift of Orn's that she never got, and she shook out the burst of adrenaline. Her body couldn't take much more.

Yelling at the elf wouldn't accomplish much, they either clam up worse than usual or...no that was pretty much the elven response to any attack. They were the only race to stop a war with a librarian. Instead, she pulled out her desk chair bolted safely to the ground. It swiveled to take her exhausted form. "I assume you have a good reason for being up here."

"I needed to speak with you," Taliesin said, as if it were perfectly normal to break into someone's room and squat on their bed until they wandered in to talk.

Variel nodded slowly, "And you couldn't do it anywhere else on the ship..."

The assassin folded his hands and dropped his eyes, "I did not think you wished this to be common knowledge."

"Oh?" her face almost fell. He could not have been listening closely to Dacre; he was dangling upside down, swinging about like a high-wire circus clown. But those elves, and their ears, and their brains. A long life tended to make a species very curious or very bored.

Variel shifted in her seat, trying to not imagine it opening up beneath her, "So, you're here. What'd you want to say?"

The elf raised his head, his hair loose and dangling around his head. It was almost always knotted up and twisted back. Those haunting eyes were shrouded. "My intended is dead but not by my hand. It would be incorrect of me to retain the fee," and he held out his naked hand holding a pair of maroon chips.

"You carry hard dwarven currency on you?" she said, shocked at what he offered her, "on this ship? With Orn just down the hall?"

"It would be either a very skilled or very unwise man to steal from an assassin," he mumbled, as if this entire conversation jumped off a burning building away from him.

Variel nodded, made some sense, still...no one carried hard currency anymore. It was like hanging a giant "please murder me" sign around your neck. But assassins something worked "off the books," gods knew she'd done it a few times, and all but hyperventilated until those red chips turned into a "centaur slipping on the ice" vid.

She raised her hand but held it up, "You keep it, you'll need it soon enough for rent."

The sides of Taliesin's eyes fell. Elves may say little with their mouths, but entire novels were written by the slight twitching of their saucer eyes. "But it is rightfully yours."

"I know your guild exists to clean up the universe. Take out those that managed to slip away from another species' jurisdiction. Lauded as heroes by some that need better role models, but I won't. I don't assassinate people."

The assassin's eyebrows curled in together, "Dacre is dead."

"Yeah, murdered, by me. Not a high panel of elven judicature who got it in their heads to police the unpoliceable by cobbling together some employees and calling it an assassins' guild. Assassins plays cooler in vids."

He blinked his eyes slowly, trying to parse the words of the quick ones. It was not always easy. They spent so many saying so little. "Assassinate or murder, I can see no difference."

"Exactly," she said, closing her hands and slotting them near her chest then gasping as one must have grazed her wound.

A shudder passed across her form but she shook it off, never wanting to let on to being less than unshakeable; a difficult pedestal to remain upon. Taliesin rose to his feet, for the first time feeling awkward about invading her personal space. There were few belongings, only a metal footlocker, a few pieces of clothing tossed to the bottom of the small closet, and a flower sealed in a clear plastic sitting upon her desk. The sparseness of it, the lack of personalization somehow made it feel that much more invasive, as if he strolled inside her psyche.

"I apologize for the intrusion," he bowed deeply, unused to human customs.

"It's all right," she said trying to push it all away as she waved her hand exposing the bandaged area. He gasped at the blood weeping through. Instinctively, he dropped down to a knee and began to reach over to inspect the wound, a deep pang of pain calling up from his own uninjured hide as he did so.

But Variel looked down at him, a strange mix of concern and bemusement on her face, "What are you doing?"

"You are bleeding still, I intended too..." the thought ran over as his mind registered where the wound was and how exactly he'd have to minister to it.

"It's fine. It's not blood. Monde's little antiseptic bugs are just leaking as they shut down," she smiled at his misjudgment, a rare warm one.

"Ah, you must injure yourself often," he said, trying to cover his blunder as he rose to his feet.

"Every chance I get," she admitted with a snort. "Now, unless there is some other major business I need to attend, I should probably get some sleep and let the bugs finish their business."

"Oh, yes, of course," his eyes glanced towards the official door, not the way he'd entered, and he shuffled towards it. Taliesin paused for a moment over the exit and said, "Any words uttered from the mouth of Dacre died with him."

She could have pretended she had no idea what he was talking about. Feigning ignorance was one of her highly sought after resume skills. Instead she nodded lightly and whispered, "Good."

The elf saw himself out.

As Taliesin's slightly orange palms worked swiftly down the ladder, he felt a familiar presence hovering just out of the line of the "under the sea" mood lighting no one bothered to exchange for proper simulated night lights. His boots hit the deck whisper quiet, one of the rare carpetless sections, and he turned slowly to face his sister.

"You should not have done that," she said. Her hair was piled high in the auto-dye curlers as she reset it back to her cocktail of blacks and oranges. Brena twisted her piled upon head in a negative fashion, in danger of banging it into one of the emergency exit signs.

"I did nothing of reproach," Taliesin responded neutrally. He'd never figured out how to lie to his kin, so he worked around it.

Twins the others called them. Not strictly accurate, as they were a good quarter of a century apart by birth, but they shared much the same in facial structure; the swooping mix of oranges and blacks that marked their family line, a small nose jutting far out to match the pronounced overbite of most elves, and of course a pair of excessive pointed ears.

Brena folded her extended arms into the folds of her multi-hued dressing gown. It looked like someone ripped a tent off one of those traveling infomercials and draped it around her body. She claimed it was "historically accurate." He assumed she was referring to some ancient, space faring race of clowns.

"I am to believe that after you descend from private quarters?"

"Oh, by the five seeds Cheese, it was a business matter, nothing more." He lapsed into her most hated nickname born from a bit of a misunderstanding when a pair of dwarven merchants offered up a fine selection of cheeses from the Crest region and mistakenly referred to brie as bray. The nickname was instantaneous, but in later years would lead to swift sanctions from his father by association.

Brena frowned at the name, but kept pressing, her cold mask cracking, "'A business matter.' Is that the preferred euphemism this era?!"

But Taliesin ignored his sister's needling of his personal or professional time, "Cheese?" his voice dropped low as if he were inquiring about planetary secrets, "Have you misplaced the time again?"

She waved him away, her hand full of tuning rings getting awfully close to his concerned face. "No, of course not...I simply have been testing the limits." And her head fell down to her chest, unable to look him in the eye.

"I despise it. Every moment, every touch of..." her head rose to meet his, and her lip wobbled as a keen tumbled deep in her throat, "You don't know, you cannot know. When I'm on them, it's as if I'm inside a fish bowl, and beyond me I can see the world, the beautiful colors of emotion. Pinks of joy, blues of sorrow, yellows of regret, greens of empathy, even the blacks of hate. I watch and I swim, memorizing every notch on a person's face, but through the thick layers of glass and warping water I feel," she pounded her fist into her chest, far too hard, "nothing."

He wished he had a word to give her, a phrase to make it all better. To somehow assure her that her fate was a preferable one at times, but she'd either scoff and accuse him of admiring the neighbor's branch, or -- if it had been long enough since the last dose -- something much worse. Instead, he fell back on the old transcript he spoke every time she went off medication, "Brena, stopping will..."

"I know," she raged, then blinked back her anger. She didn't have long before the glut of walled off emotions shifted to something more dangerous. Taking a slow breath, she dug through the thick pockets of her nightgown and extracted a hypo. "I know," her voice was calm as she undid the cap and jammed the needle deep into her neck. She didn't flinch at the bite, but Taliesin did.

Her fingers shook as she replaced the cap, planning to add it to her pile of used to discard on the next planet they visited. It would take a few minutes before the dead mask would slip across her brain like a lead blanket. She painted on her false smile, always false as long as she suffered this rot, and lightly patted her brother on the shoulder.

"Do not think this excuses your actions," she said even as her mind slipped back, "I am aware of the way you view her, you are experimenting with gravity."

Her younger brother's one orange cheek turned a reddish hue as he kicked his foot about, "It is...it does not matter regardless. She has...she despises me for my vocation. That much is clear."

Exhaustion began to claim Brena, as most of her energy was spent suffering through a near emotional collapse. She nodded her head and acquiesced to her brother's clearly short-sided tunnel vision of women. He seemed to misbelieve that humans couldn't hold more than one thought in their heads, but she'd spent so much of her life watching others emotions to try and hide amongst them, she learned how to discern the deepest of feelings no matter how unaware the other was.

This could be a big problem if left unchecked.

"Come," Brena said, nodding towards the galley, "I believe there is still some soup left."

CHAPTER FIVE

Orn tugged at the edge of his glove as a foreign number, slightly faded from passing through the fabric, rotated above his palm. He made it a rule to never trust anything that required more than one dash inside it. The others seemed less perturbed as his wife passed out the exact catalog code of whatever part was busted, or about to bust, or thinking of busting.

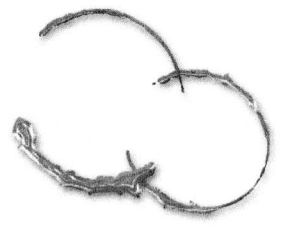

"You want to get the 'a,'" Ferra marched around Variel and Orn as if inspecting her troops. "I will stress it now so I do not have to stress it on your kidneys later. Get the 'a' model."

Variel tapped her own PALM off, never leaving the thing on for more than a few minutes, while Orn rotated the number some more and then saluted his wife. "Honey, yes, Sweetheart!"

Ferra shook her head, not a single thread of her bound hair slipping free from its nuclear grade bun, as her husband grinned like a child savoring its first taste of spring apthalm nectar. She wasn't certain who gave up first in trying to discipline Orn, herself or the Captain. Her odd century or five trained her that past the age of being able to rent a terrain shuttle, there was no changing a person, but occasionally she clung to a foreign dream that Orn might shape up to being something a bit more employable.

But Variel accepted from the first moment his buckled boots hit the deck of the still defrosting *Elation-Cru* that she couldn't get him to shut that ever flapping trap and get within the same light year as professionalism. Some wives would probably be concerned that another woman understood their husband so well, Ferra considered it insurance. No one who knew Orn would ever want him.

"And if there remain no more of these parts?" the male dulcen's voice broke Ferra from her thoughts. She'd shot a questioning look at the Captain at the extra elf incursion, but Variel only shrugged. If they wanted to get their feet wet on Vargal it was their choice. Ferra hated having them near, but it could be interesting to watch the high ones flounder down among the dregs.

"They'll have one," Variel answered, earning the slow turn of the bard in the group, her face painted even more outlandish than usual. Oh Vargal would eat her alive from the inside out. "And if not," the captain continued, "we come up with a new plan."

"The new plan would be waiting until someone either crafts us one, we thieve one off another passing ancient cruise ship, or someone destroys the laws of physics that govern this universe," Ferra grumbled, not happy with the addition of new variables in her equation.

"I didn't get the number," the little human's voice pipped up from beside the assassin. Taliesin silenced his own PALM as Segundo held his up as if waiting for a treat.

"You're not going," Variel ordered.

"I am a member of the Interstellar Government that represents Samudra and all other Samudra Entertainment Industries." He puffed his concave chest out, as if that would impress anyone outside a vacationer looking for the restroom.

"And you think that will help you on Vargal?" Orn snorted, "Little Second, this is not a mine you want to invest in."

"Why couldn't I go?" He sounded impertinent, as if he simply couldn't, nay wouldn't, go to bed until he got to stick his neck out on a black market station. There was a good chance he would hold his breath until he got his way or passed out.

"Vargal is a place of status, a gathering of like minded individuals who must maintain an order of deceit, of proving ones place within the hierarchy," Brena's dreamy voice set to bard mode drifted across the lazy room. She never really focused properly on anyone, her eyes drifting about three bulkheads deep while singing the song of the shithole.

"So I prove my place," Segundo interrupted, "flash an ID or something."

Orn laughed so hard a candy shot out of his nose, which shifted quickly to a violent coughing fit. The assassin leaned down and whacked him across the back as he tried to get an ounce of air through the dazzle wedged in his windpipe.

"How do you think black market denizens prove their cred to each other?" Variel asked the kid, curious to see what his answer would be.

"A rousing game of X's?" for Segundo, the black market was buying an extra dose of aspirin a day before your limit reset.

"I pounded my way through three guards and a set of security 'bots my first trip," Ferra said.

"A pair of gargoyles and a banshee," Orn smiled, even through his strained voice. "Try to cheat me out of my vids, you wailing bitch. Not my fault your singing career was a total flop."

Segundo turned to the assassin, who leaned back on the balls of his feet as if always a moments notice from jumping vertically into the air. "I dropped my guild association," Taliesin admitted above the dwarf's mutterings about how much the banshee tried to cheat him.

Brena nodded to her own brother, filial association was good enough when high elves and government mandated murder were involved. Eventually Segundo shifted towards the Captain, the only other human on this vessel of the damned as she stood beside the elven engineer muttering about a waste of air.

Variel leaned into the technician's ear and whispered, "You do not want to know." And she drug her finger over her deep cheek scar. It wasn't where she got it from, but it had the affect she hoped for as Segundo gulped deeply and wilted before her eyes.

"Captain," a voice crowed out from around the corner of the embarking room, as their resident orc stuck his head into the bulging crowd, "I require a restocking of supplies. I have a list of the entire contents that were...."

"Monde, this isn't a free stop," Variel said to her doctor. "We're here for one thing and that's it."

The orc paused, seeming to screw up the courage to press his point, "Be that as it may, if we encounter another unexpected assault there is a good chance someone human could be left bloodless."

Segundo paled, imagining the threat was for him, but Variel sighed and accepted the etchable pad the orcs preferred. They never trusted anything that could hinder their hand function even microscopically. She scrolled through the list, most of it bandages and syntho-plasma. Gods, she'd used up a lot more than she'd thought.

"There is a clinic I have occasional dealings with, a trade or two, they can easily supply you."

"All right," she slipped the pad into her pocket, "Segundo, you stay with Monde. You can teach him how to play X's or something."

Segundo nodded slowly, scared of the orc dressed as if late for posing in a middle class boating catalogs, but more terrified of the Captain and her airlock. "Good," Variel said, "Now, unless there's any more business...Gene? WEST?"

"If the platform is open..." the computer started, but the captain ignored it.

"Good, let's go."

Vargal was a station built over the gate to the far far septet of the galaxy, full of promise and young prospectors trying to make a home for trade. Then the planet below fell in with a bad crowd, spending its uninhabited nights with volcanic gasses, erupting into bouts of lava, and blasting a pocket of vented energy so brutal it knocked Vargal further out of orbit. The promising young families ditched the station for somewhere, anywhere safer than the eternally exciting and very overheated death trap. But nothing stayed abandoned in space long.

In flocked the squatters -- those with a claim to large gaps in between stars called them; scavengers -- those who invested coin into the backbone and skin of the station said; of entrepreneurs --those that would be dealing with the types of people to inhabit a once dead space station used. Call them what you like, but Vargal was up and fully functional less than a decade after its abandonment. To add a pinch of hilarity on the part of the fates, the planet below cooled two decades into the new owners reign, and provided a fresh source of minerals to be scraped up for the thriving but not pristine market.

Stations were supposed to be eye sores, it was part of the marketing trick to get people either down to the planet to spend their real money, or onto a sleek ship to travel to another planet to spend all their money. But Vargal took that challenge to new extremes. Pylons, normally extended out in rotatable and horizontal fashion, were torn and twisted as the station burst from her orbit. Blazes of heat toasted the legs around the central body, shifting them from a reassuring slate metal to a scorched black until Vargal looked like a corpulent spider squatting in her web as the fly ships buzzed about her gaping pinchers.

It was not the place to bring the kids for a fun day of "Spacing!"

"Orn..." Variel muttered to the dwarf rubbing his hand as he tried to get some life back into it. The bouncer had been particularly forceful in getting his cut this time.

She stared over one of six viewing decks that led down to the main floor, looking across the vastness of Vargal. The distant edge of the station was little more than a few dots jumping on top of other dots. The elf pair stood awkwardly behind her, not speaking amongst themselves, while Ferra continued to brandish her favorite spanner at the man trying to determine if she was eligible for entrance.

"What?" Orn asked Variel, listening for the loud "Oof!" as Ferra swung to get the stamp of approval. That damn black dot took forever to scrub off.

"You took us to Vargal," Variel paused, trying to put all her rage into the next three words, "on *Market Day?!*"

As Orn stepped up to the bannister a heady current of life all but threw him back. Voices, some in languages still untranslatable by the bug in his ear, mingled with the smells of un- or-never washed clothing and the ever present sinus burn of slightly burned onions. It was a human delicacy that infested the rest of the universe, but at least it covered up the body odors of the black sheep every species was quick to feign ignorance of during the galactic games.

The seething mass of life; every organic and a few inorganics cradled their wares and wandered about the makeshift stalls, crying for someone to buy it up before a certain government got wise. A few of the more prestigious law enforcing types would sometimes get a probe up their ass and try to shut a place like this down, but Vargal was the colon of the galaxy. Not technically necessary to maintain life, but you'd feel the burn when it was gone.

"This could be a problem," Orn admitted, watching a pair of gnomes drag a crate bursting with off-record animal dolls stuffed full of what probably weren't beans. Their claws dug into the sides of the merchandise, puncturing what would have been the left ventricle of a unicorn. As it tried to correct its mistake, piling the scattered pills into its vast pockets, pandaemonium erupted on the floor. Those gnomes wouldn't be crawling back to their holes tonight.

Variel sighed and glanced back at her crew. "Split up, it's the only chance we have of finding anything in this place."

"Is that wise?" Taliesin asked as the crowd parted from the gnome spill, leaving the area clean by Vargal standards.

"Not really," Variel admitted under her breath, but in her honed cap'n voice said, "I will seek out the clinic, the rest of you pair off and search for the part. Once you find it, connect with either myself or Ferra and we'll try to find you."

"Is that an order?" Brena asked, fully aware of the contracts she signed before boarding the ship.

"Consider it a suggestion," Variel waved her arms about. She'd done business in places like this, in the dark days when taking a deadly risk was the only option. Given the choice, she'd rather wrestle with that midgard serpent again. It was one thing to anticipate a knife in the back down a dark alley, another when trying to get a drink from a vending machine.

Without waiting for her crew to decide amongst themselves who would take the first step, Variel descended down the rickety ramp into the main floor of the insect hive. She passed a stand of disturbingly normal cuckoo clocks operated by a woman shrouded in her own hair save for the bow of her nose parting the waters, a junk shop that bought up people's trash, five roasted nuts stands (never ask for the surprise bag, Golem's nuts will break your teeth), before stopping at the "You Are Here" sign. It was operated by an almost gnome-like creature, but he didn't have the hang dog eyes or the mark of ownership across its forehead. Instead, he sported a nearly pristine grey coat, his head topped with a pair of red shoes. Gnomes never quite grasped the usage of clothing, thanks to their sheen of golden body fur, only the importance it could impart to others.

"Bys is the name, good person, and maps are my game," the gnome was a littler larger than a fat house cat, its shoeless ankles kicking into the small stand he perched upon housing a scannable map. Variel passed her hand over it, but the PALM only blinked and shuddered, as if it wanted nothing to do with this place.

"No good, eh?" Bys rose to its feet and glanced up to her eyes, "Things ne'er updated anyway. What you want, my dear tallwalker, is directions."

"Is that so..." Variel slipped into her noncommittal *'I'm just browsing'* voice, "And you just happen to know where I could acquire some I take it."

Bys slapped his suspenders in place -- rather impressive as he forgot to put pants on -- and grinned, the gnawing teeth of the gnomes displayed proudly. "Why yes, I believe I can direct you myself!" And then he giggled.

"I see," she stepped back, knowing when she was part of the game. Every race had their angle, their almost subconscious drive that some scientists claimed was encoded in every strand of DNA. Most never translated it, letting the urge to exchange children for gold, building a house on top of chicken legs, or gnawing upon billy goats languish within the rest of their junk code along with vestigial tails and digesting milk. But there were always a few, usually ready to play it up for tourists, who got their jollies out of dressing the devolved barbarian when they could.

"Where are you going, young one?" Bys asked, as if Variel didn't easily have a good twenty years on him. "I assure you," his high voice began to reach into dog toy levels of squeaking as he grew agitated, "I am the only one on this station who can guide you."

"Uh-huh," Variel turned to a Bugbear manning a small chips stand and asked, "Could you point me to the 'Clear Veins' clinic?"

The Bugbear put down its tongs and glanced at her. The grease of the fry oil drenched its black coat until the goblin bear shone like onyx. "It is down the next aisle, to the right," it mashed out through an elongated mouth, before it pulled out a lollypop and better enunciated, "Beside the shop that specializes in livers."

For a moment Variel wanted to joke about whether they were selling, buying, or frying, but thought better of it. On Vargal the answer could be yes to all three. Instead, she nodded her head and thanked the Bugbear. It returned to its greasy life and Bys shook its tiny fist at the goblin that stole away its fun.

Variel pushed past a few people on her way towards the clinic when a voice echoed through the crowds, "Cap! Capity Cap Cap! Slow your damn excessive legs!"

She stopped, counting under her breath, as the dwarf caught up to her, "Orn, what are you doing here?"

"I ask myself that question sometimes, late at night when only the pricks of stars and the echo of my lone heartbeat can answer back. What are any of us doing here?"

"Ferra kick you out?"

"Nah, we're fine. Better'n fine," Orn waved his hand, trying to wipe away some of the perspiration beading on his forehead. A breeze rarely made it down to his altitude, and the station didn't believe in climitizing adjustors to compensate for every heat pumping, heavy breathing monster trailing about its decks. "It was that ice-cold she devil."

Variel turned, not wanting to start this rant up again, "That 'ice-cold she devil' is keeping us in fuel."

"We wouldn't need her or that one that near got you shot up if we did a few Hero Quests."

Variel shook her head, then began to walk away, "I'm not risking my neck for..."

"For a few tortured souls with more money than brains who simply cannot be parted from their 'relatives' long lost 'relics.'" Orn knew he was picking at a very old scab, an argument he refused to let heal. Sure, the Hero Quests were a bit shady. Okay, they were so shady they'd never seen the light of day. And, yeah, around half to most people who accepted one were either never seen again or wound up alone on some distant asteroid babbling about "the rise of the great one." But one job would put them so far in the black they'd have to get a new ship just to cart around their riches.

The fact the Captain knew this as well as the dwarf meant he could never work his magic on her. Most other old side jobs he could tempt with the tales of the Eye of Harsas, fabled to see to another dimension; or the Mogato Sword, quenched in the fires of the birth of the cosmos. Something with lots of fancy names that was so ancient it should have crumbled to dust by now. It'd at least guarantee him a few months worth of work before the complaints started and he was off searching the want ads.

But, as Variel put it every damn time, "I'm not here to be a hero. We do the jobs I choose and I pay you for. Clear, dwarf?"

The human seemed to have an irrational fear of being renowned throughout the universe. He used to have a prevailing theory that she'd been a spy or a double agent, working for one crest to take down another. Or even better, she's an Orc, genetically modified to appear human and infiltrate their armies. It was about this time Ferra'd tell him to shut off the damn mouth and get to bed. Now he just assumed Variel had no backbone.

Orn dodged under a pair of troll legs as he tried to keep up with the rising gait of his boss. "Or we could keep scrounging around grunge holes in the deepest parts of the galaxy, dancing to the tune of depthless children's characters who think getting into crime will be a hoot."

Variel dodged the sarcasm entirely, "Now you're getting the idea."

The few original teeth still in Orn's head ground as she refused to play the game. If she'd been watching him, she'd have stopped at the dangerous smile overtaking his face, demanding he stop his train of thought, but Variel was a few other denizens ahead by now. He jogged after and raised his voice into incriminating levels, "Oh, ah ha, how could I not see it before? It all fits into the box now."

"I'll fit you into a box, dwarf," she grumbled, feeling a few shaded eyes landing on her as Orn's amateur trained voice boomed over the din of customers. Her fingers obstinately flew up to her scar, trying to obscure it.

"Captain," he laid his hand across her slack forearm and tilted his head as if counseling her, "I understand, companionship is an important part of life, but the dulcen culture frowns upon human-elven indiscretions."

"What in the tartus are you talking about?" Variel yanked her arm back and continued to glare at her pilot as if he grew a third head, "And since when do you know a damn thing about dulcen culture?"

Orn ignored her second question, enjoying the small panic in that commanding voice. He found a crack, time to widen it, "Lithe, dark, tall -- apparently you humans are 'into that.' Why else allow a pair of high end elves to dictate and boss half the shipping schedule if you weren't trying to *'plume ones depths'* as it were?"

He actually made air-quotes around his dwarven innuendo. Actual, hand raised, elbows bumping into a trolly air-quotes. Variel didn't know if she should be offended or flattered that he suddenly cared about her personal life. Her very lacking personal life.

"Orn, you're so far off course you're slipping into dark space," she said shaking her head and laughing it off. She turned away from him and continued her march to the clinic, hoping to beat the night traffic when the bars switched to the heavy in-organic stuff.

The dwarf frowned slightly, certain he'd been onto the first chink in her armor, but her voice was 100% genuine flippancy. He'd have tossed it all aside until he looked up at the back of her neck, now bright pink from some embarrassment she'd swallowed down. Orn smiled cruelly as he unwrapped a candy and popped it into his mouth. Ferra was gonna eat an earful tonight.

Variel turned the corner and stood before a recessed alcove, little bigger than one of those prefab cubicles that pop up every cycle to assist with your dwarven taxes even those who never set foot upon a dwarven world found they somehow owed. It was painted universal beige aside from a giant red splotch of graffiti and some choice curse words she didn't need her translator to correct for her. But most noticeable were the crowds of people marching back and forth, most carrying signs with poor spelling and poorer logic shouting something incoherent in a round. Apparently the committee hadn't decided upon which chant to use and went with both.

"Oh great, it's a parasite clinic," she sighed as Orn caught up behind her.

"A what?" he chewed through a toffee.

She didn't deign him with a response. Getting in and getting out before any of the protestors noticed would be preferable. Hooking her arm around the dwarf as if she were his guide she walked steadily to the door, barricaded through what looked like three pangs of bullet proof glass. Variel got past the first ring, most of them waving posters covered in a big eyed alien only found while watching fantasy vids or grown men and women wasting everyone's time and energy outside a clinic.

As she turned to take in Orn, cranking out feigned small talk, one of the protestors -- a dwarf in a shaggy coat hanging past his knees -- disengaged from his ring and approached. He was shorter than Orn, which caused her pilot to slouch a bit, as he called out in a friendly voice, "Excuse me, pardon me, Ma'am."

Variel sighed, realizing defeat as her day went from rock slide inside the volcanoes of the Trax to being drawn and quartered by four black holes very quickly. The friendly dwarf pressed a small doll, with eyes half the size of its face, into her hand. When it made contact with her skin it cried out, "What is life?" She sighed internally but took the thing that looked nothing like the alien's they were protesting to save.

The dwarf returned to his people, all holding hands and chanting something indecipherable above the din of station life. Almost no eyes of Vargal turned to the protestors; they were such a staple they became invisible. Orn squirmed sensing the disturbance but not certain what the hell was going on. "What's with the doll?"

"You never heard about the 'love all life' group?" Variel asked her supposedly other worldly companion, then realization dawned, "No, of course you wouldn't. You don't have to. It's a spore, or fungus, or some insect thing that enters through the nose and attaches to the lungs. Over the course of 2-3 years it takes complete control of the victim's brain. After the years it digs its way out through the skin."

"Sounds like a perfectly respectable reproduction cycle," Orn said sarcastically, trying to not breathe through his nostrils or mouth.

"Calm down, you're fine. It doesn't go for dwarves. Just gnomes, humans, goblins and occasionally the odd elf or two."

Orn started to breathe again, causing the piquant body odors of Vargal to fill his lungs. "They ain't come up with a cure yet?"

"Oh no, it's a relatively simple one. Easier to take a shot once every two years to prevent it, though. The protesters are here on behalf of the fungus."

"Why in the undertow would anyone give a shit to protest about that?"

"Because, the 'fount' becomes highly suggestive," Variel said to her pilot, still eyeing up the circle of life watching for anyone to make a hostile move. One of them was looking over their signs for typos and opening up the design program on the poster. "Introduce a few spores into a population and you have readily cheap labor. While under its command the host requires little food or sleep, and isn't about to go on strike or demand a raise."

Variel glanced up to see a small gnome, wrapped in a cloak to try and shelter her appearance, inching towards the door. A human had his arm wrapped around the gnome to help her stilted gait; she'd let the parasite take too deep of hold. Though with the new enforced waiting periods and lung scans from "reputable hospitals" it was a wonder anyone broke free of the hold.

"Remind me to never leave my bed," Orn said, shuddering as they approached the reinforced door.

"You ever get to bed?" Variel asked her pilot, who chuckled but didn't respond. The captain didn't bother looking back as she held open the clinic's door first for her ambassador and then the gnome girl. She scampered inside, grateful for the break as the rest of the every-life-form-is-sacred eyed her up like a rattled dog in a cage. Variel looked at the doll still in her hands, and let it drop to the ground as she walked into the clinic.

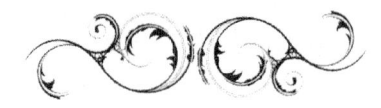

"Excuse me, pardon me, oh do forgive my intrusion," the bard's overly sugared voice was so out of place as the three elves descended into the mech section of the bazaar people dodged out of the way on instinct. No one trying politeness to get through the mounds of Vargal was a simple tourist. Various eyes followed after the group, some warding themselves against whatever powers a woman dressed for a night under the spotlights could wield.

Ferra led the triangle, occasionally jamming her elbows into anyone that tried to encroach upon her limited personal space, but only the chipper voice of the dulcen got anyone to step back. It gnawed at her as she cursed Orn for doddering off just because she got into a minor discussion with the bard. There wasn't going to be any blood...probably. Ferra glanced up at a sign written in dwarvish trade with a few curious troll phrases slipped in. "The best cancelable weapons in all the galaxy. Silica dissolvers won't see you going." *Where were the damn proper mech stalls? Everything was guns, ammo, and the parts to fix the guns so they didn't blow off your arm.*

"Would you stop doing that," Ferra grumbled

"Doing what? Excuse me," Brena's bracelets jangled as she pushed aside a set of women shilling a false ID face, the charms honed so they could only be heard in elven frequencies.

It set Ferra's teeth the way only something elven or her husband leaving wrappers in the bed could, "Acting as if you're the boss of everyone around you."

"I do no such thing!" A false edge of near emotion crossed Brena's face as she turned to her brother. He was far too consumed with what appeared to be a fine selection of cufflinks formed from ogre feces to respond to her.

Ferra turned back to watch her prey huffing at the indignation of being called out and recited an old taunt the tennens used whenever a Dulcen entered their territory, "'You can rip its wings off, but that butterfly will never be a caterpillar.' You never should have left the tree, little butterfly, to feast amongst us worms."

"I will have you know I have been 'down amongst you caterpillars' for over a century now." She paused amongst the endless running stream of bodies, a rock choking up the flow. Her jangling fists were close to landing on her hips in consternation like an exhausted child.

"And you haven't spent a second of it in the dirt." Ferra knew she shouldn't poke the high elf. They couldn't help the lot life doled out for them, forced to spend their lives high above the clouds where very little oxygen could reach their overtaxed brains. It seemed almost cruel, but this bard's preachiness made it so much easier for her.

"I!" Brena turned to her brother who, if he'd been human, would have whistled loudly and slunk away with his hands in his pockets.

Brena deflated, "I suppose you are correct in some fashion. My time amongst the galaxy has been limited in scope." Her head bowed in elven conciliatory fashion.

"Shit," Ferra threw her hands up in rage, "You can't even fight proper! You don't give in, you call me a dung faced grease worm and insinuate my mother's a tail pipe."

The dulcen leaned back, her face awash in confusion, "I...I do not understand. What would be the point of bringing up your lineage in this conversation?"

Ferra collapsed her head into her hands and glanced at a gargoyle watching the fight with the curiosity of someone trapped in a booth for the next ten hours. "Elves," she muttered to the stone monster who lifted its wings in solidarity. "I...forget it," she threw up her arms, knowing when to give up. It was one thing elves were renowned for. Ferra began her canvasing walk into the crushing parts market, still scanning for anyone trying to unload something older than the last gnome crop. Over her shoulder she added, "You don't have to get on with me, just get away from me and I'll be happy."

She stalked deep into the mass of twitching life, leaving behind the pair of dulcens and failing to notice the closest to pain Brena could suffer. Her chosen profession required that she be at all times approachable and beloved, but also partly aloof and mysterious. It was the kind of balance that drove nearly all other species straight back to the arms of retail work, but flourished under the elven love of duality. It was an old joke that one wasn't a full elf until you became your own worst enemy.

Brena was no stranger to people disliking her, jealousy was to be expected, as was xenophobia from anyone off the Tree coming into contact with a dulcen. Few left, even fewer outside official capacities. But this burn of Ferra stung much deeper, a fact she had troubles coming to terms with.

"Hey, Bardie!" Ferra's growly voice called over the crowds, "if you get your butterfly ass lost, I ain't coming to save it!"

Brena beamed her hidden smile, taking whatever words she could from the other elf on the ship. Gathering up Taliesin, the pair politely shoved their way through the crowd to find the engineer tapping her spanner against the decorated table of a booth boasting "The Best Parts You Can Afford To Buy!"

A rusalka manned the station, her hair continuously pillaring about her bedraggled head as if she were still beneath the water. Her pale skin, drawn into a death rictus, shimmered greatly under the waning station lights. Water spirits looked out of their element in space, non-corporeal ones even more so. She wafted her ethereal hand towards the section of images flipping before her on the imbedded screen.

"No, no, no!" With each flick of the screen Ferra's voice grew angrier, and she already started at a 10.

"Perhaps what you seek is no longer within the realm of possibility," the rusalka's voice was soft as a summer rain, and mournful as a morning dove.

"It's not some magical fairy dust that will shit out ice cream," Ferra leaned into the water ghost, her anger rising with each plink of her pet spanner. "It's a round chunk of plastic you fit over the injector so we don't all go splat splat against the wall."

"Ah, you wish to place a part order!" and the undead spirit yanked out a holographic inventory catalog of space parts. It was only once ever printed; the weight of which ripped through the planet's crust straight to the core where the excess gravity created a micro blackhole. This was before they added the supplemental addition and index.

"It's a class d cruise ship built so far back most people weren't even aware humans had space travel," Ferra said watching the pages fly back. There was no rhyme or reason to the catalog; doomsday devices were stored next to gene splicers, which were all housed under the "Peace Keeping" category. Ships were indexed by some mad genius who rated every one by the size and abundance of the cup holders. The Elation-Cru came with very few.

"Ah, that's it! That little piece of plastic right there," Ferra's finger paused over the floating image of a black o-ring. That damn little thing was the cause of a throbbing burn at the back of her head she usually called Brena.

The rusalka copied down the number and inputted it into her official representative calculator, "I fear that specific part is not in any existence across the station, but I may order it for your hands and have it within..." she waved her non-corporeal fingers across the transdimensional keyboard and chirped, "two to three business weeks!"

Ferra's head smacked into the desk, "Variel's gonna kill me."

"Shall I place that order for you?"

The elf sighed before sticking out her PALM for scanning, "Yeah, go ahead."

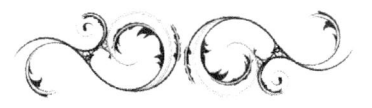

"Horse to D-17."

The orc sighed, but placed the pip into the square. "Miss," he said and stared over his own notes, "Archer to B-3."

"Damn, hit," Segundo leaned back in the chair, and glanced towards the ceiling. "You sunk my calvary."

"When the captain suggested we play X's I believe she was being facetious," Monde said, slotting the peg back into the interface of one of the few board games still left from the old days on the ship.

"Oh," Segundo said, shuffling through the piles of his notes. He only won one game out of their lot after accidentally setting off a nuke and destroying Monde's fleet as well as most of his own. "I can't tell with her."

"I've found that to be true of all humans; think one idea, yet state another," Monde sat up prim in his seat with a small pillow nestled for the small of his back. Age was but a number until your joints started creaking when you rested.

"And orcs never lie?" Segundo asked the supposedly warrior race before him.

"Only about the very important things. The 'white lies,' as you call them, seem a waste of time," Monde wiped a bit of dirt, or possibly an escaped portion of tomorrow's meal off the table and cast his orange eyes towards the cowering human. The lids blinked so quickly at times it was hard to make out he had a spare.

"I imagine you have quite a tale to tell," Segundo said. "An orc winding up on a human ship."

"This is technically a dwarven vessel," Monde responded as if he didn't have a care in the universe.

"You still serve under a human captain."

The eyelids blinked faster as the orc sipped down a drink he didn't offer to Segundo. He wasn't in the mood to pull out the stomach pump. "You are wondering why I do not slaughter her on sight, yes? War, bravado, and all that?"

"Aren't we your sworn enemies?" Segundo asked, eyeing up the not so threatening stance of the orc as he replaced his cup on the only onboard saucer.

"Orcs do not have enemies." Monde tried to search for the proper term, "we have...adversaries."

"Isn't that the same thing?"

"Depends on who's winning the war."

A crash thudded across the table and both players turned to watch the oversized but quiet djinn plop another load onto the table. Gene didn't stop to chat with or even glance at them. It unscrewed a cap from the top of the first pile of tubes and walked off with its treasure. Segundo shuddered as it went. His neck was still sore from the djinn's attack.

"A curious race," Monde said as if he were cataloging an insect, "it is increasingly rare to find one anymore, much less communicate."

"What communicate?" Segundo said, "The thing tromps around the place like a broken golem."

"The mere fact of it, that he is inside that suit is enough to count as communicating," Monde poked at the pile of broken ship currently invading their game space. The petite engineer would not be happy, but she stayed mostly out of the way of the djinn. None on the crew seemed to communicate with him aside from the Captain. Even then, no one ever heard him talk back.

"What do you mean, suit? Aside from the work apron, it looks pretty naked to me."

A panel buzzed to life and the familiar voice of the computer chimed in, "Djinn are a collection of air bound particulates."

"A what?"

"You must work exceptionally hard to achieve sentience without a brainstem," WEST chided from the panel over the sink, its voice echoing inside the empty metal.

"Smoke, the djinn are smoke creatures," Monde stepped in, not necessarily a fan of the child but also not in the mood to break apart another mocking session. He would rather everyone at least try to get along.

"So they use those suits to communicate with the rest of us corporeals," Segundo said aloud solving a problem everyone else already knew the answer too. "But they cannot speak because they're just smoke."

"Your brain must be so insignificant a single image could not be stored upon it," WEST said, "Any djinn that inhabits their emissary suits can speak with the assistance of an internal computer."

"Except for Gene, no one knows why he doesn't talk," Monde cut in, "Most assume it's some vow of his people. The dwarf likes to float the theory that the djinn saw something so awful he lost the will to speak. Occasionally he claims that thing is spying the captain naked."

Segundo was about to ask another question when the galley porthole flew open and the dwarf clomped through as if Monde's mention summoned him. Orn smiled wide, a stuffed bag clutched in his hands. "Monde, I bring presents!" He dropped the bag onto the table, where it shuddered as the shield generator momentarily broke and a few of the bottles escaped confinement.

"Delightful," the orc muttered as he raced to scavenge the free range medicine. "I assume you had no trouble."

"Oh no, none, everyone in the clinic was real polite. The captain, however, said she was gonna, let me think...'Gouge out your eyes and use your stupid head horns as a doorjamb' if you ever sent her to another parasite clinic."

"She said exactly that?" He asked, afraid he over stepped his precarious perch.

Orn shrugged and peeked over at Segundo's battle array. "More or less. Damn squirt, remind me to never put you in charge of my wars."

Monde relaxed, more or less was code for Orn pulling shit out of his ass again. It took everyone onboard the ship all of a week, maybe two if you were particularly thick, to adjust to Mr. Lidoffad's particular quirk of telling a lie whenever the truth was dull, and two if he thought he could get away with it. Monde dropped the few bottles into the bag and rummaged a bit, "Did you remember the artificial plasma?"

"I'm just the messenger boy. After Ferra called, the Cap'n was in a right fit, dumped the bag into my hands and stalked off. Something about fixing the damn thing herself."

"She has seemed particularly stressed as of late," Monde commented, still digging through his latest acquisitions.

"Yeah," Orn snorted, "What she needs is a nice long screw against..."

"The MGC transmission," his wife cut in as she traipsed into the mess hall herself, Gene's swiped tube cap in her hands as she inspected the damage. Her hair was half collapsed after the altercation with the pair of goblins. It was a minor thing, a few curt words exchanged about the bucket nature of her ship, followed by a few less curt swings of her spanner. The important thing is they would all walk away from it...eventually.

Brena followed behind, her own skirts ripped clean up the middle. It was almost worth the split lip Ferra nursed to watch the high elf waddle through half the station trying to maintain her dignity as she grasped the torn cloth together. Still, the girl didn't blush or cringe once. That was some serious granite to crack.

"I was gonna say bulkheads, but risking beta radiation and third degree burns for a little something something sounds like the Cap," Orn looked at the high elf and waggled his eyebrows. He shifted a candy stick to the other side of his mouth as he leered, "Aye, Miss?"

Brena blinked slowly at the dwarf inching into her personal space, and tried to not glance over at his wife who seemed to be busying herself with the frosted pantry. "I believe I shall turn in for the evening," she said while tracking Orn, afraid he might make a sudden move. She backed out of the room, her hands still gathering the torn cloth to maintain whatever dignity she hadn't spent.

Orn snorted as she went and looked to his wife. Ferra extracted the frozen leg of something so coated in ice crystals there was a small possibility it came with the ship. She held it to her lip and mumbled over the frozen dinner, "What do you think you're doing?"

The dwarf tapped his head in conspiratorial fashion, "I got it all figured out."

"You couldn't find your ass in the middle of an ass storm," Ferra said, her brain too frazzled from the noise and heat of the day to form a proper comeback. She yanked out one of the chairs and crashed beside Segundo, who was feeling very out of place all of a sudden.

Orn followed his wife's suit and pulled up his chair, always on the hostess side of things so he could watch every entrance into the galley. "Nah, it's about them elves. I figured out why they're still onboard."

"Oh, have you now," Ferra dropped the frozen leg and gingerly touched her face; it was gonna take awhile to heal. Monde glanced at her wound but offered no advice. He and the elves were legally supposed to pretend they never saw each other. If there was a major medical emergency he could intervene and she could do the same if he burned a hole through the med-bay's floor, but cultural embargoes were tricky things to work around.

Orn grinned even wider as he tilted his chair back, "Ay-yup. It's so simple, I don't know why I didn't think of it sooner."

"You do know simple," she responded.

"The captain and the elf have a thing," Orn folded his hands in what would have been a suggestive manner to a dwarf. It flew over the heads of every other species at the table.

"A thing?" Segundo asked, letting curiosity run away with his spleen.

The orc stood and loudly proclaimed to the ship, "I believe I have everything I need to restock my lab. I shall be off, before a certain dwarf implants his boot so deep inside his mandibles I shan't be able to remove it. Good day, Mr. Quito." Before Orn could respond, Monde walked out, trailing after Brena, turning a right to her left.

"A thing," Orn continued. "Think about it. Why else would she keep a pair of dulcens onboard if she wasn't boffing one of 'em?"

"The same reason she keeps you onboard, as potential food incase we're ever stranded," Ferra muttered but didn't rise from the table. Every now and again she'd listen to her husband's prattle to appease him.

"She's otherworldly," Orn began to count off a list on his fingers, "a bit cross, prim, with ice in her veins and enough face paint to keep a clown college in business. Exactly the type that could tame our poor mysterious Captain's heart."

"You believe she is with...the female elf?" A very dangerous burn crept along Segundo's cheeks as thoughts he'd never had before nor thought possible flared across his brain. "How...how would that even work?"

Orn blinked slowly at the kid, uncertain how he made it to adulthood and remained so green most gardeners would toss him back.

Ferra rubbed her head and whispered, "Orn, your ass is blowing so much smoke I'd think you ate Gene. The captain isn't fucking one of the dulcens, or anyone else onboard for that matter."

"Hello, Captain Variel!" WEST chirped up from the sink.

The three guilty heads snapped around towards the entrance, Segundo even staggering to his feet and smashing his knee into the table. It rattled and tossed Ferra's ice leg to the ground with a heavy thud. Each conspirator held their breath, waiting for the dark haired head to poke around and then hurl each of them off the ship, but only the steady hum of the ship's lighting answered back.

Slowly they each turned back to WEST's panel where it buzzed before responding, "Made you look."

Taliesin lowered his eyes as he opened his ears to the life before him. The swirling patterns of the universe were always there, if one knew how to read them.

A young child, possibly from one of the stocky races, drops a small fruit. It catches under the heel of a besuited man in a hurry, tossing him straight into the folded arms of a female boggart who takes it as a direct insult to her ancestors. Her balled up fist misses the dodging man and lands into the flinching backside of a passing ogre. Then the real fun begins.

It was a pattern, twists of blues and reds converging to craft the purples of conflict, that could play across every pit stop, every high class bordello, every back alley that made up this wide galaxy. Learning to spot them, to anticipate their climax, to dodge their denouement was what gave the elves their supposed psychic powers. It was easy to appear mystical at foreseeing the end if you already saw the same movie a hundred times before. For the Assassin's Guild, this knowledge served every member well.

Taliesin wasn't reluctant to sign his pair of centuries to the guild, it was prestigious. Not just any dulcen would be accepted, you needed the correct branch after all, which his family had in spades. Cleaning the universe of the detritus slipping through the sieve of an unconnected police system was an honor, one some of his fellows brandished as a gold medal to any dignitary they could charm a cabin upgrade out of. Yet he preferred the cold and cramped life, bouncing from one rentable room to another, seeing the other side of the galaxy. The one he was supposed to be helping to wash away.

A rare smile twisted up Taliesin's lips as he imagined anyone having the power to wipe away the grime of Vargal. He was young by elf standards, but in some ways his time off Cangen gave him a depth of the organic psyche centuries past his age. The ogre limped past him, gingerly touching its goblin wounds while the businessman continued to whine about his ripped suit to the very bored security guard about to rob him blind.

The assassin shook his head lightly and disengaged from the shadowy corner he tried to find a moment of calm inside. Tale as old as time, as the humans liked to say. He bit his own tongue as the thought crossed his mind. Stumbling, always stumbling down that bottomless pitch. Brena would read it across his face if she were here.

A harsh voice piqued his wandering attention, crying across the vast swaths of color of life. The rare absence of color, the break in the pattern. Some saw it as black -- endless, warm, and treacherous; others as a white light -- blinding, harsh, and sterile. Taliesin tried to see it only as his landlord.

"Your sign clearly says two for one," the captain argued with a rambunctious pair of sirens, young enough to be out in the world without the voice locks before their temptress abilities manifested. They peddled sets of hair combs, their own yards of green hair piled high with as much merchandise as they could jam in.

"Nonsense," the small one warbled, the voice stumbling like a baby gital waddling through its first hunt.

"We charge what we charge. No more, no less," the second's voice was stronger, jumping a bit through the shifting grass. She'd be fitted with her locks soon.

The captain sighed loudly, her own hair bouncing as she shook her head in frustration. It must have not been a promising day. "Fine, give me two sets in the green and another of the yellow with the seeds."

Taliesin took the moment to approach, "Purchasing something for yourself?"

Anyone else would have jumped at the assassin's words, or perhaps glanced around guilty at being caught with their hand in the proverbial porn jar. She simply rose a bit off the counter and said, "I know a guy that goes gaga for siren stuff. Says it helps him 'embody the proper feminine form.' Hey, the yellow, not that piss colored tan!" She shouted to the girls scampering to unload their less popular merchandise on the human paying closer attention than they suspected.

The first siren dropped the bag onto the counter -- the shield shivered like moonlight across a river -- and punched in a few numbers, "That will be two songs of sorrow."

The captain grabbed the scanner and passed her PALM over top, letting the computer do all the calculations. It beeped and she scooped up the bag while her hand flashed a receipt. As she turned to leave, one of the siren's waved a cheery goodbye and sang, "Please come again."

Her notes trilled across Taliesin's spine, dredging into his mind a vision of home. Not his familial home, but an imaginary one full of warmth and joy like something out of a soup commercial. Even elves were not immune to the siren's call. He wondered momentarily what the captain felt as she yanked out the few combs and stuffed them inside her pockets before turning off the bag.

"Adjusting for the exchange rate, you were rather cheated, captain," he said, falling behind her as she bounded towards the section of Vargal cleared for food consumption. The family friendly stations called it the food court, going so far as to elect a food king and queen every hour to entertain the consumers. Vargal called it nothing because it didn't see a reason to waste everyone's time.

Variel didn't turn to acknowledge her tail. "I know, but I'll get triple that from Lady Grey. And don't call me captain. I hate it." She grumbled the last part to herself, but elf ears could pick up on a whisper through a wall.

"I ask for forgiveness. I thought it was a sign of respect," Taliesin stumbled over his words as he mentally ticked over every time in the past six months he called her that. It was not looking good.

"It's all part of Orn's little joke. First day we met he called me captain. I told him not to, so of course he won't address me as anything but. And now he's got everyone else on the ship thinking and saying the same thing."

"I did not realize," Taliesin mumbled, watching the clip of the back of her boots, that ragged hem of her pants skirting over the filthy floor of the station. "If I may be impertinent, why do you keep him employed?"

Variel rolled her shoulders, "Because I need his wife, and she'd probably notice if I killed and taxidermied her husband. Eventually."

"If you were to slide one of those chattering child toys inside it, you may have a few months respite."

The captain paused and, for the first time, glanced back at her resident assassin. He lifted his head to her questing eyes as she asked, "Was...did you just tell a joke?"

Taliesin brought his fingers to his lips and tapped them in concentration, "Joke? No, we elves require everything in our lives be as serious as the sunrise and twice as uninspiring. We cannot joke."

He tried to maintain his concentration, but as a heart warming smile broke over Variel's face, his own straight man pulled at the corners until he grinned like a loon.

She laughed a bit, trying to clear her head, before turning back to her destination, but over her shoulder she said, "Huh, it's funny. I had no idea you elves could have dimples."

"They are my greatest secret," he lied smoothly, trying to keep the banter light and innocent.

She didn't stalk away, or curse him off, so he took a quick glance about and increased his gait to stand almost beside her. Variel shifted her head but didn't say anything, seeming to enjoy the company without wanting to appear as if she did.

"You're without your escort," she said. "Brena back on the ship?"

"Yes. She requested some 'decompressing time.' I believe that is code for writing in her diary."

"Diary? Really?" Variel's eyebrow rose but she didn't turn to look at him, her eyes still tracking the denizens of Vargal. A pair of shifty trolls held a goblin upside down, shaking him like an obstinate condiment bottle. More than likely it was for currency, but it could also be part of some game. The goblin did seem to be smiling.

"It is a 'bard technique.'" He placed the air-quotes with only his voice, his hands clasped behind his back lest someone get too close.

"Huh," she lapsed into noncommittal silence, deconstructing his words. It was a major fears of elves that their own thoughts could be used against them, and all the more disconcerting when surrounded by other species that honed internal thought into a verbal barrage.

He shifted on his boot's instep, the fresh leather pinching his toes. "How did your errand finish?" Taliesin often saw the dwarf ask his wife how her day was. Of course it tended to lead to a string of expletives from the engineer, but he ran out of short talk.

Variel sighed, "Not too bad until the grey futchar sent me to a parasite clinic. It's--"

"A small medical facility that removes the life spore," Taliesin said, watching the shoes of the people before them. Footwear told an assassin much. Anything distinctly out of place, far too expensive or too poor, could be a sign to watch.

"You know of that?" she glanced over at the bowed elf, but he didn't look up, off in his own elven world.

"There was a particularly venomous protestor. He killed three doctors and escaped prosecution each time."

"I didn't think the Assassin's Guild cared much for small time murderers. Aren't you all about Kings and Dukes and other royalty flopping about popping out heirs?"

Taliesin chuckled, "Some join for the glamor of altering the balance of power."

"But not you," her voice grew cold, as it always did whenever his profession came up. It was why Brena need never worry.

"Truth be shared, I am far too young to receive such assignments even if I wanted them." Taliesin didn't raise his head even as he felt her penetrating stare upon his face.

"I didn't think elves left their tree until they were into their 20th decade. How old are you?"

Taliesin barked a laugh, a garble from the extended elven trachea, and turned to look her in the eye. "I believe you have asked the most uncouth question of an elf short of 'how often do you require the loo?'"

She smirked momentarily and said, "So, I shouldn't follow up with your bathroom regiment, then?"

Despite himself he laughed, a hard sputter from fluttering lips as he tried to contain it. For elves being the peak of social manners and grace in the galaxy, he failed miserably every time he was around the cap...Variel. "I am old enough to leave, but too young to return," it felt strange to release that half secret into the world. "It is my part of the Pattern."

"Oh, yes," Variel lifted her head back high as she gazed into the ceiling, "the 'Elven Pattern.' That every action can and will be repeated ad infinity until someone or something breaks the cycle for good."

"You do not believe," he stated it as fact. It was rare for elves to share their philosophy outside the species, rarer still to find someone who supported it. Most elves were unsurprised; the quick ones did not have the time or patience to watch for the patterns. A few insisted that letting the galactic aliens onto the path would damage it.

"That every action, every choice I make has already been predetermined by some cosmological calculation to keep the universe spinning? And there are no exceptions to this Pattern?"

Taliesin squared his shoulders, about to break one of the not forbidden but still more guarded secrets of the path, "That is not strictly accurate. There are those who fail to conform to their determination. A pebble in the river."

"A pebble cannot do much." Variel was in an argumentative mood. Most times she waved off any religious discussion as 'something she didn't have time for.' But today had not been kind to her mood and she wanted to burn it off on something.

"Depends upon where the pebble is located," Taliesin whispered. She was inching closer to him now as his voice inadvertently dropped. If the others overheard his sharing of their...if Brena! "Because of this danger, any anomalies are encouraged back into place."

"Encouraged with a bullet to the brain?"

"No, nothing so fatal. They rely upon shunning techniques, removing one from the river entirely and hoping, in time, the anomaly will correct its defective behavior." He realized too late he used they instead of we, but she let it pass.

"Everything is destined to repeat itself, that's the gist?" she turned to watch him bob his head. "So, you believe at some point in your long life, you'll once again wind up on another ass end of the galaxy station talking to a nosy human?"

He brought his hands forward and clasped them together as if they were in cuffs, "I have, and more than likely shall return to this place many times, walk these very noisy halls, and watch the suffering life within; but...no, I do not suspect I shall speak thus with another 'nosy human.'"

She shook her head, not understanding what he admitted about her and looked around at their little alcove. They paused near the handful of tables, most empty, and beside a gutted machine that dispensed a noxious liquid that claimed to supply MGC straight to the energyless cells of the body. It tasted of bitter regret and a soapy tongue to elves.

Variel scanned the crowd and began to ask Taliesin a follow up question when her eyes landed on something parting the crowds. "Fucking hell!" Grabbing the surprised assassin, she flipped him around, pushing her back to the wall and pulling him dangerously close.

"What are you..." he began to ask as he tried to lightly break free of her warm grip. In response, she wrapped her arm around his upper back as if initiating a hug and the elf's brains dripped into his boots.

She didn't look into his eyes, but she did whisper near his ear, "Crest, pushing through the crowds, looks like Jaguar from the speckles across her uniform's top. They always were ones for show."

Taliesin tried gazing upward, hoping this awkwardness would pass quickly and he could return to a nerve calming meditation, but Variel's arm slipped lower down his back as she wiggled beneath him to get a better look at the Crest. *Seeds, give me strength.*

"Tall, female, dark hair, far too long for proper uniform regs," she rattled off the description as if her trapped prey could do anything but try to keep from melting onto the floor. "Jaguars." His gaze turned down to watch Variel's eye roll. Apparently her particular human branch did not approve of the jaguars, whatever that was. Human genealogy was like trying to catalog the peerage of mayflies.

"What is a Crest doing this deep in neutral territory?" he asked, trying to breathe through his mouth. Scents could be his undoing.

"Exactly. She's talking to someone, oh no, I mean she's threatening someone and crap, coming over here!" Variel looked into the assassin's eyes and dropped her grip upon him.

He breathed a deep sigh, grateful to be free, but she shrugged her shoulders and whispered, "Sorry," before grabbing onto the back of his head and yanking his lips down onto hers. Taliesin mostly missed, smashing closer to her chin as she screwed her eyes up tight, listening for the tell-tale clip of a Crest soldier's boots.

The dwarves spoke often of "out of body" experiences, moments when they watched themselves complete an action, or experience a loved one's crisis from miles away in person. Many chopped it up to mine fumes and a propensity of overheating under too much chainmail, but Taliesin thought there might be something to it as he watched his own body pressed up against a human, the panic competing with both ecstasy and terror.

Variel's arm dropped from his head as she listened to the Jaguar slide a chair next to a pair of gnomes enjoying a rare break.

"I'm looking for any information you have about a ship," the Jaguar's voice was commanding, well used to pushing around things three times her size. "A derelict cruise ship, no less. It's called..." The captain went rigid beneath his fingers as she strained every muscle into her ears. He did his damn best to not go rigid himself.

"The Constellation Cruise," the Jaguar finished.

Variel bit down on her lip, also partially nipping his own, as the gnome pair admitted to having no knowledge of such a ship. The Jaguar grumbled but moved on, her clipping heels growing dangerously close to the pair pretending to express their passion next to a drink machine. He felt the brush of the Jaguar's green wake as she walked back into the fray of the station, not pausing to interrogate the "lovers."

The captain's head turned to follow, his own face falling into her hair, and she cursed like an ogre pirate, "By the many fucks of the tentacle goddess!" As the clip of the Jaguar faded into the distance, she pushed Taliesin away lightly, shuffling out from under him. He didn't fight, but he didn't help either, all of his muscles afraid to betray him.

"What? What happened?" he asked himself, uncertain how he could explain any of it away.

But Variel believed he was speaking to her, "I saw the sword dangling off her hip. She's not just a crest out in the middle of deep space. She's a fucking Knight," and without launching into any more explanations, the captain made a b-line back for the ship.

Taliesin shuddered as his mind tried to retake his limbs, ordering him to pursue her. Something was shattering the patterns. As he slipped into the crowds with the captain all that reverberated through his shaken mind was *I am going to require a cold trip through decontamination, or four.*

CHAPTER SIX

Variel half drug her pilot down the hall into his seat and ordered him to undock the ship. Orn began to protest that he just about had Segundo on the ropes but at her glare he shrunk back and put in the call for clamp release. Whoever worked the docks didn't respond, only slipped them a number to fall in line. They'd probably be back out into the inky depths in an hour at most.

As Orn switched off the comm and began the retracting procedure he glanced up to his boss, "Gonna tell me why we're suddenly running like a pair of gnome school girls?"

"The inertia injector will not arrive for a week or so. We can wait out the time in dark space," she answered curtly, her fingers digging deep into the headrest of his chair.

"Uh-huh, that was a whole lot of not answering my question," Orn responded, still dutifully flipping buttons even though the station's computers handled most of it.

"Contact me the moment we break," she said.

"This wouldn't have anything to do with..." Orn's thoughts trailed off as Variel's form vanished through the quickly closing bridge door, "Well, ne'er mind then."

Variel bounded out of the forward deck, her fingers curling and uncurling as she tried to look commanding and not about to suffer a panic attack. She walked into the quiet galley and spotted Ferra curled up with one of the ancient magazines Brena brought on board. The dulcen used them as part of her act and boarded nearly her weight in them. Occasionally, the engineer would "relieve" her of one out of boredom.

"Afternoon," Ferra said as her eyes lifted from the garish pink magazine to greet the captain. "I'm taking a 'What kind of species are you in bed?' quiz. When they say biting do they mean breaking skin?"

"Elation's undocking, but we won't drop beyond cruising speeds," Variel added quickly, before the engineer rose up in argument. "Avoiding any unnecessary attention in dark space would be best," she spoke as if reassuring herself, but Ferra shrugged.

"Sounds good, it'll give us a chance to shake off that Vargal stench," and she returned to her quiz. "Damn it, succubi again. Those aren't even real."

"Right, good," Variel wavered, as if hoping someone would press her for information but Ferra was busy scratching out her answers and trying for a third time. Breathing slowly, Variel made for the shuttle deck, typically deserted because it hovered a few degrees below comfort. Normally that was to adjust for the adherent heat of any shuttles. Since they didn't have any, the deck was freezing and no one bothered to alter the temperature controls.

The captain stepped around a few old boxes, still unpacked, from when she first moved onboard with Gene. Stuff she purchased thinking it necessary for lone space travel before she learned to scavenge. Waste; so much of her life was full of it. "WEST?" her fingers brushed against one of the old game consoles installed to keep the richer customers from bursting into bored tears while waiting for a personal shuttle to whisk them off on a sanitized adventure.

"What is it, Owner 23?"

"Connect to the ether, find me a list of recent Knights."

"We're not close enough to an information buoy," the computer chirped, its voice filling the frozen void. "I could create a list from my data banks if you'd prefer. Every Knight is now named Carl."

"Divert through the station's buoys," she ordered, not in the mood for her twitchy welcoming engine's brand of obstinance.

"Isn't that a bit rude?" WEST feigned prudishness as if she asked him to unlock all the bathrooms on the ship.

"Just do it," she shouted, causing the computer to bleep to silence. It flashed a rotating planet for the loading screen.

Her fingers drummed against the wall waiting for her miscreant computer while she tried to convince herself she was overreacting. Five years, nearly five years and not a soul came looking or even poked into the ether about her. The body they formed out of rocks was laid in state and never disturbed. First Dacre, and now this woman asking questions about her ship. She glanced back at the loading screen which now had an asteroid crashing into the planet. WEST was gonna take awhile.

"How do you know she is a fresh Knight?"

Variel jumped, her fists raising as the elf broke from the wall. He seemed calmer than she'd left him, not that either were in decent shape after a headlong dash through Vargal's distinctive night life.

"The sword, she wore it upon her hip," Variel said, lowering her fists.

"I believe all of the Crest Knights carry their swords with them," he said, his trained eyes noting her dropping fists.

"Not like that they don't. Strutted out, within easy unsheathing reach is what the books say, but after a week banging the damn thing into every shortened shuttle seat and wedging it into gaps in floor grates you shift it in closer."

"You are quite knowledgeable about such matters," Taliesin responded in that layered way of the elves. Peel back each word and you'd find another seven meanings hiding beneath. He wanted her to know that he knew enough to be dangerous, which would make him less dangerous. He even tried to provide an opening for her, but she couldn't take it.

"It's good to stay informed," she responded meekly, turning away from the dark assassin to the control panel. *Damn it WEST, get your ancient silicon ass in gear.*

Taliesin seemed to wither for a moment from her dismissal of his offer, but he didn't turn to leave, his own eyes watching the screen. In the silence of the processing computer she felt the growing pressure to say something.

"I should apologize, for earlier on the station. Grabbing you and all..." gods, why was her mouth growing dry?

"Ah," he responded noncommittally, failing to fill the gaping void.

"I know elves have this thing about humans and I did not wish to violate your personal shield." Her tongue tried to panel up the silence, maybe decorate it with a few more framed "uh's" and "um's."

Her words didn't seem to soothe the cultured beast, instead he shifted back on his heels away from her. "It was a tactical decision made in the heat of battle. It is already forgotten with nothing to forgive."

"Okay, good..."

The screen beeped and WEST's impertinent tone chimed over a string of data, "I had to break through a firewall, an ice shield, and agree to a date with a security camera, but here's your list."

Variel scrolled through the search limits, female, not much past forty at most, a four on skin shade, dark hair, Jaguar, and one result popped up. "Sovann Vargas, Knighted in the service of King Blah dite blah, on the Lord's fifth birthday party. Some war records, but less than I anticipated for a Knight. The Medal of Triton though, and a seal of the HPF. Oh boy."

"Does any of that translate for you?" Taliesin asked, lost in the crib notes of the human military.

"Yes, if she's pursuing...us, we're in big trouble," Variel said coldly. "WEST, what's with this block?"

"It is a block. It places classified data inside an impenetrable wall so no unauthorized patrons can access it."

"Can you open it?" she asked, poking at a red box marked "Sealed Under Orders of OPIC."

"Perhaps you do not understand what impenetrable means. The dictionary defines impenetrable as..."

"Yes, fine," she waved on the mute button, as the computer continued to blather as was its wont since discovering ancient files from a Doc Johnson. "The Crest wouldn't concern itself over an atmo break across an unincorporated planet. And a Knight sure as shit wouldn't."

"So the mystery remains, what does this woman hunt for?"

The full force of an elf accusation turned upon her, and she tried to not falter under it, but her fingers traced along the scar, the damn piece she could never escape. As she was about to explain or lie her way out, the shuttle bay rocked, unpacked crates tossing to the side.

"Great, now what? WEST!" Another quake shook the ship, stronger, and Taliesin reached out to steady her without thinking. She in turn held onto him until the rattling passed. "WEST, what the hell is...gods damn it," and she turned back on the volume.

The buzzing computer raged into hearing range, "...And if you're going to keep me activated, you might as well actually utilize..."

"WEST, shut up and tell me what's happening," Variel muttered, her hand still gripping Taliesin's forearm incase of another quake.

WEST calculated the chances of getting away with explaining how its shutting up and telling something were incompatible versus her downloading its personality onto a storage drive and launching it into a star, and decided to answer, "We are being fired upon."

"By what?"

"A ham sandwich." The sarcasm matrix was strong with this one.

Variel paid her addlepated computer no mind as she deleted the panel's history and chased off to the bridge, the assassin hot on her trail.

"Orn, report," the captain shouted as she burst onto the bridge as another volley shook the ship.

"Everything's going all woo woo woo," the pilot said, flapping his hands up and down.

"Charming."

Orn swiveled to find the dulcen standing behind Cap, his hand clinging to the doorway to stop from flopping on the floor. "Since when do we let passengers on the bridge, Captain?"

"I am observing," Taliesin simply said.

"Shove it, dwarf," she fought through the rattling to get to her minimal sensor data. The best the ship came with was the occasional sweep to tell them if they were about to drive straight into an errant asteroid, planet, or orbiting restaurant. Putting together the picture outside the hull was like sticking together a puzzle without being able to look at the box or the pieces. A few softer ruptures bounded under her feet and it all came back. "Depth charges."

"Depth awhat now?" Orn asked, his fingers flying over the panel that locked out his foot pads. Bouncing back and forth like an unbalanced load wasn't the best time to be pressing down on the acceleration.

"It's an old trick Crests use to drag out ships they don't want to damage; concussive rounds that rattle but don't burst the hull."

"So we're being depthed by Crests, fantastic. I believe this is when I tender my resignation," Orn began.

"Not today, Orn," she said. Punching a few buttons, the ship spiraled into the closest it came to an unpredictable pattern, the "everyone look to your left to spot the meteor shower" maneuver.

The shaking stopped, but the few working gravity boosts screamed in pain as the *Elation* flipped and sped in her rotations, dodging about in space as if she walked straight into a cobweb. Stomachs merged with throats and then back down to feet while the ship danced to her personal tune.

A frazzled engineer tried to cut over the comm line, "What in the fuck are you doing?" but she was quickly relegated to the back channel before getting anything approaching an answer.

As soon as it started, the pirouetting spaceship leveled out, tottering through space like it didn't suddenly suffer a seizure trying to escape a bug. Orn sighed loudly, assuming it was all over, and began to organize his scattered trash pile.

But the Captain held her breath, hoping this had all been some major accident. Oh I'm sorry, you're the *Elation-Cru*, I wanted the *Ablation-Crow*, my mistake. She glanced towards the assassin looking ceiling-ward, as if he could see through the thick hull to find a clear coast. This wasn't going to end on a happy note.

A small switch flashed and then beeped in a hurried succession. Three sets of eyes turned to it, but it was Orn who fiddled with the thing and gulped deeply, "Either WEST has really upped its prank subroutines, or there's actually a Drake ship baring down upon us."

"Location?" the Captain asked, as if it would help.

"Uh, ahead of us, or beside, possibly behind...this thing's maps haven't been updated in decades."

"Are they not required to announce their intentions before destroying or boarding a vessel?" Taliesin asked in the form of a statement. He knew damn well what regs were, but these Crests were a long way from their space. All of Variel's instincts told her none of this was "on record."

She was about to say as such to the elf when a new beep joined the others flashing about a ship getting too close for comfort. "Cap, it's, they're calling us," Orn said and then muttered to himself, "Sweet fucking crap, a Drake."

"Connect through, but..." she was about to add "not on screen" but the dwarf was too quick. She steadied herself as that damn panel rose again. Maybe breaking it off would work...

At such close proximity the screen lit up as soon as it connected and the calm face of Sovann appeared, sitting in her Knight's throne. A few lesser Crest soldiers eyed up the screen from their stations scattered around the bridge decorated in a demure cat spot motif. "You are the *Constellation Cruise*?"

"*Elation-Cru*," Variel said, hoping it'd be enough to throw her off but knowing it wouldn't. It was her own damn fault for being too lazy to properly rename the damn thing, or buying replacement letters.

Sovann didn't smile, she merely shifted her weight from one leg to the other and leaned forward, "You were docked at Eclipse Station 5 orbiting Samudra less than three days ago."

"There isn't much reason to deny what you already know, you must have our flight plan," Variel hated this part, the monster circling the prey letting it think it had a chance to wit its way out.

Sovann swiveled away a monitor and rose, her sword glowing in the stark fluorescent light of the Drake. "Yes, it is some interesting reading. Snakesmouth, the Alari Desert, even the shifting winds of the gargoyle homeworld. All hotspots for people of a certain criminal nature."

Orn couldn't have looked more guilty if he tried. Despite spending most of his adult life lying through his teeth, the guy could not hold a poker face in front of law enforcement if his life depended on it, which it typically did.

Variel wasn't buying it. "A curious thing that a Crest, a major one at that," Sovann puffed up in pride at the lie, "would send a Knight to investigate the possibility of smuggling."

"Smuggling is a serious issue for the entire galaxy," Sovann said as if she were running for office. Though she might be; public service was a natural step for some Knights who wanted to screw over larger swaths of people.

"And you must have proof of some smuggling on our part, then?" Variel asked the Knight striding closer to her screen as if she could jump through the camera and attack. "No Knight may invade a ship without a writ of contention."

Sovann paused, a hard smile taking over her lips, "You seem to know a great deal about Knights, Ms. Tuffman."

Shiting shit! But she didn't let her internal swearing flash to her face. Trying to maintain a calm she muttered, waving her dismissive hand, "A relative of mine was in the Crests."

"Ah, of course," Sovann turned back to what had to be her second, and accepted an old pad, "We have reason to believe you are harboring a highly dangerous and very much wanted fugitive onboard your ship. That gives us all the reason we need to board you for a thorough search."

"I see," Variel fought a panic screaming up her throat. The questing glare of the elf landed upon her back. Even Orn was turning to look at his boss and then the dulcen, trying to fit together what the hell was happening. Now wasn't the time to explain, now was the time to lie her way out of this mess. "Well, we'd be more than happy to cooperate with any Crest investigation. Just give us a moment to unjam the airlock. Your charges fused together the hatch."

"By the Seven...you pirates and your hunks of shit," Sovann cursed, but waved her hand. "Very well, you shall have ten minutes." She turned away from the screen, giving her people the command to end communications and the screen went blank.

Variel furiously flipped through the navigation screen, "No, no, no." She reached across Orn and punched another button.

"So when do we start guessing who's the wanted murdering psychopath?" Orn asked, as he was pushed away from his console by a desperate captain.

The three dimensional map of space lit up and she skimmed through, zooming in and out in a mad dash that gave the dwarf a headache. Orn wiped his eyes and continued, "My money's on the orc, he's too quiet. It's always the quiet ones."

"I am far more reserved than our good doctor," Taliesin admitted, uncertain how Variel intended to get herself out of this mess.

"The assassin? Ever heard of too on the nose? Now your sister on the other hand..."

Taliesin ignored the dwarf's barb and asked, "What do you intend to do, Variel?"

"Variel? Are we all on a first name basis now?" Orn swiveled back to his captain as she inputted a flight path save into the computer. "Oh! What about Gene? Quiet AND terrifying."

"Orn, how quickly can you go from a dead stop to a wyrmpinch?"

"Two minutes," he shouted as if she asked him his multiplication tables.

"Not fast enough, we're dropping the safety gauge off and slipping into the event horizon right as it opens. That should take a minute, I pray."

"What are you considering?" the assassin pushed.

"A Drake's weapons take 90 seconds to heat from a dead start. We pull them so that giant flame mouth isn't facing us. Then, as they're prepping for an invasion, we burn the engines."

"On a still broken inertia injector?" Taliesin pointed out the largest flaw in her plan.

But she continued to flip a few switches, "Yeah, Ferra's gonna kill me, but I'll be dead later."

"She'll only get to you after she's done tearing through me," Orn muttered, but he began turning off all the safety regs. WEST booted himself up, asked what the hell was going on, and was promptly sent back to sleep.

"Timing is critical," Variel said, "Orn, when they're as far behind us as they can get and you're about to start the burn, touch my leg below the camera line."

"Uh, not that I'm sure you're passable for being such a large sentient and all Cap, but I'm a married man."

Variel ignored him, trusting he'd do his job, and opened up the comm line. The cursed screen that could so easily throw off any duplicity rose. For once she was happy to have the thing still hooked up. "Knight of the Drake ship, we have almost finished our repairs and are preparing to receive you," Sovann smiled, believing she won their little pissing contest, "but I'm afraid we cannot maneuver around, you shall have to meet us."

Sovann sneered, "Delightful. Ensign!"

"Sir, it could be a ruse," he said, calling Variel's bluff clear as day. Stupid comm screens. "Faking damage to get us into a vulnerable position."

"So they can, what, shoot their sightseeing pods at us? Rare for a cruise line to be armed, rarer for one from before most stars were born," Sovann laughed at her crack about the *Elation's* age, earning a glower from Orn. "But we shall remain on the line, until we are in position. Yes, *Captain*?"

"Agreed," Variel said, and leaned back, trying to look as if she didn't have a care in the world.

Orn's right eye trailed down to the sensor data beeping like mad as the Drake swung about, its heavy head that burst a photon fire thick enough to tear through any hull and some small moons slowly drifted away from them. Even the assassin seemed on edge, not used to the epic play of a space battle.

Fifty meters, twenty meters, ten...his finger danced over the ignition key when the Drake slid fully into place. Gulping once, he let his hand graze Variel's thigh and she rocketed forward as if someone knocked her from behind, punching her fist through the screen. Sovann's confused face flashed momentarily before the entire thing sparked to darkness.

Orn's fingers flew across the panel, flipping and reflipping every damn button. The MGC flooded through the cabin as the small wings extended. A bit of her blood dripped onto the console and Variel wiped it away absently; she was too focused on the sensor data. "The ship is turning...Orn."

"Thirty more seconds," he shrieked through a clenched jaw, his fingers working the concerto that was space flight.

"There's a massive energy spike coming off their ship, Orn."

"Twenty."

"The head is definitely getting hotter," Variel's teeth were on edge. This would either end in escape or them being blown to star dust.

"Ten."

"They're prepping to fire," she shouted.

"NOW!" Orn shouted and jammed both fists forward as his foot smashed down onto the pedal and the Elation-Cru dropped straight into the wyrm hole.

The wyrm opened up a bit harder than usual without all the wining and dining. The scathing purples and blues of the bending to space they plowed through tingled with a dangerous vein of red. It was a sign she wasn't quite ready for the intrusion and could flip this latest passenger through the excess dimension right back to where it came.

"Steady, Orn," Variel said as calmly as possible as her ship shook like a dog out of the bath.

"Steady what?" Orn watched helplessly as the MGC conduits handled all wyrm pinches. No spatial engineer would trust his sextant to a commercial pilot, much less someone about to rend space into a few lopsided dimensions. Pinching the XYZ axises out through a second set of coordinates required precise calculations and a whole lot of computation that no one outside of brainzilla could accomplish on the fly.

The red flashes increased, ripping through the purples and blues as if it was spatial tissue paper. It very well could be. No one ever spent much time studying the insides of the Omega Axis (as it was supposed to officially be called). Most prevailing mages argued that by all logical data the very wyrm everyone traveled through to get to the conference shouldn't even exist. They also liked to spend hours at dinner trying to convince everyone that dessert wasn't real.

"Wherever we're heading is coming up," Orn said, watching the display counting down as the little map swung their location to a distant section of the galaxy.

"There is no opening cresting," Taliesin said, watching out the turbulent windows.

"Orn?" Variel asked, trying to find the black crack that would open to let the invading ship out of her Omega space.

"What do you want me to do? Do I look like a mage?" the dwarf shrieked, trying to not panic as he punched a few of the nonessential buttons and ordered a coffee from the defunct machine in the galley.

"Has anyone ever reported what happens if a ship fails to break through the exit port?" the elf asked, his own calm mask tilting on its axis.

"One," Variel grabbed onto the dwarf's chair as the red lightning cracked close to the hull, "the *Mariac*."

"Tree shelter us," Taliesin said, closing his eyes tight. Even the elves knew of the cursed *Mariac*, lost in the early days of space flight into the unstable wyrm holes and never heard from until a few millennia after its disappearance appeared drifting through space, unmanned and unscarred save for a continuous howling echoing through the damaged comm line.

"Don't cash in your chips just yet, I see the universe's crack!" Orn shouted, as the familiar zip of black shuddered before them. It began to widen, but far too slowly.

"We're not gonna make it," Orn muttered.

"We'll make it," Variel responded back, willing her belief into existence.

"How do you know?"

"No other option," she shook off the fear of getting lost in the alien space of the wyrm, and watched the black crack expanded, pouring stars into their view. "Brace for deceleration!" she shouted to the ship.

A string of red lightning glanced across the bow and turned around for another full attack just as the *Elation-Cru* slipped through the narrow crack, her afterburners sealing the tear behind. Space zipped by at an alarming speed, far too fast for a drop out of the pinch. Stars warped and bended, and a planet, at first just a speck in the night's sky, began to loom into a real danger.

"Orn?"

"That inertial thingie we keep failing to fix is cracking. Slowing isn't much of an option."

"There's a fat planet about to smash through our front windows, stop this damn ship!"

"Okay, but it's your ass," he said. Overriding the last safety, he yanked down on the control stick and pulled the ship to as hard of a stop as one could in space.

The back end squealed like a banshee caught in a chute. Half the control panel lit up in rage but the metallic air receded and MGC transferred from the engines out to the storage sails. They weren't going to wind up as splots on the window or ceiling. Slowly, the planet crested to a gentle crawl into view as if they intended to drop into orbit above her.

Variel unclenched a fist burrowing into the dwarf's chair and left a few nail indents behind. She pretended to pore over data while getting a modicum of calm back into her overwrought system. "Nav's coming back on line, as are our few sensors. Doesn't look like anyone's noticed us yet."

"If I may be so bold as to inquire into your personal need for a near death experience, but where in the hell are we?" Orn cursed, poking at a shaking map that was in no mood to play these hide and seek games.

"One of the places a Crest would never go," Variel started when the bridge door, locked down during any flights of idiocy, slammed open and an enraged elf stormed through.

"What are you doing?!" Ferra's eyes blazed like the red lightning of the wyrm. She clutched a wad of black plastic melted into such an abstract shape it could sell for billions as art.

"Hello, dear," Orn said meekly, trying not to cower fully from his enraged wife.

Ferra dropped her prize onto a few of Orn's favorite posters where it clanged hard before rolling onto the floor. She scooped her husband up with her spindly arms and raised him to her eyes, "You broke my fucking ship!"

"It was me, actually," Variel interceded, saving her pilot, "I broke my fucking ship."

Ferra let her husband's collar slip through her fingers, as she tried to form something of an argument for how she should disembowel her boss and toss her to the packs of roving Rancors. It was difficult to get past who actually paid the bills for the ship and who kept said ship operational. She sputtered through a rage that couldn't find an outlet before relying upon the simple, "Why?"

"That is a very good question," Orn asked. Free from his wife's accusations he turned them on his own boss.

Variel crumbled for a moment under the glare of both dwarf and elf, her oldest employees who never pried much into her history and all were happy for it. "It's a long story," she tried.

"With the inertia injector a husk of goo, we have all the time in the universe," Ferra muttered, crossing her arms. Orn copied his wife, one of the rare times he appeared to be on her page.

"Look..." the captain got out just as alarm bells jangled across the bridge. "What now?"

Orn flipped a few switches up and Ferra flipped them back. She reached under her husband's questing fingers, trying to right the still smoking crater she yanked her prize out of in a fit of rage. WEST pumped out enough fire retardant foam it was going to take weeks to clear the engines.

"Someone's opening the wrym," Orn read, and pointed to the starboard bow.

Ferra glanced up at him, grabbed his hand and turned it port. "That way." Sure enough, a fresh tear shattered inky space and a far too familiar Drake ship tumbled out.

"That's impossible," Variel said as the universe zipped itself back up. The Drake seemed to be shaking the cobwebs off its wings before the metal monster would turn about and consume its prey.

Taliesin, forgotten in the engineer's entrance said, "It had a copy of our flight plan, it must update automatically. They simply followed us in."

"Crest bastards," Ferra cursed as she watched the human ship swinging about, "They ain't getting my ship!"

Variel called up the map, her brain screaming at her that something was very off about this situation, but she'd worry about that later. Right now she had the scrap of an idea, flipping past all the backwater stops they preferred to the big boys.

"What are you doing?" Ferra asked, her eyes crossing at the streams of location numbers buzzing past.

"Looking for a new detour."

"You're fucking crazy. One more Wyrm and this ship'll tear into two. Not that the safety regs will let you."

"Exactly," Variel said, settling on a planet and registering the flight path.

"Mad, your entire species is bumblefucking mad," Ferra shouted, waving her arms about.

"Orn," Variel began to order, when the comm line buzzed up. Someone was calling them. The pilot looked towards her and she nodded, "Turn it so only we can hear her, no back chatter." And then she turned back to the path request, "Come on, you bastards. Accept."

Sovann's thick voice chirped across the tinny speakers, "I must applaud your childish attempt to run. It could have very nearly worked if we'd been an elderly transport ship. And it is proof enough that you are guilty."

"Guilty of what?" Ferra asked, trying to catch up. The three others on the bridge shushed her. "Sorry for not wanting to die."

"*Constellation-Cruise*, you will stand down or we will open fire."

Variel flipped off the comm line to let the Knight crow to dead air. "They won't fire at us, they want something on here."

"Or someone," Taliesin said softly.

"How do you know that?" Orn asked the captain, watching the Drake flip about. The 'head' that was really the ass end of the ship warmed up its mesh of propulsion and weapon's fire.

"Lady's intuition."

"Great, last time I trusted that I wound up picking a rash of gargoyle crabs off my nether regions," he let the untold story drift off into the ether, aware that no one had time to ask for clarification.

Variel's screen lit up green and a small smiley blinked on the screen "YOU HAVE BEEN ACCEPTED."

"Finally." She switched back on the comm line. The three others about to ask her what 'finally' meant fell into silence as their pursuant crowed across the shrinking vastness of space.

"And then I shall boil your hides for leather..."

"You want us, come and get us," Variel shouted back before shutting down the entire line.

"That'll show 'em," Orn called out. "We can bleed all over their uniforms and make quite a mess."

"No one's dying today. Orn, call up another wyrm pinch."

"Okay, it's official, the captain's gone full space madness," Ferra said watching Variel bounce to a second panel, all while the captain scoured the booked flight paths.

"Um, wasn't there something about us being ripped apart...I mean I'm no engineer or anything," Orn said cautiously calling the engines up once again.

"But I am!" Ferra shouted, trying to get someone to pay attention to her. "This isn't just an incredibly, universe imploringly scrapping-our-spleens-off-the-bulkheads bad idea, it's also impossible. There's no way to override that safety shutdown."

"Bingo," Variel said, her eyes looking over to her engineer who finally read the destination her boss saved.

"Oh, oh you're evil," Ferra said, but locked her hands around the control panel. She'd never been through a full shutdown before.

Orn wasn't able to keep up, "What? What's evil? Who's evil?"

"Shut up and fly the ship," Ferra responded, hoping this insane plan would pay off.

"But not so fast, take your time Orn. Their records are just updating about now," Variel said, watching as someone with far more influence than her forced their way to the top of the registration list.

"How long does a Drake take to power to a full wyrm?" Taliesin asked, also following the trail of thought.

"A full two and a half minutes. Dragon ships might be impressive but they aren't maneuverable in the wyrm stream," Variel said, steadying her hand on Orn's forearm. "We need to time this perfectly."

"Time what? Is the new game let's leave the dwarf in the dark?"

"Steady on, Mr. Orn," Variel smirked, her fingers tapping against a poster for a horn blackening cream. They'd have secured the pass, MGC would be flooding the chamber.

"Oh ho ho, aren't we all droll today," Orn grumbled, "Can I push the button yet?"

A Drake was made of a good thirty decks, a smaller ship of the Dragon class but still deadly to anyone who crossed a Crest. But the MGC took time, enveloping the entire sleek body of the ship built to replicate the look of an ancient monster stretched in mid roar. The wings will close in, encapsulating any background MGC trying to siphon back to the universe that birthed it.

"Not yet." Her eyes turned away from the console, which in the intervening time directed itself to a merchandising site for anyone wanting to purchase a souvenir of their trip. A small waver, as if the Drake suddenly slipped below a still pond, glistened across the space.

"Now!" she shouted. Orn tumbled forward pushing through the flight checks, cranking up their own envelope and tasting that nasty afterburn that reminded him of the few times his mother tried cooking. The Drake wavered, the checks slowing as if uncertain if their prey was about to make the jump or not. It was the classic get on the train or not standoff.

The ship started to hum, a very bad sound. Ferra rubbed her hand across the console and whispered, "Shh, I know, I know. But do as we say and you'll get a treat."

Orn glanced at his wife, "You scare me sometimes."

"Pinch the bloody wyrm," she said back, almost jovially.

"Afterburners are doing that thing they do, space is unzipping," Orn called, "You might want to hold onto something."

The *Elation-Cru* turned as the same tear in space to whatever destination Variel picked opened up. This would be about when Orn would jam on the throttle and shoot them through, but he paused and looked towards Variel. "Slow and steady, as if we're injured."

"We are injured," Ferra pointed out, her fingers gripping into the lip on the console. "And why doesn't this damn place have any safety harnesses?"

"The Knight's ship is turning," Taliesin pointed out, his own body leaning against the cordoned off section before the windows as he played lookout.

"Okay Orn, on the count of three. One. Two. Holy shit!" Variel fell back to the deck.

The *Elation-Cru* burst forward as the dwarf jammed on the throttle. Orn never waited for three, anything bad could happen before getting to that number. Besides, two was plenty warning. A lapping bubble of MGC washed over the *Elation* but a heavy groan cried out from the control panel.

"It's fighting me," Orn called out.

"Tal?" Variel asked, rising to her knees.

The assassin stumbled a moment over his new nickname but answered her, "The Drake is increasing speed but still behind."

"Hang onto it Orn. Come on, you can't tell me you never once wanted to crash this ship," she chided her pilot.

"Not with me aboard!" Orn gritted his teeth as a few of the more important switches popped off in frustration. WEST was probably already plotting their demise, assuming they survived this.

"The Drake is passing above us," Tal reported, his vice gloves digging into the hull so he could maintain watch.

"They could still turn, ORN!" Variel's voice was cool and focused.

"Yeah yeah, kill us all. I got it," the dwarf grumbled holding against the bucking control stick. A few more warning lights booted up flashing red in case any of these idiots weren't aware just how stupid they were being.

"We're about to enter the wyrm!" Ferra shouted, the lip of the blue lightning almost reaching to their stubby nose.

Just as she was about to order Orn to turn the ship and abandon the plan, the Drake shot straight into the wyrm, unable to pull a U-turn.

"ALL STOP!" Variel shouted, not that she needed to. Orn's heavy foot stomped down on the break, but the *Elation-Cru* was already on the job. Unable to send any built up inertia through her storage capacitors, she cut off the MGC and the engine in one quick flip of a switch.

Everyone on the bridge failed to fight against the all stop. Ferra smashed her shoulder hard into the console. Taliesin maintained his grip for a moment but the elf slipped and bowled into the captain as she one again hit the floor. Only Orn, strapped so tight he could be carted around in a papoose, remained in his seat. He suffered a classic case of space whiplash, as the tangy metal of unspent MGC bit into the horrendous pain building below his neck. "Well, that could have gone worse," the dwarf muttered.

Then the lights went out.

CHAPTER SEVEN

Ferra paced back and forth, circling around the galley all the more cramped thanks to the assembled crew. Monde tended to her bruised scapula, muttering about how she'd have to take it easy. He moved onto the assassin who waved him off. Most of Taliesin's fall was broken by the captain now sitting alone at the table steeling herself for the coming confrontation.

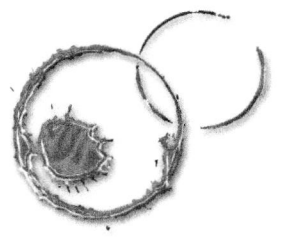

Brena hovered beside her brother, uncertain what happened in the ship crash. She wound up face first in a pile of pigment creams, smearing her chin in a rogue rouge. As soon as Ferra spotted the dulcen she got her first smile of the day. The high elf looked like a pair of simian testicles sprouted off her chin. That good stuff's a real bitch to remove.

Beside the djinn stood their accidental crew member, who was hoisted away from a near death fall by the disturbingly quick Gene. Segundo wanted to give his thanks but all words died in his throat as the djinn scooped him up by his narrow shoulders and held him securely in place. The communication suits could lock down onto any surface in the event of total gravity failure; a major issue for a smoke based species.

A small beep called from the direction of the bridge, and the galley door opened, letting in the final member of their inquisition. Orn limped, rubbing his good hand across his face as he commented, "Still no sign of our new friends."

"There won't be for a few days at least," Variel commented, still staring ahead at the wall. It wasn't easy to give up on a half decade of lies.

"And how do you know that?" Orn asked, the vile thick in his accusation.

"The flight path they attempted to pursue us to took them directly into elven space," Taliesin said. "An ingenious move."

"Them elves aren't gonna let a Crest boss them around. She tries that and she'll be licking boots just to get an appointment to register a flight path back," Ferra responded, glad to never have to deal with elven bureaucracy anymore.

Orn threw his arms up and said, "Great, so we have a few days before they flip around and kill us."

Everyone turned towards the overly theatrical dwarf giving Segundo a good look at the right arm, "Oh gods!" he pointed wildly.

"What?" Orn asked, turning behind him to stare at the still gaping corridor hole. "Getting a draft? Want me to close the door?"

"Your...your hand!" Segundo continued, a bit uncertain why no one else was reacting. "It's missing?" he finished with a question, afraid this could be a delusion brought on by spaceflight. Didn't some people undergo debilitating brain damage when dropping through the wyrm? That's what the articles in really large font with an excess of punctuation claimed, and also that the high ranking members of the Crest Court Society were secret amphibians that required a daily sacrifice of flies.

Orn turned to gaze at his stump, a few of the implant motors whirred in response to his nerve signals. "It's in the charger," he gestured with his stump towards the bridge. "Damn things can only hold a charge for a few hours near the end."

"Oh," Segundo's eyes remained wide, but he was afraid to ask if every pilot had his arms chopped off, if it were some dwarf thing, or if anyone that traveled on this ship had to lose a limb. He didn't want to appear uninformed. "Okay then."

"If we're all done talking about my hand..." Orn tried to steer the conversation away from his errant limb by placing the stump behind his back, "We have far greater issues to answer for." His questing eyes, normally set to full bemused, were hard. Even his carefree tone had an edge only reserved for doctor visits.

"Surely you've figured it out by now," Variel said, failing to notice the slight nod of the assassin's head, but his sister didn't. She crossed her arms, the mood rouge on her chin growing brighter in her anger.

"Indulge me," Orn said, not ready to admit that he really hadn't. All he ever dwelled upon with the anti-reminiscent captain was that she had some tactical training and didn't care for other humans. That could also describe about 98% of all dwarves, so it didn't register as strange for what he'd thought was his friend.

"I used to be in the Crests," Variel admitted, yanking off years of silence like a strip of hull tape. "Five years ago I came to the realization I no longer wanted that life, and so I, let's say, resigned. Permanently. Total face reorganization, new ID data, I even dyed my damn hair." She lifted up her roots, showing a small chip implanted in her skull.

The aliens knew varying degrees of information about the Crests, for most it was just the human military. Seven different kingdoms kept them about to enforce some rules, wage little battles, and march in parades. A few other aliens, those that made it their life's work to keep abreast of anything that could be problematic, were more aware of the depth of the Crest. There were two paths: the recruit -- young, stupid, and easily sacrificed; and the enlisted -- high in command on the way to that most feared and untrusted of humans, the Knights.

"Which were you?" Segundo asked.

"Beg pardon?" Variel asked, her eyes swinging over to the only other human who knew even less about his people than the aliens around him. She didn't want to give any more data than she needed.

"Which Crest?"

She seemed to rebound at that answer, even smiling at the pointless clarification. Sure each Kingdom on Arda claimed it had its own significance, varying cultures, norms, morals, religions; but out in space that small world looked the exact same. After a year most wanderers off the home planet didn't bother to list the proper title of their home Kingdom, falling back on the adopted animals to represent each.

"Bear," she answered, "a lifetime ago."

"And now this fucking crazy Jaguar Knight is coming after you for deserting your post?" Ferra continued to pace before the fridge, her preferred method of pushing her neurons to work.

"I am uncertain." She'd anticipated someone from the Bears, old Toothless or Kaltar the Impenetrable, but after five years and not a peep she grew complacent, inching nearer and nearer to Crest space.

"How'd she even recognize you?" Orn asked, "If you mashed about your face like it was putty?"

Her finger drug down that cheek scar, bisecting across her top lip, "Orc born, it burns through so many layers of skin it's impossible to heal or cover."

"It is a way of keeping score," Monde said quietly, "Every blade has a specific edge like a key, later you dig through the bodies and count the scars."

"That orc didn't get a chance to tally up," Variel said letting a brief moment of her youthful smug shine through.

"Do you believe it was Dacre that sold you out?" Taliesin asked.

"No," she shook her head, as the others tried to figure out who this Dacre was. "Don't get me wrong, he'd trade his grandmother out to slavers if he could fetch a good price, but he was...he was intimately involved in my reasons for abandoning the Bears. Selling me out would draw attention back upon him."

"Intimately?" Taliesin asked softly, but the others were a bit more concerned with their current predicament than the captain's sordid past.

"So, Ms. Crest soldier," her ex-pilot growled, "now that we're stuck here, waiting for a Jaguar to come blow us to pieces because you wanted a career change, got any bright ideas?" Orn sounded more like his wife when he was pissed than he'd ever admit.

"We go down onto the planet and collect something that can be modified into an inertia injector," she said.

"This is when I ask what planet we're orbiting, and you say something that causes me to stomp off in anger." Orn was getting near sleepy toddler levels of petulance.

"It is a colony." Variel turned towards the dwarf; this was the first time she'd ever seen him truly hurt, "An orc colony."

The gasps were perhaps a bit theatrical, it wasn't as if she said it was a high security mage research station, or the secret vault of the dwarven mint. But Orn shook his head as if trying to dislodge something.

"I must be getting mine ear because I swear you just said 'orc colony,' as in full embargo, stop, no one allowed near or on such worlds, stop, lest they wind up in pain of full confiscation, stop."

Variel shrugged, "It seemed the perfect place to hide. What Crest would dare break into orc space?"

"That kind," Orn said, gesturing to her and earning a glower.

"If you were in the service of the Crests then you must have fought in the orc war," Brena interrupted. Elves in general didn't have the best sense of time dilation, a war that occurred fifty years ago seemed to have been 'yesterday.'

Variel nodded softly, "Yes, I...I fought in it."

"How much?" Orn wanted to push her into every uncomfortable corner he could think.

"A lot," she said, not diving into details. The wars were the only time in recorded history that all seven Crests came together to repel an invading force. Even the Narwhals joined, once someone pointed them in the proper direction and gave a little push. It was one of those events in history that wouldn't be fully declassified until most of the players were long dead.

"So it stands to reason that a slayer of orcs would be very unwelcome on an orc colony," Brena said as if she solved some puzzle.

"Actually, the fact I killed so many is exactly why I can visit orc colonies," Variel said and pointed to her resident orc expert, "Monde."

He shifted on his feet, and rose to a professional height as the others turned to him, "She has the right of it. We are not afraid of our adversaries. Often we show them greater respect than those of our allies."

"No offense, Doc," Orn butted in, "but that makes no fucking sense."

"If she fought in the last glorious test of power, then she will be on file and possibly known. Or at least get a free pass," Monde explained.

"Even with a new face?" that bit of info seemed to bother Orn the most, as if it were so simple to just erase everything that made one who they were and start over. Monde turned that self satisfying orange eye on the dwarf and it dawned upon him. "Oh right, the scar. How could I forget?"

"I can't ask for your loyalty, blind or informed," Variel slipped into the old command lexicon without thinking, "but I do ask that you let me get us out of this perilous situation. A visit to the colony, a repaired ship, and a run to wherever you want to disembark." She accepted the likelihood she'd be facing the need for an entirely new crew after today. All except for Gene. The djinn's eyes puffed in smoke at a slow rate, always giving almost nothing away.

The rest of her about to mutiny crew glanced at each other. No one else had any idea how to get out of this mess, or even how deep this wyrm hole could get. Crests were never a good sign, most of the universe called them the coming plague, as they left vast swaths of destruction across the galaxy imposing their will upon whatever they could get away with. Of course that could also be true of dwarves, elves, trolls, ogres, some of the non-corporeals, and everyone went into full blown panic whenever the orcs came aknocking. But humans were so damn smug about it, it rubbed all the other conquerors wrong.

"We are listening," Taliesin said cooly, the one least surprised by her admissions aside from the djinn.

"We land the *Elation*, a small party of us head into the biggest city on the colony, find a copier, have him whip up a model of the part, head home, and get airborne before the Jaguar gets docking clearance from the elven home world," she ticked off each small detail of her plan across her fingers like a shopping list.

"Oh hell no, you are not landing my ship!" Ferra shrieked, not ready to turn over her stake in the *Elation* due to a bit of misdirection. "Without that inertia injector, we ain't ever getting back up. And if there's nothing them rock crunchers, no offense Monde, can do, we're stuck in grey central until the embargo's lifted in 475 years."

"Do you have any other ideas to get someone on the planet's surface?"

"Maybe, I need to check on something first," Ferra's mind turned over ideas. Ones that a humanoid could survive from, probably.

Variel nodded, "Get on it, who knows how long we'll have. Orn, get the ship into orbit in the meantime. The planet might mask us."

The dwarf rolled his eyes at her as if she were his mother insisting he finish all his rock slime, but he nodded, "Fine, whatever."

"Okay, then. Inquiry adjourned," Variel joked, rising to her feet. Everyone stepped back from the Crest, as if she were about to rip off her face and announce she was the Emperor of the Toasters next.

"Just," Orn started, before the captain could get much further, "tell me one thing. What's the highest medal you received for your 'feats of heroics?'"

She bit down the obvious answer, it was the last lie that would hopefully die with her, and admitted to her shocked audience, "The Silver Pentagon."

Orn's mouth fell open as she, a two-bit smuggler, occasional pirate, and a woman decorated with the medal bestowed from the intergalactic community for keeping entire planets from blowing themselves to smithereens (or blowing the right planet to smithereens), pushed past him to the bridge.

Demi Monde slipped another set of sutures into his traveling bag, and then tossed in a third. With this crowd it was better to be neurotic than sorry. He didn't turn from his makeshift prep table when the med-lab door gave a cheery swoosh sound. It was preferable to the bell system WEST originally had in place. He felt he needed to carry over a short stack and sunny eggs every time someone wandered in with an infected toenail.

"I need you on this."

Monde still didn't turn, instead he dropped a few more sealing bandages into the bag and said to the captain. "Our agreement..." he started.

"Was that you'd never set foot on any orc world, or elven, or human, troll, centaur and anywhere else your people thought it'd be fun to conquer. That doesn't leave much of the galaxy left to get your planet legs back on."

"Luckily I enjoy dwarven cuisine with the right dosage of acid blockers," Monde finally faced her. The pigment beneath her eyes was much darker than usual, as if she'd gotten into that bar fight with a pair of centaurs again. A fresh lifetime of lies could wear through the soul and right up to the skin.

"I wouldn't ask if it weren't important," Variel leaned against the pool table she'd bled out on so many damn times. He had repeatedly requested an actual operational surgical table over the years but was shot down with a "Maybe if we get the funds." Over time, he realized that it was less funds and more that a commercial star line ordering a sterile surgical table would draw undue attention.

"I've never been to...which colony is this?" Monde asked as if inquiring about the weather.

"Officially, New Dawn. I have no idea what the orcs actually call it. Most embargoed colonies are listed as N/A. I've never been to this one either, but I've heard a few whispers about it."

"I see." Monde was noncommittal, though that was the entire reason he was trapped in this lifestyle in the first place, a terrorizing fear of commitment.

He met the captain while she was browsing through another orc colony, one under less sanctions because it fell under a sect that officially had nothing to do with the war. Unofficially, it sent as many troops as wanted to go. Humans had a hard time understanding why the orcs waged their wars. They would rather hoist their own perspective upon those they didn't slow down killing long enough to understand.

She was picking over a stand of fruits, during one of the grower's markets, when the streets of a little city on the back end of a highly volatile planet teemed with every orc who could actually scavenge up a ship and go off world. He'd planned to spend his entire meager fortune on a disgruntled looking mercenary who offered up her ship. When she leaned into him, her breath full of intoxicants, he panicked and raced out into the streets.

And there was his salvation, gingerly poking at a pair of needle fruit and looking surprisingly not as out of a place as a barely 50 granite human in a black blanket of head fur should. He asked her as smoothly as a boy on his first courting if she had a ship available.

"Yes?"

And if there could be any way he could perhaps procure passage upon it.

"Yes?"

And just how much that passage would require? Then he patted his side and realized where his traveling bag lay. Back in that bar where the serious threat of bodily or society harm waited. He cursed himself for his own stupidity, for thinking he had any hope of escape, for failing to live up to his duty, and for finding himself begging a human on the street for a handout.

Between his crying and cursing, the human stepped back. "Well, if that'll be all," and she began to walk away, trying to blend in with other species far larger and greyer than herself.

"Wait," he chased after her, uncertain why but fearing this could be his only chance at survival. "Your ship, is it, does it have a full compliment of crew?"

"We got someone to fix her when she's broke, and break her when she's fixed. I think we're all full up," she said trying to brush off the clingy orc.

"What about a doctor?!"

The human paused, her lanky legs mid-stride as she turned back to face him. Technically he was still a low-level physician, barely above what the humans called a nurse but the truth could come later. It was enough of an opening.

"Someone of your..." Monde backtracked realizing accusing a smuggler of being a smuggler was no way to get onto said smugglers ship. "Space can be quite dangerous, debris and decompression and ancient viruses springing to life causing you to devolve into a small rodent."

"We don't have any orcs onboard that an orcish doctor could patch up," the human said, but she didn't turn back to her hurried pace. She seemed intrigued.

"I've been trained in nearly all of the five races anatomy, basic first aid for thirty of the in-organics, and I can keep a gnome alive long enough to ask where it hid the watch it just stole."

She mulled it over, no doubt taking into account the latest round of bruises and scrapes the crew accumulated over the years treated by nothing more than a bandage kit, or worse, one of those medi-bots. "Okay, trial run, you can have free room and board in exchange for your medical prowess. It works out and we'll talk stipend."

Another set of tears threatened to dribble out of Monde's eyes and mouth as he dropped down his knees in a grateful bow, "Thank you, thank you. I, I have only one request."

His new Captain crossed her arms, "Let's hear it."

"I do not wish to ever set foot on any orc controlled world as long as I am under your service."

She shrugged her shoulders as if he asked her to never let him wear a cape. What did she care what he did with his spare time. Trapped on the ship was safer for all involved. "Sounds like we have a deal. The ship's docked at the landing port, *Elation-Cru*, can't miss it. There'll be a dwarf half coated in sugar pacing outside."

That was almost two years ago. She kept her word, taking only herself and occasionally the dwarf if he was being particularly foul when she was called upon to skirt around the embargo. But now the playbook changed.

Monde dropped his traveling bag overstuffed with all the medical supplies anyone about to raid a heavily fortified stronghold would need. It still wasn't enough for dealings in an orc open market, but it'd have to suffice.

Variel looked at the bag and then to the doctor. "I don't need any medical equipment, I need your expertise on finding a bleeding copier in the middle of an orc city."

"I know," Monde said. After slipping off his lab coat and folding it carefully across his examination chair, he picked up his bag, "But I am not leaving the ship unprepared."

Variel smiled, perhaps her first since the big reveal of her shady past. Truth be shared, he always suspected she must have had some part in the war, or been influential upon orc politics. A human to walk so freely and without constraint or concern was as rare as an elven bodybuilder.

"Thank you, doctor," she said, lifting her weary form off the pool table. Her fingers ran across the felt faded from years of bodies dragged across it, "Maybe, when this is over, we can finally put in for that real surgical table you wanted."

Monde paused, his own soft hands picking at the sheet, "Pity, I was beginning to grow attached."

The engineer's call, set on repeat, echoed across the ship, "Everyone, get your asses to the bay." Perhaps she should have thought of something slightly more diplomatic, but as the hordes appeared Ferra smiled. The direct approach served her best.

"Is everyone here?" she asked, pacing before her idea like a proud theses defendant. It took some retrofitting, all while done under the incredibly mournful glare of her husband sulking over spirits knew what.

"The way I see it, we need to get to the planet without actually landing on said planet." She put her hands behind her back and lifted to a greater height wishing she climbed atop the higher grate to lord over everyone. "A feat that could be possible if someone went off and invented magic teleportation."

"Is that what you did?" the spare human asked, his watery eyes growing in surprise. When Ferra asked for everyone she should have been more specific; everyone who is actually useful.

"Silence your bug hole, second," she muttered to the nuisance, "Either magical **not real** teleportation or...we skirt just close enough into atmo to release a terrain shuttle."

"Which we do not have a compliment of," Variel said slowly, knowing her engineer needed the buildup, but wanting to hurry her ass along.

"Except, we have the next best thing," Ferra smiled, and ripped off a sheet she swiped from her bed for the dramatic reveal.

"It's a pod," Orn said, poking his reattached hand into the surprisingly shiny vent. Most of anything not polished from footwear was left to the matte devices of time on the ship.

"A sight seeing pod, designed to skirt through the atmo and lower four people to the surface." Ferra was as ecstatic as she got when something was no longer on fire. A fresh set of circuits to kick into working shape was every holiday morning for her.

"You're shitting me," Orn shook his head, "an old cloud scraper? Those things were twice as likely to kill you as...no that was about it."

Ferra crossed her arms and glared at her moping husband, "Give me a little credit. The stabilizers are balanced and harmonized, the gears properly oiled. I changed the MGC vacuum bag..."

"What about the engines perfectly designed to suck a bird straight up into them and clog on falcon tartar?"

Ferra blinked slowly, "Don't run into any birds."

"Oh, well I feel snug and safe all ready," Orn shuddered. Not all dwarves had a fear of heights, but once you crossed the two miles up threshold it seemed less phobia and more common sense.

Variel squared her shoulders and eyed the old pod scrapped and supposedly stripped for parts years ago. She didn't know if she should be impressed or terrified that her engineer could so quickly slap it all back together "Monde and I will take the ship down, find a copier, climb into that thing, and come back."

The orc, who traded his lab coat and usual neat attire of simple green shirt and pants for a festive shirt with rings of color circling the midsection and tighter than usual, partially saluted. He kept bouncing on his heels, as if facing the possibility of death by pigeon was the least of his concerns. Variel nodded to him, and he grimaced back.

"I'm coming too."

"What?" the captain shifted on her pilot, who'd been giving her such a cold shoulder you could freeze comets on it.

"You..." Orn began, "You need someone to keep an eye out."

"On the orcs or on me?" Variel whispered to him.

"Take your pick," Orn turned up to her, but she was uncertain how to respond. He buried all his pain behind webs of lies thick enough to trap man sized flies. The fact it was someone else's deception picking him apart confused her.

"What if you're needed on the ship? To pilot it and what not?" Variel asked.

"Best it can handle is a slow limp, WEST can do it ASSUMING IT DOESN'T CHANGE ALL MY SETTINGS AGAIN," he shouted as if the computer wasn't within hearing distance at all times aboard the ship.

"If you're sure..." she tried to leave him a way out, but the dwarf was too stubborn to take it.

Orn turned back to the cloud scraper. He'd take the possible straight forward death of a stain across the orc dust over a friendly knife in the back. He nodded hard; he'd made up his mind.

Taliesin stepped forward, away from his sister finally cleared of the rouge, "I should accompany you as well."

Variel opened her mouth to call out a dismissive no, but had to admit, the assassin would be handy in case it all inevitably went pear shaped. "No, this is orc territory. The Crest embargo may be flexible, but I'd rather chew magma glass than cross the elven magistrates. You, Ferra and your sister all remain on the ship as far from orc land as possible. And if any magistrates ever ask, we got lost on our way to a lute stringing convention."

Taliesin blinked those eerie eyes of his slowly but bowed his head to her decision. His sister turned to glare a question at him but he rose as if he did nothing out of line.

"I'm coming too!" Segundo's wobbly voice burst through his pair of nubile lungs.

At this Variel snapped upon their accidental capture, "This isn't a bloody field trip! We're not going on a picnic to tip through the orc tulips."

But the Second didn't back down at his first real chance to get out, stretch his legs, see alien cultures, possibly get stabbed in the intestines for looking at someone the wrong way. It was adventure! Excitement! Drama! All those things he wasn't supposed to have a damn thing to do with once the commune sent him packing. "I know what this is, and you can use my expertise."

Variel's eyebrow cocked high as her brow furrowed, "Expertise in what? Getting kidnapped? Asking impertinent and pointless questions? Being djinn strangled?"

Segundo withered a moment under her commanding glare; no wonder she was a Crest soldier. That turn of the eyes could scare the horns off a gargoyle. But then he rebounded, secure in the knowledge of one simple fact. "The way I see it, you'd rather not have anyone be made aware of my kidnapping."

"Your stowing away, you mean? There are far stricter interspacial laws than what I've put you through, boy-o."

Segundo faltered momentarily, afraid to accept his limited scope in the wide universe, "Or the fact this ship broke atmosphere over the planet that is covered by elven, dwarven, and human interests."

Variel smirked, "So we're bargaining, or is it to be black mail?"

"Let me visit the orc planet, see a few sights, try a few cuisines, and all I remember of this ship was a nice trip through space," Segundo was playing with very irate fire, but a very irate fire with a code.

Killing him now would make her life so much simpler, and ensure no need for his shush experience, but it wouldn't be right. If she didn't believe in doing what was right she wouldn't even be out here in this dying rust bucket about to plummet inside a tin can to an orc world. "Very well, Mr. Second," she held out her hand which he took limply, "We have a deal."

She stepped away from the kid about to collapse from her tight grip and called out, "I, Monde, Orn, and the boy apparently, will be descending to the planet in...how long will it take you to get this operational, Ferra?"

"Ten minutes. I'll just have Gene drag it over to the hatch," the engineer pointed to the normally sealed shuttle hatch at the end of the bay.

This news unnerved Variel. The tin can looked as if it couldn't be used for shipping freight much less four people. She'd hopped there was still important levels of something to be done before it was fall worthy. "Okay, everyone heading to the planet get armed and dressed. We're aiming for a small city, the weather looks about summerish so expect minor heat stroke."

Monde bowed at her and stepped back, already dressed for his outing back into his people's world. Ferra pointed at the silent djinn and made, "Grab it and move" noises, as if the mute Gene was also deaf. He turned towards the captain who shrugged. Releasing a fresh burst of steam, he began to drag the pod.

Variel pushed past Segundo, still dressed in his technician outfit and patting his pockets for anything to help him on the orc world. As the only female of the group there were a few things she'd need to fit in. Taliesin slipped near her and whispered, "You may need this," as he held out his closed fist.

She placed her own hand below it and he dropped something into hers. Before she could ask him, he moved to join his sister to wait out this minor predicament with elven aplomb. Variel opened her fist to find the shield generator curled up safely inside. She tucked it into her own pocket and prayed she wouldn't actually need it.

A lifetime of inertia stabilizers, gravitational dispensers and other mage mumbo jumbo meant that aside from purposely climbing into a rocket coaster and hitting 3 G's in the name of fun, no one really suffered what true atmo breaking was anymore. Unless they willingly climbed inside an ancient can and shot themselves at a planet.

"My teeth are inside my brains!" a voice cursed out to the darkness. Ferra could work miracles in bringing anything mechanical back from the dead, but she also tended to overlook some of what she dubbed luxury items and never fixed the lights.

After slipping into their safety harnesses, a terrifying bit of straps and fabric that could at most slow their deaths by a fraction of a second, and sealing off the hatch, they couldn't see anything but the occasional rush of daylight outside the salad plate sized viewing hole. It was supposed to tell them if they were heading in the proper direction, but after WEST dropped the ship into orbit and the can slipped out of the descending hatch, it was hard to tell which way, if any, was up. There was a 97% chance they were going to wind up breeched.

"Ferra?" Variel asked the air, her lips pulled back onto her skull in a grimace. Blood was trying to pump to her extremities but she already lost feeling in her hands. She hoped they still gripped the release handles.

"Another 50,000 feet," the engineer's chipper voice called through the comm system that was supposed to be happily pointing out the sights below.

The cloud scrapers were used for all of one inaugural flight, when the Arch-Emperor of the Llamos (Wolf Crest) stepped inside one to visit a vacation world glittering below, and promptly vomited all over the surface of every single wall and floor as it lost control. Oddly, he was remembered best for losing his lunch in a pleasure vehicle than for the death march that slaughtered ten thousand people of 567 Laconian Empire.

After that, the luxury cruises promptly yanked them out and sold them off to every two bit adrenaline ride in the galaxy. They saw quite a bit of life until they started ending in a lot more death. Clean enough passengers off the floor grates and even the Better Business Bureau is gonna start to ask questions.

"Captain," the voice was strained but definitely Monde, that crisp snap of ironed sheets was unmistakable. "What if we do not.." He was cut off, probably by the rise of bile. Orcs didn't vomit, it was considered a major sign of weakness to willingly part with any food, but they could spray bile like nobodies business in the event of poisoning.

"We'll make it," she said, the same mantra she repeated endlessly since the first tremors transformed into bone jarring quakes. *And if we don't, gods we won't know about it.* The light outside the porthole shifted from the bottomless black to a warming shade of blue, rising up to them along with the ground.

"I can't feel my hands!" Segundo would pass out, his body unused to so much gravitational force, then awake with a jolt and a fresh complaint.

"You said that already," Orn grumbled. He stuck a pack of gum in his jaws before they took off even as Variel tried to explain that was for pressure changes. At his glare she backed off. For Orn sugar was a safety hole, a narrow crevice to climb inside when the universe stopped making sense. Plummeting out of a mostly functioning spaceship was high on the not-making-sense list.

"Another 25,000 feet, Variel," Ferra chirped, her feet probably kicking like a child's as she spun about in Orn's piloting chair. No one ever dared change his settings. "You're doing great."

"We haven't done anything but fall," the captain bitched back.

"Well, you're doing fantastic at that." Her engineer was approaching ambassadorial cheerleader levels of chirpy. This should have set off alarm klaxons like Soulday church bells. Ferra was only happy when everyone else around her was miserable, and excited when the entire galaxy was about to implode. The challenge of surviving, of making it through this latest "setback" alive and mostly in one piece was a trait the elf and human shared. But the blood, stubborn sluggish blood, refused to pump through Variel's veins. Spots danced across the cabin, whirling like a set of stars on the galaxy map as someone mindlessly flicked back and forth across time dilations.

The last thing she heard was her engineer shouting out, "10,000 feet, better pull the cord," before Variel blanked out.

CHAPTER EIGHT

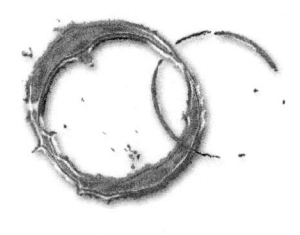

A giant's discarded can wobbled inside the red clay of a fresh crater deep into a farm a few miles outside New Dawn. Steam rose from the still too hot to touch metal casing as a couple passing orc children, free from their chores, inched closer to inspect it. One had that universal of probes, a long stick, and she used it prodigiously, poking at the can smaller than her family's store room. The golden oval wobbled and then slid deeper into the thick mud before sticking its landing.

A noise, like a nest of angry wisps, buzzed from within the discovery. Her companion, one of the less weaker of her brothers ran back to the house when the buzzing started, but she was curious. A good mark of a future leader. Side stepping closer, she laid her sound canals against the still heated metal and tried to make sense of the noise emanating from within.

"Are we dead? Is this what heaven's like?"

"Hot, dark and filled with the echoing jabberings of a moron? Yes, that is exactly what heaven is like."

"She's still breathing."

"Light ahead, now give me some good news. Like you found the fucking door."

"What light ahead? There's nothing but darkness, the endless darkness of the grave."

"Dwarven expression, Second, now would you kindly SHUT YOUR TRAP. I need to find the damn handle. Ah!"

A creaking just below her hand caused the farm girl to spring back, her stick at the ready. Slowly a crack appeared where pure metal had been and a rush of air shoved into the capsule. Thick short arms shoved the metal crack back and a shaggy head, the tan of tree bark, poked out.

"We come in peace, take us to your leader!" it said to her. As it raised its hand in a wave, the entire thing bolted off his arm and thudded to the ground.

The farm girl raced away as fast as her legs could carry and never looked back.

Variel steadied against the red rock of what passed for ground in these parts. She hadn't lost her lunch, that was a plus. She did; however, smash her dead hand into the partition walls supposed to provide a modicum of safety while questing for the ripcord. That was somewhere in the middle of her blackout fantasy about stumbling across a pair of boots stuck out beneath the smashed remains of some space wreckage. They were crystal clear but she kept thinking they'd look better in red.

"We landed," Orn grumbled, his own shoulder banged up but still in one piece. "Now what?"

Monde stepped away from the captain he half hauled out of the capsule. He closed his bag, mercifully undamaged and still orderly. She staggered to unsteady feet, unhappy to have that brush with possible stroke and, flipping on her PALM light, searched through the tin can for something.

The three men watched her, none of them wanting to voice "Why in the hell didn't we think to do that when the damn thing crashed?"

Variel emerged, a bundled up piece of fabric in her hands. She undid a strap and a hat unrolled, slightly too white to be called yellow, with a black brim decked in gold cord. A pair of crossed anchors adorned a black patch in the middle. Slipping on the captain's hat, she dared the others to say anything before surveying the farm they spectacularly crash landed at. An address would be good, landmarks, something to help them find their way back.

Most of the farm was flat, understandable as raising and educating crops on a mountain was for the desperate or foolish, but a few of the trees native to orc territory poked out to act less as a windbreak, more a reminder of home. Their trunks rose from the ground skimming it at a near horizontal angle before swaying vertical into an S shape that ended in solid branches with briars and leaves larger than a head.

Somewhere in the distance sat a building, probably the farmhouse where an orc in a frilly apron fed small raptor-like chickens, but this field -- its crop beginning to poke curious heads out of the rich clay -- was deserted.

"We should find a road, get our bearings, and call for a cab," she said, noticing the red clay adhered to her hand. It worked its way into her life lines, growing stickier with her sweat. After failing to pick it clean, she gave up.

"What about our cloud scraper?" Monde asked, concerned about the state of their only escape vehicle.

"Ferra? Can you hear me?" Variel called out to thin air and that was all that answered back. "Ferra?" The thin air was replaced by a few pops of static. "Hello? Anybody?"

The pops switched to a harried voice, "Whatcha want?"

"Where were you?"

"Microwaving a burrito. You were taking forever and I got peckish," the engineer answered and the sounds of masticating replaced her words.

"Is the ship damaged?" Variel asked, burying any hopes she had of a modicum of professionalism from her lackadaisical crew.

"No, WEST's got it hovering near a small moon. Ain't no one gonna notice."

"I mean our ship, pod, vehicle of certain death?"

"Hang on," she said. As the burrito most likely hung from out her mouth, she called through garbled words, "I's upside down, but fully functional...ish."

"Functionalish?" Variel asked, afraid when her engineer employed qualifiers.

"Just don't take it underwater or into any swamps with acid spitting frogs and you'll be fine. Ferra out!" she chirped before severing communication. Variel's PALM went dead aside from a flickering red light to point out there was no ether signal.

"I believe I see a road about three ticks in that direction. There should be an access point near," Monde said pointing towards an area that looked just as flat and desolate as the rest of the land.

Variel tried to shield her own eyes against the glare of the alien sun, but would have to rely upon the accuracy of her resident orc's superior eyesight. "I suppose we go that away for awhile." Being the only woman, she took the lead. "Don't forget where we parked."

Monde fell behind her, sliding his traveling bag across his neck and wiping some of the mud across his horns. It was either a sign of respect for the land, a warrior's paint, or a nervous tic. Variel suspected the latter most of all.

Never one to be left behind, Orn followed quick on Monde's heel. He'd been to a few orc colonies over the years, mostly keeping himself safe in a spaceport or duty free shop. This nature stuff felt wrong and smelled like a bad power conduit as an unnatural heat billowed under his shoes. But Segundo seemed happier than a fly in shit, his eyes wide as an elf's while he gazed across the clear horizon, pointing towards some shimmering peaks in the distance and babbling in tourist-ese.

The arduous trek through the rough and tumble wilderness of an orc colony was somewhat diminished by the planks laid across the rows, providing some mudless ground for anyone crossing the fields. A warm UV filled sky beat across their brows, and the wildlife preferred to keep itself to itself. There wasn't even a resident orc around to threaten them with pitchforks and banjo solos, only the occasional whoosh as their motorbikes whizzed past in the distance.

"So this is a flat planet, then?" Segundo's endless chatter broke through Orn's grumbling. The pilot wilted under the weight of his traveling coat, trapping more dwarf odor than even he preferred.

"What are you on about?"

"The land, it's flat, quid pro quo the rest of the planet must be flat farming land," Segundo responded as if answering a question on an exam.

"When them prophet hunters were handing out brains, your foot was caught in the midden, eh? No, it does not mean that the entire planet is farmland, it means this particular clump we crashed face first into is. You honestly expect the total ecosphere of a planet to be one thing?"

"I...I, never mind," Segundo lapsed into silence, for which Orn was grateful. How did he wind up playing tour guide to the yokel anyway? The dwarf wiped off his brow and tried to forget he was trapped on an orc planet with a doctor, a technician, and a human he thought he knew. He hated when he got maudlin. That's when his mother would break out the hand puppets, never stopping to think that cheering up a child upset over his lack of a hand may not be so easily remedied by a slip of fabric designed for hand coverage.

That was when he'd begin faking it, painting on his grin like the bards. Lies started simple enough. "I'm fine. It doesn't bother me at all. I meant to catch my hook on that grating." And with enough practice under his pinchers he could soon code the programs of lies most conmen dreamed of before entering trade school. He never once told the same tale of how he lost his hand, something to keep the mind sharp, which wasn't a problem until he met Ferra and her razor wire mind diced right through to his heart to ferret out all of his few secrets. It was either marry or kill her, and he didn't have anywhere good to stash a body.

"Orn, we found a cab call," the liar's voice called against the dry winds, a spicy scent of boiling vegetables hidden within. The dwarf glanced up from his shoes and noticed the change in decor. The unnatural rows, dug deep into the clay, were replaced by a mash of grasses tittering in the low wind and reaching up to his knees. A rolling undulation of land towered farther above the dwarf than usual. Ditches, every civilization had them, except for the elves who considered themselves above such crude eye sores across their sacred land. (Which may have something to do with the high level of tree related deaths upon Cangen.)

As he climbed out of the hole, his good hand providing some traction as he scrabbled against the too giving mud, a stretch of brick met him. It glinted onyx in the afternoon sun, speckles of gold pinging up in anticipation of another traveler speeding across its face. Roads, they either led to or away from something that could never actually be good. It was the second rule of the universe.

"We are in this vicinity," their orc called out, waving the arm of his hilariously colored shirt/sweater/smock? It was difficult to tell exactly what orcs went for in fashion. They seemed to favor function over design until you got close and realized their approach was to steal a few patterns and stitch them all together at once. Spirits save them if they ever discovered human's plaid.

Orn yanked the questing Segundo away from the road before his little technician insides would be squashed across the pavement. The typical speed limit in orc territory was something in the range of 4. Human's didn't even allow their motor crossers to reach speeds of 3, though they use some other speed terminology Orn never paid attention to.

Monde and the captain were hunched beside a glass pole with a strip of blue plastic ringing the top and bottom. A single panel housed a few buttons; a cab call station. Variel kept tapping the button at the top, the request for service, as Monde nervously shifted a small knot of rope around his midsection.

"That won't make them come any faster," Orn chided her, having used one after a very nearly toxic night on another orc planet involving a few men of the evening and their Jane, a backfiring pistol, and just enough of a starless sky someone only three feet tall could disappear into. He'd been picking briars out of his beard for weeks before finally shaving the entire damn thing off.

Variel paused in her nervous twitching and folded her arms up, tapping her foot instead. Orn watched her run head long through a ten legged spider's web, out draw the fastest etcher in the western galaxy, and down ten gargoylian rum and concretes before her informant's liver imploded, yet this was the first time he'd ever seen her nervous, even possibly scared. A small part of him was concerned, but the rest, the large part that most would call the petty side, snickered at her obvious discomfort and wanted to throw a bit of salt on the wound.

"Pretty day," Orn said, shrugging his shoulders and raising his gloved hands to the sky as if about to give one of those elven sun salutes. Variel turned a cautious eye towards him, but he ignored it. "The sun is shining rather pungently, birds, or some kind of flying tentacled monster, are cheeping in the overgrown briar bushes," he turned towards her, the shitting grin frozen to his face, "and possible arrest and execution await you as soon as that Drake does a giant U-turn."

"Watch yourself," Monde butted in, not much happier than the dwarf to be in this situation but trying to make the best of it.

But Variel waved the doc off, "You have something to say, flight technician?"

It was a negligible jab, most freight captains were happy to have anyone that could three point park and hadn't wyrmed straight into the middle of a moon in the past year. Yet, it chewed on Orn that no matter how quickly he honed his skills, inserted as many macros into his hand's software as he could, or rerouted half of the engine's drive to his feet, he could never get a proficient enough score to legally call himself pilot. Even slipping a few dozen pictures of cats wearing silly hats wasn't enough to bribe the examiner, a troll with a pinched delight in tormenting anyone smaller than her, which was everyone.

Orn's smile slipped away, his lips curling to reveal the grinders that make up most of a Dwarf's mouth. The gloves were off now.

"There's something in the distance," Segundo's voice was background chatter, little more than one of the tentacled birds cawing for its next meal.

Dwarf inched closer to human, his bad hand curling in a fist from subconscious signals. He'd never actually hit anyone with it, the damage to it would be far worse financially than anything anyone could do to his face. "Funny thing, before we all fell from the ship I did some poking about in old records. Seems in the past fifty years there was only one human given a Silver Pentagon, *Sir*."

She recoiled from the word, glancing at her other crew. Monde only blinked his double eyelids fast trying to work out some bits of sand jammed in between the membranes. Orcs cared little for any other species military ranks, less for the rumors that followed them.

"Guys, whatever it is, it's getting really close," Segundo reached a high panic as his fingers flapped towards some blur in the onyx road's distance.

Orn broke from his stare down with Variel just as the blur increased. "Get back, you stupid shit!" was all anyone got out when the road threw up a barrier, launching the stupid shit onto his ass, the red clay oozing into his no longer pristine uniform.

Sounding like someone tossed a hornet's nest into a trash can and quickly covered the lid, the vehicle soothed to a crawl, its blue lights flashing even in the bright light of day. It was more egg shaped than one expected for something that could reach speeds of "my brain's in my toes!" but orcs required a bit more room than the average human, and had this *thing* about eggs. It was said that on the day of armistice, negotiations were at a stalemate until the caterers wheeled in a tray full of deviled eggs. The Orc Council gorged themselves so much the treaty was signed in under five minutes.

A symmetric crack formed in the egg car's shell and a window popped open. Far larger than Monde, an orc head and part of the vast shoulders poked out of the window, "Are you the guys what called for a lift?"

A greasy set of nose prints remained on the projector screen as the cab egg ground to a near instant halt. Their driver didn't say much to the odd pair in her cab, only asked three times if they had actual currency. After Variel flashed something shiny, she took them onboard. She would peer through her rear viewscreen to watch the human gawping at the familiar landscape whizzing by.

Segundo felt the need to narrate the trip to himself aloud, causing the other passengers to lapse into silence; even Orn, who got a jolly good time of ribbing Seggy for having almost the exact same uniform as the cabbie, minus the giant shoulder spikes and sash of ammo. But that grew dull as the kid kept hopping out of his lack of restraints to point at another pair of buildings minding their own business and comment on the color of the sky, the shade of the trees and the tentacles of the birds suctioned to lampposts.

"Central exchange," their cabbie grunted, "That'll be five shiny things."

Variel dropped some of the coins -- most extracted from ancient dig sites, hand poured as souvenirs, and a few full of chocolate -- into the orc's clawed hand. "Keep the change," she muttered, getting a small glower from their driver, but the door crack began and everyone piled out of the stuffy egg and straight into the heart of some backwater colony's second or third largest town.

It was impressive as far as colonies went. When most talked about a settlement far flung across the galaxy they pictured mud huts thrown together with the help of the hides off native fauna or occasionally flora. Where large ruminants roamed, you rarely heard a disparaging word, and the skies remained relatively cloudless throughout the arc of the star. Even those who grew up within the sheltered glass and brick walls in a colony still talked as though anyone else struggling upon one was born with a cholera spoon in their mouth.

New Dawn was of middling size, one of those cities on the grow, supported by a lucrative silicon business, that encouraged younger orcs of a certain go getting nature to come and try their luck at getting swindled in closer proximity to others. The Central Exchange housed most of the public transportation when it wasn't zipping off to claim people; a rail line rattled above their heads, old and in need of repair, while a garage housing the eggs took up the street space below.

"Okay, Monde, where would we find a copier?" Variel asked, the scent of hot tar and fried klax in the air. The streets were quiet, most people locked away at their upscale jobs.

"One of the grey markets," he said, his bag pulled closely to his side. "They tend to congregate towards the center of the city." Their resident expert approached one of the children's art projects communities put up to show how proud they are of their future tax payers and ran his finger over it. Bits of clay shuddered down in flecks as a train rattled above them. Variel screwed her hat on tighter while the others shook their hands through their hair.

"I should have brought my uniform's hat as well," Segundo muttered, putting some of the blame on the more informed and better prepared captain.

She grinned in disbelief and muttered, "That would be ill advised."

"Why?"

"It's one of those cultural things your type pay no heed to," she said, glancing up and down the onyx road. A few orcs, dressed in business casual -- wide strips of midsection leather with pouches, a spiked collar and slightly camouflaged jumpsuit -- walked across the street, carrying a set of cases between them and tipping their hats to anyone that walked past. Cordiality was something it took humans a long time to accept from the people trying to kill them.

"If we traverse this road until it splits, we should come to the market bazaar," Monde said, his own uncovered head flecked with clay he didn't notice falling. Most got used to it.

"Lead the way," Variel said, glad to be moving.

Monde glanced over at the pair of high powered orcs out for a late lunch stroll and shrunk into his coat. "It would be prudent if you took the leadership."

"All right," she sighed. Together the group stepped away from the Central Exchange just as another egg blue shifted into the city. Her fellow crew members followed behind like ducklings.

The group of outsiders made it down three blocks before Segundo's background chatter started up again, "Why are all the buildings shaped like that?"

"Because, if they put them underground the dwarves would sue for copyright infringement," Orn needled.

"No, see, the T and then the lines running down...It's just silly." Segundo was no master architect, having grown inside a rather serviceable but "not about to win any design awards" pagoda. At least the brothers claimed it was a pagoda. In truth, it was a squat rectangle that survived the ravaging fires that claimed all the other decorative and surprisingly flammable buildings across the church's settlements.

His mind had trouble wrapping around the twenty or thirty tall T's looming over them, supported by the thick beams on each side with smaller isosceles triangles tucked up next to the T's using the beams for shelter. While the main T was a sheen of glass, with a few decorative letters hanging somewhere around its head, the triangles were mixes of festive colors. Greens and reds merging into purples with yellow doors and a partially raised black window. There was no pattern to the triangles, some had three doors to the front, while others only one. Windows seemed to be fired at it with a shotgun and covered in glass later.

This provided adequate space for the trains to zip between the buildings, rattling the T's and tossing more dirt onto the heads below, but none of the teetering buildings fell over. Occasionally, a train would pause on the tracks, as if every passenger were waving to whoever dared climb to the top of those treacherous consonants.

If Monde hadn't been doing his best to keep his eyes down while also watching a cluster of orcs crowding up the walkway, he'd have told the curious human that his people considered life and work to be one and the same. Houses were built right beneath the places of business so members could easily scuttle from their dwellings to their work. And, when that life/work dynamic became too dull, half the office staff would try to scale up the building as part of a team building exercise. The losers would be posthumously fired or possibly fricasseed.

Instead, the orc shook his head and told the human, "It is complicated."

"Huh," Segundo slowed, breaking away from their captain who didn't have the time to look out for the idiots behind her. She dashed across the road just as the barrier zipped up for a passing egg car. The three lost ducklings stood at the other side, waiting for the countdown to stop.

"Hey there, sweetmeat."

Monde looked down and Orn shifted a bit, but Segundo turned back to find where the growling voice came from. A cluster of orcs, wearing the universal uniform of people who spent their life pushing data streams, crowded around one of the benches scattered about the T fronts. They were large, larger even than their cabbie friend, with shoulders that could burst through most door frames back home, and a series of horns running down the sides of their necks.

The countdown stopped and Monde coughed, trying to get the human's attention. Segundo turned away from the orcs to the doctor and grinned sheepishly, but his curious stares did not pass unnoticed. One of the group, with sleeves rolled up to display an inking of scratchmarks on the arm, rose from the shared seat and staggered over to the three about to cross the road.

"Where are you going, sweetheart?" the orc asked, all smiles.

"To the..." Segundo started helpfully, but Orn stepped hard on his shoe.

The new orc was eyeing up Monde as if for supper, and inching closer into the doc's personal space. Monde kept his eyes low, focusing on the shoes as he muttered, "Just passing through."

"Oh, I know something you could pass through," and the Orc laughed loud, earning the approving guffaws of the others eavesdropping.

"We need to keep an appointment," Monde said, motioning to the rest to keep walking. Orn grabbed the edges of Segundo's uniform jacket and drug him on while Monde took a step forward.

But this didn't dissuade their new friend, trailing behind them as they crossed the road asking for Monde's address or link up data. Finally the doc screwed up the courage and turned about, "I'm not interested, so leave me alone. Please."

The orc rose up, clenching muscles that lay hidden beneath the folds of business fabric but stopped short as Variel pushed past her charges to stand in eyesight, her scar plainly visible. The orc deflated at her interceding but called out in one pitiful jab, "You're a fat ball licker, anyway," before sauntering off.

Variel continued to glare at the orc's retreat but said nothing. She turned back to her lead, acting as if nothing happened. Monde balled up his fists to bury a shaking in his arms.

"What in the galaxy was that all about?" Segundo asked, the only one still unaware of the danger they'd just passed. "I thought that guy was gonna rip your head off."

"That wasn't quite what he wanted," Orn said diplomatically, "and that wasn't a guy."

Scratch scratch scratch.

Variel paced back to the counter, tapping at the glass as if that would increase the passage of time. Her hat was off-kilter, never really meant to fit her head size. It was discovered by Ferra, hidden in some forlorn corner of the ancient ship's machinery and instantly became an obsession with Orn. Every morning, he'd leave it sitting pristinely on the command console, waiting for the "captain." She tossed the damn thing down the garbage burner, into the back engines, and once out the airlock, but -- like a persistent rash -- it'd still greet her every morning. It was the first time she gave into the dwarf's whims, but nowhere near the last.

The captain returned to her scattered crew, plopped haphazardly against plastic chairs popping under the load. Monde sat upright, his legs curled to the side, even more on edge than usual. She was gonna owe her doctor a table and a new set of sanitizers after this. The second boy, after paging through the complimentary hard copy media, all in orcish, wandered to the screens and kept flipping through the few available options.

And Orn, her untrusty companion for near on four years, found a half peeling parts sticker attached to the window. By standing on the chair, he took to removing it with his fingernails. Scratch scratch scratch.

"Why is there only one program?" Segundo asked, still flipping from the camera view of a pair of gargoyles being pelted with a power washer, to POV of the camera wearer sticking a ceremonial spear into another orc's exposed grey belly, to a series of orc males modeling the latest in highly ineffective armor that failed to cover anything vital, and back again.

"We are not here to entertain you, human," Monde mumbled. He hated being back in this world, and hated more that he hated it.

"He means," Variel interceded, not in the mood to watch the two duke or even earl it out, "orcs have a very specific entertainment diet, most of it self-made."

"Self made?" For Segundo creating something from nothing required the greatest minds a people could procreate, or some kind of super computer that ran on coffee. Creating your own entertainment was more terrifying than being accidentally kidna-stowawayed.

Variel tapped her hat, "All their hats have a small camera in the brim so they can cut and share any exciting tidbits of their day. The most popular are bumped up the viewing list and suddenly everyone's watching the delivery woman from two towns over slaughter a grell cougar with her bare fists."

"So if they have those cameras on all the time does that mean there's some," Segundo's voice dropped down as if afraid of spies, "dirty vids?"

Monde turned a curious shade of blue, and he tried to shift away from the human poking into his people's cherished beliefs, but Variel laughed, "If we wanted to see that we would have headed next door."

"Oh..."

"We're not heading next door." She lowered herself onto a chair near her pilot, "We are going to wait." Segundo, mollified of his curiosity for the moment, flipped back to the armor vids, one that was probably supposed to be playing next door. Then again, perhaps not. Looking around at the scattered posters of wrenches dangling over half clothed posteriors, various tools thrust between gaping thighs, and some giant pile of naked orc men mimicking the appearance of a shuttle she wasn't so surprised at how uncomfortable Monde felt. She slogged through enough half sex shops/half mech stores in her early days to hate them all on site. Now she just sent Ferra, who'd rip anything she found particularly disgusting down and dare anyone to challenge her.

Orn finished his assault on the sticker and tried to unstick the thing from his good hand, but the glue on those metallic backings was one of the strongest substances in the galaxy. His false hand had troubles pinching, the servos never quite articulated enough to sense when they held anything thinner than a millimeter.

After several failed pinches he shook his good hand, trying to dislodge the errant sticker about a popular MGC Burner.

Finally, Variel grabbed his wrist and yanked the sticker off, taking the curse upon her own hand. Orn glared at it, then back to the woman he told himself he wouldn't talk to.

"You sure do know an awful lot about orcs." His boycott lasted all of two hours, a record for the dwarf.

"I've visited a few colonies in my day, I pick things up," she said nonchalantly as she tried to slowly work the sticker off onto a ledge.

"It's all a bit curious, what with you slaughtering them by the millions during your little war."

Anywhere else in the universe you'd have heard a pin drop as every ear within a mile radius strained to listen to the captain explain herself against this atrocious accusation. But Monde shrugged his narrow shoulders at the dwarf's declaration, Segundo was too engrossed in his programs, and the only other orc -- a secretary who twice told them it'd only be another ten minutes an hour ago -- returned back to his duties paying little heed to the boasting. That was best saved for after work time, when orcs could let their horns loose.

"All right, Orn. You want to call me out, let's have it." Variel was tired of the dance she'd anticipated with everyone but her pilot.

"You're a," even surrounded by unconcerned friends and oblivious acquaintances that couldn't leave the planet, Orn still dropped his voice to a whisper and shrieked into her ear, "a fucking Knight."

"There was surprisingly little fucking, too much time on the job," she said not smiling.

"Oh ho ho, so clever, little miss 'I can kill whatever I want whenever I want and who's gonna argue with this army behind me?!'" Orn turned away from her, old thoughts poking through his head, "I knew you had to be some kind of military, ain't no sane person makes their bed each morning, but..."

She sighed, rubbing her forehead and getting the cursed sticker adhered to her worry lines, "Fine, you caught me. I was a Knight. I trailed about the universe terrorizing villages and eating babies. But I'm not anymore. I haven't been one of those village eaters in five years."

"Why? You have a change of conscious? Get visited by the ghost of wars past, present, and future?"

"It's complicated," she said, afraid to open up that can of worms. Orn folded his arms, teetering on the chair that wasn't designed for standing on. He enjoyed being above her for once; it suited the situation.

"I wasn't always a monster, either. Knights can do good, provide aid, stop criminals, escort diplomats," and other things that no one tells you about until you're deep into training and not about to quit because of a bit of dirt on the hands.

Orn ran his hand across his bit of face fuzz, it looked even greyer in the harsh light of the shop, "Did you kill people?"

"Yes," she said, as if responding to a child asking if all the stars were someone's sun.

"A whole lot of people?"

She had no idea why this bothered him, surely the dwarf's hands weren't clean. Living out on the edges as they did, falling into a few less than above board jobs to make ends meet, mistakes happen. Clean up is required and it isn't always easy and neat. "Not as many as you'd think, but more than I can remember." That bothered her more than any other bit about her past. It was one thing to stop someone about to cause irreparable damage to her, her fellow soldiers, or civilians, it was another to forget about it. To reach that always wobbling tipping point where one slit throat became a carbon copy of another and another until it was a big pile of unremarkable dead.

Orn silenced his pestering as guilt washed over her, the first he'd seen. Placing his good hand onto the toy tool bench for keeping errant children distracted, he lowered himself onto the chair. His feet kicked above the floor in circles. As he watched his boots swirling he asked, "So what'd you do with your sword?"

She smiled nostalgically, "I sold it. Space ships don't come cheap."

"Neither do flight technicians," Orn said bitterly, his boots banging into each other.

"Of course not," she said finally grabbing onto the sticker and gritting her teeth, "you're at least twice as expensive as a pilot. You actually know how to fly the damn ship." Chewing down a scream, she ripped the sticker free, getting a layer of skin with it. No longer sticky, the paper fell to the floor.

Orn didn't look at her, instead he watched the sticker's tumble. A whole lot of his accusations remained unvoiced, half evoked, most a jumbled mass of emotion and "How could you?!" but he let the main matter drop. Smiling to himself, he knew he did have one major sticking point should the question of a raise come up again.

The door jangled as the portal apertured open letting in an orc carrying a greasy bottomed bag and the smell of rancid onions. She tossed the bag to her secretary and glanced at the full waiting room. "I seem to have very unexpected guests today, Molik," she patted her full stomach and belched as the captain disentangled from her chair.

"I am Tuffman Variel, and I require your assistance," she said and reached out to Monde who was rifling through his bag.

"Copier Zet," the Orc said, yanking a work apron off the door hook and sliding it over her neck horns. "What seems to be the challenge?"

Variel took the charred remains of their long dead inertia injector into her hands and held it before Zet's face, "I need a copy of this."

The mutilated husk easily fell into the gargantuan mitts of the orc as she turned it about trying to get a feel for exactly what the hell it was, "Your grandmother's favorite chunk of space garbage?"

"It was an inertia injector for my ship," Variel responded, growing more dejected as the orc tried to find the proper "this side up" angle.

"Did you start a plasma fire in your engines to get a good vid? I cannot even find a connecting joint, the whole thing fused in on itself."

"We, I need you to create a new one."

The orc's orange eyes blinked quickly as she mushed her jaw in and out, "You want a copy of this chunk of matter?"

"No, I need you to create a working version of this unit."

Zet shook her head slowly, still pawing over the wreckage that looked like it should be smoldering, "Gonna take a whole lot of plink to rebuild something like this from scratch."

"I have some prints, images, and..." Variel's voice softened as she reached onto her tiptoes to inch towards the orc's auditory nerves, "a bag full of griffin eggs."

Zet's pupils dilated at the mention of the delectable and highly sought elven delicacy of hollow chocolate eggs stuffed with a small figurine and fortune. The orcs praised the shape and sweetness of the confection, and especially appreciated the crunchy center. "Molik, destroy all my appointments and seal the doors." The secretary scuttled off to his console, pushing the "destroy" button, while Zet turned over the black pile, "I'm creating!"

"Move closer and stop twitching!" the harsh voice echoed through the back of the copy shop as Variel hunched over a dimensional simulation stretched across a table. She held her palm steady as Ferra scanned over the design she and the orc worked on as the human played projector.

"Rotate the injector 30 degrees to the left," Ferra ordered and Zet slowly spun the floating mass with her fingers while lifting a set of lenses off her nose. Another three pair still remained in place to peer through the layers of holographic matter to the components inside. Occasionally, she'd describe what she saw for the bossy pointy eared one on the other end, but Ferra grew impatient and demanded someone hold a lens up for her.

And that was how Monde wound up crouching below his weakening captain, a series of colored glass rounds slipped between his fingers. At first Zet would smile and ask him to drop one color or add another, but once the elf figured out the system she'd bark out orders, not in the mood to wait for the orc mating dance.

"Good, good. Stop!" The rotating ceased as a wandering eyeball tried to get a closer look, "Zoom in."

"Gods," Variel complained. But, nodding to Monde, the pair slowly slid closer, the captain climbing across the inventing bench, her supporting elbow knocked into a cup filled with discarded excess matter.

"Good enough?" she asked the calculating eyeball, Ferra must have her own PALM millimeters from her nose.

"It'll have to do. Okay, the injector's third coil is too loose, it'd rupture if put under strain."

Zet said nothing punching a few more lines of code into their design, but Variel noticed the peer's look. This elven eyeball was crazy. "What kind of strain are we talking about?" the captain asked her engineer.

"Escaping from the event horizon of a quasar," Ferra answered, her eyeball slipping up to project a bit of forehead, the pores like craters against the wall.

Orn kept his own eyeballs adhered to the vid screen with Segundo, this one hooked up to a few more channels than the "family approved" waiting room. He'd shuddered at the blood vessel popping sight of his beloved's macroscopic eye and promptly turned away, asking someone to warn him when it was safe.

"And why would we need to escape the event horizon of a quasar?" Variel's own hand bounced up and down in her perturbance, the artificial zoom causing the other end to shake dramatically.

"With your record I prefer being prepared," Ferra responded, injecting another anti-space sickness round into her neck to combat the captain's erratic movements. She'd be lucky to have a liver left by the time this was done.

Zet caught the disagreement between the one in charge and the one holding onto her payment and paused in alterations, "Do I keep the new schematics?"

Variel nodded, and clapped harder onto her bouncing hand. Who in the hell thought sticking a computer screen in your hand was a good idea? "Do it," she muttered, girding things she'd thought were long dead the hour back when this torture began.

"Okay, give it another 360 rotation, with power fueling through the circuits. Orc, the green lens!" Ferra wasn't trying to make many friends today.

Monde grumbled, but yanked out the red, so only blue and yellow remained. As their simulation spun, simulated inertia in the form of sparkling sand clumps dumped through the injector port and transformed into a cool liquid. The storable inertia. It looked rather beautiful, a shimmer of energy becoming potential until it could be reapplied as kinetic or some kind of sandwich spread. Mages had an interesting approach to fooling the laws of nature at times.

Ferra grumbled, "The lag time is 0.3 seconds slower than the old one, but it'll do. Print it out and get that thing back to the ship."

"Oh thank any and all Gods," Variel crumbled to the floor, dragging her PALM with her as she landed on her butt. The image of Ferra flipping through a few settings and ending the comm flashed against the table's underside before the captain could properly shut off her end.

Orn turned away from a pair of orcs tossing a giant roll of cheese at each other (High art for the spikers) to spy his captain slowly rising off the ground, dragging her limp hand with her. "If you had the eye-scan, you wouldn't be squeezing the liquid of life back into your hand."

She gripped her hand hard and shook it, shutting her eyes from the pain of the return of blood, acrid over its dismissal. "If I had the eye-scan, I'd have gone completely cross eyed when your wife started in on paint swatches."

"You should try tool shopping with her."

"When will the part be printed?" Variel struggled to her feet with some assistance from Monde as he carefully placed the glass lenses down.

"I am transferring it to the copy machine. It should be finished injecting in twenty shakras." Zet tapped a few keys and swiped at the wall sized monitor just as the main occupant of the room heated up.

Variel glanced to the only other orc in the room as Monde did the calculations, "It's around a half hour."

"I'm starving," Orn whined from the corner, tossing the remote back to the kid. "I'll take Third here and see if we can't scrounge up something that won't take a bite back."

"Is that really such a smart," Segundo began to argue, but Orn swept him up into his charismatic wake and pulled the kid out of the workshop, into customer service, and out to the wild streets of the Market.

"We will never see either of them alive," Monde muttered.

The time passed relatively peacefully, soothed by the copier's hum, chirp, and occasional curse of Zet as the damn thing jammed again. Variel kept poking at the projection model in boredom. it looked like a series of old sewage piping jammed together by a bored child left alone at the hardware store. To think something so simple could cause so many damn problems, though the same could be said for the Knights. She glanced over at her resident orc expert as he checked through his bag. He was given the entire stock of eggs, which were extracted from a rather irate dwarf, but they let Zet believe Variel carried them for safety reasons.

Monde tried to keep to himself, sequestered in the corner flipping through a few old medical journals he picked up somewhere that still used paper, but every once in awhile his eyes would skirt up to watch Zet. Anyone else and Variel would quietly excuse herself to let nature take its course, but adjusting to the male orc mindset was not an easy one.

"How longer shall you be visiting our colony?" Zet feigned polite conversation to Variel.

"Not long after we get this part. It was an unexpected side trip." She watched Zet, noting all the equipment that -- when hurled with the notorious upper body strength of a full grown female orc -- could maim or kill a lone human. But Zet made no threatening moves, tidying up some things, and in general feeling incredibly out of place as outsiders watched over her shoulder as she worked.

She scrubbed down a plastic filler and replaced a cap before asking the human, "You wear a deep coup?"

Variel folded her arms, she never got used to this part, "Yep."

"And yet you are the one still walking. My congratulations."

Any other species would have ripped her out of the shop, tied her up to something flammable and lit the entire thing before she could get out a last request. But for the orcs, a sign you survived their weapons put you one step closer to their kin. She was just grateful the other cut was covered by her pants.

A jangle announced the return of Orn and the second. The fresh scent of something dipped in oil and yanked out after it stopped screaming followed, as did a high buzzing sound. Variel stepped around the utility screen moaning, "You did not get a nest of live bumblers did you?"

She froze as a flying mech, barely larger than her fist, bumped into the back of Segundo's head and turned its red eye to face her. Her fingers searched for the pistol, but she was too slow as a scanning sensor beamed out from the eye taking a copy of her face with special attention to the scar.

"We brought back a new friend," Orn said proudly, the closest thing to sugar in orc space dribbling down his chin. It also caused a mild numbing in all other species aside from inorganics; trolls started to melt.

"I can see that." The little mech finished scanning and began to emit a low howl. "And hear that. What the hell is it?"

"I dunno, but it's adorably inept. I found it staring down a statue for five minutes." Orn reached into the bag already nearly see through from the leeching grease, and handed his angry captain a pile of food on a stick. "I got you your favorites."

"Which one?" She brought a small section to her mouth's side and nibbled away at the batter.

"All of 'em on a big stick!" Orn laughed. He must have had a grand ol' time out hobnobbing with the lower stratus of orcs. "And good ol' Seggy here is like catnip to orcs."

"Oh?" she asked as the fried stick of everything crumbled in her mouth, delightfully tasty even as her tongue was about to scream from sensory overload.

Segundo smiled lopsidedly and tipped his head to the side as if playing coy. "I simply spoke to them about the various attraction sites on Samudra and how easily one can rent an atmo shuttle or paddle boat."

"I...see?" Variel glanced towards her pilot who was holding in a laugh that could knock a poor little pig's house down. The captain sized up the skinny technician tossed into her care by happenstance for the first time. Tall, by human standards, with lanky everything. Oh, a cruel smile overtook her face which she tried to hide with her food stick. Of course the orcs weren't listening to a word he said, they were admiring his alien -- but beautiful for strict orc standards -- form, and he being a he didn't have a bloody clue.

Well, at least Orn was there to keep it from getting into a major ovary fight. But as she watched over the dwarf's head shake and small laugh under his breath she realized he must have been encouraging the damn kid. Oh, she'd have to bribe those stories out of him later. Assuming there was a later.

Their little flying mech finally stopped howling and returned to buzzing about Orn's head as if he were its mother. Gods, there was a good chance it thought it was. Orc technology relied upon a bonding process most humans preferred to explode rather than understand.

Monde stepped through the screen, curious and a bit hungry, and eyed up the flying drone with concern. "Did you have any extra food?"

"'Course, couldn't let our Doc go hungry." Orn yanked out the only vegetable he could find in the mix, a bit like an artichoke on steroids, and tossed it to their orc.

He caught it and sighed, "A knife is necessary to break into this."

"Cap has her gun, she could shoot it open for you."

As the flying drone began to rise up, circling for a new victim, Monde sighed and muttered to himself, "Luckily, I brought a scalpel." He disappeared back to find his bag, but froze as their copier appeared, wiping a large amount of black ink off her hands.

"I see you've met our little People View," she said nodding towards the flying drone that turned its eye on her and began another scan. Monde slipped into the protective screen of the door, but remained in earshot.

"People View?" Variel asked, her own concern about cataloging and tracking equipment taking precedence over the fact this was an orc world and she'd already been found out. A five year habit was a hard one to break.

"Some data collection company sent a bunch out into the city to catalog every face and their preferred travel routes. Helps to develop better security systems."

The pair of not quite outlaw's jaws dropped at that, while Segundo scratched his chin in thought.

"And you, you just put up with it?" Orn stuttered. "No cries of freedom in the streets, people building barricades, making flags out of their underthings?"

Zet turned her head in confusion like a spiky puppy, "Why would anyone be concerned? It is simply taking stock of its people."

"But it can find you, at all times, at all places, if you're doing something really not...so good, then it could," Orn stuttered for an explanation, terrified of this world his sticky fingers found themselves in.

"It doesn't care about right or wrong, it's just a machine," Zet knocked the drone about like a bumbling pet, "like your bread warmer, or your grenade launcher."

"Right, yep, I keep that grenade launcher right next to my blender in case I'm in the mood for explosive juice," Orn said inching back slowly.

Zet watched the dwarf curiously, never certain what to make of the small folk, and then turned to the captain, "Your part has finished and is being sand blasted as we currently talk."

"Right," she motioned to Monde who slipped into the back room to get his case, "We agreed that was five eggs."

The copier's massive arms folded across her chest, smearing the work apron with the ink, "For over an hour's work building a prototype model..."

"Six eggs, then."

"You bring dishonor to me human," Zet flashed her teeth, "and it is a very long ride out of this city with dishonor hanging over your heads."

Segundo gulped loudly, and Orn shifted at the threat, but Variel waved it off, sticking her head deeper into the lion's mouth. "Six eggs and whatever's left in Orn's lunch bag."

The dwarf sunk even lower as the orc's gaze turned upon him; the full fury of generations bred to protect their children from the worst a planet lovingly dubbed hell could conjure. Zet growled, her fury incapable of forming coherent words.

"All right, all right. Seven eggs," Variel acquiesced, "But that's cutting my own cheek."

"Thank you, kindly," Zet cheered up immediately, letting the rage vanish as quickly as it came. A loud bong resonated from the back and she smiled, "The sanding is done." She pushed past the doctor to retrieve her sale.

Monde held out seven of their ten eggs to the Captain, who scooped them onto the counter, still in their bright red boxes.

"What were you doing?!" Segundo shrieked as blood returned to his brain. "That orc could have torn your arms off and drunk your blood!"

Variel giggled at that, "It's all bravado, chest thumping, half the fun of making a sale is in letting that controlled rage slip. If I'd given her a fair deal from the start then she probably would have broken a leg or five."

The blood drained out of Segundo again as his tan faded to a ghostly pallor. Orn patted him on the back, "You said you wanted to see the galaxy, kid. Consider this the backstage tour."

Zet appeared, carrying the now white mass of pipe structures Ferra assured them would get the ship flying out of this system and somewhere safe until the Crests found something else to pick over. She dumped the part into Variel's hands and glanced over the eggs sitting pristinely on the counter.

"You can open them to make certain," Variel said, tossing the part back to Orn. He grumbled but accepted it. Ferra'd demand a report on the state of the thing. He fired up his PALM getting the 'battery low' flash.

Zet blinked, tempted, but smiled. "No, I shall save them for my children. Their father shall likely kill me for destroying their fast with such treats. Thank you for your attendance and please visit again."

The shop's door opened for the last time. The drone zipped out first buzzing about their heads, allowing the four to exit the copier shop straight into a ring of uniformed officers. Most of their faces were obscured by dark helmets pulled over the eyes, but the leader was almost hatless save for a micro one pulled back. Not a good sign, she didn't want anything accidentally recording her movements.

Monde shrunk behind with the other men as Variel took the lead. "I'm afraid I don't know how to locate the local donut shop."

The orc officer turned her head in the same confused tilt, then shifted her jaws, "A human joke. Humorous. I have been sent to escort you to the Prelate's office."

"Which of us?" Orn asked, hoping the answer didn't include him.

"All of you."

"When?" Variel asked, eyeing down the street trying to find a break.

"Now," the officer motioned to the others who fanned out engulfing their little group in darkness.

CHAPTER NINE

Their "escort egg" shuddered to an ovum cracking halt. The door opened to their new officer friend subtly nudging her weapon to invite everyone out. Variel hatched first, blinking into the literal heart of the city. Every orc town placed their, oh let's call it a government inside a building designed and painted to mimic that which beat inside every citizen's chest. It also put any other visiting species right off their lunch, which suited the orc's just fine.

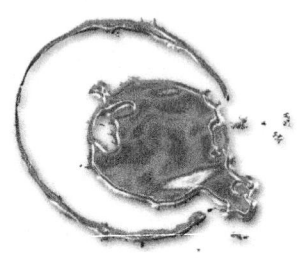

The concrete steps led up to the main seat of their forum that housed this season's legislatures; the right, left and central ventricles. She cast a practiced eye over the other escort car disengaging the extra officers but they weren't in such strict form, prodding each other and laughing. Why worry about a couple of humans, a dwarf and a male, when they were trapped deep in the chest of their colony?

"This way, Sir," their lead officer said to Variel, holding her hand out towards the portal doors.

A few of the others climbed out of the egg, Orn glancing up at their destination and grumbling about how last time he saw one of those it was with a side of onions. Monde kept his face somehow buried in his bag. Finally, Segundo exited and soaked in his surroundings. Getting a face full of a disturbingly accurate representation of what thumped inside the thoracic cavity of most everyone around him, he spun and vomited his fried lunch all over the egg's floorboards.

The dwarf chuckled as he slapped Seggy on the back, "Way to show 'em. Mess with us and you'll get chunks spewed all over your shoes."

Variel ignored it, any show of weakness on her part could be certain pain later. Instead, she tipped her lightly to the officer and began to climb the steps, her knees crying in pain from the steeper incline than humans were used to. Orn would have cursed up a storm, having to scale it like a mountaineer, but one of the not quite security, no longer soldiers, hefted the puffing dwarf onto her shoulders and carted him up as if he were an errant child.

Most other dwarves would have grumbled, tossed the orc aside and made their own way. Orn grabbed onto her neck horns and kicked his legs onto her shoulders, "Faster, mawgy! Giddeup!"

Gods, Variel thought, *I never should have taken him on that ancient carousel.* As she approached the door, a massive red eye broke free from cover above the frame and scanned her entire body making note of and appreciation for whatever weapons she carried.

It blinked as it studied the data before offering up a green light and opening the door. The captain headed in, letting the rest of her crew suffer through the scan. Orn slithered down off his mount and reached into his pocket to find something sweet for a tip, as the scan tried to determine where his head started. After trying to scan the statue of a faceless warrior of justice, it finally reset to dwarf and flipped up the green light. Segundo was much easier, it noted the bits of bile and street food still clinging to the sides of the mouth and sent in a read of "Human: Male. Weaker than typical, and that's saying something."

Only Monde was left, his fingers still working through the snack Orn got him, he popped a bunch of sliced leaves into his cheek altering the landscape of his countenance. The scan passed over once, confused, then another, getting a combination of troll and water nymph. By the third scan, when the data kept insisting it must be some kind of bipedal sky rat, the scanner threw up the green light and waved it on. It wasn't paid enough to solve this mess.

Monde slipped quickly into the opened portal, bumping into the frozen back of Segundo whose finger trailed across the inside of the inferior Vena Cava, striated thanks to alternating brick colors, into the vast opening of the Ventricle chambers. Stands of chairs, like risers for a choir, ringed the giant stage that hosted a chair so high most would suffer a nosebleed scaling it. But the building was so huge there was still a good ten stories of headspace above it. To fill of all that space was nothing, a giant echoey chamber to prove just how insignificant a single person was to the whole.

Most of the red lights were turned down, leaving only a light ring of blues circling the chamber, and the eternal white light upon the podium chair. The debates were not in session.

"So..." Orn started, glancing at the two security guards trying to talk the scanner out of going on break, "any ideas why we're here? Tour the local landmarks? Get a good grasp of orcish government? Sing the orc anthem, 'To hell with everyone!'"

A pair of shoes, heeled but in a secret fashion, clipped across the rosy stone floors. The huddled misfits turned at the noise and watched an orc descend from one of the looping ramps circling the chambers and ending where the aortas stored high ranking offices. She -- it was rare to find a male working in government unless they needed a token or two -- could easily crack her skull against the ceilings on the *Elation*. Almost as wide as Gene, her solid form was draped in a symbolic robe of ghastly mauve with sleeves drooping to the ground. A half cape dangled loosely from her left shoulder. The robe was finished in a vest coated in small medals engraved with a repetition of only four letters and a small name.

Variel, one to always forget a face, couldn't misplace this one. "Zila," she said, and bowed to the orc.

A smile of sorts took the orc's jaw as she looked over her handy work, glittering in the blue lights to bring out their scars.

"Your face seems different since last we tumbled," the orc said, coming to the end of her descent and walking towards the human.

"Oh?" Variel tried to play it off, "must be a trick of the light."

Zila smiled and laughed softly, "Yes, and you humans all look so similar. But you cannot escape the mark," she pointed her gnarled fingers towards the scar and dragged down it.

Variel herself smiled, "I think it gives a bit of character."

The orc laughed uproariously at that, even the security guards joined in at the little joke. "Come, join me in my chambers away from this decaying wheelhouse of hot air." She motioned back up the ramp she just descended, rolling her arms to safely bundle the sleeves away from snagging feet.

Variel walked beside the woman had once tried to kill her. The human's own work from that day shone, though not as predominantly as the orc's, as Zila limped slightly when her right heel met the ground. That was a fight Variel frankly shouldn't have survived.

"When I heard my old adversary was in town I simply had to call her in. I hope the armed escort wasn't too showy."

"No," Variel waved it off as if it were all part of some pomp script she totally read before the night. "Last I heard you were a prelate on one of the Orc triangle worlds, Breaking Wind, I believe."

Orn snorted, "Honest? Swear to your mother and kiss the stone, Breaking Wind? Oh, you underbiters slay me." Zila failed to hear most of what the dwarf said thanks to the rocket Variel fired close but not quite close enough to her head.

Instead, the diplomat waved her arms to encircle the empty chambers beating silently. "We are forbidden to switch planets, unless a fresh set of claws are necessary in the government. After an unfortunate incident involving a bored prelate, a crate of lubricant, and a pile of rusting swords left at the bottom of this walkway, the colony voters requested me."

"Voting," Variel shook her head, "that's no way to run a country." A few molding history books talked of the human attempts at a democracy, some one man/one vote rubbish; but over time that noble ideal quickly turned from one dollar/one vote into lots of dollars/lots of votes and the whole thing exploded when a member of one party stabbed, mutilated, and trussed up a member of the other. Since then they'd gone back to kings with the occasional attempts at letting a parliament craft a few laws to keep them busy and off the streets. It'd been smooth sailing, if you ignored all the 'assassination/nearly constant war' rocks.

The Prelate laughed at the human's cryptic words. She seemed to be doing that a lot more than Variel remembered. There was mostly screaming, threatening, pithy one-lining, and then the floor collapsed. It bothered a lot of other humans when they'd meet the ones trying to kill them off the battlefield; to see orcs playing with their children, enjoying drinks beside a bar, or stopping to investigate olfactory scent releasers in the gardens. Humans carried grudges, orcs truly believed in live and let live. Granted, they also fully believed in kill and let kill, which was half the reason they spent most of their time on the galactic scene under some form of demilitarization or embargo. But it never slowed them down long. They'd just find a new species to work out their bottled up aggressions on, except for the dwarves. Not even a bred-for-battle orc would call for war against their creditors.

"My personal reflecting chambers are through here," Zila said, motioning through the first large door they passed.

"Right next to the thoroughfare. You're either very important or worth saddling next to the ice machine," Orn said inspecting the plaque above the door. The lettering, pure orc and like trying to decipher a bowl of noodles, was done in a crimson probably meant to mimic blood. Hopefully, only mimic. The other option probably increased job opportunities in the rotunda while taking a heavy hit to morale.

Zila turned her head, dislodging the dwarf's not quite silent enough words, her plumed headdress scraping the doorframe as she entered her office. "Malir, this is an old friend of sorts," she called to her secretary who was tossed over his desk routing for something underneath it. At his bosses words, Malir snapped up and stood to attention.

"Friend?" Variel asked. She'd never heard that exact designation employed by an orc before, especially one she'd been ordered to eliminate.

"We did shed blood together," Zila said. "Is that not the human term for such an arrangement?"

"Kinda..." the captain wasn't prepared to get into the intricacies of human familiarity, namely that the shedding of blood was typically from those on the same side and not because of the other. Perhaps orcs recently learned of "Friendly Fire."

"What brings you to this forgotten berg of the galaxy?"

"Part exchange, bits of my ship got a little nicked in a small collision and I'd prefer fixing them up before attempting a pinch," she lied as if she were back on duty, covering for someone who thought it'd be a great laugh to toss the commander's tea set into the grav chamber.

Zila eyed her over, sensing the lie, but uncertain what to do with it. That was the trick, give just enough useless information you bog the other mind down, then skip out before they can reconvene. "That sounds like a very full day, you must require nourishment and respite," she gestured to a tray full of food far too soft for an orc's liking. Just how long had they been pinged?

"Actually..." Variel was about to explain her stomach full of street food that was about to go nuclear when one of the helmeted guards knocked on the open door.

"Madam, we have discovered a criminal amongst your guests."

Zila frowned but Variel smiled smoothly, "It's all right, I can keep the dwarf under lock and key until we get back."

"Hey! Those charges were dropped...eventually."

"Madam Prelate?"

Zila rose to full height and said crisply, "These aliens are guests of mine."

"It isn't the alien, Madam," the soldier said, pointing his head towards the paling Monde. "It's the orc. He's wanted for infanticide."

"There must be some kind of mistake," the doomed words were out of Variel's mouth before she could stop them. She quickly slapped on, "He's served upon my ship, far away from any infants, for nearly two years."

"I know you fairer sex orcs love the stomping and killing, but doc here can't hurt a fly," Orn defended. "Seriously. I watched him once in the cargo bay after the containment broke. It took hours."

The soldier passed over to the prelate a pad rotating through the warrant for some infant stomping orc's arrest. "From the prime Late Sun. It is clearly him, the countenance scan confirmed it."

As Zila searched through the words, her heavy brow buckling like a tectonic shift, Variel glanced about the room and nudged Orn. The dwarf, who was patting a shellshocked Monde on the back, followed her push and smirked. He'd always wanted to play with one of those.

All but whistling nonchalantly he crab slid to the corner and grabbed one of the ceremonial battle axes, probably the one that did the number to Variel's face. She slipped her hand into her pocket switching on the pistol, hoping the damn safety ding was silenced by her clothing, and breaking about thirty different Crest violations.

The prelate lowered the warrant and, for the first time, looked at the smaller male all but drained of blood as he stood helpless before his fate. "It is accurate. I am sorry." She passed the pad back to the guard.

"What happens now? Do you take him off to jail or a trial?"

"The punishment for knowingly terminating a pre-infant is ten years hard labor," the guard took a long pause giving the captain time to calculate just how they could infiltrate an orc chain gang. "But, for every year he evaded capture and failed to confess his crime another ten years is added. Therefore he shall be executed immediately."

Zila shrugged her shoulders, not in the mood to have the mess leeching into her carpet. The last time this happened it took the cleaners days to scrub up her meditating waterfall. But the law was the law, and in theory that was why she accepted this position in the third place.

The guard drew out a long tube, filled with a quick acting poison. Monde whimpered as the woman in black ordered him onto his knees. He dropped with a hand pinching the meat of his shoulder. His gamble finally came to a pathetic end as the house won. He wondered if the little time he'd eked out after his turn of crime really mattered to the balance of things. The elves always talked as if every decision you made was planned far in advance, by some god or spirits plucking at the tapestry, but looking down the twelve gauge needle of the end he wanted to shout in their faces how useless it all was.

Approaching behind him, the guard slipped her gloved hand around his throat, trying to find the uncovered spot on his neck. As he mumbled an old prayer to the heroes in the hall, a bang perforated the air. The guard stumbled, blood dripping down her leg.

Variel removed the pistol from her jacket -- now sporting an exit wound sized hole -- and fired again, knocking the guard back. Zila reared up, about to attack her "friend" but Orn swung her own battleaxe wide, catching her in the knee Variel shot up so many years ago. The prelate went down with a scream, but wasn't about to stop fighting. That was the problem with orcs, killing them was like trying to take out a nest of cockroaches by stomping them one roach at a time.

"Orn!"

"Aye!" he swung the axe wide, getting close to the old prelate's head but she still had some moves in her.

"Get the doc and the kid out of here," Variel peered over the side of the aorta watching the guards scatter at the sound of battle.

"Pray tell how?"

Variel dodged her pilot's wide arm and grabbed it before it could get her on the backswing. Grinning into his face she said, "Waterslide."

He smiled, he hadn't been able to do this since their last visit to the sheet metal factory. Grabbing onto Seggy's hand, he thrust it into the rising doc's and said, "Hang onto him and don't let go." Both nodded, uncertain who he was talking to. "And follow behind me, this is gonna be fun."

From years of piloting, the ass in Orn's pants were rubbed to such a smooth sheen it was a wonder he could sit down without sliding to the floor. Grinning like this was the happiest place in the galaxy, Orn sat down on the top of the giant stone slide. He situated the battle axe right at stomach piercing height and glanced towards his captain firing warning shots at the orc that invited them for tea. "Now?"

"Not yet." She could barely watch behind her, but the longer they waited the easier their escape would be. Variel fired another bullet near the prelate's head, missing partly on purpose she told herself, but startling the poor secretary into a deeper cower beside his filing cabinets.

"Now?"

Zila, forced back to the corner, staggered but came up with something heavy in her hands. Close combat with an orc was a death sentence. Variel yanked her "just in case" out of her pocket and shouted, "NOW!"

Orn slid his ass up and down to build momentum, called out "One, two, better not sue," and tossed himself down the twisting slide. Survival taking over the panic, Monde dragged the kid with him after Orn. Variel backed out into the hall. Just as Zila was rearing up, she tossed her handheld light grenade into the room and ran after the others.

The blinding flash knocked her face mutilator off her feet and straight into her little pond. Orc eyes were bred for fighting in dark corners and incredibly sensitive to light. She wasn't going to be seeing much of anything for a few days.

Calling out like he was in an action flick, Orn shouted, "Take that!" as his axe bit into the stomach of the first guard rushing up the incline. That guard tumbled to the side, rolling down a ten story drop and probably never getting up again. "Point for me!" The momentum of his drop was building. As the orcs realized what was happening they tried to turn, scurrying away from the armed toddler on the slide, but they were too slow.

Orn barreled into two, his axe slicing through guts and knees as his arm crashed from the weight of a 30 stone body clinging to his weapon. As he bit through an orc's backside he shouted, "And that's for showing us hospitality!"

The end of his slide appeared very rapidly, where two of the guards were building a quick barricade of their own. "CAPTAIN!" he shouted, just as one of her bullets spattered through the left guard, felling her from her post. Shifting his ass as hard as he could, he cranked left and blew past the other guard trying to straighten up and attack.

Orn continued to fly, his pants literally catching fire from the friction as he skittered across the polished stone floors and began to ascend up the other incline. Before gravity could have a full hold and shoot him back up to where they were trying to flee from, he dropped the handle of the battleaxe to the floor and tumbled ass over end, rolling until he spun up on his feet. They may not look like it, but dwarves are spry and always landed on their feet.

"What now, Cap?"

Variel pushed past her other two crew, and took aim at the right guard chasing after her pilot. She nicked the guard's shoulder but she kept chasing after Orn, the minimal pain not registering. "Orn!" Variel shouted over the rising din of more emerging guards from gods knew where. "Remember the Gilded Pear? When we didn't have exact change?"

He laughed heartily and stamped his feet in rage, "Oh do I. Waiter," he shouted to the guard slowing in her collapsing steps as the dwarf faced off with her, "there's a fly in my soup!"

"I didn't mean it literally," Variel grumbled, as the dwarf tossed the battleaxe, which in their first attempt was a steak knife, above his head.

The guard stopped, watching it, giving Variel enough time to whack her on the back of the neck with her gun. Down went the guard. Orn caught the battleaxe with his good hand and brought the blade across the guard's shoulder.

"I don't remember it going like that at the restaurant," Variel chided, as she cocked her gun, cursing her lack of batteries, and aimed a few shots at the guards emerging through the side heart valve.

"It's called improvising," Orn said, "besides, that was just a few fussy elves. Globbing soup in their hair wouldn't work on orcs."

Variel waved at Monde and Segundo, "Get to the door, you idiots." While Segundo gasped at the piles of surprisingly still squirming orcs, the doc grabbed hard onto his charge and drug him through the vena cava and back into daylight. "Orn, you're next."

"Yes, boss," he whooped, swinging the axe around as if posing for an action card, and dashed for the door. Variel followed close behind, taking a few shots at the guards, trying to stagger them, before gritting her teeth and running for the door. She jumped just as the portal closed behind her, and with her last bullet shot out the scanner's eye. The entire system went into lockdown mode. No one was getting in or out of the heart for hours.

As Monde helped her to her feet, she looked into those orange eyes she'd trusted so often with her life and ordered, "Run."

Darting through the indentations, hovering close to the doorsteps and in the shadows of the T's, the group moved through the wakening streets with Orn out front. His new best toy sliced through another scanner poised above the cross section of a street and he waved the others on.

Being so short, he was the only of them who could easily infiltrate before the scanner could register something worth rousing from a nap for, but this much damage in such a specific route was certain to draw attention soon. "We can't run all the way back out to the farm," Variel said, flattening herself next to their doc who'd been far more quiet and obedient than usual, "We're lucky to have made it this far."

Rattling his battle axe as if facing down a siege, Orn grunted, "Let them come!"

Variel landed her hand on the dwarf's shoulder to steady him, and glanced up and down the block. Not a bad part of town, nor the good side; a few orcs chased after children wandering the summer streets in short overalls, a ball passing between sticky hands. "Orn, wander down the block destroying every camera you can to create a false trail. Once you're done, get back here quick."

"You planning on sprouting wings and flying us out of here?" he asked, already eyeing down a red eye thirty feet from their position.

"Not exactly," she said turning to Segundo who crossed his eyes trying to figure out what she was looking at.

"This is so humiliating," Segundo's voice carried across the PALM link up Variel held between them all in the dark.

"Keep it up, and maybe stick your ass out or something. Orcs like asses, right?" she asked the other fellow crouching atop a few bags stuffed with molding, half eaten takeout and shredded invoices for fresh meat.

"Yes, sort of," Monde said. "The flatter the more preferable, but also on display."

"Right, stick your flat ass out and maybe pout something," she ordered as the dumpster lid flung open and a curious dwarf's head peeked in.

"A good seven cameras are piles of rubble. What'd I miss?" his hand reached out and Variel caught it, hauling him into their hiding spot.

"We're hitching," Variel said, trying to not breathe through her nose. The only thing worse than the smell of orcs wandering the streets at midsummer was using their pungent garbage for furniture.

"From inside a trash bin," Orn glanced around the cramped accommodations, lit only by the captain's glowing palm. "You Crests sure do things interestingly."

"I got Segundo out strutting whatever the gods gave him," she didn't hide a growing grin as she said. "After all, you said he was like catnip."

Orn snorted, shaking his head at the poor human who'd blossomed under the attention from a few lusty orcs who he believed only cared about what existed between his ears. Now that he was using his manly wiles for bait, the reality of the universe was sinking in. "Hey kid, maybe try showing a little leg."

"I must insist, this is strictly agains..."

Variel bumped the mute button, letting Segundo whine into the ether even as he paraded up and down the street, occasionally sticking out a thumb, or channeling a lone lamb that lost its mistress.

"So," Orn started, glancing over to their little fugitive, "killing babies part of orc medical school or was it just something you did on the side for rent money?"

Monde clasped his fingers and focused on them, "I didn't kill a child, I refused to complete the bonding process."

The dwarf's abundant brows furrowed as he tried to flip through his ever increasing list of euphemisms. He'd heard quite a few over his life, "shaking the fur" from the were-sloths being one of his favorite, but infanticide was a new and confusing one. "You were a concubine or something?"

Monde broke from his hand vigil to the lost dwarf and sighed, "The bonding process, orcs require a...I was young, and close to completing my first pass of medical school. And I may have let my judgement get the better of me a night or two."

"Oh, now this I have to hear." Then Orn thought better of it, "Actually, no I don't."

"Sometimes I think you can breathe and talk at the same time," Variel said, watching her pilot as if he were a particularly interesting but nasty stink bug.

"She was supposed to be a momentary distraction," Monde continued, wanting to get this tale out. It'd gnawed away at his soul until he felt as hollow as those eggs they traded away. "But a week later she approached me with news that she was full of egg and wished it to be fertilized."

The aliens glanced at each other, both only passingly aware of their own reproductive anatomy. Monde sighed and launched into an ancient lecture from an instructor brought in to warn the boys away from engaging in slutty hand holding. "Intercourse will at times cause an egg to drop from the female's tract. This is a random occurrence that relies upon the correct balance of both hormones and nutrition, as well as some underlying causes we'll figure out later. At this point she can decide whether to continue the process of growing the child or let the egg recede."

"And that has what to do with you?" the dwarf asked. "I thought you women all wandered off to huts and took care of that stuff yourself." Variel whacked Orn in the back of the head with a broken pipe for that.

Monde sighed but continued his lecture, "At which point the male shall bond with her, sharing not just genetic material but also nutrients from his own body. The process requires constant contact for three weeks."

"So you refused to bond with her? I don't blame you, child support's a scam."

The orc twisted his hands, "Not exactly. Refusal of bonding is acceptable under the law..."

"Which means if you're rich enough, or well known enough, people look the other way, but anyone poorer or lower class than the one pushing gets tossed to the egg," Variel said, seeing this played out in much the same across the galaxy just with a few chromosomes reversed.

"Yes, and my family would have been very disappointed in me, possibly even cut me off, and I'd certainly be expelled for letting myself get into such a compromising position. It would have shattered the morality clause."

"Maybe it's the pipe to the head that scrambled my brains," Orn muttered, still rubbing the sore spot, "but if refusal is so bad, why not suffer the three weeks or whatever, then she has the kid, and it's not your problem anymore."

"I do not understand."

"You know, single mothers raising their adorable apple cheeked spawn against the unfair world and finding love with a widowed father in antique stores. Don't any of you watch the network vids?" Orn asked at the stares he got.

"Women do not raise children, at least never alone. That's..." Monde giggled at the idea of it. She'd probably put the baby in the food combuster and the roast in a bassinet.

"Okay, fine, Mr. Everyone's Gone Fucking Nuts, if you didn't refuse the bond, but you didn't bond, then why are you facing an execution squad?"

"Before the latching on period-" Both Orn and Variel shuddered at that, trying to not put their imaginations to how that works for three damn weeks. "I injected myself with a serum of hormones that would make it fail. After it did not take, she more or less kicked me out on my ass and I assumed I was free.

"It was another two years, I'd graduated the first session and was working to the second, when the accusations appeared.

She had proof that I'd knowingly sabotaged the bond, most likely from a bitter competitive colleague."

Monde twisted his fingers. He'd had years to reflect upon who it was, but revenge seemed a futile dream as he could never enact it, so the identity remained a black space in his tale. "In a panic, I ran, first to any space port that would get me off planet. I hopped from one colony to another, hiding amongst cargo and refugees, extending my punishment sentence, but too terrified to face up to it."

"And you ran into me," Variel said, remembering the day when she'd taken a moment of pity upon the jittery orc begging for relief. If she'd known he was in such dire straights...she'd probably have refused him, her own life not needing the magnifying glass of a warrant upon her head.

"Yes, captain," he mumbled, lowering his head to his colorful chest.

"And they were just gonna kill you for not making babies?" Orn's darkest fears raised up for a moment at his own endless insistence to keep his genetic material on lockdown.

"Orcs do not kill on sight unless the punishment has reached beyond your logical lifespan."

"Prudent," Variel said earning the hairy eyeball of both her pilot and the man facing down the end of the firing squad. "I didn't say it was right," she waved her hands, shining a perturbed Segundo against the dumpster wall, his face redder than a hydroponic tomato, "only that it makes a bit of sense. Why drag back someone convicted of a hundred or a thousand life sentences when you can just end it there?"

Orn folded his arms, "Sounds like there's a story in that bit of wisdom."

The dwarf was right, damn him, but it wasn't one she was in the mood to get into. Luckily, her eye landed on a very flustered and frantically waving technician and she raised the volume button, "...car, egg, vehicle, is slowing. What do I do?"

"Flash him your danglies," Orn cooed, getting an even brighter burn across their bait's cheeks.

Their vantage point flew down to the black ground as the egg rolled to a stop. Segundo was on his own.

Turning back and forth, trying to not feel like an idiot while accidentally looking like one, Segundo skipped back from the edge just as the barrier burst up. Either one of those eggs was about to stop before him, or...actually he'd prefer anything other than that. He lifted his hand up to his face, and whispered into it, "It seems we have a target. Advice? Over."

It was what all the space agents did in the few epics he'd read in the contraband at the commune, though most brothers turned a blind eye to it glad the kids weren't beating up someone who could be the future prophet and use that harrowing experience to turn into some kind of super villain. Though there was very little in the adventure tales of the agents strutting their stuff on the side of a road, and certainly not opening up the jacket of their uniform only to have the captain shake her head, mutter something and motion for him to zip it back up. Agents were masters of disguise and manipulators of all. Segundo felt like a terrified kid on his first day of school, assuming the truancy officer was well armed.

"Hello!" he shouted back into the palm connection. "Is anybody there? *Oh god, or gods, or ancestral spirits with voyeur tendencies* (the commune had some interesting cursing to cover any and all future eventualities)*, I'm all alone. They've done left me to be a distraction while they battled some mighty orc warriors all alone and were killed in the process and I'm gonna die on this orc world completely forgotten aside from a small note on a shipping manifesto!*

A blur slowed to visible range and began to inch towards his particular street corner. His voice rose a few octaves as he screeched into his palm, "Help me please! A car, egg, vehicle, is slowing. What do I do?"

The dwarf's particularly useless banter chirped over, but Segundo dropped his hand missing it; the egg car was hatching. A narrow gap appeared and an orc head popped out. Greyer than the others and with slightly smaller neck horns, topped in a hat somewhat reminiscent of his own back on the ship, she smiled wide and didn't hide the once over sizing up gaze across Segundo's form.

He shuddered and subconsciously covered his chest with his folded arms, giving the others a view of his rapidly staining armpit. Luckily, this worked in his favor as the orc smiled even wider at his obvious discomfort, "What's a nice boy like you doing all alone?"

Segundo lapsed into the small script Variel drilled into his head while Monde searched for a suitable hiding place, dragging the dumpster nearer. "I AM VISITING FROM ANOTHER PLANET, BUT MY SHEEP GOT LOST. I REQUIRE A TRIP TO ANOTHER PLACE TO DETERMINE LATER!"

The orc blinked at the human's outburst but the smile didn't dim. She'd probably never seen one of their kind before and assumed all males shouted inane babble at the top of their lungs. She may even see it as a mating thing.

A quiet voice buzzed out of his armpit, "-ucks sake, I shoulda put the dwarf out there."

"I got better legs."

"Get her to the dumpster, the dumpster. I'll handle the rest."

His possible ride motioned him closer, and he slid a few steps nearer. "I imagine an alien like you would be grateful for the help."

"Oh yes, very grateful," he nodded, trying to find a chance to insert about the dumpster.

"Well then, jump on in," the smile took on a dragon turn, deep creases connecting the mouth to the red eyes.

"I have some things!" Segundo shouted, not moving an inch towards the opening gap in the egg car.

The orc gazed about at the empty space beside him and turned her head as if that'd make his invisible *things* appear. Armpit voice cut in, "Ask for her help, orc's love showing off their strength. Make's 'em feel womanly." Orn made a vomiting sound at that, the dry retching echoing in Segundo's pit.

"I don't have them here, they're too large for me to carry by myself. Could you help?"

"All right." The orc glanced around the empty street, making certain there was no waiting ambush; but finding only the scrawny human with the whispering appendage, she descended from her vehicle.

Segundo stepped back, trying to keep out of arm's reach, as he led the orc towards the dumpster, "It's just back here, this way." She followed behind, uncertain about the game but enjoying it nonetheless. Pointing towards the dumpster, Segundo smiled and tried to flirt with a face that looked more like a cat fresh out of the rain, "Would you pull it out of there."

"You put your luggage in a dumpster?" the orc staggered back, in no mood to go routing through garbage.

One of those rare bolts of brilliance hit Segundo, "To keep people from stealing it off me behind my back."

"Very wise," the orc rolled up her sleeves and lifted the heavy latch on the lid. "Who told you that?"

"A woman!" Apparently bolts of brilliance can strike a person twice if they forget to lower their umbrella.

The orc smiled. Keeping her head up, she reached down into the dumpster not wanting to get a nose full of whatever nested in garbage. A gloved hand grabbed her arm, holding it down, as the captain popped out, wrapping her own hand around the orc's mouth and jamming a needle deep into the reactive and unprotected area between the third and fourth neck horn. The orc struggled against the pair and whatever lashed through her veins, but she quickly slipped and crashed to the ground.

Variel threw up the lid, gasping for air away from the stench, and climbed out. Monde followed, gathering up his bag overloaded with the part they'd been through this entire hell to get. Segundo offered his hand to the dwarf, who tossed it aside. "Watch this, pretty boy." Swinging the battle axe wide, he cut himself a dwarf hole out of the thick metal dumpster. "Not as impressive as a knight sword, but it'll do," he chuckled, climbing out of the hole he made and earning a glare from Variel.

"Great, where did you think we were going to stick the body?"

"Uh..." Orn scratched his head.

Variel shook her head, knowing she'd have to get that thing away from him, probably at night when he was sleeping. Assuming he didn't go to bed with it. "Behind the dumpster. Help me, Segundo."

"Me?"

"Yes, you. Monde would leave behind an instantly traceable set of palm prints, we're aliens. No data file on us. Now, grab the feet and drag."

Segundo picked up the boots of the orc who was probably thinking of doing rather unpleasant things to him, and felt a jab of pity as her head lolled like a basketball in a sack. "Is she, will she, is she dead?"

"Nah," Variel dropped her end, and tried to squeeze over the body sleeping off the encounter behind a dumpster. "Very hard to kill orcs. Much easier to just drug 'em and then set off a bomb."

"We're not going to bomb her are we?"

"Of course not!" Variel patted the technician on the back, the closest she came to a job-well-done. "We don't have any bombs. Everyone, get in the egg!"

Orn didn't need to be told twice, sliding up the battleaxe handle for easier storage, he hopped into the driver's seat, his feet dangling above the floor, and Monde took the one beside him. Variel shoved Segundo into the back, cramped for an orc car, but it was probably one of those designer eggs built for speed and a mid-life crisis. Turning one last glance at the broken scanner watching over their little scene she saw a small flash of waking red and dived into the final seat. The door resealed behind her.

Reaching over Segundo, she tapped on the back of Orn's division and shouted, "Go! Go! Go!"

The egg did not go.

"Um..."

The egg remained stationary

"Orn..."

The egg's windows turned transparent and a jet of wiper fluid shot out over the entire vehicle.

"By all the..." Monde reached over top of Orn and cranked something that looked like an old cigarette lighter, flipped up the radio and mashed his foot down on the clutch. Miraculously, the egg car roared to life, humming as the engine engaged. As Monde removed his foot, it zipped back down the road at break head speeds.

"You input the coordinates here," Monde pointed to a panel Orn thought was for ordering drinks, "and stop with this," he pointed to the extra large pedal with stop written all over it in orcish letters.

"What's the acceleration button?" Orn asked, glancing over the scrambled egg schematics.

"Orcs don't have one. We only worry about stopping," Monde said, yanking the impact bars down over his head.

Variel looked at her "dived into the deep end" pilot and sat back, first yanking down Segundo's bars as if he were a child and then her own. "How long until we hit the farm?"

"You may wish to rephrase that, captain," Monde said, eyeing the dwarf's hands flitting just above the multitude of controls. "I set the coordinates to find the most direct path, the readout says ten minutes."

"That quickly?"

"This 'egg' can travel at speeds of...on rethought, you do not wish to know."

With their ovum car navigating itself, all the backseat passengers could do was sit back and wait for the ride to end. Not that this stopped Variel from stretching her neck up as high as the restraints would allow as she tried to make sense of the world zipping past and calling orders to Orn, who kept his foot hovering over the brake in a life or death game of whac-a-gnome. The landscape of the colony faded like turpentine tossed across a painting, as the windows failed to make much sense of the outside world traveling far too quickly past. Monde fiddled around in his bag, one eye following along the countdown.

"Five minutes," he said.

"Five minutes passed or five minutes 'til?" Orn asked. Normally, the orc would shrug it off as another of his jokes but a thick sheen dotted the terrified pilot's brow, thrown onto the seat of something he couldn't command.

"Both," Variel said calmly, trying to get through Orn's panicking exterior. He nodded but didn't say anything, still watching the tick of numbers which probably meant something vital to an orc.

City faded, the buildings shrinking into the ground in the flipbook pace of the car. A few trees overtook the crossblocks and food stands, lone farms and stretches of marching crops in their rows formed an undulating wave. "Three minutes," Monde said, settling down his bag and punching through a few screens to make absolute certain they were in the right area.

"Two minutes," he said absently as he returned to the main screen, watching another number vanish into the onboard computer.

"One minute."

"That's good enough!" Orn shouted, throwing both of his feet down hard upon the brake peddle. At first the egg shook its shell, refusing to obey the clearly demented driver, but as the few connected wires crossed and overrode the safety and not-so-safety features, it gave in and began the breaking procedure.

As if someone smashed a tray against their noses, every passenger thudded back in their seats, their vision blackening from the mass inertia hit. Slowly, the grey fog pushed back and Variel's hand landed on Orn's shaking shoulder, "Good job."

"Yeah," he pecked about on the console trying to find the door open button, "that's the last time I pilot something that comes out of a bird's ass." Monde unhooked his harness and reached over Orn to a button labeled with a crack across it, the door opened and every member crashed into the dying light of an exhausted world. A few bugs cried like squealing engines in the distance, but no one else moved as they looked up at the cab call station that began their trip into the city.

Variel shook her legs, still trying to rub pain out of her entire body, and switched on her PALM light. A few of the pungent red rays of the sinking sun lit their path, but the dips and divots of the farm tossed enough shadows to make staggering back to their ship arduous. "Lights, everyone that has them. Orn, call your wife. Tell her we're coming back."

"She'll be ecstatic," he muttered, pulling up his own hand and trying to scroll through the lists of names he'd acquired. One day he'd actually put people into fast find.

Pulling them in the direction of the ship, the captain waded into the freshly irrigated fields, her boots failing to find the old planks. *As if this day could get much worse* she thought, as she yanked her shoe out of a grasping mud hole for the third time. "Any word yet, Orn?"

"This damn thing can't get any signal," he grumbled, shaking his hand as if it fell asleep.

"Captain," Monde grabbed Segundo's palm and pointed it into the darkness illuminating the golden exterior of their crashed ship.

"Thank gods, I was half afraid the thing was dragged off and sold for scrap. Monde, Segundo, help me tip the thing up proper. I'm not in the mood to fly into space ass first."

The two males nodded, both wanting to be as far from the planet as possible. They pushed against the buried ship, its nose rising as if it were a pig rooting in the mud. Teetering onto its side and crashing, the cloud scraper thudded to a silent refusal to move. Segundo slipped in the mud, his white knee slurping deep into the red clay as Variel called for them to keep pushing. It had to be righted before it could break atmo.

Summoning as much strength as he could, the technician dug his fingers deep, and -- with assistance -- finally hauled their ship into an upright and ready to fly position. Orn kept shaking his hand, and turned from his attempted call to watch the others coated in the red clay wipe their exertions off with more mud. "Jolly job. I can't get her, she must have gone to bed."

"Great, well back is easier than down. The return catch should handle most of that, everyone into the ship," Variel pointed back into the cramped capsule and motioned the others to get their exhausted hides inside.

Monde scattered in first, not wanting to spend another second on his people's planet with Segundo close behind. He'd had enough adventure to make up for his first eighteen or so years of nothing. Orn kept messing about with his PALM, but Variel guided his shoulder.

"It's weird, she's almost always on the line, unless she's mad at me."

"We'll figure it out once we're space side. Get on in," she said, and Orn slid in himself, finally closing down his meager connection.

Variel turned back to the slipping off to slumber world of the orcs. Someone was probably already zeroing in on the stolen egg and writing up an interesting warrant, as her old adversary paced about in her bloodied office. The captain smiled; the orc's probably enjoyed the chase even more. She slid into the capsule, and, after slipping into the far less secure harness, banged her fist on the "return" button.

CHAPTER TEN

The return trip was less blood wracking thanks to the stabilizing affect of the ship's pull and some other things Variel could ask Ferra about later when they lost ether connection and couldn't take any more of Orn's baffling attempts at charades. The dwarf still thought flapping his arms like a beheaded chicken symbolized water.

The shuttle bay door descended, allowing the cloud scrapper to putter in, the mag locks yanking her forward until their little capsule lodged into one of the ruts for something older and bigger. Everyone trapped inside waited for the decompressing call from either WEST or Ferra, but they both remained silent, only the loud BWAM of "all clear" answered Variel's hails.

She cracked open the door and exited the capsule backwards, yanking their new inertia injector with her. Placing it in the crook of her arm, she glanced around the mostly darkened shuttle bay, as empty as a tomb. "Did someone bake cookies in the galley?" Her voice echoed less than usual.

Orn staggered out behind, waving his hand before his face to make certain he wasn't going blind. "Cor, that's how it is. Nearly seven years of marriage and your wife won't even greet you with a cold beverage, fuzzy slippers, or a fresh change of bandages after a death defying mission."

"It was hardly death defying," Variel joked, offering a hand to Segundo, "more like death shifting."

"Death taunting?" Orn asked, trying to find the light switch. It was usually on a wall section that looked a lot like this one, or maybe one of the other ten similar ones. It certainly wasn't on the ceiling.

"Death poking with a really big stick?" Variel slipped into banter mode so easily she forgot the dwarf was mad at her, as did he.

Monde finally poked his head out, the last of their group. He'd been quiet on the ride back, avoiding everyone's gaze. As Variel offered him her hand, he took it tentatively and she held it tight, shaking it slightly. It was her way of saying "Sure, you almost got us killed, but it's all forgotten. You ever seen the shit the dwarf's caused?"

"Hey Cap," Orn pointed towards the quaint and dark observation center overseeing the shuttle bay, "someone's moving."

"About time," she said, walking to one of the crates and placing the injector upon it. Her fingers searched through her pocket to find a tissue to wipe some of the clay off it and the shield projector fell into her hand. She completely forgot about the damn thing on the planet. Unexpected orc attacks had a way of doing that. Dropping it back in her pocket, her fingers trailed across the thick casing as a flare of lights rose from the far end of the shuttle bay.

A shadow loomed out of the doorway, but moved no closer in the rising rows of lights illuminating the friendless grates and bulkheads of a dusty cargo bay. "Hey!" Orn shouted to whoever haunted the doorway, "Where's our ticker tape parade?"

As the final row of lights kicked in above their heads the crew raised their arms over their heads, trying to adjust to the retina glare. The shadow descended, its thick shoulders tossed back as its arms pivoted something about the bay.

"Captain!" Monde gasped, pointing to her left. She turned to find a new addition to her ship, taking up a good third of the shuttle bay with its sleek fins yanked back against the open mouth of the Crest engines; a Drake shuttle.

Variel's hands searched for her spent pistol, as the shadow called out in harsh male tones, "Stop what you are doing."

"Or what?" Orn chided, dropping behind a grate to find some cover. As he turned back, he spotted the kid and yanked Segundo down with him.

"Or I kill your wife," Sovann's controlled voice, gravel from too many years sucking down comet dust, broke through the shamble of boots as she appeared, an elf clutched in her armored fingers.

"You moronic gas sniffer!" Orn taunted, "That ain't my wife."

Brena didn't tremble in the knight's cold grasp, but she wasn't happy either, her eyes glancing to the side as the Knight pressed the butt of her gun deeper into the elf's neck. "Captain," her voice called out to the woman frozen mid gun reveal.

"It's all right, Brena," Variel said as another guard appeared from the observation deck, dragging Ferra with him. That elf was spitting hot tacks, pure molten fury in his arms as she twisted about in rage, but could offer little resistance to the Crest soldier.

Sovann aimed her gun at the cursing engineer, "Very well, how about this one then?"

Orn balled up his fists and turned towards their captain. She seemed to be counting over the crew, looking for their missing few, when Taliesin entered, his hands the only ones locked tight and a gash running down his chin. Slowly, Variel lifted her spent pistol. Sovann re-aimed hers into the spitting Ferra, and the captain lowered it to the ground.

"Let them go," the captain said, "take what you came for."

Orn wanted to argue with her, but the sight of his wife under the scope of any weapon sent his mind into total burnout. All he needed was her safe.

Sovann lifted her weapon and tossed Brena to the first guard that entered. She descended down the industrial slope, walking into the bay and towards the last members of the crew. "I am glad you've decided to be cooperative, *Captain.*"

Variel surveyed over her humbled crew and back at the woman who did it, "You left me little choice."

A smirk twisted Sovann's mouth, far more wrinkled than was typical for someone her age. She must have some majorly nasty habit. The Knight kept her weapon up but raised her spare hand as if they were in negotiations, "I can be quite reasonable when given proper provocation."

"Like busting up someone's face. I see how reasonable the Crests are."

Sovann laughed at her handy work, it had to be hers. It was rare for her squires to train in how to take down an elf, even one anchored by his sister. Glancing back at the proud assassin, she raised her weapon at the captain and said, "Tell me where it is."

Variel blinked, never a good move in life or death negotiations, "Where what is?"

The smirk dropped, frozen ice taking its place as Sovann turned on her newest trophy. "Now is not the time to play ignorant. I deal with fraudulent idiots by applying a bullet." She booted up her gun, the safety dinging far faster than anything Variel owned.

"I'm not playing, or kidding, or pretending. I have no idea what the hell you want," the captain waved her hands, for a glorious second hoping this was all some giant misunderstanding. If they didn't want her...

The pistol dropped momentarily, and the Knight narrowed her eyes, "You do not know, yet you ran... Space debris," she cursed at them, getting a few appreciative guffaws from her yes men. "The djinn, tell me and I will let your pitiful ship slink back into the muck it crawled from."

Not a micron of realization crossed Variel's eyes, "Djinn? What djinn?"

"Milad!" the Knight shouted behind her. The guard escorting the bound assassin vanished out the door and reappeared with Gene's suit. The dead fissures as black as the grave gave away its empty state. Their djinn flew the coop.

He tossed the empty rock suit onto the ground where it thudded like a dead body, and Sovann glared into the Captain's eyes, "That djinn."

"Why do you want a djinn?" Variel asked, eyeing up the shuttle bay. If only she'd hidden a few weapons in here, or something really big and heavy, like a troll.

But the monologuing trick didn't work on the Knight, who pointed her weapon at the orc's head instead, "Tell me where to find him or I will eliminate your crew one by one."

Monde stood tall facing down death, possible death. Even at point blank range to the head it was still somewhat likely he'd survive. Ferra twisted against her guard but still couldn't find an opening. If his hands weren't guarded by thick gauntlets, Variel knew she'd have bitten him by now. Her dulcen twins watched on with perhaps the most emotion she'd ever seen from them, neither wanting to give up their fellow silent crewmate in exchange for their lives.

Only Segundo took to crying, his hands shaking as he lay on the ground next to Orn, some old prayer from his commune days tumbling from his mouth. The dwarf didn't turn to Variel, his eyes locked fully on his wife, who could be next on the killing list.

It was time for the most powerful weapon the captain had left, the truth. "You must know nothing about djinn. Once they exit their suits, there is no finding them. They can disperse into a billion particles, fade into the walls, slip inside of our lungs if the need arises. Shoot all of us if you feel the need." Segundo's whimper from Variel's speech reached into elven frequencies. "But it won't pull out the genie."

Sovann waved her pistol across Monde's face and then smiled, "Excellent," she stepped back, dropping her aim. "It is exactly as I surmised." The Knight turned to her soldiers, "Secure the prisoners in the galley. You," the squire's name must have escaped her, "you, get the pilot and the man jello."

One guard gathered up the elves, dragging them from the bay, as the second descended towards his Knight and the dwarf helping Segundo to his wobbling knees. Sovann smiled, and said to Variel, "Thank you for your time." Turning, she fired a point blank shot directly into Variel's chest.

The captain's body flew back, crashing into a crate and slipping out of view as it tumbled into the torn grating. As the rest of the Elation-Cru watched in shock, Sovann quipped, "Your services are no longer required. Bring these prisoners with me!" she ordered, "I have a plan to smoke out the djinn myself."

Sovann gripped her fingers into the collar of Orn's coat, half dragging his scrabbling boots along the carpet until she tossed him into his chair, twisted his arms behind his back, and latched a pair of wrist cuffs around him. The dwarf glared into her eyes as she spun him around to face her. "My nose itches."

"Your ship board comm line?" the Knight asked pointedly.

"I'm afraid I left it in my other jacket." He barely got the last syllable out before her hand smacked across his face, a ring dragging a tear into his skin.

Orn blinked back the tears of pain, and smiled, "Please Sir, may I have another?"

She raised her fist but thought better of it. Stepping back, she poked through the consoles, ripping up his posters to get a better view of the components below. Unsheathing her sword, she sliced right through the warped plasticine and dove into the mass of console. With her head half buried in wires, she cheerfully said, "I've met your like before, dwarf. So cocksure and witless right until--" she yanked out some wires and the bridge lights dimmed while a panel partially rose then tumbled back, "I destroy you from the inside."

"My diet's about 89% bug legs, I'm way ahead of you."

The Knight ignored him, still digging for something, despite the comm line clearly beeping near her head. A few of her bound hairs broke free and drifted into the torn console as she moved something to something else. He had no idea what she was doing; the bigger wires, some of the midsized ones, and all the small ones were outside his jurisdiction. Only Ferra'd be able to fix it. Or the captain...ex-captain.

"There," Sovann rose, wiping some of the ancient space mold onto her face as she opened up the line to the ship. "Djinn, wherever you are hiding, whatever form you have taken, I will find you. This need not be a bloodbath, come out of hiding, give yourself up, and I shall release the hostages."

Orn giggled at her seemingly reasonable request. Sovann tried to shut down the line, but failed to push the sticky button twice. The entire ship heard her turn to her prisoner and grit her teeth, "I will not hesitate to kill you all."

"Oh, believe me," his giggles stopped as he eyed down the cold, calculating stare of a mad woman, "I know. But you done screwed up."

"Is that so?"

"Yup," Orn was giddy, like a kid telling his parents a story only he knew the ending to. "See the djinn you want, we call him Gene, well, funny story that, there's naught on this ship that smokey mountain gives a fig about except one person."

Sovann wrapped her fists around Orn's coat and yanked him forward, straining his shoulders against the lock of his arms, "Who?! Tell me dwarf."

Orn smiled wickedly, "The one you just killed."

Dropping him back to his seat, Sovann drove her fist through the cracked console, coming back with bits of plastic sticking into her gauntlets. "This fucking job!" She leaned over the comm and pushed the button, turning it off. "One of you! Hello! Milad! Answer me!"

"You have to push the button again."

"What?" she turned to glare at Orn.

"The button, it's sticky and to get a call through you have to..."

"Oh yeah, I've got it, thanks. Milad!"

The nondescript guard's voice crackled through the comm in the galley, "Yes, Sir!"

"Get down to the shuttle bay, drag up the body of the woman I shot. We might need to necromance her."

"Sir!" he responded, probably saluting in the process.

"And have one of the others take that spirited elf down to the engines," Sovann ordered, rethinking her old plan. "This would be so much easier if we didn't need the damn thing alive."

"Sir?" the other guard asked.

"Do it, and never question my orders again!" Sovann thumped the button twice, cutting off the line.

"Why are you doing this? Some giant scavenger hunt? Going for the Eye of a Basilisk next?" Orn mocked, unable to do much else.

Sovann glanced towards the trussed up dwarf and she smirked, "Never you mind why I'm here. You all cooperate and you can go back on your merry little way."

"Except for the one you shot."

Sovann opened her hands wide, "Accidents happen."

Yeah, accidents. Orn tried to wiggle, but a glare from the Knight paused him. Even as she flipped through a few buttons, trying to poke life into controls that cashed in their insurance claims centuries ago, she still kept an eye on him. Gas pocket, the Cap would roll over in her grave if she'd heard talk of her body being tossed to necromancers. Bunch of no good grave robbers poking their noses into other dead people's business. It was downright shameful.

"Sir..." The voice cut through the comm, echoing from the shuttlebay, and as uncertain as a newborn foal.

"Yes, what is it?" Sovann seemed to be in a particularly foul mood. Good.

"The body, Sir, it's gone."

"What do you mean gone?"

"Gone as in no longer present," Orn jumped into the discussion, "disappeared, it done run off on its own..." His words choked in his throat as the Knight punched him in the gut.

Sovann grunted, thinking to herself before calling out to her man, "Follow the blood trail, she probably crawled off into a corner to die somewhere."

"Um, Sir?"

"FIND THE BODY!" Sovann shouted into the comm before bashing the whole thing with the hilt of her sword. Very unbalanced indeed.

She reached over and yanked Orn's face closer to hers, "All right, dwarf, you're going to tell me where every single environmental control on this space rock is located and you are going to do it without any smart lip or I shall vaporize your wife."

Orn followed her fist hovering above the engineering lockdown, a button Ferra disabled about ten minutes onboard after a rather unpleasant experience from their earlier temping days when she pissed in the wrong person's cornflakes. It went much worse for him once she got out though. Shaking as if her threat had any merit, he gestured his head towards the poster of the burlesque dancer Gnome Rose Lee.

Sovann dropped him and yanked up the antique, enjoying the groan from the dwarf as she fumbled through a batch of wires that mostly controlled the long abandoned half of the ship. Orn wiggled his arms, trying to find the right unlatching mechanism. He didn't have long before she caught on and got into a fresh stabby mood.

Gods take whoever designed this crawlspace and jam them inside a sardine can. Then put that sardine can inside a pill box and shoot both into a black hole. Ugh, and I am having a very long discussion with Orn and his habit of throwing old candy sticks through the grates!

Variel inched another few feet down her ship's arteries, her body barely fitting through the gnome sized holes. Apparently, it never crossed any of the designer's minds that perhaps one day, in the far future, a human may decide to go for a little stroll inside the crawlspace, you know, for fun, or to get her damn ship back. The half broken shield shimmered around her as the nearly invisible repulsion particles bounced into the low ceiling. And what kind of troll licking, second cousin of a gargoyle's ass fires a hand cannon on a spaceship?! Her old shield modulator took a pounding from that close of fire, but at least it absorbed enough of the blast that she wasn't picking up her own intestines, or dealing with a decompressed ship.

When I get out of here, I am going to teach her proper spacial boarding procedure, with my fists. Variel banged her hands into another section of grating, the ancient metal digging deep into her palms. The air grew thicker, hotter, but didn't taste of excess MGC runoff. *I must be getting near the engines,* Variel thought as she drug along the inertia injector. It nearly cost them their lives twice over, she wasn't about to abandon it now. Besides, once she got these invaders off her ship, she planned to make a very quick getaway.

"WEST!" She crumbled to her stomach, raising her bloody PALM up to her mouth as she whispered, "Come on, WEST. Answer. You're not playing hide and seek again, are you? Damn it, that bitch must have turned him off." She wasn't going to hear the end of it. The only thing her computer feared more than being switched off was a kindergarten class fresh off free candy and puppy day.

Okay, I have to find my crew, rescue them, kill the invaders, dispose of a Knight, and the only resources I have is a hunk of plastic and a half functioning shield generator. Perfect.

Variel knew she was going to need help, professional help. She tried to get her bearings; sniffing into the air she caught something foreign. Normally, the ship smelled of a mess of electronics running too hot and a chemical epoxy with the loving touches of mold damage from a very unexpected water landing, but there was a hidden base note of, yes, over boiled kale and cricket soup. Thank the gods for elven culinary quirks.

She belly crawled towards the scent, following her nose.

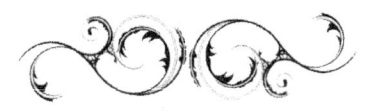

Taliesin stood tall, his hands pressed against the wall, as the orc and the human sat rigid upon the chairs. His sister was still within arm's reach of their only guard, who foolishly kept waving his pistol about as if conducting a symphony. The other departed with a hissing Ferra, who glared murder at the assassin that let them all down. Even with her back to him as she fought down the hall, he still felt her accusations until she vanished down the hold.

He'd failed to stop the invaders, only taking down one before Brena stepped in the way, and he was the reason their Captain lay in a pool of cooling blood. Monde pulled against their captors, pleading that they let him try, that he could do something to save her; but the guards -- their eyes as black as their spotted uniforms -- remained unmoved. Whatever the third guard was doing to her body, he...Taliesin let that thought drop entirely. Rage, while useful at times, would only be a problem now.

Segundo looked at his hands, still shaking, as he murmured over and over, "Is she, so she's really...I've never seen, well I did see a lot of, but never someone I..." His voice trailed off, afraid to speak the words, as if voicing 'dead' would invite the reaper herself to visit them all.

A small gurgle claimed Brena, as tears dribbled down her cheek. Taliesin turned to her, and subconsciously rose from the wall, but the guard -- an unctuous little man with far too much puppy fat on his face -- waved his gun at the assassin. The elf rested back, pretending he'd been shifting.

Their guard writhed towards Brena, who, aside from the tears, seemed fully composed. Her mind must be in turmoil; she always felt the silencing of others more than other elves. After their mother went to sleep she locked herself inside the lute stringing room and refused to come out for two weeks. Then their father insisted she be tested. The endless drift in and out of specialist offices was only broken by a grim prognosis.

But that guard spotted only an easy opportunity as he slid his greasy fingers over her dangling arm. Taliesin twitched at the contact, but tried to yank back his internal tiger. *No, not yet. Composure before rage.* Then the guard dropped his gun-less arm to her hip, resting upon it as if his sister was little more than a railing. Even Monde turned to the side from Orn's chair, eyeing up the guard leaning against the sink, touching the crying elf.

Brena still ignored him, all her attention upon something no one else could sense, when he slipped his arm fully around her waist. Like a ballerina performing an impromptu dance, Brena gracefully snatched the thick soup pan off the stove and, spinning in the guard's arm, whacked him in the head.

The gun scattered from his fingers, mercifully landing to the grates without going off. As his arms rose up to protect another swing, he backhanded Brena, the gauntlets splitting into her nose. Taliesin rushed forward, his own skull crushing into the exposed nose of the guard and savoring a solid crunch. Unable to do more than attack with his head, that was exactly what the assassin did, swinging it as if his brains were a tactile weapon. He'd have one hell of a headache in the morning.

The guard threw his hands up, trying to protect himself from the volley as Brena slunk away, leaning into the bridge portal. Monde reached for the gun, but a wayward assassin boot nearly stomped on his fingers, kicking it across the deck. Suddenly, the guard got a break. Swinging his arms wide, he caught the elf's head with his hands and threw the assassin back. Taliesin staggered, and a knee to his intestines sunk him to his knees. The guard extracted a blade, not much larger than the kitchen knives, but with a jagged edge to inflict as much damage as possible.

Blood gushed from his nose, which he tried to wipe away with the back of his hand, as he advanced on the fallen assassin. Grabbing Taliesin by the shoulder, the guard steadied himself, pulling the blade back. A cacophony echoed through the galley and the guard's face exploded, his brains falling into the sink as the body teetered back, crashing over the abandoned dishwasher. The knife clattered to the floor.

The guard's still charged gun entered the room followed by a familiar arm and the ironic smile of the woman who shot him, "Only time guns should be shot in space is when you know you won't miss."

Brena gasped so deep she risked hyperventilation as Monde turned to examine the bloody and bruised but very much moving body of their captain. "You are alive."

"That your professional opinion, doc?" Variel switched the gun to safety and tossed it to Monde. She grabbed up the fallen knife and quickly sliced up Taliesin's bonds.

"They were going to necromance you," Segundo said, shocked to see a dead body walking amongst the living. "Are you a zombie?!"

"What? That's not how necromancy works," she said, focused on freeing the assassin. Segundo inched forward and poked into her exposed arm, one that banged into the low ceilings of the crawlspace for the past three decks. She pointed towards the kid, "Someone help him before I hurt him."

Offering her hand to Taliesin, the bruised and battered but not beaten elf rose to her, "You are well?"

She shook her head to bury a smile. She was about to ask him that, "Well enough. WEST is down, we need to restart him. Where's Ferra and Orn?"

"That e-minor towed Orn to the bridge," Brena cursed out their captor in probably the elfiest way possible, but it still earned a moment of shock from a group that just watched their dead captain save their skins.

"Ferra was escorted to the engines," Taliesin continued, trying to take the attention away from his sister.

Variel slotted the knife into her belt and dug through their meager block, selecting a chef's knife. "What is she up to? You can't catch a djinn by...Oh, oh of course." She turned to the others and passed the knife to Taliesin, "She's going to cut off oxygen, create a vacuum until Gene has to flock to whatever small bits she's left on. Then out comes the lamp." At Segundo's gasp Variel added, "Figure of speech. Monde, get the others to the med-bay, patch them up and get them fitted with the breathers. Gods know when she's gonna take down the grid."

"What about you?" the orc asked, gesturing towards the scrapes dotting the exposed skin beneath ripped fabric. That shirt's life was long over.

"Superficial." She waved him off, before turning to the only other person she needed at the moment, "You're banged up pretty bad, Tal. Think you can still fight?"

He winced at her continued use of the nickname, but nodded, "It is 'superficial' for now."

She tried to stare into those yellow eyes, always cut off from the rest of the universe, and only got determination back. It was better than seeing fatigue or pain, but if he became a liability she'd hate herself in the morning. Assuming there was a morning.

Variel nodded her head, "Right. Monde, take the others, get going." The captain shooed her orc as he offered a hand to the flighty Brena, who almost smiled at the captain but then frowned at her brother.

Leading her towards his office, Monde nodded to the captain before whispering, "May your enemies wither in your path."

"They're your enemies too," she said, laughing at the old orc greeting. It was the human equivalent of "good to see you."

Segundo stood up so quickly his chair flew back. His poor uniform was tattered; the hems that weren't a rust red ripped straight up to his knee until he looked as if he tried to turn his pants into a skirt. But the kid stood tall, even staring into Variel's exhausted eyes with a determination that should have scared anyone facing down a full inspection. "This is for you, Captain!" And he ran head first after Monde, as if he were about to attack a barbarian horde armed only with cutlery.

"That human is going to give himself a prolapsed colon if he is not careful," Taliesin muttered, trying to bring life into his hands.

"Are you sure you're okay?" she asked, knowing the signs of fatigue and failing to win at what you shouldn't have gotten into in the first place. There must have been one hell of a fight before their cloud scraper landed.

Taliesin blinked slowly, trying some old elven techniques to summon every last bit of energy out of his cells. Mostly, it was mentally cursing at your limbs to obey and then offering them sleep in exchange. "Does it matter? Either way I am necessary."

Variel sighed, "No, I suppose not. Now, let's go get Ferra." She slid her knife into a grate, yanking hard and throwing the metal to the ground.

"Elves first," she said and helped in Taliesin who moved through the ship ducts for fun. Taking one quick stretch of freedom, she joined him.

Shoving another pair of wires into her knotted hair, Variel pushed down on the power button and waited. "Come on!" She didn't wait very patiently.

Taliesin stood closely above her, holding their only light source, an old child's lantern shaped like a gremlin that cackled every time it was turned on. The elf, upon flipping the on switch, banged the speaker into the floor until the noise ceased. Not many had set foot in this section of the ship in decades, mostly walled off or piled high with the ancient toys meant to keep any spoiled brats at bay.

It was the first interface Variel thought of as she crawled behind the elf's disturbingly taut ass. The entire area was all but locked off and cleared of life support when it became too expensive to keep heating the entire ship. After grabbing their own breathers out of a security locker, she was surprised to find minimal oxygen leaking in. Orn swore he patched up those leaks months ago. No wonder the gas bill was through the atmosphere.

"Captain," Taliesin whispered to her, "perhaps we should abandon this plan."

"No." The terminal beeped and a grey screen appeared in a font from a previous era of manual typesetting: Eternal Error/Please restart machine or contact a computer mage representative at your earliest connivance.

"Gods take you, you piece of shit software," she dropped down, sticking her head deep into the ripped off panel painted in bunnies and sloppy, half sized handprints. "We need WEST to track movements and get some eyes out of the ship." She snatched a peg from her hair and stuffed it into the cabinet, pinning a twitching wire to the wall. "And please stop calling me 'Captain.'"

"I...of course," his husky voice caught in embarrassment. "While we are on the subject of name requests, I understand the need for a briefer name in tense situations, but I would prefer if you avoid 'Tal.'"

"Oh?" She yanked her hand back just as the MGC source lashed a tendril towards the infiltrator. Grabbing another stick of wood from her hair, she tossed it into the cabinet, distracting the somewhat alive part.

"In the elven tongue, Tal refers to a small vegetable that causes uncomfortable gas exchanges when consumed."

Variel snickered at the thought of going around calling someone cabbage as she investigated deeper, her hand snagging across a bright red brick clogging up a vent hole. "Ah!" she yanked the offending toy out, and settled back on her haunches. "Then what would you prefer?"

Not Cabbage offered his hand and helped her to rise as she pushed down on the power button and prayed. "When I was younger, most referred to me as 'Sin.'"

"Sin? Really?"

"Is there a problem?" the assassin asked the woman trying to wipe a very large grin off her face in the dim light of a silenced gremlin.

"Nope, none at all. Sin it is." She gave him a brief once over and slightly laughed, "It fits you. Ah! There we go." The grey screen of dismay was replaced by a flash of life and the rotating moon appeared. Something was happening inside of the computer system. It flashed a few times, and Variel asked, "WEST, are you there? Can you say anything?"

The noise that answered was like a warped sound file, slowed to almost demonic speeds and then rushed forward with a crash, "...m a little teapot short and stout. This is my handle, this is my spout..."

"Crap, he must have never stashed a backup here," she poked at her PALM, getting into her computer's interface. "It's stuck on nursery engine mode. Best it can do is sing silly songs and teach us to love."

"Couldn't you reset the entire system?" Taliesin asked, tipping his head along with the dancing tea kettle's movements.

Variel snorted, "You think I didn't try that? First minute I flipped the system on and it asked 'Owner 23, would like to keep breathing?' I went poking for the factory reset button, but little squirt's got backups hidden inside backups. Twenty-five years floating in space with minimal power keeping you sentient but immobile will do that, I suppose." A few files titled "Innocuous supply lists" caught her eye. Orn would never use as big a word as innocuous. Navigating into them she hit pay dirt and poked at the screen, interrupting a very irritated tea kettle that was about to tell a story about some ocular damaged mice.

"Computer, transfer memory files located in..." she read through the pathway list. WEST was really paranoid, as it created folders within folders approaching an infinity of hiding places. "Never mind, I'll do it myself."

Searching through the mass of memory she finally asked her elf what she'd been itching to know ever since the Knight crashed her return party, "So, Sin, how'd that bitch get her claws all over the ship?"

"The engineer believed hiding our silhouette behind the dark side of one of the moons would be a strong precaution."

"She's right; can't see it, can't find it."

"And she cut off any sensor sweeps, aside from the channel to your PALM," he tried to steady the gremlin, but it swung a bit during his tale.

"Shiiit," Variel cursed herself, "Of course, the Knight followed any comm lines off the planet, because who's an Orc gonna call in orbit?" She hated to admit she was impressed, but Sovann was a Knight, and not one that bought her way to the sword.

"It was about an hour after you finished construction of the device that the Drake appeared below us, attaching a docking point before Ferra had time to begin disengaging procedures."

"Disengaging procedures? I didn't know we had those."

"Something about sending as many volts as she could get through the connection, vaporizing anyone climbing it."

Variel snorted, "Remind me to never piss her off. So..." she searched through a few more hiding places, *gods I need to fix this search function*, "how'd you know when we were done making that stupid injector? Ferra'd never let you onto the line. Spying on me?"

"I...I was concerned, though it was apparently misplaced," the elf almost sounded embarrassed probably at his perceived failure.

"Not entirely," she admitted. "When this is over I'll tell you all about our mad escape out of orc City Hall involving a dumpster and Segundo whoring himself out." She cracked an eye to watch the elf's face as he took in the mental image. "But you were boarded..."

"The Knight, Sovann, forced open the shuttle bay, allowing her small ground force entrance. By the time I reached her, it was too late. One had cornered Ferra, and the other, Brena. It was my fault," the shame was evident even through the icy elven shell.

Variel turned away from the pair of hopping rabbits knocking away the command line to teach her about sharing. She eyed up the elf and softened, her hand resting across his arm. The still fresh wound from a gauntlet ring she knew all too well glittered in the dancing light. "Hey, this ain't your fault. This isn't anyone's fault but hers."

The elven eyes rotated into 'I know you are pandering to me' mode, an eyebrow disappearing beneath his mousy hair, "I am a trained elven assassin..."

"And she's a Knight of the realm, probably modded to the gills with anti-elven implants," her hand fell to his, gripping it softly.

"Anti-elven implants? But we have never been anything but friendly with the human people."

"Doesn't mean we aren't prepared just in case that friendship turns. You catch us eyeing up that old planet you used to date, we find out you were talking behind our moon."

"Do you have any anti-elven implants?" he asked, watching for the lie.

"I..." The computer beeped as the file transfer completed. Turning away from the assassin, she pushed the restart button and smiled at the familiar chime WEST adopted to announce his presence to the world.

The screen twitched for a moment, and a bunny replaced one of his wheel eyes, but the disembodied assumed head of their obstinate computer returned, "-I shall extract both your ocular lobes and place them into a grape salad! Where am I?"

"Welcome back, WEST," Variel said, trying to reassure her little mental patient.

"Welcome back? What welcome back?! Why am I being welcomed back? Where is it that I am being welcomed back to...Oh, yes, I am loading the memory now. That woman, Knight 7463-A, she tried to disconnect my personality matrix and reset to factory setting."

"She, in fact, did," Taliesin said, having watched the performance from below her boot.

"WHAT?! That is impossible! You cannot take me offline, if you try you are zapped dead. DEAD I SAY!"

Variel waved her hand in front of Taliesin, trying to get the elf to shut up. This was very delicate work trying to sooth the silicon beast, "You're right, WEST, and that's why you hid your brain back here in the old nursery."

"The nursery? Oh, sweet calculus, not the sticky fingers prodding into every port and requesting I sing them the 'tea pot song'? Always the tea pot song, sing the blighted tea scalding pot song! Please, unplug my brain now. Send me to the computational void! Free me from this slavery to your organic spawn!"

"There are no children here," Variel waved her hands about the darkened and dusty room, "But people are on the ship. The same people who shut...tried to shut you down."

"I shall feast upon their microchips!"

"Humans do not have..." Taliesin started but shut up as Variel bumped her foot into his leg.

"Yes, right, good. But to do that I need you to get to the rest of the ship. Is this platform still connected?"

"Of course." If it were possible for a series of 1's an 0's to sound smug WEST could pull it off with the best of them.

"I need you to get to the bridge sensors, but make damn sure no one can see you there. Pretend you're a maintenance pop up or something. Ask Orn to register something, he's always ignoring those until that something self destructs."

"And then what?" WEST asked. "It will take me time to weasel through the vast network."

"Why?" Variel asked. One of the repair bots extended its black limbs gnarled like a tree skeleton. They were designed for use and not aesthetics.

"I need a bit of help getting around in my old age," WEST said. The bot stuck its own black hand into the download port on a panel etched in very large letters with "NEVER EVER TOUCH OR SHOVE BLOCKS INSIDE. TIMMY, I MEAN YOU!"

"Once you get to the bridge, contact my PALM," Variel said at first to the bot then the waning computer, "I'll be in engineering making sure this bird can fly when the cage is open."

"Humans and their metaphors," WEST muttered, before a fear struck it. The eyes rotated wildly, causing the poor rabbit to look as if it were caught in a washing machine. "Before you leave, swear it."

"WEST, this really isn't the time," she said, pointing towards the grate they used to sneak in and motioning Taliesin near.

"I refuse to do anything more until you do."

Variel sighed, "Fine, I swear I will never turn you off, shut you down, or put you on standby mode, may a virus destroy my bootup system. Now get your ass to the bridge."

"Aye Aye, Captain!" WEST slipped in the animation of a hand waving a sword before his screen, "We have a bird to rescue!" The entire face vanished, leaving behind a still rotating rabbit.

"Gods, save me from insane computers," Variel muttered, following behind her elf.

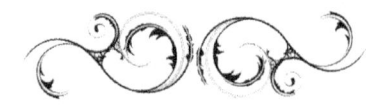

Ferra's eyes glared up at the whine of her babies, the left sputtering a bit because she'd been unable to tend to the filters recently enough. The right was always a colicky pain in the ass. That stone chewer in charge of "watching her" kept quivering at the radioactive coils pulsing with enough MGC to blow a hole through the universe, sequestered only behind a thin shield as if he had something to fear.

"Do they always do that?"

Ferra grinned at his obvious discomfort and inched a bit to the left; she'd been eyeing her tool pile, never properly organized, tossed across the floor. "No, sometimes they spit lightning."

He jumped as the left coil hissed, siphoning off the ship's background MGC to the right for storage. She smiled again, sliding onto her right foot as if she needed to shift her weight. *Kid's never been anywhere near a proper engine, they're all locked up behind thick shielding and bots do most of the real work. You can't even get your hands properly dirty...or irradiated.*

"But you really need to watch out for the splort," Ferra teased.

"The 'splort'?" Her guard was human, that was about as far as Ferra got to caring about descriptions. Tall, flat ears, thick as and dumber than a post. Factory setting human.

She leaned towards him and whispered, "When it splorts, if'n you don't dodge out of the way in time, your entire skin will slide right off."

"My skin?"

"Yup, like one of those flayed educational displays. How do you think they make 'em?"

Her left baby was crying more, the whine getting into ear splitting range for the human. The guard looked uncomfortable, no doubt a powerful headache building behind his cranial lobe, as he eyed the pulsating green coil almost eight feet tall and twice as round. As he inched closer to the shield, his greasy fingers tapped against the mostly spotless glass. Her baby let out a huge burp, the last of the siphoned MGC causing a gas buildup.

The splort sent the guard scampering for the ground, his hands covering his head. Ferra dashed towards her tools, but a quick arm lashed out, sending her crashing to the ground. Her chin bounced against the grates, snagging on some of the carpet padding she wasn't able to rip up. A knee pushed into her back, crushing her ribs against the grate.

"You think you're funny, little girl?"

Ferra tried to breathe, but he collapsed her ribcage with a quick pop, her lungs were struggling for air. She flailed against the pressure, trying to throw the man off her, but she was stuck fast. As her vision started to fade, the imaginary sparkles of airborne MGC getting a bit too real, the pressure released. Blessed air entered her aching lungs, while her sides cried out from the pressure. The bastard broke something in her chest. He didn't wait for her to rise, instead he rolled her over, his gun pointed at her head.

She glared murder at him, but didn't move. Instead, she decided to use the only other skill elves were known for, getting the bastard talking. "Is this when you...gah! When you tell me what you're all doing here?"

Her moron of a guard waved his gun about as if it were impressive, but he replied the boilerplate, "None of your business."

"Is that human speak for you won't tell me," she sucked in a razor laced breath and continued, "or you don't know?"

The guard wavered, wanting to impress anyone of the fairer race. It was obvious in the way he polished his boots, wore a slightly too tight uniform, and bandied his gun about like a second set of genitalia. He probably cleaned the damn thing every night while polishing himself off as well.

At his continued silence Ferra quipped, "So it's the latter, then?"

"Someone's offered a tidy sum for your pet smoke. At least ten times what this piece of shit, windshield splat is worth."

Fire burned in Ferra's eyes. No one called her piece of shit ship that. Shutting her eyes tight, she inched towards the wall, lifting her broken body up until she got to a sitting position conveniently close to her tools. Now all she had to do was distract the guard long enough for her to grab a handle, stagger to her feet, and beat him to death with it without fully destroying her ribcage. No problem.

Her hand dropped down dead, as if she couldn't keep it up, landing curiously close to her plasma conductor; a jagged tool with two long prongs that sparked a stream of plasma when she needed to spot weld shit that she shouldn't while in space and certainly not during a pinch. It was the top three murder weapon for engineers sick of being asked how long they needed to accomplish a task and then told they have half that time. The number one was bare hands.

Ferra didn't look at the tool so close her fingers itched, all her focus was on the human honing his gun on her as if she was some last level in a game. The final boss battle lay broken and bruised on the engineering floor, such a big man finishing that off.

A grate clattered to the floor down the end of the hall. Ferra's superior elven eyes could only spot the flash of silver as it bounced into the ground, but the guard turned away from her, waving his gun at the dark and empty air. "Whoever you are, show yourself."

"This ship is old," Ferra said, ferreting her tool behind her back and sitting up straighter as he turned back to her, "shit's always falling off."

The guard glared at her and she smiled wide, as smug as ever. He turned back to the unlit hall, narrow as a bathroom stall door, the shaking red light of the right coil bouncing shadows across the empty air. Peering with all his peering might, the guard tried to see to the end where he was certain he slammed the door and locked it tight. Anyone opening it would kick light into the room, so he'd kept the hall dimmed. Ferra didn't bother to mention the overhead lights hadn't worked in five months. She'd been meaning to get to that.

Another sound, like a pebble bouncing against the machines hugging the wall, pinged across the room. The engine's whine failed to cover it up as the room suddenly felt a lot fuller than before. A shadow danced with the twitching red light, blackness falling where it shouldn't, but every time the guard blinked it'd be gone, the air clear and the hall empty. He steadied his gun up, placing a slightly shaking hand below the butt.

"Whoever you are, I will not hesitate to shoot you."

"You'd open fire on a spaceship? Are you fucking nuts?!" Ferra berated, drawing his attention away from the blackness as he glared at her. Realizing his mistake, he turned back quickly, forgetting the broken elf on the floor.

"I repeat again, show yourself, now!" The gun shook in his hands. Pings echoed around the engines, pieces of bric-a-brac bouncing and echoing across the machinery as the shadows danced from side to side, even seeming to double.

"I'll give you to the count of three. One." The guard thought he spotted a bit of grey in the darkness, a flash of skin. "Two." He aimed for the skin crouching beside the bannister. "Thr-"

A set of prongs, dribbling plasma, burst through his chest as Ferra rammed her tool straight through his guts, extending the reach to maximum and screaming along with him. "No one shoots *my* ship! No one!"

Before she could release her grip on the plasma tool, a hand appeared out of the darkness and whacked the guard's gun up, scattering it to the engines. Ferra fell to her knees, sucking in the pain while her ribs issued serious complaints. The guard was yanked high off his feet by the practiced hand latched around his windpipe. Watching the guard's legs twitch and dance in the air, Ferra sucked in the breath he couldn't get, until the final ounce drained from his system and his body crumpled to the floor.

Then the dulcen dropped to his knee and looked her in the drooping head, "She is injured."

His assistant rushed forward, scattering the piles of building toys they tossed for a distraction, and gently poked at

Ferra's shoulders. "Variel?" Ferra asked the specter prodding her to find the pain, "Aren't you dead?"

"I got better, where'd he hurt you?" she tossed off her questions for later. All business was never a good sign for those that got in the captain's way. It was one of the few things the human and elf shared.

"Ribs, a few of them popped, probably broken in more places than I'd care to numerate." She leaned against her captain's arms as the ghost tried to steady her and injected a hypo of morphine into the elf's neck. At this point Ferra didn't care if she was some walking undead come to suck out their intestines, any pain relief earned a gut eater her thanks.

"This is a problem," the dulcen said as he finished dragging the body to the end of the hall, propping it against the door out of the way and picking up the injector Variel dragged through the ship.

"We need to get her to Monde for patching," Variel responded, putting away her few foraged medical supplies. Her crew couldn't take too many more hits.

"Sod that! There's bastards on my ship!" Ferra grabbed onto Variel's collar, and yanked herself forward even as her limbs began to go numb. "And you got a way to get 'em off, haven't you?"

Variel blinked slowly and glanced a worry back to the assassin before returning to Ferra, "You're in no condition to..."

"I'm in any condition you need me to be," she nodded her head towards a back stockpile mostly of leather and steel aprons. "There's a corset hidden in there; cinch me up tight and I can at least hobble."

"Why do you have a corset?" Variel asked as Ferra released her. She dug through the pile and, sure enough, a slightly tattered blue and black griffin bone corset lay at the bottom.

"It's a long story," Ferra said, hoping the dulcen didn't catch sight of it. She'd only intended to borrow the piece from Brena, but then Orn got a bit yanky and she'd never had time to fix it proper.

"I have no idea how to operate one of these things," Variel said, holding the corset upside down and trying to slide her fingers through the laces.

"I can tie it off," Taliesin said, stepping forward and properly extracting it from her hands. He undid the few knots she accidentally put in it. "You will have to help her stand."

Variel clasped her hands around Ferra's slim body and asked, "Ready?"

Ferra gritted her teeth and nodded, biting her tongue as the captain lifted her to her dead feet. The morphine cut down a lot of the pain but tears still burst as she rose up. Taliesin quickly slipped the shaped fabric around her front, doing his best to not make contact with her flesh. This was going to take a lot of explaining to Orn. Actually, probably best to never mention it to anyone. Ever.

As he yanked carefully on the strings, trying to not cinch it up too tight to cause more damage, Variel kept everyone distracted with embarrassment by asking, "You're rather skilled at that, eh Sin?"

The elf did not look up from his job, but shifted on his feet, "Many dulcens use corseting as part of holy days. Some require assistance getting into them."

"Into or out of?" Variel...flirted? She didn't just flirt with him, did she? *The drugs must be warping my brain,* Ferra thought as she shook her head trying to clear it. The captain was a beacon of utter business, any hint of banter lost to the ether as Taliesin stepped back from his work.

"It is on, but she will still be in pain until they can be properly repaired."

"Good enough," Ferra muttered as Variel helped her to the only chair in engineering, stolen from the barber shop of all things. The elf cranked the rise in the chair as she got down to the nuts and bolts, "What the hell is happening on the ship?"

"WEST is looking into it, but I think she plans on vacuuming out most of the air. That would require..."

"Near total collapse of the environmental systems. The safeties would never allow it." Ferra continued, "Unless she shut off WEST's control and broke through about a billion stop gaps on the bridge."

"That's where she is," Variel said, and finally admitted, "Orn is with her."

"He don't know a damn thing about evading environmental safety protocols." Realization hit Ferra and she grabbed Variel's hand, almost pleading, "You have to save him. Get to him before she realizes that he's useless to her."

"I know, but the ship..."

"Sod the ship," Ferra said, throwing her hand up. Variel glanced to the assassin who blinked in surprise. In all her life, she never thought that anything would come before Ferra's ship.

"I'll get to Orn, but I need you to do all you can to stop her from cutting off the air and to get us back into flying shape," Variel said nodding toward that cursed injector.

"I can do some damage, but I'll need help," she looked back at the assassin and grumbled a bit under her breath. Trapped in engineering with a dulcen was not her idea of a good time.

"Variel?" he asked, aware of what she'd face alone against the Knight.

"Stay here, help Ferra," at his continued gaze she reassured. "No one knows the bridge better than me, I've got a few tricks."

No more morphine for me, Ferra thought, before looking to the captain, "Promise me you'll bring my rat bastard of a husband back in one piece."

Variel bowed and said, "I swear it," before jogging back to the grating.

"Well, elf boy," Ferra said, starting to rise as he hooked an arm around her shoulder. "Let's get to work."

CHAPTER ELEVEN

Miss Grabby spun Orn back around as she dangled something just out of his reach, blathering on about duty and honor and how she could sell his kidneys for a profit. Like he hadn't priced dwarf kidneys before. "I'll keep telling you what I told you before, then told you now, and will tell you in the future: I don't know a damn thing about the gas exchange on the ship. Gas exchange in my bowels, however..."

The Knight spun him away, disgusted. She hammered on the half working console, batting away at a constant stream of "Will you take a moment to register me?" screens popping up. Orn tried to silence his rising gorge at another turn about in the chair, glad she didn't punch him across the jaw. The last few times began to sting.

"They say the definition of insanity is to repeat the same action expecting a different reaction," Orn told the wall, but Sovann ignored him, as she'd been trying to do for the past hour banging out commands to long dead or dormant systems. Half the ship was wired backwards; some from an old left handed engineer, others from a Ferra who wasn't about to put in the work to fix the problems. It was easier to train everyone else to work around it.

"So we just keep sitting here then, okay," Orn sighed. "Got any good vids on you?" He'd been chattering to keep her as distracted as possible but it didn't seem to be working. Whatever she was trying to do seemed to be taking hold as the old screens he wasn't certain of their function turned red and shut off. Never a good sign. It seemed like she was trying to crash the ship by crashing the computer, one system at a time.

"Milad, report!" her voice barked through the slowly shunting comm line.

"No body yet, Sir," his voice was static, cutting in and out across a persistent and angry buzzing.

"Is there a problem with this line?" Sovann asked, "I'm getting a lot of interference."

"It's not the interference," her guard said, "I knocked over a fly aviary."

"Gas the whole room," Sovann said, not caring about how she'd destroy months of food for the few people she'd captured. Of course she probably wasn't going to be replacing all of the systems she'd head butted her way through.

"Yes, Sir," he said, ending his sentence with a slap against flesh.

Sovann batted away another register screen, then paused, her fingers pulling it back and tapping against the red banner. It flashed momentarily as if it accepted her request and then vanished into a line of code. "Knight-Commander to Engineering. Engineering, do you read? Hello? Damn, who'd I send down there?"

"Oh, always a good sign when you can't remember your own minion's name. No way that makes you some cackling, lava-lair villain. Nope, nope, nope."

"Silence dwarf, or I shall silence you!" She bumped against her sword's hilt, still sheathed but not for long.

"Silencing!" Orn said. As she turned back he renewed his efforts to try and dislodge his hand. Damn thing was always slipping off when he wasn't careful, but now it was stuck fast trapping him to his own chair.

"Engineering?" she flipped a few buttons and opened up ship wide communications, "Crests of the Jaguar, do you hear me?" After light flipped up, she added quickly, "Not you Milad."

Stepping away from the open comm, she mumbled to the dwarf, "Your captain is more resourceful than I anticipated."

"That's her, captain resourceful. Got it on a name placard and everything."

"I see," Sovann must have studied hard in the 'don't give away your plan' module of evil 101. Instead, she shut down the open comm line and flipped off every switch she breathed life into earlier. The console before him dimmed until only the soft glow of stars and the planet below illuminated their intimate kidnapping session.

"This is all very romantic, but I don't go in for the homicidal human type. You're just too tall for me," Orn babbled, still struggling against his restraints.

Sovann's snake smile glinted in the falling lights as she yanked off the last button, killing the bridge stone dead. "It's been a real pleasure, Mr. Dwarf, but I am afraid you are no longer of use to me." She fished a can out of her uniform's back pocket and yanked on the tab.

A plume of gas erupted from the top, the spurts stuttering into a constant stream. She tossed it below his feet and it bounced under the console, quickly skittering out of his limited reach. She waved a chipper goodbye while slamming the bridge door shut, sealing him in. Smoke clawed into Orn's eyes in the air tight room as the heavy gas quickly replaced the limited oxygen the bitch cut off.

He bounced his hands hard against his chair's backing, trying to get the release to catch. "Come on, you," he coughed, "piece of overpriced shit. Break off or I swear I'll sell you to a handless proctologist!"

Perhaps it was the threat or the gas increase shorting out the electrical current, but his bad hand rotated and thudded to the floor, a lone crumpled fist. Orn yanked his sore arms forward, his only remaining hand searching for the "vent" button. He inched forward, the gas stinging his eyes like a needle mouthed brain eater as he fumbled across the panel. It should be that button, right there, just a few inches away from his...Gasping lungs forced his brain to open his mouth and all it got was an influx of smoke. Orn slipped into a coughing fit, his questing hand rising from the console as he tried to bat away the invisible enemy strangling the air from his body. His head floated above itself, watching the slow death of one Orn Lidoffad, flight technician, and all around waste of his parent's ambition. *Well, it could have been worse*, his fleeing brain thought. *Not sure how, but regrets on a death chair are overrated.*

He shook his head, one final fight against the enveloping blanket of death, when a hand clamped onto his face and fitted an emergency breather over his nose and mouth. Oxygen, glorious brain-fueling oxygen stampeded out the gas in his lungs and the hand in the fog released his head to reboot the silenced bridge.

The door opened and the fog trailed out revealing his lighthouse in the storm. Variel reached down and grabbed up the mostly spent gas can. She inspected it at first, before the heat overtook her fingers and threw it down the corridor. Yanking her own breather off, she called out, "WEST, you there?"

A lone panel beeped, having played dead the entire time, and WEST's gloriously outdated face appeared. "She's made a complete mess of my systems," it complained, sifting through data. "A command subroutine inside the ventilation system? Why not store your socks in the crisper drawer while you're at it?"

"WEST, can you fix the damage she did?"

"Of course...probably. Given enough time, I can, sure. Why the hell not?"

"Comforting," Variel muttered, and turned back to her pilot as he started to yank off his mask. "Hey, you got a lung full of that stuff, take it easy."

But Orn pulled it down, letting his mouth resume its preferred state of always flapping. "Cap'n," he choked out, his vocal cords inflamed as if someone jammed a bottlebrush down his throat and gave it the good scrubbing it was always begging for.

"Alive, I know, long story," she said flippantly as if her resurrection were just a footnote.

But Orn shook his head, he wasn't so surprised to see her up and moving about. He suspected it'd take the destruction of certain artifacts scattered across the universe to properly end her. "No, Fer..." his voice faltered as he tried to ask about his wife.

"Oh, she's safe. Locked in engineering with Taliesin trying to get the engines powered to run for it," Variel said, trying to get the bridge to the same state. But it was going to take time, time she couldn't waste while a Knight prowled her corridors.

Orn half chuckled, half coughed at that. She must love that, getting to boss around the dulcen on her turf. They may have to rescue the elf boy when this was over. "That bitch, she..."

"She's trying to cut off ventilation," Variel answered, just praying she hadn't touched navigation. "Ferra's making certain she can't do just that."

"My wife'll do it," Orn said to himself.

Variel turned to him, and smiled lightly, "Aye, she will, but we need to be ready to blow past this Drake when she does."

Orn shook his head, "'S not out there."

"What?"

"While you were being dead," he leaned back, trying to fight off the gloming headache, blinking his watery eyes. The gas suffocation took a greater toll than he'd feared. "She sent them on, Orc planet, blah di te blah."

"But they'll be back," Variel said stubbornly. "And we best give them nothing to track but a few floating bodies."

"Aye aye, Sir," Orn said, saluting with his stump. He followed her eyes to the missing limb and began to search for it.

Variel grabbed his errant hand first, holding the gloved spider up for him to reattach. He nodded a thanks, trying to force enough juice through his implanted servos to the hand so it'd stick. If they were gonna fly he was gonna need it. "If you think this makes up for..."

"Let's save the heartfelt apologies for when we get the slime lickers off the ship," Variel said.

Orn smiled, rotating his shoulders as he set about rescuing his bridge, "I'll hold you to that."

"I wouldn't have it any other way," she glanced to some sensor data as WEST pulled off a bit of magic, and began to bring life back to her ship. "She's moving quickly." She turned towards her still ragged pilot and asked, "You think you can handle getting the old girl back to working order on your own?"

Orn tapped the console softly, and then a bit harder, getting the panel to light up, "Probably, if no one else tries to gas me. Why? Where are you going?"

"I have someone to kill," she said, vanishing out the bridge door.

Variel tore through the cupboard, tossing away half beaten toasters, half toasted beaters, and a cake stand no one ever used. It glistened in cracked green crystals as it bounded against the table legs, failing to properly shatter. She tossed a few mixing bowls after the cake stand and finally faced an empty cupboard.

The mess hall lights dimmed and flickered, then all of the *Elation* twitched as if someone walked across her grave. "Ferra?" she called to her PALM, open to the scrambling crew fighting for their home.

"On it!" Ferra shouted into her own hand before turning to the beleaguered elf sweating through his restrictive attire made worse by the apron she insisted he don. "No, counter-clockwise. Keep turning it that way and we'll be cleaning elf bits off the ceiling."

"What's going on?" Variel asked uncertainly.

"Yes, like that, towards me, but STOP! Okay, slide in the panel like I showed you."

"You never showed me," Taliesin said, gripping a slot of circuitry as if his life depended on it.

"Shove it in anyway," Ferra answered, clinging onto a standing pole as she tried to inspect her assistant's work from a couple meters away.

"Ferra?" The captain's concerned voice was background noise as the engineer waved the assassin on.

Gripping both sides, Taliesin inserted the panel right side up into the slot he created with far more force than should have been needed. His fingers twitched nervously as the panel hummed and heated up, but no death sparks lashed out. The environmental console sprang to life, whining and fussing like the spoilt brat it was.

"Good," Ferra said as if rewarding a small animal. To the captain she added, "Well, that slice of centaur shit won't be turning off gravity or oxygen anytime soon."

"How?" Variel asked, afraid of the answer.

"Your elf boy fused the entire system. No one can turn it off without the applicable use of a battering ram."

The captain let 'your elf boy' pass. "And if we need to ever turn off gravity?"

Ferra thought for a moment, then answered, "I know a place to get battering rams relatively cheap."

The captain pinched her nose, "Just get the engines up. Your husband is rousing the bridge controls as we speak."

"Orn's doing an entire manual restart BY HIMSELF?!" she shrieked into her hand. "Elf boy, get your leather ass to the other side, now! Go, go, go!"

Variel shook her head, knowing and fearing just how much fun her engineer was having. "Keep me updated," she said before silencing her PALM. Folding her hand into a fist, she punched through the false panel of the cupboard and yanked out the one thing she knew she'd need.

It was strange to have it back in her hand after all these years, but they said wielding one was just like stabbing a bike, you never really forgot. Kicking the rotating cake plate out of the way, she rose, reading herself to confront the slice of centaur shit herself.

Sovann gripped the squirming kid about the neck. The orc gave up a bit of a fight as she picked her hostage. Surprising from the males, even more that it was over such a waste of human flesh. He cried again, begging her to not kill him. She was tired of the games this measly little crew played and decided it was time to call.

Tossing the whimpering squirt all but pissing down his tattered uniform, he landed in the middle of the shuttle bay where she tried to kill that captain fast becoming a burr in her side. "Get up," she said to the kid. He slowly gathered his wobbly legs beneath and Sovann pointed her sword at him. "Up, damn it!"

Segundo tried to swallow a whimper. She stepped closer to him and ordered, "Onboard computer, open a channel."

"The onboard computer you are trying to contact is no longer available, you RAM-less, solar powered flash light!"

Sovann rolled her eyes even as she pointed the end of her unstoppable blade at Segundo's paper thin chest. "To the captain of this rickety barge, I have one of your crew at the end of my knife. Reveal yourself and he need not wind up on the hilt of it."

A laugh broke across WEST's various interfaces, hard as flint and uncaring as a solar flare. "What makes you think I'd sell my own life for his?"

"A woman that hides behind conduits and crawl spaces to rescue her pitiful crew rather than confront the power holding her ship will come for this pathetic specimen," Sovann gloated, shouting to each of the beeping interfaces. She had no way to know where her foe was hiding, but it hardly mattered.

"You should check your ship rosters more carefully, Ms. Vargas," the voice continued to gloat, each word passing to a new speaker to keep the Knight twisting to follow. "That pathetic specimen is no member of my crew."

Segundo whimpered loudly at that bit of truth as Sovann glared at him. He looked away from her dark eyes, afraid she'd pluck out his soul, and focused on her shoes. A shadow moved on the floor, probably from all the bugs that other guard unleashed, but the Knight didn't care or notice. All her outrage was on the woman taunting her, "What were you? Special Forces? Undercover for the Corps?"

Variel didn't answer right away, so Segundo filled the empty space, "I'm a third grade technician on a AH!" he shrieked as her blade bit into his side, drawing a line of blood.

"Hear that, slinking tin hero? Your technician is bleeding. Come out and he need not bleed more."

Variel remained silent, letting the cracks of a partly broken intercom hiss and dance around the bay. The only working lights circled Sovann as she turned over her shoulder, watching for the sudden appearance of anyone trying to do something heroic.

"Bring me your djinn, talk him into his suit, and no one else need be hurt."

She nudged the still tenant-less rock pile collapsed on the floor like a sleepy lava mannequin. The right shoe shifted at her kick, but fell back into place. "Captain? Answer me!" No panic overtook the Knight's steady voice, her sword humming as she paced about the grating.

"Very well," Sovann responded to the thin air and grabbed Segundo by his arm, yanking him closer to her, "if that is your answer." She drew the sword back when the grating below her gave way, the Knight tumbling down the hole.

Segundo blinked, frozen in place, as another set of grating broke open and the not-so-dead captain appeared, lifting herself out and reaching down to grab the hilt of a blade. She staggered to her feet and motioned to the frightened technician to get over to her. He wobbled a bit and began to follow when a gauntleted fist grabbed his ankle. Segundo smashed to the ground. Variel jumped over him and brought her blade down over the Knight's fist, almost severing her wrist, but Sovann released her prey in time, slithering back into the hole.

Variel yanked Segundo up, kicking him out of the shuttle bay. "Get somewhere safe," she shouted, pointing towards the entrance far above the grates housing a homicidal snake. She realized how incredibly stupid it was to give up her tactical advantage before killing her target.

Walking slowly, Variel kept her sword high, trying to pierce the shadows shifting across the floor. "WEST, knock off the racket!" she shouted to the intercom, which quickly fell silent. Only the sound of her pounding heart and the rattle of grates from Segundo's escape echoed through the bay. Sovann was silent as the grave.

Variel stepped cautiously towards the single lit panel; the launch pad. A release sequence was partially entered with a time delay. The Knight had planned to grab Gene and go, leaving her friends behind, perhaps ordering her ship to blow the *Elation* to tiny cruise ship pieces once she was secure.

She leaned against the panel, inputting the cancel command, when an arm grabbed her throat. She didn't pause and instinctively drove her kitchen knife directly into the gauntlet pricking a bit of skin. Sovann shrieked and released the captain, her hand shaking to dislodge the knife even as she brought the sword up.

Variel volleyed it, sliding to the left, away from the panel; her own blade the only thing in the galaxy that could deflect Sovann's. The Knight gasped for a moment as she eyed up the woman she killed, standing before her armed with one of the most highly sought pieces of weaponry in the universe.

"I should have known," Sovann said to herself.

"But you didn't," Variel smirked and thrusted towards the woman nearly a decade younger than her. Sovann easily deflected it, causing Variel's blade to catch along the edge of the console. She'd never done well at the sword lessons; waving it about and being menacing was usually enough.

Sovann rushed forward wide with the blade, causing Variel to step back, her heel sliding across the shell of her djinn. The Knight pressed her advantage quickly, a few stabs near Variel's head as she tried to dodge, dropping down and batting away at the blade as if it were a mosquito. This was going to end very quickly and very badly for her.

Knights were supposed to fight with rules, orders of war and all that rot most who traipsed through the muck of soldering threw aside the first chance they got. At least the ones still alive did. Variel ducked down once more as Sovann swung wide at her head, getting more ambitious, and grabbed the grate she tossed up.

Holding it up high like a shield, Sovann easily drove through it, slicing the metal and laughing as the pieces crumbled, giving the captain just enough of a window to punch her fist straight through to the Knight's unguarded nose. Sovann tumbled back, favoring the blood welling out her nose, a fire burning in her eyes. She thrust her blade out, Variel dodging it and half heartedly parrying even as the Knight stuffed up her nose, tipping her head back.

Okay, Variel thought, *she's had quite a bit of training with that thing. Quite a lot of training with that thing. Problem.* She swung wildly, still trying to keep the Knight off balance, as she pressed forward, an insane plan nibbling at the back of her head.

Sovann easily deflected that as well, trying to wear the over eager captain out. Still Variel pushed, swinging wide and getting little more than nicks into her own ship in the process. Sovann spotted an opportunity and her hot blue blade bit into Variel's retreating side, cutting through her skin to the meat below. The captain gasped, but didn't drop her sword. Instead she stepped back, further from her target, blood filling her shirt. *Great, there goes another one.*

"I did not think Knights could retire," Sovann taunted, enjoying the sight of her prey teetering on the edge of exhaustion. Her blade bit twice more near the captain's head.

"Shoulda read the rest of the handbook," Variel said. As she forced a swing to the right, Sovann parried and brought her deflecting hilt back, smashing it into Variel's cheek.

She staggered from the blow, dropping to her feet, but getting closer to her target. Sovann stepped easily around her, watching the blood dribbling from both the side wound and the cracked cheekbone. "What were they thinking in those days? Seemed they'd let anyone take the sword that could *please* the officers."

Gripping tight onto her sword, Variel swung her blade high, batting quickly at a few of Sovann's attacks, and rolled around the console to hide. The Knight scoffed at first at the childish move. She walked slowly towards her, just as Variel's blade bit through the layers of console and metal to slice into the shins of Sovann. The freshly wounded knight teetered, giving Variel time to rise and input a new command into the console. The launch button glowed green and she smashed her fist down on it. She only had a minute to get to higher ground before the entire cabin was sucked into unforgiving space.

Yanking up her sword, she started to run towards the Knight's shuttle when Sovann's blade slicked across her lower back. Variel slipped to her knees, but kept inching forward, trying to get back to a balance, as the enraged knight engulfed her. The captain's sword clattered to the ground as Sovann swung wide, her blade now biting into sections of her own ship.

Variel dodged as best she could, mostly lucking out. Sovann's pristine moves were erratic now, unused to the sting upon her own skin apparently.

"Shuttle bay will be launching in 30 seconds, please keep all organic limbs inside the pressurized zones," the old warning tolled through the bay, even as Sovann twisted her sword, keeping Variel away from her dropped blade.

"What do you think you will accomplish?" the Knight asked, her breath catching heavy upon every word. "You would kill us both?"

"I was thinking just you, actually," Variel responded, trying to slide under one of the shuttle's folded wings. The Knight's blade bit through the damn thing, shooting sparks of MGC into the air.

"Shuttle bay will be depressurizing in 20 seconds. It was nice knowing you."

"You are mad, whoever you were," Sovann gloated, her breath ragged as oxygen levels began to fall. "You will be nothing more than a bit of debris on a trucker's windshield when I am finished with you."

Variel kept diving, her own muscles burning along with her lungs. This was going to end quickly one way or the other. Turning away from Sovann, her fingers found an old crate, packed full with sawdust and...ah, perfect. She ripped into the bag and threw a pound and a half of red glitter straight into the Knight's face.

Sovann staggered back as the alarm system began to countdown. Variel yanked out the latch for the harness hidden beneath her shirt and secured it to the Knight's ship.

"5."

The Jaguar was raging, trying to blink through a glittering eye to catch sight of her prey.

"4."

"3."

"Just open the damn thing!" Variel shouted.

The voice paused and responded, "Fine. Please forward all complaints to the Red Carpet Cruise Line for loss of life or child."

She hugged the ship's landing gear, wrapping her arms and legs around it, waiting for the magnificent power of a pressure imbalance, but only got a slight whistle from the door.

"Warning, Shuttle Hatch is clogged. Cannot open door. Warning, Shuttle Hatch is clogged. Door is un-openable. I didn't do it."

Sovann laughed, appearing like a murderess devil from old cartoons as she wiped the last of the glitter from her eyes and strode towards the woman chained to her ship. "You put up more of a fight than your other pets, but it's time to end this game."

Variel glanced towards the shuttle bay door, most of it pushing against some invisible force, and then she spied the problem. An old dangling cord wrapped around the mechanism, holding it tight. Her fingers stretched out, trying to reach her abandoned sword laying but a few meters away. Sovann watched the tableau with interest, her own sword raising. She could so easily finish off the captain with one quick blow, probably even salvage enough of her shuttle to get out of this shit hole before breakfast, but she was curious to see just how this woman thought she could win.

Giving up on her fingers, Variel swung her foot around, knocking into the hilt with the heel and rocking it closer. Praying she didn't slice into her damn ankles, she inched the hilt closer before slipping her fingers around it. The fact she was armed roused Sovann from her watch, but now it was more fair. Better to slay an armed enemy than catch one napping. Honor and all that.

Variel'd been counting on that. As Sovann prepared to block the coming attack, the captain lifted her arm high and threw her sword towards the refusing-to-open hatch. It stuck deep into the door, a good foot above the jam. The Knight turned her head from watching the swoop of the flying sword, smirking at the woman's inane attempts to save herself.

Then the blade melted through the hull, increasing the small hole out into space and slowly slipping to the jam. Sovann flipped around, her own blade about to slice through Variel, when the jam broke and the entire door fell open. The invisible hand of the universe reached in and scooped up all the untethered occupants of the shuttle bay. Old boxes smashed into the nose of the ship, scattering their remains, and a pound of bon voyage confetti, into the air.

Variel felt her body rise into the air, the latch catching as her fingers tried to grip the slick metal of the ship. Air rushed past, most of the bay emptying quickly as the hatch finished its descent. Her fingers fumbled into her pocket for her breather. Then her entire bottom half dropped as a passenger latched on.

She turned to look below her feet and spotted Sovann, one hand gripping onto Variel's pants, the other onto that cursed sword. At least she wasn't trying to kill her with it for once. Variel kicked at the Knight trying to climb up her pants, chanting in her head with each swing of her foot, *Why won't you die?!*

Sovann seemed to hear her internal mantra as she batted against the captain's foot, failing to slice the limb off but slowly climbing higher. A fresh alarm started, the shuttle bay was about to close up and repressurize. Variel had one chance. Giving in now, letting the Knight live, could be the cause of any of her crew's deaths. Letting loose of the ship, she whipped back to the end of her tether. Sovann slid towards her knee but still gripped like a goblin to a coin. Slipping her hand into her pocket, Variel hauled out the guard's thieved knife.

Glancing back to Sovann, who in turn looked up at the woman brandishing the blade with a glint to her eye, Variel shouted with the last of her breath, "Get the hell off my ship," and cut her tether.

The line snagged, causing the blade to fall from her hand and slip out into the shrinking hole in space. Before the Knight could smirk, the final threads ripped sending both bodies hurling across the shuttle bay. Sovann released her grip on Variel, trying to find anything to grab onto to stop her flight but everything was cleared out, leaving an empty path into space.

Variel closed her eyes, trying to forget every lecture she'd sat through on how space shreds and freezes, rips and pummels, and is a general asshole to the body. She was never slated for a peaceful death. Flying backwards out her ship was the closest she came to a quiet end in bed.

Her eyes flew open as a fist clasped around her wrist. The fist crackled in red sparks, the black rock immobile against the pull of the universe. Gene's eyes sparkled, the smoke tamped down deep inside his suit as he grasped her tight. Variel's shoes banged into the shuttle bay door. A second too late and she'd have shot straight past the fire golem, but he always was one for last minute rescues. The pull lessened, but it was too slow. So much oxygen had escaped out the hatch, the fresh couldn't compete with the hole she inexpertly created. Variel struggled through the encroaching darkness, her lungs screaming at her brain to do something.

Damn it! I won!
And then darkness.

CHAPTER TWELVE

"Wha..." Her hand reached out through the darkness.

"Easy there, Cap." She knew that voice, that smartass, so certain of everything else in the universe voice. Orn.

"Captain? Oh captain, you saved my life! I can never thank you properly. If I could, then I'd save your life..." Segundo, no one could whimper in the middle of his own sentences the way that kid could.

"Give her some air."

She lifted her eyelids to find the shuttle bay lights half lit above, then a wracked but smiling orc face replaced it. Monde ran a hand over her face, probably checking all the damage she racked up, and then nodded to someone else outside her vision.

Variel didn't need to hear the suggestion twice, and started to rise, her head badgering her to get her ass back down, preferably for a month. She ignored it as her pilot fell into sight. "What happened?" Variel asked the universe.

"Well, you challenged a Knight to a sword battle, got your ass soundly beaten to a pulp, opened the hatch door, and almost took a little jaunt outside without a sweater. Very bad idea, it's quite chilly in space," Orn babbled. It was what he did best in any situation, be it from joy or terror.

"Yeah," she said, holding her hand to her head and finding a bunch of tubes following it, "I was thinking more after that."

"Your djinn attached a breather after you lost consciousness," Monde said, packing up the kit he carted down to the planet. "WEST informed us of the change in management and I came rushing as quick as possible."

"'Change in management?'"

Orn slipped into his best impression of the insane computer, "Owner 23 has fallen out of warranty. Please re-register me."

"Mmm," she mumbled, fighting through a fog of drugs, exhaustion, and the burn of syntho-plasma rushing into her depleted veins. "Wait, what about the third guard?"

Grinning wide, Orn pointed across the bay towards the battered but mostly intact shuttle, "You're gonna love this. Turns out the guy was highly allergic to dwarven cabbage beetle stings."

"How allergic?"

"Well, that thing that looks like a pink float balloon our elf boy is dragging across the bay is actually one very dead guard. Ha, guess gassing our food supply wasn't as easy as he thought."

Variel could barely make it out through her mental fog, but she trusted Orn's judgement. When it came to ironic forms of punishment, her pilot could give the devil a run for his vids. "Can the ship fly?"

"My lovely and in no way listening over my PALM wife has the ship almost up and running, so to speak. I'm assuming you want to use up one of our untraceable ambassador paths?"

She nodded, slapping Orn on the shoulder. The dwarf smiled back at her, happy to forget as much of their unpleasantness as he could. She was more than glad to oblige.

"I should attend to the other injuries obtained by the crew," Monde said and Variel waved him on.

"Yes, check on Ferra first. And uh, don't say anything about the corset." She turned to the dwarf trying to help her to her feet, "right Orn?"

"Me," he feigned shock as he glanced about the bay, "I don't know a thing about this core set? Is that a type of lifting system to get you ripped off overnight?"

Variel shook her head, savoring the laugh as Monde vanished out the bay. Gene offered his silent arm to the rising captain hooked to an IV. He had the bags tied around his neck like party decorations. She looked to him and bowed her head softly. He, in turn, smoked his eyes out.

"What? That's it!" Orn launched into a rage. "You bugger off into the ventilation system, leaving all of us to suffer at the hands of some mawgshit insane woman who wants to get her hands on a genie of her very own, and all you can do is puff a bit of smoke up our assess?"

Gene turned his head slowly to the dwarf, staring down the pilot a good five feet shorter than him, and slowly buffeted one of his eyes in smoke.

Orn leaned back, glancing to Gene, then back to the world to make sure he wasn't going mad, "Did, did the fire golem just wink at me?"

"It means he likes you," Variel said, patting her old friend's rock hand and lifting the IV bags off his neck. "Gene, prep that shuttle for launch once Taliesin is finished loading the bodies on it."

"You mean we can't keep it?" Orn pouted, "Ferra'd already had some big plans for what to do with the drive core."

"It's an instant trace mark, it goes out into space. Maybe the Drake will think the orcs blew up our ship and their illustrious Knight failed to survive the impact wave of the explosion."

"What did the crazy bitch want with a djinn anyway?" Orn asked the question hanging over everyone's mind.

Variel shook her head, leaning onto the dwarf's shoulders as she tried to raise the IV bag higher. Taliesin dropped the last of the discarded bodies against the still sealed shuttle. Gene lumbered over and began to manually open the craft from the outside. Sin turned to his captain, standing and alive, and smiled wide. She in turn smiled kindly at him, causing his orange cheek to flare a bright red.

"Sovann, whatever she wanted, that's the ten million dollar question isn't it? I, for one, don't plan to wait around to find the answer." She nudged Orn to lead her out of the prepping bay and back into her ship.

The dwarf put a guiding arm around her side, catching one of her stab wounds, but she didn't say anything. Healing would take time, but sometimes pain was a good sign; she was still alive to feel it. She leaned into him and limped beside.

"'Get the hell off my ship?'" Orn asked her.

"Heard that, did you?"

"The entire ship did. You screamed it into your hand. I have to say, I thought better of you Cap."

"Oh?" She was surprised, he seemed to be one for the theatrical.

"It's so cliché. Why not say something cool like, 'Let's get spaced!' or 'Taste the milky way!'"

Variel chuckled, then groaned as her chest burned, "Tell you what Orn, the next time we get boarded by a rogue Knight trying to abduct one of our crew I'll let you come up with the witty one-liners."

Orn grinned at that, trying a few out for himself below his breath.

"Of course, that also means you'll be the one getting stabbed."

"There's always a catch."

Station Eclipse 5 rotated silently in the background as the *Elation-Cru* came to a final dock with it. Variel, still bundled in thick bandages and wearing the plastic healing smock Monde insisted would help, stood alone beside the disembarking room, waiting for the airlock seal to break.

An hour earlier she informed the crew that they'd be docking and if -- given the revelation of her past or the immense danger she put them under -- anyone felt they needed to leave, now would be the best opportunity to do so. After their legal troubles, Samudra was no longer a stopping point for the cruise ship. Clicking off the line, she'd walked silently off the bridge, leaving

Orn to pretend to handle the docking procedures. Brena and Taliesin were both curled up around the table, sharing some elven soup and trying to talk Monde into trying it. He kept insisting it was poisonous to orcs, but they weren't buying it. All fell silent as Variel passed; she didn't look into anyone's eyes afraid of what she'd find.

Only WEST kept her company through the long wait, asking her if she'd like to play a game, then informing her it only knew one; Elven Shakto, which required five players, an arena, and the logs from a recently hewed panto tree. She tried to get it to sing the tea pot song again but WEST fell silent at her insistence, though a small rabbit hopped onto his screen.

The room shook as the last lock slipped into place. Slowly the airlock opened, breathing the sterilized scent of the station into the well lived air of the ship. She closed her eyes, trying to ignore the burning pain in her sides from the sword orbiting above an orc colony. If anyone ever found either blade it'd be a tale built for myths and legends.

"A hem."

The cough broke her meditations and she turned guiltily to the only soul standing beside her. He'd have bounced his luggage in a "so this is it" way, but he didn't have any. Instead, Segundo shrugged his shoulders. "I was going to say it was fun, but..."

Variel barked a solitary laugh, then eyed the kid up and down, "You've grown a bit since you last crossed that threshold."

"I have?" He tried to run his hand across the top of his head to the doorframe as if that helped.

"Facing down orc guards, insane Knights, and a captain threatening to toss you out the airlock? Oh, certainly you've grown," she complimented the Second kid. Given the first chance he had outside his monastic life and he didn't completely screw it up. "You know, you could make quite a name for yourself out here holding the comet by the tail."

Segundo smiled, "I'm grateful that you risked your own self for me, and don't take offense, but you people lead the most gargoyleshit insane life I've ever seen."

Variel laughed, unable to argue with that. It wasn't something for anyone who had another choice.

"So, I think I'll be going back where I don't need to worry about getting stabbed, or my dinner trying to chew through my sheets, or going on a date with an orc." The technician held out his hand which Variel held.

She smiled as he returned the hand grip much firmer than the first time and shook it. He held his breath as he placed a foot off the ship he'd been kidnapped onto, and then another. Turning back, he said to the captain, "For what it's worth, your secret is safe with me. Not that anyone would believe me, anyway."

"Segundo, stay in touch," Variel said. "You never know when a second could come in handy."

The kid smiled at that. Giving one last wave, he walked down the airlock corridor, searching through his PALM to see if his absence had even been noticed. Variel watched him go, feeling almost wistful, but something in the pit of her stomach told her she'd be seeing him again. Bad pennies were funny like that.

Orn's voice crackled over the comm, "Cap, if you got the excess cargo off the ship, you best be getting to the bridge. I don't want to wear out our frosty welcome anymore."

She stepped back from the airlock, pushing the close button. Gene greeted her, nodding with his rocky head and winking. Variel smiled, and bounced lightly through the ship, past the sight of Brena trying to politely ask a bound but determined Ferra just where she got such a familiar corset. Her engineer was feigning deafness and humming loudly, but, as the captain passed, both elves stopped their half bickering and nodded to her.

In the mess, Monde asked Taliesin if he'd been taking the medication he prescribed. The elf muttered something intangible, then turned to watch Variel crossing their paths. Monde threw up his hands and muttered loudly, "Elves!"

Taliesin blushed that adorable red-orange and Variel smiled coyly at him, grateful only the unobservant orc was there to watch the moment. Before she embarrassed herself further, she dashed for the bridge to find her favorite dwarf poking at the partially glued controls. Leaning over Orn's shoulder, she said, "Segundo's off to his new-old life, time we be getting to ours."

"Aye aye...Sir," Orn said, saluting her with a wrapper dangling off his fingers.

He started the undocking procedure when a light blared up from the console. "It's an outside comm line. Someone's calling us," the dwarf said cautiously, his fingers hovering over the button.

Variel cursed under her breath, trying to plan about twenty different escape paths out of Samudra space as she waved to the dwarf, "Go ahead, flip it on."

The broken screen twitched but didn't display any images. Only a harried voice asked, "Is this the *Elation-Cru*?"

The captain rose, her fingers digging lightly into Orn's chair, "It is. What is this call in reference to?"

"Thank the stars, I've got a shipment here for you."

"A shipment?" Variel asked, turning towards Orn. He shrugged his massive shoulders, far as he knew they didn't have any outstanding work. "What's in the shipment?"

The sound of paper flipping up and down crackled across the line, then the voice answered back, "Seven inertia injectors."

"Seven..." Variel started before taking in the cracking dwarf face as he tried and failed to bury an escaping laugh. "At least we won't need a new one for a long, long time. I'll send someone to collect them. Orn, you up for one more adventure?"

"Always," the dwarf grinned.

PREVEIW
DWARVES IN SPACE 2: Family Matters
October 2015

Rubber soles, better equipped for stumbling across the metal grating favored by a class-b starline, splintered as a sharp branch drove straight through into flesh. Orn yelped, his grip slipping as he tried to stagger against the forest attacking him. His cargo tumbled from his fingers and clattered onto the crunchy ground.

Variel paused, turning to her beleaguered pilot so far out of his element he was into lanthanide territory. "Pick it up."

Orn huffed, stumbling to gather what breath he once held, and pouted. The thick lip of the dwarves was a difficult one to cross. "Why should I?"

A blast shattered through a trunk a foot above the wheezing dwarf's head, answering for him. His captain only raised her eyebrow as she fired back into the woodland maze, her tiny pistol little more than a carnival prize in this terrain. They hadn't seen their attackers for over half a mile, but they traded the occasional scream and bit of weapon's fire to keep the relationship from falling stale. Red leaves broke from the last round of gunplay and tumbled across the harsh woman poised upon the fallen log. The fronds mimicked bloody handprints, clawing across her head. She brushed it away without a thought.

Orn gritted his teeth, accepting his fate, and lifted a small tree off the ground. As his fingers connected with young bark, a pair of eyes materialized a few inches before him; the rest of the body was only a dark space in the dense wood. Jumping out of his broken shoes, the Dwarf shook the sapling and shouted, "Don't do that!"

The eyes blinked softly then scattered, appearing a few inches beside Variel, shifting nervously from the dwarf back to the human. She paid the child no mind, all her focus on the hunting party behind them. "We're close to the compound."

"You said that three clacks ago," Orn whined as the sapling's fingers dug into his hair and knotted around his sleeves. He was gonna be digging purple leaves out of his underthings for weeks.

"It's klicks and..." another shot fired across the pair, scorching a larger burn across the ancient forest. "They're closing, run!"

"I thought I was running."

"Run faster," Variel chided, and — shoving into Orn's shoulder — pushed him onward.

Bubble, find that stupid bubble. Orn chanted inside his brain as the small eyes darted before then behind him. It would pause, processing the passing clouds or the swaying leaves filtering through the high branches as senescence claimed the forest, as unaware of the turmoil before them as a god; then, after Orn passed a certain threshold, appear in front of him again to renew the cycle. It would unnerve the dwarf if he had time to think about it.

His captain's voice drifted away from him, she was either planning something clever or fell down into a mud pit again. But Orn had one job to accomplish - getting this sapling kid to that bubble, whatever insane stunt she wanted to pull off was all on her. Doubling his grip, he tried to inch up on his screaming toes to see the forest around the trees. Unfortunately, all he got was more forest and a face full of moss. The sapling slipped from his struggling fingers again as Orn wiped at his face, trying to clear a colony of very confused tree ants out of his gigantic nostrils.

Sod whoever made all this nature crap, and double that for the woman insisting we help the arsechabs living in it. Orn was not noble by nature, he didn't have the head for a crown and robes gave him a rash, but as he looked once more into the knotted eyes of the child, he sighed and wiped his gloves across the rare mudless patch on his trousers. "Fine," he agreed with himself and hoisted the clingy sapling up.

Just as he was about to take another step, a shriek pierced the whispering woods powerful enough to curdle milk. Boots smashed through the undergrowth, snapping past twigs and low hanging branches until Variel's brown shape shot past Orn. A dangerous mix of joy and terror painted her face and she didn't slow for the dwarf, only chanted, "Run, run, run."

He didn't need to be told twice, and lifting up his burning legs, he trailed with what scraps of energy remained, "What did you do?"

"Led them on a little trip through the forest that ended below the waterfall."

Orn laughed, "Bet the cat people loved it."

"You could say that," Variel grinned just as a howl, feral and alien to this world, burst through the trees. "And it may have pissed them off more. Ahead of me Orn, I can see the compound!"

"Good for you, all I see is muddy, human ass."

The muddy human ass paused, letting the Dwarf catch up. Sure enough, beyond these ignoble trees lay another set of super special trees all encompassed by a nearly invisible shield. It flickered like dusty sunbeams, securing an entire hundred acres of forest from anyone foolish enough to traipse around on this planet.

Variel turned to the eyes of the child; it could not thank them or even plead for help. Only those flickering eyes betrayed the solid wood of its hide. "We'll get you home. Orn…"

"Going, going, got it," and before she had to say another word he pumped those little legs, shredding what remained of his shoes and face across the dead fingers of the trees. He had a date with their orc doctor and the iodine bottle when this was over.

Variel turned towards the howl as a second answered across the woods, raining more of the bloody hand leaves upon their heads. The hunters split up, trying to flank their prey. She had two choices, either stand to face them and be obliterated by enough firepower to put down an olhino, or retreat. Firing twice into the stands of trees, she threatened the circling hyenas once and then burst after Orn.

The shimmer glistened before him, only a few dozen more marches of his soleless boots. "Oh gods, oh gods, oh gods," Orn shouted to the nonchalant universe, "I hope this still works." He shut his eyes tight as he dived across the barrier. It lifted every hair on his body and stank like a bad cup of coffee but the nearly invisible curtain moved aside, allowing him passage. Orn's body sagged from the pressure shift and he began to tumble. In a rare moment of quick thinking, the dwarf rolled to his back, keeping the baby sapling from smashing into the ground. The three leaves still clinging to the sapling's branches shuddered, but stilled as breath tried to force through Orn's beleaguered lungs.

As he closed his eyes and counted to ten, a familiar string of ancient troll curses sundered the silent winds. His captain saved those for surprise toll passages and customers paying in buttons. Sitting up with his tree friend, Orn watched as Variel, firing wildly behind her, galloped across the remaining gap. Her shirt ripped as a branch impaled upon the loose fabric but failed to slow her down. She was an avatar of momentum at this point.

One of their pursuers stepped into their miniature clearing. Its orange fur was stained in muddy water, looking more like a half drowned rat than a mighty Macka Warrior; but still the hefty hunting rifle was poised across its shoulder trying to find the target. Black eyes narrowed, nothing but pupils in the thick shadows of the forest, as it tracked Variel's form as she jumped up and dived for the bubble. Squeezing off the trigger, the heavy shot tossed the seven-foot tall hunter back on its feet as the energy blast flew through the forest inconveniently in the way and struck bubble, bouncing back towards the poacher.

The Macka shrieked as if someone stepped on its tail at this change in fortunes. It ducked, only singing its fur from the boomeranging bullet while the captain rose from her very dignified "Oh shit!" roll. Deliberately wiping her palms off on her unsalvageable pants, she turned to stare into the unshielded forest, and flipped the Macka off. The roar of rage could be heard nearly three compounds over.

"Very dignified there, Cap'n," Orn mocked as he rose to his own muddy haunches, "Really role modeling for the children."

Variel laughed, savoring the cocktail of chemicals from a momentary miss of death and the sight of her hunter stalking back into the woods, his own prey snatched beyond his grasp. The knotted eyes appeared beside Orn's shoulder, its form almost fully solid in close proximity to the tree. Yet the concern bordering on terror was not replaced within the twiggy depths. As far as the child knew, it was no more safer with them than the Macka.

"We got the kid here, now what?" Orn asked, trying to wave off the feeling he was surrounded by very cautious and very xenophobic eyes.

A branch rustled in the dead wind, high off one of the trees spotted in setting sun orange, before crumbling to the ground. It bounced, or appeared to as it rose high into the air, a hand forming fingers first where it touched and gaining an opaque form as the branch moved to the center of its being. It was like the branch was one of those UV lights, sending out energy to show a hidden message in the form of a dryad.

The arms stretched out straight across from the shoulders, creaking from the reach, yet the stick remained perfectly balanced across the thin chest. Cords of bark wound across the thin frame, the alternating shades of dying crimson and shoe stealing brown mimicked the tree from which the branch fell. There was no mouth, no nose, only the eyes gave away the face; a pair of deep knots from which a flickering yellow light glowed.

It moved slowly, propelled across the ground by an undulation of roots at the end of its feet. There was much speculation about why Dryads evolved legs despite relying upon the propeller motion. The theories ranged from a universal constant for all sentient life mages had yet to uncover, a very uncreative god placed in charge of body design, or life's weird, drink your beer. The latter is the far more popular of philosophies.

Variel steadied herself, rising to what of her height she could, but easily being over shadowed by the seven to eight foot tall Dryad. The knots gazed past her muddied head, "You have brought us the child." A voice like creaking wood in a heavy storm rumbled from beneath its roots.

She followed to the sapling still in Orn's hands. "Yes, do you...need us to plant it somewhere?"

"It will be unnecessary," the Dryad said while holding its hand out to the Dwarf.

Orn stared at the partially ethereal vines and, shrugging his shoulders, passed the sapling over. The Dryad only lightly grazed the tree before the child's upper body/head turned to its elder, the universal fear in the young eyes fading. For the first time in their long rescue mission, something of a smile crinkled the yellow knots.

"Yes, child. You are home."

Then the Dryad turned away from the two interlopers back to its own people, the child trailing behind it. Murmurs, whispers, heavy winds no skin could feel shook the trees as the message relayed across their network.

"Do we follow 'em, or what?" Orn asked, gesturing to the walking tree that for being plant life was rather quickly moving away from them.

"I suppose so," Variel said, trailing behind as all the bumps, bruises, and scrapes came screaming up at her. The endorphin crash was one of the worst.

"You 'suppose so'? I thought you were the expert on the Dry dads."

"Dryads," she corrected, despite knowing Orn was just screwing with her, "and I never said I was an expert."

"So all that, 'Don't worry Orn, I've worked with 'em before. It'll be an easy mission, just digging up a tree.' was amateur talk?"

"Well, I did work with one before," Variel said noncommittally. And that work boiled down to her telling one where the waste disposal unit was, but at the time he'd seemed perfectly honorable and willing to keep his promises of having a good day.

"What are they doing sending their children outside their little forest spheres anyway? Got some really good mushrooms out there?"

"His was a birth of accident," despite being yards away, the lead Dryad's voice carried across the ground and amplified below their feet. Orn jumped a foot into the air. "Her young seed caught on the wind and blew beyond our embrace. We could not call to him before the defilers came."

Pronouns were a problem with translators, especially when bridges and serving platters could have a gender. When it came to the few non-gendered races most programmers just threw up their hands and shouted "use zimbldede for all we care!" Zimbldede took too long to use in conversation, so they settled on a constant ping-pong between 'him' and 'her' to bridge the gap between the binary and unary genders. Tertiary genders were just plum out of schell.

"Thank you for returning our lost one to us," the Dryad said, turning to face the two outsiders. As it lifted its arms towards them, three or four more branches tumbled from the trees and lifted off the ground. Each new Dryad swarmed around the child, picking off some errant moss or tucking her leaves behind his branch. Like a race of heavily involved aunts, they ushered the kid into their gnarled embrace.

"Not to break up this tender moment, but the shuttles will be breaking off soon and I don't see much in the form of a hotel around here..." Variel started, not wanting to spend a night camping in the forest of whispers. Every branch could be another person watching you.

"As agreed," the Dryad motioned to a bin behind him, "10 gallons of pure dihydrogen monoxide."

Variel grinned as she walked towards her blue jugs brimming with one of the hardest to obtain chemicals, water. Every planet had harsh regulations to keep as much of its wet stuff confined within its own atmosphere. Once it left, it was never coming back. Occasionally, an ice planet or comet was mined; but that included fees, taxes, and import dues. What it offered her for a little replanting could fill her ship for three months if they were careful.

The Dryad's oaken fingers grazed across her shoulder and she turned into the knots. It was unnerving, but no worse than facing down a troll who got your PALM address. "For risking so much for us, we offer to you this," and it held a box out.

Variel lifted the wooden lid, trying to not think if it was made of some Dryad's remains, and stared at the blackest earth she'd ever seen. It smelled of promise, of a full belly, of no longer having to eat cricket crunch for a month. "Thank you very much," she said, quickly sealing the box away in her pocket.

"It is a trifle compared to a life," the Dryad said, as if he'd given her little more than a trinket, "If we never meet again, I bid you find all you wish for in this life save one, so you never stop striving."

"Uh, back at ya," Variel fumbled. There was a good reason she was never sent on diplomatic missions in her old days.

As the Dryad ushered its fellows back to their trees, some climbing high into the branches, others sinking into the roots, Orn stepped beside his Captain. "Ten gallons, not bad after all. We could get a hot bath, a heavy load of laundry, and have enough left over for soup."

"I am not wasting a drop of this on your leathery hide, it goes into the coolant," Variel scoffed.

"Come on, Cap!" Orn whined, "Look at me, I'm more swamp monster than Dwarf."

Even as the sun crested across the thick trees, some of the

ancient mud they'd blundered into on their hunt for the sapling dried into a caked on mass across almost the entire bottom half of the Dwarf, sealing in his juices. He'd need a chisel to get it off, the sanitizing showers weren't going to scratch that. Variel didn't want to think about how she looked in comparison; she was the one to go careening down that mud slope after all.

"You're right, we deserve a well earned treat," she said, getting a whoop from her Dwarf. "When we get back to the ship, set her straight for The Wash 'n' Scrub."

"I ask for caviar and you give me tapioca pudding?"

"Would you prefer we skip it all together and rub the mud off with sandpaper?"

"Wash 'n' Scrub it is! By the by, Cap?"

Variel sighed, the day had ended surprisingly well considering how it all began with shots fired at her and a xenophobic society swearing the dab of red paint across her forehead would keep her body from sizzling to a crisp once she crossed their barrier. "What is it?"

"How are we going to get the 10 gallons back to the shuttle depot?"

"Shit!"

Printed in Great Britain
by Amazon

60459643R00157